Soft as Water

Soft as Water

B. ROBERT CONKLIN

Skip the Preface
publishing

Columbus, Ohio

SOFT AS WATER
Copyright © 2024 by Robert B. Conklin

ISBN: 979-8-9872301-4-5 (Paperback Version)

Library of Congress Control Number: 2024902048

Cover art:
Photo 146764778 | Artwork by Ilkin Guliyev | Dreamstime.com

First Edition

For more information, visit:
www.skipthepreface.com

"Nothing in the world
is as soft and yielding as water.
Yet for dissolving the hard and inflexible,
nothing can surpass it."

—Lao-tzu, *Tao Te Ching*
Trans. Stephen Mitchell

"Jazz flows like water. Jazz never seems to begin or end …
Jazz is a conversation, a give and take …
Jazz is abandon."

—Nat Wolff, American actor and musician

Chapter 1

The apartment came with its very own ghost, which was fine by Will Archer, because he already knew what it was like to be dead. Not doornail dead. Or zombie dead. Or brain dead. Just clinically dead on an ambulance gurney after the accident, a delayed reaction to the rupture of his chest wall by a malfunctioning airbag.

He would hate to disappoint anyone if asked. No, he didn't see the proverbial light at the end of a tunnel, even though Utica teems with underground waterways haunted by the spirits of freedom seekers who died during passage. He came across no one he knew who had preceded him to the afterlife. There was no voice beckoning him back to the world of the living, telling him it wasn't his time. There had been nothing, not even blackness: just a void in his existence while emergency technicians tried to electrocute his heart back into a rhythm with a portable defibrillator.

Later at the hospital, when he learned what had happened from two police officers who had shown up to interrogate him, he wished they hadn't been so persistent.

If there was a ghost, it wasn't introducing itself, not right away, as his landlady, a Mrs. Gossett, showed him around, laying down the rules of the house. She had a lively, wizened face framed by a bouffant of blue-gray hair—Will guessed she was the near side of 70—and wore a blue robe and house slippers to match.

There weren't any other apartments to be had on this side of the Ohio River. And this was the address he had carried in his pocket on a scrap of notepaper coming down from Erie. It was the address his new employer had given him over the phone.

The village of East Orange, West Virginia, where he was taking up residence, had a certain Mayberry quietude about it. In comparison, New Bloomfield on the Ohio side of the river, where he was to begin his new job the next day, seemed an older cousin of the "school of hard knocks" variety.

His lodgings were in an old gabled Victorian house with steep slate roofs guarded by the shade of giant sycamores. In fact, it was called the Victorian Arms, as advertised on a bronze plaque out front. The house had been subdivided into apartments that they passed on their way up the stairs.

One door on the second floor opened onto nothingness, a straight plunge down twenty feet to a spiked iron fence. Mrs. Gossett showed it to him on the way up to the third story in case he lost his way and stepped through it by accident. The fire escape, having rusted through, had been removed some decades ago. The ladder had posed a greater hazard to her tenants' well-being than a fire would.

"Wouldn't want to lose a new tenant so soon," she said drily, and he had made an attempt to laugh. He hadn't much experience with older people—his own parents had died in their forties in a ferry accident, and he had never known his grandparents—but he figured it was always wise to humor senior citizens.

"Do you go by William?" she asked politely as he followed her up the last flight of stairs to a cramped landing. "Or can I call you Bill?"

"Will is fine," he corrected her, more tersely than he had intended.

A naked bulb dangling from a high ceiling provided the only source of illumination. Will wondered who replaced the bulb when the light went out. It would take a tall stepladder and a firm sense of balance.

"Will it is then," she said cheerily, sorting through a ring of keys at the door to apartment #9, a lucky number, he hoped, despite his trepidation with heights. "Ah," she said, holding a skeletal key up to view with fingers that were equally skeletal, white, and sinewy. "Where there's a will there's a way."

Surely she didn't think this was the first time he had heard this proverb applied to his name.

She handed over the key as Will set down his duffle bag on the couch along with his laptop and a suit in its plastic sheath, which he draped over the back of a chair. He had graduated college in this suit, married Abbey, attended Joel's baptism. It was a relic of his former life, something he carried from Utica to Erie, and now from Erie to this little dot of a town on the Ohio River. The laptop didn't violate his rule about handheld electronics. It wasn't exactly something you could be scrolling while driving.

"You have wifi?" he inquired.

"The house may be ancient," she replied, "but it is equipped with modern conveniences. Think of the reviews I would get on Yelp without wifi."

The first thing he did was unzip an outside flap of his luggage and pull out a 5" x 7" photograph in a gilt frame. It showed a pale, white face, beardless, topped with a business cut, and beside it, a young, brown-skinned woman, bright and smiling, cradling on her hip a small boy with a curly mop of black hair, maybe three years old. Instinctively, he ran his hand through the nest of a beard he had grown since, wearing it as he would a disguise.

"Sibyl—that is, Mrs. Waxman—didn't mention you have a family," she said, studying the photograph around his shoulder, as he propped it on a desktop. "Will they be joining you then? There's only the one bedroom, I'm afraid."

"No," Will said sadly, "they won't."

"I'm sorry," she replied, lowering her eyes. "I don't want you to get the impression I'm nosy."

"Are you?" Will asked, trying to lighten the mood.

"Of course," she answered, smiling. "All landladies are. It's their nature."

She placed a hand lightly on his, and then Will knew that everything would be all right between them, after all.

"Come along now," she said, removing her hand. "Let me show you the rest of the apartment."

There wasn't much to show. The apartment was old-fashioned, its quaintness matched only by its mustiness. The living room seemed comfortable enough despite its hardwood floor covered with a threadbare carpet that fell short of the baseboards, which looked as though they had been gnawed by rats. He hoped the rats had found different accommodations by now.

Beyond lay a small room inside a corner turret with a ceiling that rose into a six-sided dome. This, he could tell, was meant to be the bedroom. It offered a wonderful view of the river, wide and smooth-flowing, and the silver suspension bridge he had crossed, keeping an eye out for closed-circuit cameras. Going on fifteen years since 9/11, homeland security was still very tight, but he doubted inland river crossings were monitored 24/7.

"Now about that ghost," his landlady said from the living room, as he emerged from the turret.

She described noises in the night, a low, vibrant humming, like the sound produced by a wax-paper comb, climbing and descending a musical scale. Thumps, as of footsteps, pacing the floorboards, back and forth, back and forth, like the steady metronome of a grandfather clock. Loud wails like a police siren, moving from one part of the apartment to the other. Rattles, as if a loose collection of bones were coming apart at the joints. All of these sounds, added together, have cost her more than one tenant over the years asking for a refund of their deposit.

"Don't worry," Will said, looking around the room at some of the details that were filling in the overall picture: an exposed pipe running vertically up a wall, the high plaster ceiling with spider-web cracks running through it, old-style push-button light switches. He worried about insulation fraying from copper wires behind the walls. "I'm used to living with ghosts." He glanced at three faces in the photograph on the desk. Some ghosts, he knew, were still among the living—himself included. "Who's it a ghost of, do you know?"

"You'll be getting acquainted soon enough," his landlady answered. "At your new job, I should say."

"Oh?"

"It's the ghost of your employer's son."

"Mrs. Waxman's? You mean Jamaal Waxman?"

Jamaal Waxman, saxophonist extraordinaire. He only knew the name because it was also the name of his new place of employment: The Jamaal Waxman Memorial Museum. Jamaal had been a young jazzman dead these past twenty years, give or take. It was his memory that his mother, Sibyl Waxman, was working hard to keep alive. And here he was, just another ghost.

"He died in this very room. On the couch, in fact." Will glanced at the small settee with plump velvet cushions. Just enough room for two. A lovers' couch. "I was the first to find him. A misfortunate occurrence."

"How did he die?"

"Overdose," she said simply. "Heroin. Are you a drinking man, Will?"

"No," Will answered curtly, the word as blunt as a hammer blow. If he hadn't been drinking—and texting—the accident wouldn't have occurred. Two people—mother and child— would still be alive.

"Surely, you must have some vice. Do you smoke?"

"Now and then."

"Well, you must come join me for a cigarette—now and then." Her eyes were as bright as Christmas bulbs. She must have been something, Will reckoned, back in her youth.

He escorted her to the doorway, where she paused.

"I do hope you have better luck than the previous two curators," she said solemnly. "They stayed in this very room, as well. The previous curator—would you like to know how he died?"

"The fire escape?" Will wondered, recalling the door to nowhere.

"Drowned in his bath."

"Right, well, I'll have to take my chances." And he meant it. He didn't have much choice. His money was tight, and he was grateful for a job that paid twice the minimum wage. The only downside was it didn't offer healthcare, so he'd hung onto a Golden Rule policy under an assumed name for emergency treatment. He never knew when a seizure would be severe enough to send him to a hospital.

"And the one before that?" Looking him straight in the eye. "Do you know what happened to him, young man that he was?"

"Changing a light bulb?" Will responded, trying to make light of what he perceived as an absurd line of questioning. He presumed anyone foolhardy enough to attempt it on the stairs would be taking a chance with limb, minimally, and probably life as well.

She shook her head slowly from side to side. If her goal was to unnerve him, she was succeeding all too well.

"A vehicle at a crosswalk. A very clear case of hit and run. Both young men like yourself. You're a married man?"

"No—"

"Ah, but you still wear a ring."

Will held out his hand, as though showing off the gold band on a shop-at-home network.

"I'm sorry," she said, lowering her eyes. "There I go, prying again." She made a move as though to touch his shoulder—or God forbid, his cheek—but, perhaps thinking better of it, brought her hand back to her side. "Just be careful. Always watch your back, Will. Always."

Fortunately, this was something he had put a lot of practice into, and he almost said as much. Still, you could never be too careful.

"Well, thanks for the advice, Mrs. Gossett. Or do you have a first name you go by?"

"It's Phyllis. But I prefer to be addressed by my last name. It was my late husband's. That way I'm always reminded of whom I lost."

"Of course." Why was he not surprised by the mention of yet another death? They appeared to come with the territory.

"Don't forget," she said lightly, her tone brightening, as she backed through the doorway onto the landing as though to perform a curtsy. "Lights out at eleven."

"Eleven?" Will wondered if he was hearing her right.

"I'm joking, Will," she said, pulling the door closed on her exit. As though she were a Cheshire cat, the last thing he saw was her smile.

***

Feeling a migraine coming on, Will hoped to circumvent it through sleep. His landlady's joke became a self-fulfilling prophecy: lights out at eleven after all.

He swallowed a couple of antihistamines as a sleep aid and plunged immediately into dream. In this one, he was climbing a skyscraper: One World Trade Center, testament to the Twin Towers that were lost. Scaling the glass panels without rope or plungers. Just his hands and bare feet—a human fly. He was only a few feet from the top when a young Black man in a white robe looked down at him.

"Hello, roomie!"

"Jamaal?" he asked, but the man only smiled, flashing a set of perfect teeth. One of the incisors glittered brilliant gold.

"Just let go," he advised, still smiling.

"What?"

"Let go and fall back. You'll feel so much better if you do."

Will tried to hang on more tightly but started to lose his grip.

"Don't worry," Jamaal said, bending his head. "Just start counting backwards. You'll be dead before you hit bottom. And then you can join them."

"Them?"

"Isn't that what you want? So you can beg their forgiveness?"

His fingers lost their grip and he fell away into nothingness, but this isn't what panicked him. He didn't know from which number he should start counting.

He felt a *whoosh!* as the bottom dropped out of his existence, then woke in bed with a start. It took him a moment to orient himself to his new surroundings. Part of him thought he was still drowsing on the bus coming down from Erie.

Eyes wide open, he heard a thrumming sound, faint at first, but growing louder, and climbing a scale. It went through one octave and reached a crescendo before descending again. But there was something peaceful about it, something lulling.

Just the pipes, he thought, turning over in bed. *The pipes, the pipes are calling,* he hummed lightly to himself before falling asleep.

Chapter 2

Everything was out to put her in a bad mood this a.m. Not just the weather—another rainy morning. Her toaster zapped the bread coal black. Little Joel, just turned five, had woken up with a chronic cough, so she voice-mailed his preschool, then texted her partner at the gallery to let her know she wouldn't be coming into work. Even her horoscope on her smartphone was bad: *Expect an untimely visit.* But that was late last night, when Daryl had arrived.

She began picking up a few things off the floor—paper plate pasted with frosting, broken plastic fork, tossed-aside noisemaker. Amazing the amount of damage a collection of preschoolers—little Joel's friends—could cause, even with their mothers (and one father) present. They had offered to help clean up, but she had waved them off.

When she threw open the curtains, she found Daryl lying back in the recliner, blending in with the shadows. He squinted up at her, adjusting his eyes to the fresh shock of light.

"Hello, Abbey. You look even better in the morning, I'd swear. Not a lot of women can vouch as much."

She had to admit, he was no slouch when it came to charm. It's probably the main thing that reunited them after her year studying abroad—in England, where her heart still lay. It didn't take long, though, to find out he was cheating on her, and that's when she met Alan. He didn't seem her type at all: polo shirt, wrinkle-free Dockers, laced Keds. A prototypical frat boy. He always came across as so clean-cut, so chaste. But not chaste enough. A semester before they graduated, she got knocked up and they got married—in that order. It always made her wonder if Alan hadn't married her just to do the right thing.

"What are you still doing here? I thought you'd left."

She went back to picking up after the party.

"Thought maybe you could put me up for a few days."

"What makes you think I'd want to do that?"

"You know, now that what's-his-name is out of the picture."

"What's-his-name is my husband. And he's not out anywhere."

Funny, though, she hadn't discussed him at length last night. As a topic of conversation, he had been readily dismissed.

"Where's Pax, still MIA?"

"Yeah, but his name's Alan."

She never did care for his college nickname: Pax.

"Come on, Abbey. You can confide in me." He took a sip from a half-empty beer bottle he found on an end table. "What's it been now, a year? You ever think of filing for divorce?"

"On what grounds?"

"I don't know, like abandonment."

Yep, it was turning out to be just that sort of a morning, for sure.

It was almost as if he had planned it—and knowing Daryl, he probably had. Showing up at the tail end of Joel's birthday party so that she couldn't exactly turn him out without creating a scene in front of the lingering guests. Afterward, she had agreed to a glass of wine—he had brought the bottle. This was after she had put Joel to bed.

And then, she winced at the thought of it, one thing had led to another, as it always did with her ex-boyfriend, pre-Alan, and before she knew it, she was out of her clothes and on the couch with Daryl on top of her, hammering away as though he were nailing shingles to a roof.

It had been twelve months after all. Twelve long months. Eighteen, if you take the accident into account, following which Alan had lost all interest in sex. She had needs. No, let's call them requirements. It made it sound more clinical, less a matter of emotion.

She suspected she knew what lay beneath it all: a means of retaliation, of getting back at her renegade spouse for all the upheaval his disappearance had brought to her life—*their* lives, hers and Joel's. It was as if she were saying with each reciprocating thrust, each pulsation: "Take that, Alan Paxton, wherever you are." *Whoever* you are.

She pulled down a bunch of streamers from the ceiling. Opened a trashcan in the kitchenette with her foot.

"I'm not looking to start anything," she said. "What happened last night, that's all there will be to it."

"Right, what happens in Utica, stays in Utica," he said with a grin.

"It never happened. It was a fluke. A mistake."

"Didn't feel like a mistake to me," he said, coming up from behind, wrapping his arms around her, pressing her against the Formica counter.

"I can give you fifteen minutes to be out of here. Or else I'm calling the police."

Daryl laughed, backing away, hands in the air where she could see them.

"Come on, Abbey. There's no reason to be that drastic. I didn't say I wanted to start over. But I can leave, if you want."

Same old Daryl. Everything was always so "oh, come on" with him.

He began stuffing items into a Power Rangers backpack—so typically school-boyish; he never had grown up—his only luggage. The man liked to travel light. Spare pair of socks, stick of deodorant, disposable razor.

Something was wrong. It couldn't be this easy.

"Just thought I might be of some help to you."

"Help?"

"Must be rough, single mom and all."

So here it was coming. An offer. But of what?

"I'm gathering you want him back."

Abbey shrugged, exposing a bare shoulder above the loose neck of her sweatshirt. She wasn't sure what she would do if he were to turn back up: hug him or strangle him.

Despite her ambivalence, she worried about him the way a mother goose would a stray gosling. She had been trying to find him for a year now. She didn't have confidence about Alan's ability to survive in the wild. He was too much the gentleman. Boy Scout. He would get trampled, taken, run over, fleeced. She'd developed a social network with hundreds of "friends" spread across the country. There had been several leads. A few photos posted. Resemblances, sightings. It was like discovering Elvis in a laundromat, Bigfoot in a patch of woods. It didn't take much investigation to uncover the leads as spurious.

But then there had been that close call a month ago in Erie, PA. He had made the mistake—or was it?—of using their joint credit card to make a purchase. After all this time gone missing, was he trying to leave a clue to his whereabouts? Was he trying to reassure her he still thought of them as together: joint? The total had been so small, so negligible.

"Most likely someone stole his credit card and is just testing the water," Daryl had suggested when she told him about it over the phone.

"What water?"

"You know, seeing if anyone will notice before making more purchases."

Call it intuition, but the date of the sale taking place on their wedding anniversary seemed too coincidental. She brought up a record of the receipt online and discovered he had bought one each of their favorite candy bars: his a Milky Way, hers a Butterfinger.

Abbey insisted the purchase confirmed he was alive and well—and perhaps a touch remorseful?—residing in Erie, just 285 miles and four hours and twenty-five minutes due west of Utica on I-90 according to Google Maps.

She was all packed and ready to drag Joel along on a rescue mission, but Daryl showed up on her doorstep, with his usual perfect timing, offering to go as her proxy to track him down.

"It's not like finding Waldo," he told her. "It'll take some detective work."

Erie was a small enough town, but at the end of a week, Daryl had very little to report. He'd hung out at the Wal-Mart where the sale had been transacted, browsing aisles, staking out the parking lot. He'd knocked on doors in the vicinity, shown a photo of Alan around local bars, coffee shops, coming up with blank stares, shakes of the head. He'd pursued a single lead based on a glimmer of recognition from a homeless man who claimed Alan had been a "regular," twice daily contributing a dollar to the "cause," coming and going. This led him to a pay-by-the-week Microtel across the street, but when he followed up with the manager, bribing her with a twenty, he hadn't found Paxton in the list of residents. Nevertheless, he left a calling card and a copy of the photo, in case the manager should detect a resemblance, but no surprise, he never received a return call.

A year of searching and all Abbey had to show for it was a credit card statement on one end bracketed by a parting note on the other. Alan had left it on a Saturday morning Abbey had rolled over to find her husband missing in bed, only to come across a page carefully torn from a yellow legal pad attached to the refrigerator with a magnet, no less, explaining how he had to give them up—the two people who meant everything to him—a way to atone for the wife and child he had taken from another man. The sheer selfishness of his so-called "penance"—depriving himself of wife and son without seeming to care about their deprivation of husband and father—continued to enrage her, like a shark incessantly roiling through her subconscious, always restless, never asleep.

"I don't think you'll find him the way you've been going about it," Daryl told Abbey, helping himself to a swig of orange juice directly out of the carton from the fridge. "If he's smart, and I'm guessing he is, he would have changed his appearance. If he's smarter, and I'm not sure that he is, he would have moved to a large city, even one close by, say, Buffalo. He'd do what he could to blend in, take a low-profile job. But he's bound to surface, sometime or other. Because there's one thing you can lay a bet on—"

"His seizures," Abbey interjected, popping a couple of slices of fresh bread into the toaster to reboot her breakfast.

"They're his calling card in a way."

Abbey nodded her head, agreeing. That was the one big thing that concerned her: his seizures.

"I'm worried, though. We're not going to be here at the end of the month."

"No?" Daryl poured himself a cup of coffee that was still percolating.

"What if he decides to return and finds new homeowners?"

"Moving are you?"

"It's not just the mortgage. It's the property taxes. I've found something smaller. Which reminds me. Think you'll be around to help us pack?"

"Mama?" she heard behind her and turned her head abruptly. It was Joel, fresh out of bed.

She ran up to him with open arms. Felt his forehead. Warm.

"I'm sorry, were we making too much noise?"

Joel glanced skeptically at the strange man who had moved to a stool at the kitchen counter. He shrank behind his mother so as to eclipse the man's view.

"Momma, I'm thirsty."

His voice sounded hoarse. She picked him up with some effort and carried him to the kitchen table.

"Joel, this is Daryl. You remember him? From your party? He's a friend of mine. Say 'hello,' won't you?"

"Hello," he said in a tentative voice, following directions.

"Hello, little man," Daryl said. *Little man*—it was Alan's pet name for him.

"Sit tight," Abbey instructed. "And I'll find you some cough syrup."

"Are you feeling sick?" the strange man asked.

Joel nodded his head.

"I think so. If Mommy says I am."

"A good answer," Daryl said, smiling. "Always do as Mommy says."

"Are you going to find my Daddy?" Joel asked.

Daryl looked at Abbey.

Abbey knelt next to Joel in his chair, measuring pink medicine into the small plastic cup that came with the bottle.

"Did you overhear us talking?" she asked.

Joel nodded.

"Is Daddy lost?"

Abbey tilted the medicine into his mouth, cradling the back of his head with her free hand.

"You must miss him," Daryl said, crouching down to look

him in the eye.

"He has brown skin, Mommy," Joel observed, pointing. "Just like you and me."

"Joel, it isn't polite to talk about people," Abbey chided, but Daryl only smiled.

"My daddy has white skin," Joel said to Daryl.

"I know about your daddy," Daryl told him. "I know just what he looks like."

"Did you see the pictures in Mommy's picture book?"

"No, but we went to school together—"

"No, you didn't," Abbey countered.

"True, I never actually met him, just saw him with your mother from a—"

A knock at the door kept Daryl from explaining anything further.

It was Don Perritt.

Once or twice a week, he showed up on her welcome mat with donuts or bagels. It was his way of remembering, she figured. Ever since the accident. Or rather ever since Alan had left, six months following the accident. At first, his timing had struck her as oddly coincidental. But soon enough, his visits became routine. Over the course of a year, they had come to share a measure of loneliness. They were both victims of loss, although his was so much more unfathomable.

He was very stiff, very formal, Old School, standing at the threshold in a sweater vest in the middle of June, no less, waiting as usual for an invitation to step inside.

"Hello, Donald."

Abbey was very formal too. They still called each other by their given names in full.

"Hello, Abigail." And looking past her, "Hello, young man." He always addressed Joel in this manner. His way of being friendly. "I brought custard-filled and chocolate-covered this time. They were out of the old-fashioned."

Daryl rose and came over. He was still in his T-shirt and long flannel pants, his version of pajamas. By the look on Don Perritt's face, he sent a shockwave through her visitor's nervous system.

"I apologize, I didn't see you had company."

"No reason to. Daryl was just getting ready to leave." Although, she thought, it hardly looked it. "Daryl, this is Mr. Perritt."

Perritt clutched the box of donuts without extending his hand in greeting. His fingers were long and delicate, perfect complements to the violin he played in the symphony orchestra. "I'm so sorry to intrude. I must be going."

And with an abrupt bow from the waist, he turned around and left.

"Boy oh boy," Daryl said, looking after his departure, "it sure didn't take you long to start playing the field again."

"I am not playing the field," Abbey said, coming up and closing the door. "I feel sorry for him. It was his wife and child that, you know—"

She nodded at Joel to indicate the sensitive nature of the topic.

"That's the widower, is it?" Daryl prompted, understanding.

"Yes, and daughterless," Abbey whispered, her head averted in case her son had acquired the ability to read lips.

"I'm five!" Joel decided to announce. He held up all five fingers proudly. *To lose a child!* Abbey looked sympathetically at her son. "Look, see? My whole hand!"

"So you are," Daryl commented. "So you are."

***

At the end of the block, Don Perritt stood looking back at the long row of houses he had passed. They reminded him of breadboxes, virtually identical in shape and size and floor plan.

He tilted his head back, watched the wind sweep fragments of low clouds across a mottled gray sky. He had choked on his breath when he first saw the outlines of a man in the background, thinking it might be Alan returned from the land of shadows.

And if it had been Alan, if he were to return, Perritt knew he had only one course of action open to him. He would not murder Alan as he thought he might have right after the accident. No, he would take from him the two things he held most precious, just as his own wife and child had been taken from him.

Chapter 3

New Bloomfield was the kind of small town even a dog might run away from if it had the chance, but Will had run to it, lured by nothing more than the prospect of a new job he had found through a Craigslist posting. Nailed it right over the phone without a face-to-face interview, speaking with a Mrs. Waxman.

"When can you start, dear?"

"Aren't you going to ask me more about my qualifications?"

"Oh, I have a way of telling these things about people from their tone of voice. I'm sort of psychic that way."

A little laugh at the end—a *tee-hee* that he had found unsettling. But that hadn't stopped him from crossing the OH/PA boundary to pursue the offer.

Crossing the bridge, he removed his wedding ring and deposited it in a pocket of his suit jacket. It pained him to tuck it away. It was something a less faithful man might do at a singles bar. But the fewer questions at his new place of work, the better.

At the bottom of the bridge on the Ohio side, a huge sinkhole had opened in the pavement and swallowed a car. He had encountered it yesterday coming from the bus depot and had asked a couple of bystanders about it. Even though it happened a few days ago, it was still the talk of the town. The car was stuck vertically in the bottom, like the relic of an archeological dig, and the hole was cordoned off with yellow police tape until the vehicle could be removed and the pit filled in. The woman driver, he learned, had not been found, buried somewhere down there with the wreckage. The theory was she had crawled out, disoriented, and plunged bodily into another hole.

He passed it quickly, following the directions in the email his employer had forwarded, clear as a treasure map: X marks the spot. The marquee was hand painted. Calligraphic red letters beckoned the visitor to "JAMAAL WAXMAN MEMORIAL MUSEUM." A sign taped to a window advertised the admission: Adults $5, Children $2. But the 5 and 2 had been crossed out and replaced with 2.50 and 0.50, respectively.

Spray-painted over the glass entranceway was a black swastika extending to the bricks on either side. Somehow, he didn't think it was meant to be a selling point. He pushed through, tinkling a bell, another angel getting its wings.

"Anyone home?" he called out, but no one answered.

He paused to examine two long exhibit cases. One case displayed memorabilia. Penciled-in sheet music. A leather jacket. A pair of gloves that looked nothing more than winter mittens, except that the finger and thumb tips were sliced off. A photograph on the wall explained it, showing a young man who he assumed to be Jamaal standing in the snow wearing a Santa hat, playing his sax next to a dangling bucket for charity.

In the other case lay what must be the museum's prized possession: a saxophone, gold-plated. The gold—was it real? He studied it from various angles, hoping the play of light would give him a clue.

From the back of the museum, he heard a toilet flush, then the running of a tap. Moments later, a young woman came through a dividing curtain, as though appearing on stage. She took three swift strides toward him, holding out her hand, a huge smile crossing the warm, deep brown of her face.

"Hello!" she exclaimed. "I heard you come in, but I was, you know, indisposed. So you're the new curator, are you?"

Will nodded.

"Hey!" she said in the same exuberant voice. "You're not

wearing pink. Didn't you get the email about it being a pink day?"

She was a walking advertisement for pinkness. Pink knee-high stockings, pink shoelaces, pink plaid skirt in two different blushes of pink, pink blouse, pink beaded necklace—all held in place with the finishing touch, a pink bow that tied frazzles of shoulder length hair in a tight knot as though constraining the tension of a spring. Will wondered what would happen if you undid the bow. Would she explode into a shower of pink confetti?

"I was so, so glad when I got the email," she said. "Pink is my favorite color. Now if only we can find you something pink to wear. Mrs. Waxman won't like it if you aren't dressed in pink."

"So you're not Mrs. Waxman?" Will asked, comprehending,

"Do I look like some old lady in her sixties?" she asked, giggling. "I'm Amanda—Mandy, for short." She led him back through the curtain to the rear half of the museum. "But don't tell her I said that," she said, suddenly turning. "The part about her being old."

"Promise," Will said, raising his favored hand, his left.

She started rooting around in cupboards and drawers for something pink, he presumed. All the while, she filled him in on who she was and wasn't.

In three minutes, he found out she was an intern, but she usually worked in the afternoons, only three days a week, Monday, Wednesday, and Friday, but she came in early this morning because Mrs. Waxman asked her to because she couldn't make it because of a meeting she was attending somewhere, she didn't know where, and ordinarily, she wasn't a morning person, she liked to sleep in as much as she could—beauty sleep, she called it—but she liked working here and maybe Will would too. Oh, and did she mention she didn't have a girlfriend? So if Will happened to know of anyone …

As he listened to her—all that energy—he had to smile. She

reminded him a little of Abbey. Not so much in the way she dressed—Abbey was never this flashy—but in the way his wife was so warm, so animated, so social from the get-go of their relationship. He always felt like a sloth in comparison.

"Here's something," she said. From the back of a drawer, she pulled out a pink handkerchief. Within seconds, she had folded it into sharp angles, as though making a paper airplane. "There!" she said, maneuvering it into the breast pocket of his suit jacket, a remarkable piece of origami. "Pretty in pink," she said, plucking at its tips.

Will felt himself flushing as pink as the handkerchief as she dusted some lint—hopefully not dandruff—from his shoulder.

"Now," she said, tilting her head with a critical stare, "if we could only do something about that hair. Not to mention that beard! I've been known to trim a lock or two if you want to avoid the cost of a barber." She checked her watch with its pink wristband. "Well, better get crackin'."

"Yes," Will agreed. "Better get."

He studied the typed list of duties she pointed out tacked to a bulletin board:

> 1. Open and close museum.
> 2. Put on soundtrack.
> 3. Greet guests/conduct tours.
> 4. Answer emails.
> 5. Dust shelves, empty trash, etc.
> 6. Play video upon patron request.
> 7. Pop popcorn.

One other duty had been penciled in at the bottom:

> 8. Clean graffiti.

The soundtrack, he was told, comprised a single CD, Jamaal's only recorded album titled *Wax of Sax*. Copies in vinyl cases were on display, for sale at a bargain basement price.

"You'll get tired of it in no time," Mandy told him, "the same old notes going around and around on repeat."

"So just the one album?"

Mandy nodded.

"And that makes his memory worth preserving?" He couldn't help sounding skeptical.

"It does to his mother. There was a retrospective in the local paper a couple of years ago, spreading the same old rumors about his demise." Mandy took hold of his elbow. "You have to understand, this is a very small town, and what happened was the scandal of the century—the previous century, that is."

"How so?"

"His love interest threw herself from the bridge and Jamaal died from an overdose. Everyone believes he killed himself out of despair, except his mother. I guess she felt it was time to act."

"And what is it you do here?" Will asked.

Mandy pulled him by his tie into a sealed-off back room where a large table held hundreds of photographs.

"They're for a scrapbook Mrs. Waxman wants to publish. Reprints mostly," Mandy informed him, holding up a photo. In it, a young Black man in shirt and tie had one arm around a young, white, red-haired woman in a taffeta gown. "Pre-cell-phone version of selfies. Digicams had just come out. Flip-phones weren't even in vogue. Can you imagine?"

"Looks like they might have gone a little overboard."

Mandy held up an X-Acto knife with the steadiness of a doctor preparing for surgery.

"Anyway … I revise history."

With one continuous movement, like peeling an apple, she excised the image of the woman and tossed it into a drawer.

"Who is she?"

"Jamaal's big love interest. Mrs. Waxman blames her for her

son's death."

"Wouldn't photoshopping the digital images be easier?"

Mandy viewed him critically with an arched, thinly penciled brow.

"You're a smart one," she answered. "Hopefully not too smart for the job. There is one more thing."

She led him by his tie back out of the room, flicking off the light and closing the door behind them. She handed him a vinyl record in a sleeve she selected from the top of a stack: *Essence of Jazz*, Vol. 1: *The Early Years*. "Homework. There are nine records in all. Mrs. Waxman wants you to listen to them in your spare time at home."

"So I can pretend I'm an authority?" Fortunately, his apartment came with an old turntable in a cabinet, so he had something to play it on.

"A jazz aficionado. Correct!"

Next, she sat him at the computer at a small desk along a wall in the back. There was a space for creating his very own password, and Will typed and then retyped abbey4ever while Mandy promised not to look.

"Now," she said, turning back around, "all you have to do is scroll through the emails and respond to each one that deserves a response."

"Are there ones that don't?"

"Well," she said, hesitantly, "there's the spam mail, and the phishes. Oh, did I mention the hate mail?"

"No," Will said, "I don't believe you did."

"We get a lot of hate mail. Death threats, too." She considered him seriously, inspecting him as she would a flower arrangement. "I hope you're not too put off by death threats."

Will laughed. It had been so long since anyone, or anything, had made him laugh that the sound sounded strange, foreign, as though a canary had been trapped down the mine of his throat all this time and only now had sucked in enough oxygen to make a peep.

"As long as they're not directed at me."

"Oh, well, they won't be. Not at first, anyway."

"Do you know who they're from?" he asked, more seriously. After all—death threats.

"Mrs. Waxman has a theory they're all from the same person. Someone with a vendetta against her or her son." She took hold of his shoulder and gave it a squeeze. "Come on, I'll show you where we keep the cleansers and scrub brushes."

"Ah, yes. For number eight on the to-do list, right?"

"Hey! You're catching on fast. Any questions?"

Before he could reply, Mandy informed him she needed to leave post haste or be late for class.

"Will you be changing clothes first?" he asked.

She gave him a dumbfounded look.

"No, why?"

"No reason."

He could imagine the sensation she would create in whatever lecture hall was her destination. Or were the other students used to her dress code by now?

***

After she left, Will jumped right to cleaning the graffiti with only a short break for lunch. Mandy's X-Acto knife, he discovered, worked best on removing the graffiti from the glass of the door, although its *squeak-squeak-squeak* was an irritant as he scraped at the paint.

There was a time not so long ago when he had used just such an implement in a half-hearted attempt to slice open a vein, so he was pleased to be using one now for such a constructive purpose. Maybe it was a sign his mind was on a good course?

Chapter 4

His employer showed up at a quarter past one.

"You must be William," he heard a woman's voice, bright and cheery as a robin's, coming up behind him as he stood outside, scrubbing the graffiti with bucket and brush.

Will turned to size up a stout older woman with a white leather handbag that she held defensively the way a running back would a football. Her eyes were hidden behind sunglasses with plastic frames—pink, of course. She wore a wide-brimmed white straw hat with a pink ribbon anchoring it under her chin.

"Hello," Will said, lowering his scrub brush to shake hands. "You're Mrs. Waxman?"

Her eyebrows, finely plucked, rose into two half arches of apparent surprise. The hand she had held out to meet his dropped to her side.

Tsk, tsk, she clicked against the roof of her mouth.

"I'm sorry this had to be your first impression of your new workplace." She took in the swastika over the tops of her sunglasses. "What do they think, I'm Jewish? A burning cross would be more apropos, don't you think?"

"Maybe if you had some solvent," Will volunteered, "the paint would come off more easily?"

"Here I am, trying to restore my son's reputation to the community," she continued, "and they just keep on tearing it back down."

"So this isn't the first time?"

"That the museum's been vandalized? Let's just say it's not uncommon."

"Have you reported it to the police?"

"Tut! The police," she said, waving off the notion. "The police around here aren't good for anything except chasing after out-of-towners going faster than 25."

Now Will decided it was safe to at least smile.

"They weren't any help twenty years ago, nineteen to be exact, this coming July, when my poor Jamaal died. So they're not going to be any help with this kind of thing, I shouldn't say."

"I thought he—" Will began to say, but stopped short, left wondering how the police would be of any help with death by overdose.

But as soon as he saw her expression, he decided against further remarks. She had the look a maddened bull might have before charging.

"Thought he—what? What was it you were going to say?"

"Nothing. Just that Mrs. Gossett told me—how he died."

"And what did she tell you?" she prodded, opening her purse and beginning to rummage through it.

"Only that he—"

"Killed himself?"

Will shook his head solemnly, as though he were in a church.

"No—not that. Overdose."

"Nothing could be further from the truth," she said, still sorting through her purse. "That boy was clean. He had cleaned himself up. He was murdered."

"I see. I'm sorry. I hadn't realized—"

"Love," she said, bringing out a tube of lipstick. "Love of the wrong sort of woman—that's what killed him." She unscrewed the lid and applied a fresh layer to top and bottom, using the storefront as a mirror. "You do believe what I'm telling you, do you not?"

Will looked at her reflection as she paused with her lipstick—

a bright, lively pink, of course—holding it an inch or so from her upper lip. He was reminded of the way Abbey would grimace, inspecting her appearance in her vanity mirror back in Utica. Their complexions were similar, as well, accentuating the comparison, even though Abbey was so much younger.

"Yes or no? Every question requires an answer."

"Is it a prerequisite for the job?" Will asked, trying to detect a chink in his employer's sudden armor of seriousness.

"You could say," she said simply, putting her lipstick back in her purse.

Will weighed the options.

Stay put or pack up?

Suck up or quit?

Job or no job?

Settle in or move out?

"I guess I'd require more proof."

He watched apprehensively as her eyebrows arched once more, but this time there was a smile that broadened her freshly coated lips.

"Ah, it's just what my son would have said. You're a skeptic, a questioner of authority, I see. Just like Jamaal was. Well, well. Is it proof you require?" She pulled open the door, ushering Will inside. "Seek and ye shall find, William. Seek and ye shall find."

So, Will thought. This is how it's going to be around here. Every day a test. But at least he still had a job. For now.

"There is one more thing," she said as Will went back to scrubbing the door. "I'll need your driver's license. For a background check."

"Oh? But I thought—I mean, I'm already hired, right?"

"It's strictly routine," she said. "Merely a formality. Unless …" She studied him over the frame of her sunglasses. "You have something to hide?"

"No, no," he said quickly—maybe too quickly—opening his wallet. He had two to choose from, and he handed over the one that was his preferred identity.

Fortunately, the real William Archer, drifter that he was in life, had never been convicted of a felony—not even a misdemeanor. Up until the night his head had been on the receiving end of a cue stick at a bar in Erie, PA.

He found him in the "police beat" of the local paper in Erie. Same age at the time: 26. Former occupation: drifter. Current occupation: deceased. The news item carried his name, place of origin, and a request for any known next of kin. This left a window of opportunity wherein he was able to purchase the dead man's Social Security number online armed with nothing more than the man's legal name, date of birth, and last known permanent address.

It amazed him how cheaply a dead person's life cost and how eagerly he had stepped into his new identity. As Alan Paxton, he had played by an orderly set of rules. His life was more laid out, more rigid—with home and hearth, wife and child—as though plotted on a Monopoly board.

As Will Archer, he was a nowhere man: no attachments, no permanent relationships, no ties to any one place. He had reimagined himself as an on-the-road biker, an easy rider, moving along the map on two-lane country roads. There had been no left-of-center accidents, no head-on-collisions, no homicides. Plus, on a motorcycle, he didn't believe you could text and ride at the same time. Even if you could manage the trick, he would have kept both gloved hands on the handlebars.

Truth be told, he would have been content to stay in Erie if it hadn't been for a calling card left at the front-desk of the motel where he was staying. He was on good terms with the manager, an Indian woman in her thirties, who pulled him aside one morning to inform him someone had been looking for him, showing his photo, which she recognized despite his recent growth of beard. She handed him the business card that had been left with her and told him to be careful, to watch his back.

The business card advertised the services of one Daryl Harris, Repossession Agent. He recognized the name immediately—it had to be the same guy who had dated Abbey before they met. It was too coincidental. He had never met him up close, though Abbey had pointed him out from a distance as they crossed the quad at college. So Abbey was onto him, sending an ex-boyfriend to track him down. This is what prompted his emigrating from Erie: the fear of being found out.

"I'll have it back to you by the end of the day," Mrs. Waxman told him as he let his hand drop to his side. "So you can drive home."

"I don't drive," Will said simply. Ever since the accident, he would have added, but it would have meant explaining too much.

"Yet you have a license."

"It's just for identification."

"That might become a problem when they demolish the bridge."

"They're going to demolish it?"

"It's unsafe. You've seen the sinkhole, I'm sure. You'll need to start thinking about how you're going to cross the river when they do. The bridge upstream—the new one they're building—is quite a hike."

"Maybe I could buy a boat," he thought out loud.

His employer looked him up and down as though measuring him for a suit.

"You might. Then again, you might think about buying a car. I know a place where you could get a good deal. Used, not new."

***

That evening, he ate a starving poet's dinner—a slice of cheddar with a stale dinner roll washed down with a half glass of milk—in the turret, with its view of the river, rolling gently along in the dying light. It was full of windows with a ceiling that rose into a six-sided dome, a feature that led him to nickname it the Hex Room. Finished eating, he leaned back on the futon that formed his bed with a yellow ledger on his lap, opened to a blank page.

One thing that had stuck from his outpatient visits following the accident was the notion of journaling. It would help speed the road to recovery, one of the counselors had advised the group. And he had taken the suggestion to his fingertips, studiously logging a new entry each day.

When he opened his eyes, it was a quarter to midnight. He awoke to a rattling sound from the other room. He sat up, looking around, feeling disoriented. He turned on a light and glanced at his ledger. On it, he had written a single word in bold block letters:

ESSENCE

He must have done this unconsciously. He'd been listening to *Essence of Jazz*, a worn needle scratching out old melodies by luminaries such as Louis Armstrong and lesser knowns like Coleman Hawkins, but it wasn't something he remembered writing.

"Who's out there?" he called into the dark. He had bought a handgun before he left Utica, when he was still Alan Paxton, but he hadn't unpacked it, and his duffle bag wasn't within easy reach.

The rattling from the other room persisted. It seemed to have a rhythm to it, like a set of maracas.

Rats, he thought, attempting to reassure himself.

Rising, he decided to investigate. Taking a breath to steel his nerves, he took a step into the outer room. The rattling stopped for a moment, then started right up again. He found the source right away. It was coming from the desk, more specifically, the top drawer of a stack of three on the left-hand side.

He put his hand on the knob to give it a pull, but it wouldn't come free. It was stuck—or locked. He noticed a keyhole above it in the wooden frame that held it in place. As soon as he let go of the knob, the drawer started rattling again. It seemed agitated. Back and forth, up and down, just an eighth of an inch or so all around, enough space to allow it to rattle and bang and tap.

He opened the drawer below it, and it came out easily, smoothly. Nothing inside. He pulled it all the way out and set it on the floor, then looked underneath. He didn't perceive any hole that would let a rodent enter. He cautiously reached back inside and discovered there was about an inch of space between the back of the drawer and the back of the desk. So that might account for it.

Will sat back in a swivel chair that squeaked as he rotated back and forth, and studied the problem rationally.

The rattling persisted, as though taunting him.

He decided the best way to deal with a spirit of the dearly departed was to talk with it reasonably.

"Hello, Jamaal, is it?"

A quick knock of the drawer in response.

"Listen, if we're going to start sharing quarters, we better lay out some ground rules."

As though in answer, the drawer gave a tentative shake, then stopped.

"What do you say to no banging around past midnight? That's generally when I like to be asleep by."

Correction: That's when he tried to fall asleep. More often, he lay awake in the cruel embrace of insomnia. Tonight had been an exception to the rule. Typically, whenever he closed his eyes, he saw a pair of headlights coming at him, slicing through his vision, making him swerve hard in the darkness to avoid collision.

The drawer gave another rattle, then paused.

Will was about to return to his bed, when it rattled once more, as though playing a game.

"All right, old mole," Will said, steeling his nerves. "What is it you've woken me up for, then?"

The drawer gave one violent, heaving shake that made Will jump back in his seat.

He heard a loud smack hit the floor and looked down to see the photograph containing his wife and child upside down.

"That was uncalled for," he said with resentment.

When he picked it up, he noticed a crack running jagged through the glass, cutting diagonally through Abbey's smile and running over the top of Joel's head. A true Anglophile, Abbey had wanted to name their child Geoff, but Will had thought it too stuffy, too … British, so she compromised for a more American-sounding Joel.

Scrutinizing his image, he noted that his pallor hadn't improved since the photo was taken—his "ghostliness," as Abbey laughingly referred to the difference between their skin tones. He blamed it on a cubicle workspace with limited exposure to sunlight. Maybe he should have done more father-son activities with Joel outdoors.

He stared at the photograph for a long time until the drawer rattled, shaking him out of his reverie. "Sorry, but see? No tears. I'm tear-free, like a baby shampoo."

He retreated to the Hex Room to find a new place for the photo, deciding on a windowsill. Propping it in place, he looked out at the bridge. Strings of white lights along its cables lit up like a carnival ride at a fair.

A solitary figure caught his eye—that of a young woman. But that was all he could make out from this distance.

She paused near the center of the bridge, where it rose to its apex between its two buttresses, white floodlights illuminating the towering pylons. He watched with apprehension as she climbed up onto the outer rail.

The rattling behind him was fervent, insistent, until he passed it, crossing into the other room. He slipped on his shoes and ran down the winding staircase. When he reached the bottom step, Mrs. Gossett's apartment door opened suddenly, startling him, before he could cross the foyer.

"Will!" she exclaimed, pinching her bathrobe shut at the neck. "I heard your footsteps on the stairs. The way you were clomping, I thought perhaps a smoke alarm—"

"I'm sorry, I can't talk. There's a woman. On the bridge."

"Will, please. Wait a moment. Slow down."

She took hold of Will's arm before he could pass, but he shook her off. Or tried to—her grip was surprisingly viselike.

"I think she might be intending to jump."

His landlady shook her head.

"Doubtful. It's not like she hasn't pulled this stunt a thousand times before."

"Stunt?"

"Almost nightly. So there's really little danger. Even the police have stopped taking her seriously."

Will let himself be coaxed to a standstill at the main entranceway, his hand on the doorknob.

"The best thing you can do is come back inside. Why don't you join me for a cup of tea? Or maybe something stronger?"

"No, I really feel—"

He pulled the heavy wooden door open wide enough to step through, but his landlady called after him.

"Will—please. Wait, won't you? I won't be but a second. And then, if you're determined, well, then you can go."

Her eyes fastened on him, attempting to hold him in place, as she backed through the foyer into her apartment.

It didn't take her long to come back out, extending something long and limp. At first he thought it might be one of her several cats that had free roam of the place, upstairs and down. Narrowing his eyes, it came into focus as a crocheted shawl.

"I'm sorry, I don't think it's something I would—"

"Not for you. It's for her. It's a cold night out."

True, there was a nip in the air, stirred by the river.

Will took it, feeling the material. Loosely woven dark wool, it seemed cobweb fragile, as though it could come apart in his hands. Not much defense against cold weather.

"It was her mother's," she said, as though this explained everything. "Something I've had in my chifforobe for a very long time."

"Who is she?"

"You really don't want to know. Best you could do is go back to bed. She's a siren. You'll find yourself drawn to her, and then, it will take all you can do to keep from going down with her, to keep from drowning."

Surely, his landlady was being overdramatic, a lonely woman spinning fairytales out of the air.

She gave Will a forlorn, parting look, then turned and stepped back into the foyer.

"Wait a second," he said, pausing on the threshold. "Does she have a name?"

"Of course she has a name," she answered as though Will had asked something absurd. "Her name is Essence."

Chapter 5

Head tucked down against the night's chill as he crossed the bridge, his gaze was perfectly aimed to be caught by a pair of slippers, fuzzy pink ones, lying side by side, set neatly together, the toes squared off, as though they had been transported from under a bed.

When he looked up, he saw her. She seemed a perfect statue, an outgrowth of the bridge, figurehead of a sailing ship. Standing atop the rail, she clutched a suspending cable, leaning out into nothingness, just the darkness of the night.

Her eyes were half closed. She could have been resting inside a dream. She was dressed in nothing but a thin satiny robe—a shade of green beneath the shimmering lights of the bridge—tied loosely at her waist.

He coughed into his fist.

"Essence?" he asked, tentatively.

She turned her head slowly, looking down at him, pupils myopic within a hazel rim. Far from alarmed, her face seemed inviting, a warm slice of pie peeking out between loose strands of hair that danced with an electric current. It seemed the sort of face more at home on a pile of pillows than perched a hundred feet above a river at night. The coils of dark hair radiated a reddish tint. Freckles dotted the light russet brown of her cheeks.

"Dare me to jump?" she asked with a sly smile. Suspended as she was, she had a faraway look, as though lost in a cloud.

"Were you planning on it?" he asked, trying to defuse the question, looking uneasily at what seemed a light grip on the cable—all that separated being from nothingness.

"No," she said, turning back toward the water. "Not tonight. I'm just practicing. Scared of heights?"

"A little," he admitted, keeping his eyes on hers.

"Or maybe you're the opposite—like me—and afraid you'll let yourself be drawn over."

He knew just what she meant: the temptation to give way to gravity. A counselor from his outpatient group had called it "high-place phenomenon." The French have a more poetic term for it: *l'appel du vide. Call of the void.* But for Will, it was more than a call. *Allure* of the void. A physical attraction—a definite pull.

"Can I help you down?" he asked, trying to downplay the urgency in his voice.

"Do you know how high this bridge is?"

Looking tentatively over the rail, he saw the river swimming dark and wide below.

"Not offhand."

"One hundred and five feet," she replied, swaying to and fro. "Or thirty-two meters, if you're into metric. And do you know how long it would take you to drop to your death?"

Will considered the question the way he would a math problem, but his mind came up blank.

"Only 2.56 seconds," she answered for him. "That's if you weigh what I do, but a woman doesn't divulge her weight." She was right about that. Abbey had always kept hers a closely guarded secret. "And do you know how fast you'd be going on impact? About 55 miles per hour. It's called the 'splat factor.'"

"It sounds like you've done your homework."

"Google makes it easy," she answered. "Too bad they're going to destroy it."

"So I've heard."

"They've already got a replacement for it." She tossed her head toward the new bridge lit up with bright floodlights far upstream. Wider and sturdier, it boasted four lanes and the promise of a quick bypass of both towns on opposite sides of the river as though to avoid a plague. "But I think it's quainter to jump from an antique bridge like this, don't you?"

"Let me help you down," he suggested once more. All her talk of jumping and falling and splatting was making Will nervous.

She held out her free hand, and he took hold of it, firmly leading her off the railing to the walkway. Her hand felt soft, as smooth as tissue paper, and he let go reluctantly, her fingers sliding out of his grasp. He bent down and brought up her slippers, handing her one.

"Do I know you?" she asked, beginning to let go of her smile, cocking her head to the side, studying him at an odd angle as she slid on her slipper. "I know a lot of men," she said with a knowing sort of look, "but I don't seem to recognize your face."

He held out the other slipper, but she didn't take it.

"What's that?" she asked, studying his other hand.

He extended the shawl.

"Something my landlady gave me to give to you," Will explained. "In case you catch cold."

"Something borrowed, something blue," she said dreamily, making Will wonder if she wasn't maybe drunk or drugged. "This looks old, but you look new."

"Well—" He had it in mind to say something, but then whatever it was went right out again. He hadn't been anticipating a rhyme. "You don't want it? The shawl?"

The young woman shook her head. At first he thought it was a sign of refusal, but as she lifted her chin, it seemed she was only tousling her hair out, letting it catch in the breeze.

"It's your mother's."

"My mother's?" she asked, eyes widening, then narrowing with suspicion. "Did you know my mother?"

"No," he answered.

"No," she agreed. "You couldn't have. You're much too young to have known her. You would have been just a boy. Like I was. Except I was a girl, of course. A little, helpless baby girl."

She began walking, backward at first, pulling her robe together, then turning and walking more quickly.

"Can I walk you?" he asked, taking a step forward.

"No, that won't be necessary. I know the way."

"Wait! Your slipper."

He started to follow her—an awkward Prince Charming—but she broke into a run, racing along at a halting pace with just the one slipper on her foot. It was a hundred yards to the foot of the bridge on the Ohio side, and she already had a good distance on him, when she stopped and turned, as though waiting for him to catch up.

Before he could reach her, she crossed the street, racing along the edge of the giant sinkhole in the pavement. Will circled it warily, keeping his eyes on her as she skipped along a sidewalk that led to a park.

"Hey! Wait up! I just want to talk."

Silhouettes turned into recognizable shapes: pointed gables of a gazebo, raised arm of a statue. A creaking sound lured him through a grove of trees. He emerged into a clearing to find a set of playground equipment, glistening silver in the light of a nearly full moon. Louder now: *creak-creak*. Chains of a swing.

As he approached, he could make out one fuzzy foot, the flow of a robe, her hair flying freely as she tilted her head far back on the downswings, then pumped forward on the upswings.

Before he could utter a word, she jumped from the swing without slowing, like a kamikaze, then sprang up in the darkness.

He extended the pink slipper in a gesture of good will. The shawl was draped over his forearm in the manner of a maître de.

As he came up to her, she reached out and tapped him on the shoulder.

"Tag, you're it!" she said with a mischievous smile.

Turning, she sprinted through the park. For a moment, Will stood stock still, dumbfounded, then chased after her, slipper in hand. At least the slipper made him seem less of a stalker and more of a Good Samaritan, trying to do the right thing.

Coming out of the trees, he saw her crossing a boulevard that bordered the park. On the far side, she passed through an opening between twin wings of an iron gate anchored by white pillars.

A gated community? Will wondered.

As he advanced, the gate began to close, automatically. He heard the faint whir of a motor.

Silently, she stood on the far side of the gate, peering through the bars. He ran across the street and slipped through just before it clanked shut. Then she was off again, running like a nymph across a wide lawn.

Following in her footsteps, he thought he had intruded upon a cemetery. As he wended his way through, he saw what he had mistaken for tombstones were statues. Imitation Greco-Roman, by the looks of the torsos and draped shoulders, the naked breasts and shrunken genitals, the lopped-off arms. They exuded a shimmer of whiteness in the night courtesy of a fickle moon playing hide and seek among clouds.

On the other side of the lawn sat a mansion. Stopping for a moment, Will made out three distinct stories, four large chimneys, dozens of windows, mostly dark, only two of them lit. Not a gated community after all, but an estate?

He spotted her climbing a rainspout with the agility of a spider. Springing into a run, he toppled headfirst over a hedge he hadn't made out in the dark. Spilling onto the lawn, he came up all prickles and thorns. As he looked up, a light went on in a second-story window.

At the same time, spotlights went on in the yard.

They were so bright, he winced, and he waited for the migraine that was bound to ensue whenever his optic nerves were stimulated by such a burst of light. When his eyes adjusted, he squinted at the house and spotted two white shapes with black stripes, low to the ground, rounding a corner. Ghostly, they wove their way in and out of shadows. His instinct was to freeze in place. It wasn't obvious what they were at first. His first thought was *dogs*, but they seemed too lithe and agile for dogs. Cats maybe, but big cats. *Very* big cats.

On impulse, he turned and ran. His only hope was to make it to a line of trees sprouting along the fence that enclosed the yard, but the tigers were already closing in. As though playing a game, they had outdistanced him and were now circling back around. He hid behind the last of the statues—a whitewashed giant of a woman—pressing his back hard against it, his spirit draining away like water. And that's not all that was draining. He felt something warm trickle down his inseam.

The tigers came around from either side like mirror images, identical twins. As though knowing they could take their time with their prey, they began closing in—slowly.

On impulse, Will tossed up the slipper and shawl, then leaped, catching hold of an edge that was thankfully not smooth granite, as he had anticipated, but rough sandstone. Digging in with his fingernails, he did an awkward pull-up, scrambling with the tips of his tennis shoes to find a foothold. He pushed and pulled and squirmed until he made it onto a narrow ledge formed by the statue's crossed arms, which cradled a pair of enormous breasts. Peering down, he saw the tigers had arrived.

One rose on its rear feet, reaching as far as Will's foothold, and began sharpening its claws on the sandstone.

"Nice kitty," Will whispered.

As though to prove him wrong, the other tiger batted down its twin. A small fight blistered with bared teeth and bent-back ears, until the one tiger backed down and rolled onto its back. Will watched with distrust as they began a playful tussle.

Struggling to keep his balance, he stood up on the statue and waved his arms over his head, calling out, "Hello! Help! Someone! Please!"

In answer, the spotlights went off. So did the light in the second-story window—Essence's room, he gathered.

As though responding to a whistle, inaudible to humans, the tigers perked up their ears and ran off toward the mansion. He was thankful they were gone, but he didn't risk climbing back down. The gate was too far off, the mansion an equal distance away. And even if he made it to the front door, it didn't mean it would open for someone knocking so late at night.

Every few minutes, he called out, but after a while he gave up in futility. This was the first time in the past year and a half he regretted his personal ban on cell phones. Eventually, he decided there was nothing to do but hunker down for the night.

As though in a dream, he stood and relieved himself over the edge—his pants had dried out from his earlier false start—thinking he must look so much like a fountain. Finished, he curled up in the arms of the statue, his head on the pink slipper he had inanely thought to rescue ahead of himself. The shawl he pulled over his shoulders against the night air that hung heavy with dew. His whole body felt like a blob of freshly poured rubber so that he didn't mind the hard contours of the statue's massive arms that formed his bed.

Chapter 6

He awoke to birdsong and a stiff neck, as though it were a twisted slinky. He had an aerial view of a crisp, white lawn, dew glazing it like icing on a cake.

It took him a moment to realize where he was: still in the arms of a voluptuous statue, a giant-sized fertility goddess.

"Ahem," he heard from somewhere below.

He peered over the edge of the arms that held him.

What he saw surprised him, but he was getting used to surprises: a tall man, maybe mid-forties, clean-shaven, in a black tuxedo, neatly pressed, wearing a Crocodile Dundee type of hat at a slant.

"G'day, mate," he said in an accent to match his hat. "How ya goin' up there?"

How ya goin'? Did he mean how was he going to get down? A good question.

"Sleep all right then?"

"Well—" Will began.

"Madame requests the honor of your presence. Soon as you're suitably disposed, that is."

"Madame?"

"Mrs. Warner, of course. The lady of the house."

"Er—" Will uttered, but was unable to contain a yawn, and by the time he gave his neck a couple of twists so sharp the bones cricked, he forgot what he meant to say.

"Shall I tell her to expect you soon then?"

"What about the tigers?"

"Crimson and Clover?" The man gave a broad smile. "Mere

pussycats, I assure you. Besides, you're too scrawny for their taste."

Scrawny? Will protested inside his head. He was at least as tall as this man standing below him, although in comparison, he came across as more welter weight.

"Not enough meat on you. At any rate, they've already had their breakfast."

"So they're back in their cage?" Will asked, hopeful that such a cage existed.

"They're nocturnal, you see," the man said, not giving Will the benefit of a direct answer. "They enjoy a bit of a romp at night."

"So it's safe to come down?"

He wasn't willing to take any chances.

"Absolutely, dear boy."

Dear boy?

"There's a loo as you enter to the left. Give you a chance to freshen up before attending her Grace."

"Her Grace?" Will remembered what he had wanted to say. "But I need to go home, I need to change. Tell her—tell her Grace I'd love to … oblige her." Will stumbled over his words, feeling somehow that the strange formality of the situation required him to seek an appropriate manner of speaking. "However, I have business to attend to."

"Come now," the man responded. "It's still quite early. Crack of dawn, in fact. And her Grace does not take refusals lightly. Best to come down and tidy up a bit, don't you think?"

With this final suggestion, the man spun on his heel and walked back toward the mansion.

Will followed a few minutes after, cautiously crossing the wide lawn, easily the acreage of a golf green. In the daylight, the mansion didn't seem so alien or forbidding. Nevertheless, he approached the front entrance cautiously and, after a moment's hesitation, rang the bell.

The door opened slowly and, as it turned out, automatically. No one was behind it. Crossing the threshold was like stepping into a different world: an entrance hall five times the size of the foyer at the Victorian Arms. He still held the shawl in one hand, the slipper in the other.

Recalling the directions of the butler—if that's what he was—he hooked a left directly into a bathroom. "Loo" was too small a word to describe its enormity. All tiled with an impossibly high ceiling. A large tub raised on ornate feet. Everything in marble and silver with glitters of gold.

A quick glance in the huge ornate-framed mirror told him his beard could use some grooming, and then he saw that shaving equipment had been laid out.

At first, he planned merely to tidy up: trim the undergrowth, shave his cheekbones. But the straight edge of the razor was so sleek, so smooth, before he could catch himself, he had drawn it down in one fluid motion from cheek to jaw, creating a distinct mismatch with the opposite half of his face. Oh, well, he shrugged. Might as well continue.

Finished with a rough draft, he busied himself with the fine-tuning, running the straight edge carefully over the contours of his face through a lather of cream, the edge so sharp, it felt as sheer as silk. Only three small nicks for the worse, which he patched with a half-used stick of lip balm from the medicine cabinet. True, he hadn't planned on eradicating his beard when he started, but there it was: an entirely revised version of his features.

Having taken so much time on his face, he decided a shower would feel oh so good. He turned on the faucets, running the water over his hand, letting the moment linger. Adjusting the temperature, he felt caught in a web of time, thinking back to filling the tub when he lived with his wife and child. Giving baths to their boy. Adding bubbles and toys. The whole process of bath time. Tantrums and tears when soap got in little Joel's eye. Protests about having his hair washed. Now that he's turning five, did he still make such a fuss?

Five! The date came to him—June 17th—and he realized he had missed his son's birthday the day before. How could he have let the date slip by without recognition? Too busy getting settled and warding off tigers, he supposed. Tears rose and a sob caught in his throat. He lifted his face and flushed out his eye sockets with a spray of warm water. *Oh that this too, too solid flesh would melt* … and simply vanish with a gurgle down the drain.

When he stepped out of the shower, he found that his regular clothes were gone. Hanging from a hook on the door was a lavender suit with lilac shirt and purple tie. His underwear had been substituted with boxers with mauve polka-dots, adhering to a theme. Replacing his sweat socks was a pair of plum dress socks that stretched halfway up his calf. That's probably what the garters were for: holding his socks up. But he had no experience with garters, except at his wedding.

What could this be but some sort of trap? Here he was accepting attire from a benefactress he hadn't yet met. It would be wrong to don it. On the other hand, what choice did he have except to leave the premises wrapped in a towel—and vulnerable to predators should they happen to be lurking about.

All showered and shaved—and feeling a tad foolish in such a flamboyant outfit—he left the humidity of the bath for the chill of the foyer. From there, he entered an enormous room adorned with couches and tables and shelves and lamps all in discrete gatherings and clumps so that, if he didn't know he was in a private residence, he would have thought he had entered the exhibits of a furniture store.

"Won't you please take a seat?" he heard, unnervingly close—so close, he jumped.

Looking down, he saw a woman in a wheelchair. A wide-mouthed vessel behind her caught a rivulet of water from a marble fountain in the wall, outlined by a frieze of cherubs.

She wheeled her chair closer, and he did as beckoned, finding a seat in an overstuffed settee.

The woman had a very dignified look. Her gray hair was perfectly coifed. Her dress was sealed at her throat with a pin capped with a gemstone. The sunglasses added a touch of mystery.

"Would you care for tea? Coffee? Milk?"

At this last suggestion, she gave a whiff of a smile that quickly dissipated into the tightened wrinkles around her mouth.

"Milk, please," he mumbled, feeling ill at ease.

"Milk it is then, Mr.—"

"Archer," he said, half rising. "Will Archer. And you are Mrs. Warner?"

"One and the same," she answered, ringing a tiny silver bell.

At once, as though out of a hidden compartment, the man he had encountered earlier reappeared, minus his Aussie hat—a butler, after all.

"Jenkins, please, milk for the gentleman."

"Milk without a cuppa tea to go with it?"

"Two percent."

"Of course, Mum. Be back in a jiffy."

The same trace of a smile from Jenkins.

"So, Mr. Archer," his hostess said, wheeling her chair closer so that their knees almost touched. "You will need to explain to me what you were doing on my property overnight."

Will hesitated, unsure how to respond. He looked away. His eyes roamed the room, alighting on a portrait above the fireplace, yards away. It was a large portrait in a gilded frame—of a young woman with flaming red hair piled high above a long, white neck, like a swan's, protruding from bare shoulders. The portrait reminded him of the woman Mandy was excising from photos at the museum.

"You obviously are not a burglar. Or, if you are, you are not a very cautious one. Either that, or highly inept."

That same arch of the eyebrow. That same half-smile.

"Yes, ma'am, well, about that—" Will cleared his throat, prelude to a more formal approach. "I mean, no, ma'am." He brought the pink slipper forward as evidence. "Actually—there was a young woman I was following. She left this behind. I brought it, thinking to return it."

Words weren't forming the way he hoped. He must sound like a stalker—however one should sound.

"Whatever it is, you may set it on the table beside you. Jenkins will see to it."

Whatever it is? Ah, so she can't see. Will made a motion with his hand to be sure, then felt foolish making such a crude test of her eyesight.

"It's a slipper," he informed her. "She left it behind last night. On the bridge."

"This young woman. What did she look like?"

"Like that portrait," he said, pointing at the painting. "Only, not quite. Different."

He meant the obvious difference in race. But there was something about the eyes, he decided. Something in the way she looked aloof, superior—yet playful, impish at the same time.

"My only daughter."

"I'm sorry?"

"Fortune, my daughter. You are not the first to remark on the resemblance."

"She's beautiful."

"Was beautiful," Mrs. Warner corrected.

Past tense: *was*.

Out of nervousness, Will picked up a blue marble he found on the low table beside the settee, placing it in his palm. It gave him a sense of stability, anchored within the folds of his lifelines.

Jenkins walked in with a tray holding a ceramic kettle and a pitcher of milk. He proceeded to pour tea into a small cup. Then he did the same with the pitcher, filling a tall glass.

"There you go," he said jovially. "Reckon you're dry as a drover's dog."

Indeed, Will found he was thirsty. He guzzled the milk, draining the glass in a series of gulps, hoping he wasn't coming across as boorish. He felt he was failing to perform some important protocol. There was no doubt a ritual associated with one's morning teatime about which he was completely ignorant.

"Jenkins, will you be so kind as to wake my granddaughter," the matriarch said quietly.

At the mention, Will choked. He set the glass down, coughing.

"Are you all right?" she asked, leaning toward him and placing long, thin fingers on his knee with precision. She must be adept at judging where her visitors are positioned based on the sound of their voice.

"Yes, yes," he gasped, trying to contain his spasm. "It's only—it's nothing. You mentioned—"

"Essence. My granddaughter."

"And the woman?" Will queried, regaining his voice. "In the painting?"

"Her mother. Fortune. Forgive me, but I thought I had already made this perfectly clear."

Will massaged the marble inside his palm the way he would a rubber ball to alleviate stress.

"She's dead, you may have gathered," she continued, an echo

of remorse in her voice. "She died tragically."

"I'm sorry," he said, meaning it, taking a fresh gander at the portrait.

"She threw herself from the bridge."

"The suspension bridge?"

"It was midnight nineteen years ago on the Fourth of July. Independence Day. Nineteen hundred and ninety-seven. A date engraved on my memory as though it were yesterday. She was only nineteen. So young, so young. Thankfully, she didn't carry the baby over the rail. She left her behind, swaddled in her carrier, barely five months old."

"Essence?" he inquired for confirmation, but she ignored him, her reverie requiring no audience.

"It was Jenkins who found her, who brought her back to be raised by me, her maternal grandmother." She lifted her head and turned it toward Will, as though she had momentarily regained her sight. "What is your impression? Do you think I have done a good job raising her?"

Will didn't have an answer for that.

Down the grand staircase came the young woman he had met on the bridge. She wore the same satin robe, loosely tied. Jenkins followed a step behind and a head above.

"Ah, Essence," Mrs. Warner said, as her granddaughter approached, padding across the carpet in bare feet. Did she possess super hearing? Or was there an aroma of Essence in the air?

Her granddaughter took up a position behind a velvet chair, leaning against it for support. She seemed on the verge of returning to sleep standing up.

"This gentleman claims to have met you last night. Have you made his acquaintance?"

Essence looked up, but vaguely. She stared through half-lidded pupils and then shook her head, slowly.

"She's indicatin' the negative, Mum," the butler said.

"Thank you, Jenkins. And this slipper? Please, raise the slipper in question, if you would." Will did as instructed, feeling like a courtroom defendant. "Does this slipper belong to you?"

Essence took in the slipper with the same languid gaze that, candle-like, melted within a dreaminess closed to the world.

Again, she shook her head.

"Same response as before—"

"Acknowledged," Mrs. Warner said, cutting him off, before he could say "Mum," Will presumed. "That will be all. You may go back to sleep, if you wish, my dear."

"But wait a second!" Will exclaimed, rising. The words came out in an automatic burst. His standing up was involuntary, too. "Essence," he said, advancing toward the forlorn figure on the stairs, "you remember me, don't you? We met on the bridge."

"Careful, mate," Jenkins said, intervening. He was as tall as Will, but better built, a muscular tautness to his neck and shoulders, his feet positioned in a stolid boxer's stance that looked immovable. "Best you return to your seat."

"I'm sorry," Essence murmured, turning her face away. "But I don't—" Her voice trailed off as she took to the stairs.

Jenkins led her away by the elbow, guiding her up the staircase. She stumbled halfway up, and he took hold of her more forcefully under her armpit.

"She's lying, of course," Mrs. Warner said with a long exhale, as Will retook his position on the edge of the settee. "Or perhaps 'lying' is too strong a word. She has a tendency to disremember. Every other night, it seems, she slips out of bed. There's no confining her. She has a Houdini's touch for escaping all of our restraints."

Will pictured straightjackets, bed straps, chains dangling on a dungeon wall.

"She tends to sleep half the day away, I'm afraid. And when she awakes, she claims no memory of the night before. So, you see, she chooses not to remember."

Will felt disappointed by this inability of Essence to retain her memories in the short term. It made him feel like a wisp of steam, an evaporating phantom.

"Let me attempt to reassure you," she went on, shifting tack. "Your quest is not unfounded. The slipper is indeed one of hers. She is very fond of her 'pink fuzzies' as she calls them. And now, I must reveal my little joke. I already know who you are."

"You do?"

"Yes, and thus the reason for your attire."

Will pulled the tie through his fingers, examining the fabric, a lustrous silk.

"It will be a purple day today," she announced. "You would have received the email by now, as have I."

Right, Will thought. That is, if the wi-fi at the Victorian Arms wasn't so fitful, putting his laptop into sleep mode before it had a chance to connect.

"So you're aware of my job at the museum."

"Of course. As the largest investor in the enterprise, I keep close tabs on its operation. Besides, I think it important that we grandmothers keep in touch from time to time."

She could only be referring to Sybil Waxman, Jamaal's mother. This made him surmise that Essence was as much Jamaal's daughter as Fortune's. The pairing of the grandmothers—the one so full-bodied and assertive, and this one so eccentric and sinewy—hadn't clicked till now.

"It was a pleasure making your acquaintance," she said by way of dismissal.

Will rose, pulled by a set of strings. He backed away, as though retreating from a royal presence.

"Well, thanks for the milk, and it was nice meeting you. And the suit, too. I'll make sure to return it."

"No need, no need," she said, waving her hand in adieu. "It was my late husband's."

As he turned to go, Mrs. Warner called from her chair.

"Before you leave, would you be so kind as to put my eye back where you found it?"

Will stopped, momentarily confused. It took him a second to realize what she meant. Slowly, he unclenched his palm to reveal the round blue marble, glistening with a coat of perspiration.

Great, now he wasn't only a stalker but a kleptomaniac. So much for first impressions.

"I'm sorry, I didn't realize—"

"I'm joking, Mr. Archer. It's merely a marble."

By this time, Jenkins had returned to his employer's side.

"I have excellent hearing," the old lady said. "If I had a gun, I could shoot you and drop you like a stone." Then, as an afterthought, "Do you think I should put our theory to the test?"

Will didn't answer, unsure if the question was directed toward him or her butler.

"I'm not sure the young man appreciates your sense of humor," Jenkins remarked.

Will came back into the room and returned the marble to its table. He also handed over the shawl.

"What's this?" she asked, rubbing the fabric between bony fingers.

"Something of Fortune's."

"Thank you, Mr. Archer," she said after a moment's reflection. "If you would be so kind as to allow my manservant to show you to the door, now that our little interview is concluded."

Interview?

Will was confused as well as chagrined. He never felt so off balance, except when having met Mrs. Waxman. He left reluc-tantly, crossing the lawn with frequent looks back at the house, only partly in fear of the tigers. In particular, he scanned the sec-ond-story balcony which Essence had climbed to the night be-fore. He wished for a last glance—but not to remember her by. He had a feeling hers was a face he would encounter again.

***

Essence watched the Grandmother open her bedroom door without knocking and wheel herself in. On her lap was the pink slipper.

She stopped in the middle of the room, several feet from her bed. Essence wondered how the Grandmother always knew where and when to stop, despite new obstacles she set in her path every day: a stack of books, an armada of figurines, a hillock of dirty laundry. She must have radar. Invisible antennae.

Without speaking, the Grandmother began clapping, slowly, in mock applause.

"An amazing performance you put on this morning, my dear. Simply spectacular."

But it wasn't a performance—not really. Out of her early morning bleariness, the whole living room scene had appeared surreal, part of a lingering dream. There was the man she had met during the night, sitting there in a new suit with purple flour-ishes, sipping a milk with the Grandmother. Recognizable, de-spite a freshly shaven face that looked painfully tender to the touch. It hadn't been what she was expecting when Jenkins had come to her room to retrieve her.

She took the slipper that the Grandmother proffered and sat back on the edge of her bed beneath its four-poster canopy, spread out above like an enormous tent.

"You will not be seeing this William Archer again, is that clear?"

"Oh," Essence responded, "is that his name?"

She could tell by the way the Grandmother's mouth tensed, the crinkles at the corners deepening, that she was silently cursing herself for revealing a name she thought her granddaughter already knew.

She wheeled herself more closely, leaning her head forward.

"You must promise me never to see him again."

"Yes, Grandmother," she complied. It was always best to agree to the old woman's demands. There would always be opportunities to disobey them. "But why?"

"I suspect he has been recruited by Nana Other."

She meant her other grandmother: Sybil Waxman.

"Recruited? For what reason?"

The Grandmother waited, as though listening to her heartbeat. It had been known to flutter in moments of excitement.

"She wants him to solve the riddle of her son's death."

"You mean, my father. Why can't you ever say it?"

The Grandmother ignored the question.

"She has suspicions. And I am afraid to find out where her suspicions will lead."

"Where could they lead?"

"It would bring up too much ugliness. Your mother's reputation would be sullied once more. It's a cold, cold case, and it's best to leave it that way."

"You mean the rape."

The Grandmother nodded.

"It doesn't bother me as much as it bothers you," Essence said, "being the child of a rape victim."

"You mustn't talk about it," the Grandmother snapped. "You mustn't bring it up."

"Why not? You've got the whole town believing it."

Essence knew this was partly the Grandmother's motive for

funding the museum. Having spread the rumor, she worried about the fallout attached to her daughter's reputation.

"You know what I think, don't you? I don't think she was raped. I've been to the museum. I've seen the photos of my father, the two of them together. He doesn't look that kind of man."

"He was a heroin addict. There was no telling what the drug made him do—of what he was capable."

"I'll bet my mother asked for it. I bet she got on her knees and begged."

The Grandmother slapped her once, harshly, across the face—her aim perfect.

"I'm sorry to lash out, but must you always be so disagreeable, my dear? Now, promise me!" Her tone became as insistent as a razor held to her granddaughter's throat.

"Okay, Grandmother, I promise."

"Raise your right hand."

She raised her left.

"Swear on your mother's grave."

"She doesn't have a grave."

And this much was true. Her mother's ashes resided in a silver urn on the mantelpiece beneath her portrait.

"You're impossible!" The Grandmother wheeled even closer and held out her hand—the same one she had just struck her with—for Essence to take in hers. "Pray with me, child."

Essence rolled her eyes at the ceiling as, taking the Grandmother's hand, old Florence Warner rolled out a prayer, one of many she used on these sorts of occasions, whenever her granddaughter's soul was in jeopardy. And Essence, dutifully, mumbled along, the lines sounding memorized, rehearsed, as though she were a little girl taking part in a school play.

Chapter 7

The bullets drilled through the rear windshield, blasting out a hole as big as his head. They sounded off in quick succession: *boom, boom, boom, boom, boom, boom!* Good thing his head was in the process of ducking.

Daryl didn't have a gun with which to return fire—not that he would if he could. He'd exchanged it for a digital camera with telephoto lens. Pictures were the only targets he preferred to shoot these days.

Usually, his job as a repo agent wasn't this exciting, but this was Philadelphia, birthplace of the nation's freedom, and this particular debtor wasn't fond of the idea that freedom came with a price: that is, a monthly car payment on a Porsche that was nine installments overdue. Thus, the gunfire.

Disgruntled debtors came with the territory—but not typically wielding weapons of this make and caliber. His assailant was a young woman—Caucasian—standing braced in the middle of the road beneath a streetlamp. He viewed her in the rearview mirror when she was exchanging magazines, her hair blowing in the wind, her shoulders square. Under different circumstances, he might have put the car in reverse and invited her to hop in for a ride. She seemed just his type of woman.

Not that any woman compared to Abbey. Daryl had always felt protective of Abbey. Even when she had dumped him for Alan after returning stateside from her year studying overseas. England had changed her, made her more self-assured, more determined. Thus, her mono focus on finding her missing spouse. With his last visit to Utica—one he recalled with especial fondness, given what had transpired between them before he was metaphorically kicked to the curb—he had been handed an extra assignment: to repossess Abbey's husband.

Tracking down vehicles was much easier than people. The lender made it easy, giving Daryl the GPS tracking code and a spare fob for keyless ignition. Except this particular owner had refused to cooperate by leaving the Porsche unattended for more than a couple of minutes at a time as she made a series of in-and-out pitstops: hair salon, convenience mart, party favor outlet, real estate office, USPS branch, even a public library.

"It's like she's playing cat and mouse," the young woman riding shotgun observed. Asuka was his latest accomplice, whom he recruited from a bevy of girlfriends, and the occasional down-on-his-luck guy friend, who looked forward to the joyride he would treat them to before taking over the wheel. Then they would have the lesser joy of following behind in his old, reliable, slightly beat-up Chrysler to the impound lot back in Utica. To make up for it, he gave them a little something for their trouble: a decent cut of the payout each car retrieval earned.

Daryl had developed the same feeling that the car owner knew he was on her tail and was taunting him, daring him to take what she falsely believed to be hers—and not the bank's.

"Want me to try approaching her?" Asuka asked.

Daryl sized her up. His passenger was tall and thin and wiry.

"I know what you mean by 'approaching,'" Daryl confided. "Have you ever considered that your mixed martial arts moves are only feeding the stereotype of your birth?"

"Can I help it if I'm half Japanese on my mom's side? I'm supposed to what? Give up a hobby I enjoy?"

Daryl reflected that on more than one occasion, her "hobby" had left the vehicle owner prostrate on cold cement. He didn't wish to risk another breach of the peace.

Plus, there was the problem of the gate now that his quarry had eluded pursuit back to the safety of her protected neighborhood. Obtaining the keycode from entering traffic posed little difficulty with his telephoto lens, but Daryl could anticipate the suspicions he would arouse from the adolescent guard in his little glass booth protecting a white-flight community such as this.

He had returned under cover of night—well, almost morning. He and Asuka had hung out at a local bar past closing, when he had her drop him off curbside and drive off to their rendezvous at a 7-Eleven across town.

Wearing dark clothes, he easily hopped the fence, luckily without pulling a hamstring—old sports injury—and found the Porsche sitting like fair game in the owner's driveway. The owner had caught up with him, on foot—more specifically, barefoot—when he had to wait at the iron gate for it to open automatically—but ever so slowly. And that's when the shooting began, the guard looking up dumfounded from his cell phone—a look Daryl was sure he mirrored.

Daryl pulled the car into the convenience mart—the cloak of twilight was fast dissolving—and hopped out. Brushing bits of glass from the back of his head, he made it to the bathroom, only to find it occupied.

Several long minutes later, having relieved himself, he bought a box of Twinkies, then headed back to the Porsche, where he found a small crowd had gathered. He should have found a better hiding place for it, but when you've got to go, well, impatience had got the better of him.

"This your car?" a tall, greasy-haired, tattooed dude asked him point blank.

"Wish I were rich enough to afford a car like that," Daryl responded with a laugh.

He backed off to the other side of the parking lot where he

consumed the whole box, stuffing one Twinkie at a time into his craw. One thing he observed about being shot at: it made you ravenous for junk food! There was nothing better to do while waiting for Asuka to arrive. Where the hell was she, anyway?

He made a call to his employer on his cell.

"Problem?" asked the voice belonging to a person he had never met face to face, just like Charlie out of *Charlie's Angels*.

"I've got the merchandise, but it's damaged goods," Daryl reported.

"Take it to …" He wrote down on a sales receipt an address that would repair windshields with no questions asked. Presumably, this business of having your windshield shot out wasn't such an uncommon occurrence as he thought.

"Worse than that, the cops."

He watched with some apprehension as a uniformed officer exited the convenience store, munching a Kristy Kreme and sipping a coffee.

"Show him your credentials, you've got every right to repossess said silver Porsche."

"Silver, did you say?"

Daryl squinted, thinking the predawn light was playing tricks with his eyes. The car he had followed throughout the previous day had indeed been silver. Absconding with it, he couldn't differentiate its color in the dark. Beneath the bright lights of the service station, he could see that the car was as blue as a map of the Pacific Ocean.

"Read off the license plate for me," Charlie requested.

Daryl read off the numbers and letters.

"It seems you've got the wrong car."

"What do you mean, 'wrong car'?"

"The car you want is BAD 4 U."

Yes, Daryl thought. Everything about this was turning bad.

The only thing the two license plates had in common, aside from the same number of letters and digits, was the first letter: B. In his haste, he hadn't bothered to read further. He had made the assumption that there would be only one Porsche of this make and model in the vicinity. What he hadn't counted on was copycat neighbors.

That explained why the fob for keyless ignition he had been supplied with hadn't worked. To start the car, he had been forced to perform a relay attack single-handedly with amplifier and transponder that required back-and-forth trips to the owner's front door to pick up the signal of her fob that he hoped was on the other side. It was, but the delay gave her ample opportunity to challenge him through her doorbell camera and grab a weapon.

"I would strongly advise abandoning said vehicle and moving away from the premises casually without attracting attention," his employer intoned.

Too late. Some of the onlookers were waving and pointing in his direction as the cop took a closer look at the windshield. Asuka chose that moment to pull up with the Chrysler, but Daryl shrugged off the questioning look she gave him as he backed away from the parking lot.

"I'll try again tonight," Daryl told his employer.

"Don't bother. You've been compromised. I'll send someone else."

The phone call left him feeling humiliated and worried about his reputation. Keeping his eye on the police officer, as he quite audibly radioed in a possible stolen car, Daryl slinked off through a windbreaker of scraggly pine trees, passed an abandoned Dairy Queen, and hoofed on down the block, where Asuka picked him up as though he were any old hitchhiker.

"What was that all about?"

After Daryl explained, she seemed both delighted and upset

by the incident: delighted the assignment came with so much action, upset she had missed it.

"Now what?" she asked rather petulantly, no doubt feeling cheated out of a cut of the proceeds plus a chance to sit behind the wheel of a Porsche.

"Don't know about you, but I'm beat. What say we find an out-of-the-way motel to recuperate?"

"Okay, but no funny business. I have a boyfriend."

Daryl raised his right hand and swore: "No funny business. Agreed."

At their motel room, funny business concluded, Daryl decided to turn his attention to his new pet project: the problem of Alan Paxton. How exactly to flush him out?

The trail, if ever there was one, would be as cold by now as Hansel and Gretel's path of breadcrumbs. But Daryl had promised Abbey he would do what he could to locate him, given his investigative skills as a repossession agent.

Daryl was aware of the efforts Abbey had made to get Alan or to get him to contact her. His Facebook site had been deactivated, so she made a habit of posting appeals on her own social media sites, messages he had not responded to—ever. She kept dipping into the ceaseless trickle of Internet traffic, hoping to snare some clue as to her husband's whereabouts. She was still counting on people coming to her: Abigail Paxton. What Daryl proposed was a way of getting people to come to him: as Alan.

All he needed was his laptop and a decent headshot.

Fortunately, he had both. The laptop is something he brought along to scan license plates in between repos. The photo, courtesy of Abbey, he'd been carrying around on his phone ever since Alan had gone missing. It was an easy matter of plugging it in as the profile picture of a new social media page he created for one Alan Paxton. Status: married. Child: one. Education: B.A. Occupation: Auto claims examiner. Nickname:

Pax. He created a stream of additional posts with more photos—family affairs—Abbey had transmitted, giving his life a visual backstory.

In the descriptor field, he considered adding a few hobbies and interests, unusual ones, as a sort of payback for stealing Abbey away from him all those years ago: Chia pet collector, Candy Crush Saga addict, trainspotter, bedwetter. But he didn't think Abbey would appreciate the fun.

He stared at the photo on the screen, sizing up the features—so clean-cut, so boyish, so … white. He still couldn't believe Abbey had gone for someone like this: a frat boy no less. And not for the last time, he lamented ever losing her, but he could only blame himself for being so noncommittal at the time—not that time had changed his outlook on relationships. His M.O. was still very fly-by-night. Only Abbey had come close to tempting him into something more permanent.

"Coming back to bed?" Asuka called from the Queen-sized mattress where she sprawled on top of the covers, naked beneath a towel she had loosely wrapped around her torso following a shower. Very loosely. Like Daryl, she hadn't packed so much as a toothbrush, never mind a change of clothes, assuming she would be back in Utica by nightfall.

Daryl knew what she meant by "bed": more funny business.

"What about your boyfriend?" Daryl had asked upon her first invitation, but she had only smirked with a twitch of her long black hair.

He checked his watch: only 2:30 in the afternoon.

"Just a sec," he told her, finishing up. "All right, Mr. Paxton." Daryl addressed the blue eyes staring back at him from the computer screen. "Time to bring you to life."

A single click of the Enter key and …

Voila! Alan was back online again.

Chapter 8

There were only two death threats this morning—in between requests for hours of operation—loaded with racial slurs, and packed tight with exclamation points, as though with sticks of dynamite, explosive in ALL CAPS. The milder of the salutations referred to the proprietor of the museum as SUPREME BITCH-LADY. The other was less kind.

Will printed these off to be stored in a special folder dedicated to accumulating proof of racial targeting for a police investigation that was continually put on hold for lack of traceable email addresses. Apparently, the perpetrator was using publicly available computers—presumably at a library or Internet café—to create and then delete accounts.

He was threading the printouts through an old-fashioned printer, the kind with perforated holes along each side—trying to correct a jam that had folded one half of the seamed paper like a Japanese fan—when Mandy startled him with a "Ta-da!" and a twirl of a taffeta gown.

"You shaved your beard!" she exclaimed, waltzing up to him. "I barely recognize you." She rubbed her fingers over his chin as though polishing a doorknob.

"I guess it was time for a change," he felt the need to explain. A change back to his former appearance, he might have added. Had this been his intention subconsciously—a return to his previous self?

"Oh, my goodness! I know it's a purple day and all, but aren't you taking it a little too far? First a shave, and now this?" She made a flourish of her hands that swept over him like bird wings from head to toe, taking in the color of the clothes Mrs. Warner had set out for him. Had it only been just this morning? It felt so long ago.

"Me? What about you?"

"What about me?"

She was dressed in purple from a violet headband to the lavender bows on the toes of her shoes. He had to admire her dedication to Mrs. Waxman's color principle. So far she was nailing it down as though competing in a beauty pageant.

"Nothing, except we're a perfect match for a prom date."

Her pout relaxed into a smile, as she ducked into the adjoining archival room to begin sorting through photos.

"Mind if I look through them?" he asked, following her in.

"Go ahead, they're not copyrighted or anything."

He was particularly interested in the women she was cutting out. Most were the same person whose portrait he had observed in the mansion that morning.

"Fortune," he said aloud.

"As in money?" Mandy asked without looking up. "I'm afraid this job doesn't pay all that well. I'm just an intern."

"No, I meant Fortune Warner."

"Oh." She paused with the X-Acto knife. This time she took in Will with a more serious assessment. "What about her?"

"I met her daughter."

"Essence?" Mandy asked, going back to her work.

"Do you know her?"

"Yes, I know her. Or rather, know of her." She'd only met her a few times. They took a course together at the college, a small Bible school in town. But she dropped out before the end of the semester. "She keeps a low profile," Mandy added, then lowered her voice an octave, as though to reveal a secret, "... by day. By night, she's a regular Blanche DuBois."

***

At eleven, on the dot, the bell tinkled furiously, as the proprietor charged into the museum.

"Mrs. Waxman!" Will said, startled for the second time that day. He had cleaned as much of the graffiti out front as he ever hoped would come off without more heavy-duty equipment, such as a sandblaster, and was just on the point of dusting the glass cases, beginning with the one that contained Jamaal's golden sax.

"William, please, a word!" she said between breaths, which heaved from her chest in a series of huffs.

She led him through the back room past Mandy, who was finishing up with the photographs. Mandy gave him a worried look as they passed out the back door into a narrow alley behind the museum.

It took Mrs. Waxman a moment to catch her breath. As soon as she did, she got right to the point.

"I've just been informed you've been hanging out with my granddaughter."

"I wouldn't call it 'hanging out' exactly," Will said, defensiveness creeping into his voice.

"No, no, you misunderstand me. I'm not angry."

"No?"

"Quite the contrary, I'm elated."

This made Will more confused than before. He would have had an easier time understanding her anger.

"And you want to know why?" Her mouth broadened into a palpable bloom. "It's because you have an opportunity. Two opportunities, as a matter of fact."

"I do?"

Will looked back and forth toward either end of the alley, where rectangles of sky were showing. He wanted to make sure there was an escape route, if need be.

"First, you have the opportunity to look after my grand-daughter."

"Essence?" he asked, just to be clear.

"Yes, yes," she said, giving his shoulder a hard shove, which was probably meant to be playful. "She needs protecting."

"Like, from enemies?"

"No, no, no. From herself, William. From herself. She's her own worst enemy, as the saying goes."

From what Will had gathered at the top of the bridge the night before, he had little trouble believing this to be the case.

"You mentioned a second opportunity?"

"Yes: to look for clues."

"Clues?"

"The next time you set foot in the Warner mansion."

"I'm not sure there will be a next time."

"Why ever not?" She jutted her lower lip into a terrific pout. "Surely, you plan on calling on my granddaughter again?"

"I haven't really—"

"And now you know where she lives."

"Yeah, but I—"

"So of course you'll be setting foot in the Warner place again. What could be more natural? And when you do, you can start looking for clues."

"What sort of clues?"

"Clues that would help explain the death of my son. As to his murder."

"You mean—" Will had to stop himself to let the thought formulate. If she wanted him to find clues, this must mean she suspected someone living there of homicide. And as far as he knew, there were only three residents of the Warner mansion: Essence, old Mrs. Warner, and ... "You think the butler did it?"

"How droll," she said, giving him another playful push. "This isn't a mystery novel. I don't know what clues exactly. All I do know is Florence Warner is hiding something, keeping something from me."

"What makes you say that?"

"She's the biggest financial backer of my little museum. Why would she invest so heavily in Jamaal's memory unless she felt some measure of guilt?"

It seemed a logical question. Will studied it from various angles for flaws, while Mrs. Waxman dug in her purse.

"Here," she said, producing a business card. "My cell phone number is on it. In case you ever need to call."

"Outside business hours? Why would I—"

"In case of an emergency. I've already lost two curators. I don't plan on losing a third."

When they stepped back inside, Mandy was already positioned with a camera, which she aimed directly at him and shouted, "Smile!"

Before he could ward off the flash, it impacted his brain like a letter opener slicing through soft tissue. When he reopened his eyes, he found himself laid out on the floor with Mandy hovering over him.

"Are you all right?" she asked. "I'm so, so sorry. I only wanted to get a spontaneous shot—you know, unrehearsed. For the website. Our social media page. I just hate it when a smile looks rehearsed—that's all. I didn't know you were going to—"

Mrs. Waxman came into view, cell phone at her ear.

"How is he?" she asked.

The room was spinning counterclockwise, as though to wind back time, and it took Will a moment to orient himself to the situation.

"It's all right," he said, trying to sit up. Mandy placed an arm behind his back, helping him upright, and Mrs. Waxman crouched down beside him, still on the phone.

"I think he's all right now," she spoke into it, eyeing him critically. "He's coming around. I'll call you back if I need to."

"It's just a headache," he said, feeling embarrassed.

"Some headache," his employer said, sounding impressed.

"It was more than 'just a headache,'" Mandy said. She brought a Dixie cup of water to his lips, and he took a sip. "You had some kind of seizure."

"It happens sometimes," he said. "I'm feeling all right now."

"Just … happens?" Mandy inquired.

"Anything sudden or unexpected—a bright light, a loud noise."

"I'm so sorry. If I'd known."

Mrs. Waxman and Mandy helped him to his feet.

"I hereby grant you the afternoon off," Mrs. Waxman announced.

"But the museum. Who will—"

"Let me worry about that. Mandy, dear, will you lock up after us? William, I'll be driving you home."

"I can walk," Will said, taking a step, but having to steady himself by gripping a chair back.

"Sure you can," she said. "Which is why I insist."

Chapter 9

Will lay all that afternoon in bed with the shades drawn, luxuriating in the dimness, brain like a teabag steeping in a cup of warm water. He kept a washrag over his eyes. It was the rattling of the drawer that awoke him from a restless sleep.

The ghost was starting early tonight. It had just turned dusk.

Moving into the living room, he inspected the desk. Perhaps it wasn't the drawer that was rattling after all, but something inside. Shaking of dice? Bunch of loose marbles?

The apartment came equipped with a shelf full of board games: Monopoly, Life, Sorry, Parcheesi, checkers, chess, and—he had noted it when he first unpacked—a Ouija board minus the one essential element for communicating with the spirit world: its planchette. Working around this difficulty, he found a tumbler—what he wouldn't give for a brace of Scotch straight up, if only his conscience would permit it—and drew a V with a Sharpie on its rim for a pointer. He coated the board with cooking spray from the kitchen cupboard to reduce friction and tested the drinking glass for mobility, moving it upside down with his fingertips on the bottom. It glided as smoothly as a skater on ice.

He placed a notepad and pen nearby in case he needed to take dictation. The heading on the notepad that had come with the apartment was the name and address of a hotel: Brass Pineapple, Charleston, SC. He wondered if it was somewhere Jamaal had stayed on the road. As though understanding what Will was about to do, the desk drawer stopped its rattling.

Nothing happened at first, and he wasn't surprised. He wasn't a great believer in William Fuld's talking board as a link to another dimension. The few times he had toyed with it, when he was much younger, he suspected the person opposite him of cheating or else their collective unconscious of taking over. But here he was playing solo. He gave the glass a friendly nudge, and it slid directly to the space on the board that said, "Hello."

"Hi," Will responded. "Are you Jamaal?"

Immediately, as though impelled, the glass pointed to *Yes.*

"Are you happy where you are?"

This was the first question that occurred to him. He felt a little foolish for speaking it out loud. Shouldn't a ghost be able to understand you telepathically?

A sharp move to the opposite corner of the board: *No.*

"Is there something you want to tell me?"

Yes.

"What is it? I'm ready."

He kept the fingers of one hand lightly on the bottom of the inverted glass. With his other, he picked up the pen.

S-A-V

—and stopped.

"Save? Save who?"

E-S-S

It stopped moving again, as though short on psychic energy.

"Essence?"

Immediate *Yes.*

"From jumping?"

Yes.

"From drowning?"

Yes.

"From—"

The glass took control, and Will jotted down the letters in sequence.

M-T-H-R

The glass paused, and Will deciphered what he had written.

"Mother? Her mother?"

But this didn't make any sense, her mother being dead.

The glass started moving again.

F-A-T

"Mother fat?"

He thought of the weight Abbey had complained about putting put on with her pregnancy.

"You want to prevent her getting pregnant?"

Immediately, it added an *E*.

"Fate," he understood. "Mother's fate? Fortune's?"

Yes.

A thought occurred to Will, and he spoke it aloud.

"Was she murdered?"

The glass moved to *Yes* then *No*, then rested in between.

"You're not sure?"

The glass repeated the movements.

"Maybe?"

Yes.

"Were *you* murdered?" To Will's mind, it seemed a logical follow-up.

Again, the same movements, the glass coming to rest in between *Yes* and *No*.

"Who would have wanted you dead?"

M-A-N-Y

"But who specifically?"

A long pause ensued, making Will think their conversation was at an end. Before he could lift his fingers, the glass moved to two different letters in succession.

P-G

"P-G?" The smallest word he could come up with to fill in the blank was "pig," and that made him think of ... "The cops?

The police wanted you dead?"

The glass moved forcefully, deliberately, rapidly between the two letters, over and over, as though in confirmation.

P-G-P-G-P-G-P-G-P-

The glass flew out from under Will's fingers and slammed against the wall near the entrance to the Hex Room, shattering into several sharp fragments.

Their session decidedly over, Will went to pick up the pieces with dustpan and broom. Glancing out the window, he saw the girl on the bridge, standing on the walkway, not hanging from a cable this time. She was facing his direction, staring toward his dormer window. Despite the distance that separated them, he felt exposed, vulnerable, naked. And yet … attracted.

***

By the time he arrived at the bridge, she was gone.

He hurried down the walkway to the Ohio side past the gaping hole in the street that had swallowed a car with its woman driver. He ducked into an alley to let a car rumble past crammed with loud teens looking for trouble—one of them threw a beer bottle in his direction—then hightailed it to the park.

Hearing the familiar *creak-creak-creak* of the chains, he came across Essence swinging. This time she was wearing a loose-fitting tee and pair of shorts.

"You came," she said, gliding back and forth. "I was hoping you'd know where to find me."

"Well, here I am."

He got on the swing beside her and pulled back on the chains, idly, without trying to match the height of her arcs.

"I'm sorry about this morning," she said, glancing his way. "I barely recognized you without your beard."

"It was just something I did without deciding to. You know, on impulse."

"Would you say you're impulsive in general?"

"Well, er—" Will began, fumbling for an answer.

She stopped pumping and brought the swing to a standstill, dragging her feet, until she was evenly matched with Will. She reached across and ran her fingers over his face, sparking an electric current that trilled through his neck and ran down his spinal column on a wire.

"I like it," she said. "Nevertheless, I should have been … nicer. But I'm on sedatives. I wasn't quite myself."

"Are you on sedatives now?"

"Uh-huh. I'm almost always on one pill or another. Antidepressants, antianxiety, anti just about anything you can think of. My doctors seem to be trying to erase my personality."

"Are they succeeding?"

To this, she didn't have an answer, but went back to swinging, renewing her pull on the chains. Will decided not to compete, lacking the energy to keep up with her.

"You know they're going to close it off in two weeks' time, don't you?" she said, in passing. "They're going to demolish it— or start to," she added on the upswing. "That gives us just two weeks. Seventeen days to be precise."

"Us?" Will wondered if had heard her right.

She jumped off the swing, landing like a cat on all fours, then sprang up. This time she didn't run out of the park but sauntered along with her hands clasped behind her, making movements as though ice skating.

He caught up with her, walking beside her without knowing what to say, but feeling he should say something. He felt out of place, like a single training wheel on the side of a bicycle.

"So this suicide you're planning …"

"I didn't say I was going to kill myself. I'm just going to jump and let fate decide the rest."

"It's a hundred feet to the river," he reminded her.

"One hundred and five," she corrected him.

"The odds …"

"I know the odds. I've beat them before."

"You've attempted suicide before?"

Their conversation seemed so nonchalant. They could be talking about the latest episode of a TV show.

"Twice now. The first time was my wrists in the bath, but not deep."

"And the second time?"

"An overdose. Not overly dramatic."

"So you like drama?"

"Yes, you could say that."

"Is this why you're telling me all this, so I might try to save you?"

She stopped, turning to face him. They were just outside the halo thrown by a streetlamp. He could see an unmistakable pout.

"I don't need saving, William."

Oh, so she knew his name. He was momentarily confused. Had they been formally introduced?

"Please, you can call me Will."

Their conversation had become so low-spoken that it was in danger of becoming absorbed by the sounds of the night: crickets, peepers, a chorus of leafhoppers.

"Is this all just some sort of game?"

"No, I wouldn't call it that."

"A need for attention then?"

"I won't deny it. I do like attention. But it's more than that—or maybe less. I need freedom. I need to be free. And I'm running out of options."

"Options?"

"It would take too long to explain."

She began walking again, skipping along. He had to jog to keep up until they crossed the street to the gate of the mansion.

"Well, goodnight … Will," she said with a smile, turning to enter the code.

"Wait a second. Do you have to go so soon? I felt we were just starting to—"

"Get to know each other? I'd like that, but unfortunately, duty calls."

"Duty?"

"My grandmother. You've met Jenkins. He's given me a heads up she'll be making the rounds tonight, knocking to make sure I'm in bed."

"And if you're not?" he asked, knowing his voice held a plaintive note like a piano key stretched out for resonance.

In lieu of an answer, she came up to him and draped both arms around his neck. Her face was so close that in the light from the streetlamp, he could make out the patchwork of freckles crossing her nose. Her breath was light and easy, emitting a scent of peppermint. With her eyes closed, she found his mouth and gave him a long, languorous kiss, not deep, but full and wet and supple.

At first, he kept his own lips static. They could be made of cardboard for all the response, the reciprocity, he allowed.

Gradually, he allowed her to pry his lips apart with a darting tongue. After what seemed minutes, she withdrew her mouth and stepped backward with a grin.

The gate had swung fully open behind her. Thankfully, there was no sign of the tigers.

"What was that for?" he asked, abashed by his own reaction. An image of Abbey crossed his mind. She didn't seem pleased.

"Haven't you been listening?" she asked, still smiling, as she backed away. "If you want to get to know me, you'd better hurry."

This time, he didn't follow her through the gate as it began to swing shut. He waited on the outside, looking in, feeling like a prisoner in reverse, a prisoner of his own longing.

***

After Will left the Victorian Arms for the evening, Phyllis Gossett went inside her papered sitting room. She dusted off her husband's urn on the mantel, then set the duster aside and powered on her computer.

The contact information of the person she was searching for was right there on the museum's website. She was listed as an intern along with one William Archer as curator. Will's phone number was the party line for the Victorian Arms. No surprise there, as he didn't possess a cell phone. The intern's was a mobile number.

As she took a seat, one of her cats hopped on her lap but she shooed it off.

"Not now, pussy, dearest. Mama has an important call to make."

The cat seemed put off, but she ignored it. She picked up the phone and dialed the number she had underscored with her fingernail on the computer screen.

The phone rang three times.

"Hello?" a young woman's voice enthused into the receiver, as though grateful someone had thought to call her.

She took a deep breath before responding.

"Yes, hello, Amanda? Amanda Anders? My name is Phyllis Gossett. I run the Victorian Arms apartments. Will Archer is one of my tenants … Oh, no, he's fine. There's nothing the matter. However, I have a proposition for you … No, I can't discuss it over the phone. It would be better if we were to meet face to face. In fact, I think it's time we were better acquainted."

Chapter 10

On Sunday, his first free day, Will went to a florist's and bought a bunch of daffodils. He waited outside the gate of Essence's manor with them, staring up at a security camera that must be beaming his lovely visage onto a surveillance monitor.

A migraine had prevented his setting out to find her the evening before, and he hoped she didn't regard his no-show as an insult. Without a phone number, he had no way to schedule what he had considered an open invitation to see her again.

He stared across the wide green lawn, seeking a sign. But the windows were dark, revealing nothing from within. He started to feel foolish, holding a bouquet of daffodils. Maybe he would leave them outside the bars as a testament. A testament to what, though, he didn't know.

"Are they out yet?"

The voice came from below. It belonged to a small boy who looked like one of the Little Rascals. A sprout of hair sprang out of his head like the stem of a radish.

"The tigers? I haven't seen them."

The boy was eating popcorn from a bag, as though waiting for a matinee. He proffered the bag, but Will declined.

"That means they're still asleep in their cage."

"You live around here?" he asked. The boy's bike was parked without its kickstand, lying in the grass like a sleeping pony.

"Sometimes they come right up to the fence," the boy said, ignoring the question. "But you shouldn't feed them. Just like you shouldn't feed geese, not really."

"But you feed them?"

"Yes, sir. I feed them popcorn. They like it with butter but no salt. I experimented."

A big word for such a small kid.

"So you're on pretty good terms with them, are you?"

"Terms?"

"You know, friends?"

The boy thought about this for a moment, munching another handful of popcorn.

"They're too big to be friends," he concluded. "Friends are kids my size."

At the mention of size, Will had a brainstorm for special delivery of his bouquet. Of course, it depended on the tigers being safely tucked away for the time being. He wouldn't want to be brought up on charges of child endangerment—or worse.

"Think you could squeeze through the bars?" he asked.

The boy gave him a quizzical look.

"You mean trespassing?"

Another big word. The boy was a walking dictionary.

"Well, yes. That's one word for it."

"That would be dishonorable."

Will let loose a heavy sigh. What was he thinking? Would he send his own son on such a perilous mission? He should just throw the flowers away, forget about this whole futile quest. The ghost had instructed him to save his daughter, not court her.

"A knight is all about honor," the boy informed him.

"You're a knight, are you?"

"Yes, sir. My name is Lance."

"Ah, short for Lancelot." Will knelt down, facing the boy. "How old are you, Lance?"

The boy held up one finger at a time until all were extended on one hand and added two more on the other.

"I don't need any other fingers," he said.

Seven, Will thought. Two years older than Joel. Would Abbey let their son wander about like this unsupervised? He thought not, but this was one of the benefits of a small town, he assumed—the illusion of safety, even with tigers prowling about.

"Can you do me a favor? If you see a young woman come out on the lawn, can you wave to her, and if she comes to the gate, can you give her these?" Will handed Lance the bouquet. "And please say they're from Will."

"What will you pay me?"

"Here." Will dug in his pocket. "Here's a dollar."

"Two dollars would be better."

Aside from the one-dollar bill, all he had was a five.

"You drive a hard bargain for a little guy."

After paying up, Will moved down the sidewalk, backward, staring toward the gate until he was forced to round a corner.

Whether he was being monitored or not, he couldn't be sure.

***

But he was. From a room, one wall of which was tiered with closed-circuit television screens, showing various views inside and outside the mansion. Essence stared at one of the monitors, as Jenkins came up behind her.

"Ah, I see your friend is back, Missy."

She hated it when he called her "Missy," his pet name for her since childhood. It sounded so diminutive, reducing her to a ceramic figurine on a music box lid.

"He looks different in broad daylight."

"Should I sic Crimson and Clover on him?"

Essence glanced at another monitor showing the tiger cage. Both animals were stretched out, side by side, in their litter of straw. A couple of gnawed bones lay beside them.

"No." She turned toward him, seeking evidence he was joking. "Anyway, he isn't inside the gate."

"Of course, Missy. No worries. Should you need me to dispose of him, however …"

Essence smiled.

"I like him. I think I might keep him as a playmate."

At this, Jenkins rolled his eyes into his wide forehead framed by immaculately groomed hair.

"Do you really think you need another … playmate? Don't you have enough already?"

"Do I detect a hint of jealousy?" she teased.

It was true, though. She did have plenty of playmates: plebes from the Bible college, salesmen traveling through town, married men cheating on their wives, even the occasional off-duty policeman. But it wasn't all fun and games. Some of them sought her out because she helped them. With their problems, their issues. A few of them were really sad cases. Others, believe it or not, just wanted to talk.

And not just men—the occasional woman, as well. Lonely-hearts, risking or seeking danger, whose needs were different, more sensual than sexual. In all honesty, she took more pleasure in their company than that of the men. But like their male counterparts, they knew where to find her, in the park, and she stayed hidden in the shadows, listening as they whispered her name like a code word, evaluating their silhouettes, deciding whether to let them discover her. It was Jenkins who should know, after all.

She suspected him of following behind. Always at a distance. Creeping around trees. Hiding behind bushes. Was he a voyeur? Did he get a thrill out of it? Or was he there to protect her if the need arose? A third possibility had crossed her mind: that it wasn't her he enjoyed watching but her male consorts.

Nine times out of ten—excepting those nights when the Grandmother made her own rounds—he let her escape, climbing off her balcony and down the rainspout, never reporting her to the Grandmother, who she was sure must hear rumors of her nocturnal escapades, her gossip vine ran so thick through the town with its long, strangling tendrils. The Grandmother even had Jenkins install a set of bars that fasten against the balcony door, but her mistake was letting Jenkins, like a zookeeper, possess the spare key. Without eyes, short of testing Essence's door before she turned in for the night, she could only take Jenkins's word for the security of the premises.

They had tried it with her mother, after all. Keeping her as penned in as the tigers, with disastrous results. July 4th, Independence Day—but what a drastic means of achieving it! Jumping from the summit of the bridge at midnight. Out of despair. Unrequited love. Her lover failing to meet her, as she'd hoped. Uncaringly, her mother had gone without her, leaving her in her bassinet on the bridge to be raised in some strange matriarch's household—an act of selfishness that Essence found unforgiveable.

He lingered in the doorway, leaning against the jamb on an elbow, forearm raised above his head, an attempt to appear casual, even though it was evident he was staring with a gaze that was difficult to read. A secret longing? Disguised amore? It seemed underpinned with sadness, as though bottling his disappointment in her.

"You poor, poor devil," she said, coming up to him and running a scarf around his neck. "You were in love with my mother, and now you can't keep your eyes off me."

She meant it only in jest, but he took the bait too seriously, like a carp to a lure.

"No offense, but you're nothing like your mum. She was a sweetheart, a genuine angel, while you, you're nothing but a …"

"Say it, why don't you?" Essence challenged him, but Jenkins regrouped, collecting his cool.

"Back home, there's a word for a certain type of woman

that's bandied about. Down Under they'd call you a 'molly.'"

"Is that so?" she said, pulling her scarf free. She didn't have an exact translation, but she could tell it wasn't meant as a compliment. "And you're such a gentleman?"

He brushed past her into the room, spinning her around like a toy top, and began adjusting the dials of the monitors. Unhappy at being ignored, she decided on a different approach.

She jutted her chin at the monitor showing Will Archer handing over a bouquet of flowers in black and white to a small boy whom she recognized as a regular onlooker outside the gate.

"What if I told you I was turning over a new leaf? You know, mending my ways. Settling down with just one person."

Jenkins studied her with weary eyes. He looked younger than his forty-seven years. Despite his hair graying at the temples, he was in tip-top shape, the result of a daily workout regimen. He was twenty years younger when her mother died. She had seen the photographs. A dashing young man. Stunningly handsome. Had he been in love with her mother? Had her barb struck a nerve?

"I'd say be careful what you wish for … Missy."

"I am," she replied, moving out the door. "I always am."

And she was.

She went down the hall to her bedroom, one of the few rooms in the entire mansion that wasn't subject to Jenkins's surveillance.

And a good thing, too. It allowed her to count the Grandmother's money and dream, dream, dream. Just to start the dreaming process all over again, she removed a white vinyl valise with two brass snaps from the top shelf of her closet, virtually identical to the valise her grandmother kept in hers. The case was a precaution in case she was found out and had to make a quick exchange.

She was nineteen, the same age as her mother when she died. To emulate her mother on the anniversary of her plunge into oblivion has been a thought, incubating in her mind for a very long time. Except, unlike her mother, she had a different idea for escape.

Opening the case, she stared at its contents as though for the first time. The case contained fifty bundles of banknotes of the same denomination. Each bundle contained 100 notes held together with a paper band. Each note was a crisp $20 bill.

This was the Grandmother's emergency fund. Thank God for an old woman who didn't trust money managers or stockbrokers enough to negate the need to keep cold, hard cash stashed in her bedroom. Except the cash wasn't cold or hard. It was warm to the touch and felt more like linen than paper. It had taken her several surreptitious trips to stationery shops to find just the right surrogate that had the feel of real money.

At first, she had ordered a stack of prop money, fake bills used on movie sets or theater stages. But it didn't have the right texture. Her grandmother would easily tell the difference. Her fingers might be thin and brittle, but her fingertips were as sensitive as a cat's whiskers. She had finally settled on an acid-free archival quality paper with a "rag" texture. There was no need to counterfeit Andrew Jackson's portrait. The "bills" could retain their ivory blankness.

What kept her from immediately fleeing with the contents was her certainty that the Grandmother would use Jenkins to track her down and bring her forcibly home, as she had several times in the past. She could never get far without money, and now that she had it, she still doubted she could ever get far enough away to elude pursuit.

This was why she had been preparing for a jump from the bridge that would never take place. Rather she was preparing others by appearing on the bridge at midnight, climbing onto the rail for any passerby to see. They wouldn't find a body. There would be no body to find. By the time they gave up the search, she would be somewhere far away. Warm places came to mind: Jamaica, Tahiti, the Bahamas.

What she needed, though, was someone who would testify to witnessing her plunge. Someone she could confide her troubles to. Not exactly a patsy. Just someone who would sympathize with her to the point of lying for her and maintaining her fiction forever. Someone who was on her side. And now she thought she had found this special someone.

Stretched out on her bed, propped by pillows, Essence cradled her phone. Sometimes it seemed her phone was her only real friend. Of course she had other "friends" she met in chat rooms—pseudonymous nobodies with strange, inventive handles: asuzu23, wac-man44. More often than not, their discourse devolved into sexting, which she found trivial and boring.

Her phone, on the other hand, didn't want anything from her except to assist. It always listened to her, although its need for clarification could be annoying.

She spoke into it, waking it up.

Its response was immediate.

"Hello, Mistress of Darkness."

This was her current Nickname of the Week. She had programmed it that way. She had meant it as a joke, but it was starting to grow on her.

"How can I help?"

She leaned over it, speaking as clearly as she could, enunciating each syllable.

"What can you tell me about William Archer?"

Chapter 11

"Joel?"

No answer.

A strange silence came from the back bedroom. The sound of his playing—vocalizations of zapping lasers and descending bombs and aeronautical whooshes—had ceased. Maybe he had fallen asleep?

The last Abbey had seen him, he had been playing in his new bedroom. It was their very first day in their new home—a townhouse in a large apartment complex with a pond and pool and, most significantly, a playground. Daryl was still on the road, so friends had helped her pack up their house the past couple of days and move the furniture and boxes into the new place. And here they were—or here she was—in her bedroom unpacking.

She was in the middle of sorting through the contents of a shoebox that held Alan's mementoes—his "memory box," he called it. A handful of print photos. Birthday cards from her to him. Four joint birthday cards from them to Joel—the last one delivered mere days before he abandoned them. A favorite pacifier of Joel's that had taken a year of coaxing to wean him from. A pair of booties that they had always intended to have bronzed. As she reviewed each item in turn, she felt a volatile mixture of nostalgia and anger. The nostalgia needed no explanation, but the anger? Possibly at the aborted nature of the box. No new memories, it seemed, would be forthcoming.

As she replaced the contents, it struck her how there were very few reminders of their time together—just the two of them. A single Valentine's Day greeting attached to a Milky Way bar still in its wrapper, long gone stale. A pair of ticket stubs commemorating the one and only concert they had attended as a dating couple.

She reflected on their very first encounter when they bumped trays in the college cafeteria and her apple leaped to the floor. They had clunked heads when they both stooped down at the same time to retrieve it. From there, it was a toboggan ride through two semesters of dating, the end of it bookmarked by college graduation with her hiding her balloon of a second trimester pregnancy behind a billowing gown. They hadn't had time to discover each other, to trace the contours of each other's individuality, before Joel had come along.

And there it was, at the very bottom of the box where she had buried it: the parting note Alan had affixed to the refrigerator on the morning he disappeared from her life—their lives—seemingly forever.

She had made the mistake of revealing it to the detective she had contacted to file a missing person report. The presence of such a note signified conscious intent, not evidence of someone MIA. Same thing when she approached the media; outlet after outlet discarded her predicament as that of a delinquent husband, nothing very special about it. Except when one journalist learned this was the same Alan Paxton half responsible for the fatal accident that had occurred six months prior. Abbey could imagine the headline, DEADBEAT DAD WHO KILLED MOTHER-DAUGHTER ON THE LAM, and aborted the interview.

That he wasn't a deadbeat, just the opposite, made him even less newsworthy. A noble gesture, cashing out his 401(k), compromised as it was by the early withdrawal penalty, but it kept her afloat the couple of months it took her to build up a clientele for yoga classes, which she began teaching in between exhibits at the gallery. Maybe Alan had figured it would last longer than it did. He wasn't very good with finances. She was the one who did all of their bookkeeping.

Painful as the message was, she wasn't sure how long she had been transfixed by the tight, neat penmanship—in cursive, no less—carefully riding the thin blue lines of the yellow sheet of paper. A cloud darkened the room, erasing the strip of sunlight that had spread across the floor, shaking her out of her reverie. This was when she called for Joel without a response. Half-tempted to crumple the goodbye note in her fist, she instead folded it into thirds and placed it back in the box.

She stood up. Her left leg had fallen asleep, the way she had tucked it beneath her. She crossed the hall and peeked into the small room, cluttered with action figures and Lego blocks and rubber band-propelled toys.

She called down from the top of the stairs: "Joel!"

She suppressed a rising panic, as she made her way down the stairs, clutching the rail, because of the prickling in her foot.

Out the back sliding door, there was a small patio, enclosed within a privacy fence, with a space where a gate should have been. So he could have easily snuck out of the apartment. But where? And why?

She started her search by rounding the pool. One large-bellied man was asleep on a deck chair, stretched out under his newspaper as a sun block. Two teens, a boy in Speedos and a girl in a shockingly stringy bikini were splashing around, but thankfully there were no small bodies floating or lying on the bottom. No lifeguard on duty, she noted. Swim at your own risk.

Next she tried the playground full of shiny equipment. And there was Joel! Thank God! But who was that with him?

That's odd, she thought, as she approached, slowly, step by step, then more hurriedly, her pace quickening, in case this man-ifestation of Joel should prove a mirage and evaporate.

"Donald!" she exclaimed, coming up behind the slim, white

statuette of a man in a turtleneck extending his long, thin, delicate violinist's fingers in what?—encouragement?—as he stood at the bottom of a tall slide at the top of which sat Joel.

Perritt turned around. Abbey was used to men looking her up and down, peeling off layers of clothing with their gaze, but Perritt's eyes were so level, so cold, he could just as easily have been sizing her up for a coffin.

***

When in disgrace with fortune and men's eyes—that line darted through Perritt's mind again as it so often did these past eighteen months. But Shakespeare had it wrong, didn't he? It was more the case he was in disgrace with women's eyes—or one woman's set of eyes in particular—and here she was approaching him hurriedly. He could detect her nervousness, the way it breathed out of her nostrils in short bursts. And this was the last thing he wanted, to cause her discomfort, distress, unease.

"Yes, hello," he said, trying to put on a cheerful demeanor. "Mrs. Paxton, I presume."

His attempt at levity fell flat.

"What are you doing here?" she asked. Looking beyond and above him, she spotted her son. "Joel! Are you all right?"

"Yes, Mama," he answered, and Perritt hoped this would sound a reassuring note.

"With regard to your first question," he said, with measured cadence, "I happen to live here."

"You live … here?" Abbey asked. "But, when? Since when? We just moved in."

"I've been here for—" He paused, letting the thought trail off. "Like you, I presume, I found my former residence to be too accommodating for a single person, although, of course, you have your son."

"Watch me, Mama!"

Mama, Perritt thought. How cute. His daughter had been nine, going on ten. Her "Mama" days long past. Her "Dada" days, too.

They both watched him go down the slide, arms in the air. Abbey rushed over to be there when he landed, which he did perfectly, both feet on the ground. She picked him up by the shoulders and, short of shaking him, let him hang there as she scolded him.

"What were you thinking, leaving the apartment like that. Don't ever, ever do this again. Do you understand me?"

"Yes, Mama," Joel said and started crying.

"Please, don't cry." She pulled him close and let him bury his eyes into her shoulder, which was bare, her shirt sleeveless, the beautiful brown of her skin complementing the light mocha of her son's complexion.

"I don't know what made you think you could just go waltzing out of the apartment in a strange neighborhood where anyone—" She stopped short, casting a glance at Perritt.

"I do hope we are better acquainted that you don't think of me as just anyone," Perritt said, adding a lump of sweetness to the iced tea of his voice.

Abbey nodded.

"I didn't mean to offend," she said.

"No offense taken," Perritt said, adopting a smile.

"I heard other kids," Joel said. "That's why I went down. And when I looked out the door, they waved at me, and ..." He looked around, still tearful. "I don't know where they went."

"I heard them, too," Abbey said. "I just didn't think you would follow them out the door."

"I was prepared to escort the young lad back to your residence," Perritt said. "If it's any consolation."

"Yes, of course. I should thank you."

But he could tell by her eyes that she was still distrustful. What could he do, what could he say, to regain her trust? Had he ever had it to begin with? Would she have contacted him to let him know where she had moved? Or had the purpose of her move been to escape his acquaintanceship?

"My phone number is still the same," he said, fishing for an answer.

"Oh," Abbey said, coming out of a thought, as though out of a cloud. "Yeah, right. I was planning to call. We were only just getting settled."

"I could have helped you move," Perritt said. "I could still be of help, if you'd like."

"No, that's all right. We're almost done unpacking."

"Then I insist you let me take you out to dinner tonight. Or I could bring over pizza?"

"Pizza!" Joel said, snapping out of his funk.

"Maybe not tonight," she said. "I've got a lot of things to do."

"Aw," Joel complained. "But Mama, pizza!"

"Some other time then," Perritt said, gracious in the wake of rejection.

He watched Abbey tug little Joel away from the playground and back toward their apartment. He waited until they were out of sight around a corner of a quadruplex before he strode through the complex in the opposite direction. His car was parked outside the rental office, and he stopped inside, sidling up to the tall counter where a clerk stood on the other side, watching a small television set.

"Back again," she observed. "See anything that suits your fancy?"

"Yes, please," Perritt cleared his throat. "I noticed an end unit that appears to be vacant."

Chapter 12

Was she only a mirage? This was how Will felt crossing the bridge this night. For two nights in a row it rained so heavily, he hadn't ventured out. Having missed two opportunities to reunite, he had a feeling of time running out, the month of June carrying him along like a moving sidewalk at an airport.

A crowd had been standing around the hole in the pavement at the end of the bridge earlier that day, peering and pointing, as Will passed by. A backhoe was parked beside it, just outside the perimeter of yellow tape, awaiting instructions to proceed with filling in the enormous pit that threatened to swallow other stray motorists. The only thing preventing it from doing its duty was the husband of the woman who had disappeared.

Someone had seen him step over the tape and descend feet first into the pit as though climbing into a grave, which in a sense, he had. There was a small opening at the bottom of the pit where a body could squeeze through like toothpaste through a tube. Will could imagine the scrunched shoulders, the wriggling hips, the blind eyes peering into absolute darkness.

A county engineer had been brought to the scene and, after consulting an enormous map of the town's sewer system, concluded that the man might have entered into the complex of obsolete pipes that were used to carry water or waste as far back as the late 1800s. With the multitude of interconnections, both active and not, it was impossible to predict where the man might emerge, if ever he did.

In some ways, it seemed very romantic, an act of self-sacrifice. What could Will do as he passed at this late hour but silently wish the man well in quest of his wife, Orpheus in pursuit of Eurydice, hoping to rescue her from the underworld?

He found her on the swings, barefoot, wearing a thin, satiny robe that shimmered in starlight.

"Essence?" he sang out.

"Will," she shouted, "is that you?"

"Yes," he said, hesitantly, as though he had forgotten their appointment. "I'm here."

"Where have you been?"

"Well, I—the storms the past two nights. I didn't think—"

"Afraid of a few raindrops, were you? It's okay," she said, as though helping him out of his quandary. "You wouldn't have found me in any case. I was being held hostage."

"Hostage?"

"By my grandmother," she said, as he came a step closer so that he caught a whiff of perfume. "She insisted I sit with her. Night after night. And Jenkins kept me locked up so I couldn't easily escape."

"That's terrible."

"It's not that bad," she said without slowing. "If you don't mind listening to Bible-thumping televangelists on cable while she keeps hold of your hands praying for your everlasting soul."

"So you managed to get away?"

"I bribed my jailer. So now I'm free as a bird!"

She leaped from the swing, as she had before, and sped off into the dark. Laughing, she ran to the merry-go-round, giving it a twirl and leaping on. Bemused, Will walked over to join her. He hadn't been on one since he was a kid. He gave it a couple of pushes to set her spinning faster, and although it wobbled and creaked, it did the job as she held onto the bars, leaning way back, letting her hair fly in the whirlwind it created.

He hopped on, ending up on the opposite side, but as he

tried to make his way over, she turned and rolled off the edge, springing right back up in the dark.

"Catch me if you can," she taunted him.

"I think I can," he said, but when he got off the merry-go-round, he had trouble standing straight, and before his dizziness dissolved, she was off and running through the trees. Still wobbly, he chased after her, but she had already disappeared, blending in with the shadows. As he paused, he heard a rustling of leaves.

"Essence?" The rustling stopped. Maybe it was nothing more than a squirrel rearranging its nest.

Eyes adjusting to the darkness, he made out a figure in the trees and went in after it, but tripped over a root, slipped, and fell to his knees in a reservoir of mud.

He heard a giggle and looked up to discover the source. Focusing, his eyes processed Essence in the darkness, staring down at him, her hands holding her sides.

"So not funny," he said, knowing his voice sounded as cross as a schoolmaster's. "The least you could do is help me up?"

She held out her hand, and Will took it. She was stronger than she looked, for someone so light on her feet.

As she pulled him free, his feet slipped, and she fell into his arms, pressing herself against him, so that he stumbled and almost fell, regaining his footing at the last moment. She stayed against him, though, wrapping her arms around his neck, nuzzling her nose, like that of a puppy, into his shoulder.

A surge rushed through him, filling his senses. It was her perfume, he decided, a fragrance of purple blossoms. He could almost picture the petals, although he couldn't quite name the flower. Not violets, something else, rising on a vine: *clematis.*

She kissed his neck, her lips open and wet, then worked the kiss over to his mouth, where it lingered, teasing him with her tongue. Slowly she unbuttoned his shirt, and he let her work her fingers on down, unzipping his pants, but halfway down, he recovered his sense of self and took hold of her wrist, but lightly.

"No," he said gently. An image went through his mind of another face, but then he remembered a splinter of glass had cut across it where it had fallen from his desktop.

"No?" she asked, opening her robe, her breasts falling free, round and supple. He looked her up and down, assessing her nakedness, appreciating what she revealed. "Are you sure?"

But Will stood mute and motionless. He could have been a garden gnome for all the resistance he made, as he let his pants fall to his knees.

"I would have pegged you for boxers," she said, smiling.

"Disappointed?"

She pulled the band of his briefs, letting him spring free.

"Not at all," she said, fondling him.

"Here?" he asked, glancing around self-consciously. "In the open?"

"You have protection?" she asked, disregarding his question.

Will shook his head, knowing the fantasy would now end, the dream dissolve.

"No matter."

As though conducting a magic trick, she reached inside a pocket of her robe and produced a condom, which she slipped on him. She let her robe fall from her shoulders and, lowering herself, she took him by the hand, pulling him toward her. He dropped to his knees, between her raised legs, so that they were both in the mud.

He tried to rise, so he could free them both, as though from a tar pit.

"It's all right," she said, smiling. "It's as soft as a bed."

Wriggling and squirming, she found her comfort zone, like

settling into a mattress, then reached out and guided him inside her, where it felt like a rich, foamy lather, washing him clean.

Afterward, they exchanged the mud pit for a patch of dry leaves. There, he lay beside her in the dark, staring through a web of branches at a maroon sky, she on her side, snuggled against him, her arm across his chest.

"Why did you come here tonight?" she asked. "Do you still think you can save me?"

"From what you're planning?" He rolled over onto his side. "I hope to convince you."

"Convince me?"

"I don't want to sound paternal—"

"Given the circumstances, I'd rather you didn't."

Will laughed. Wrong choice of words.

"But you have your whole life in front of you. You're young. You have everything to live for. You—" He didn't know what else to say without progressing through a series of clichés from self-help books.

"Is that the advice you'd give to a bird in a cage?"

"And your grandmother is your jailer?"

"Her and Jenkins, yes. He's her yes-man. If they had their way, I'd never be allowed out of the house. I was schooled by tutors up until a year ago. And now I've spent a year languishing because they can't make up their minds about letting me attend college, even the one here in town."

"You couldn't just leave, run away?"

"Please, I'm nineteen, it wouldn't be running away. But no, I can't. They won't let me."

"How could they stop you?"

Essence turned, facing him, propping her head on her arm.

"A year ago, after my second attempt, I spent a month in a hospital, a nuthouse."

"Psychiatric ward?"

"They've since arranged for a court to have me declared mentally incompetent to live on my own. If I leave, they have every right to track me down and bring me back and imprison me. Her networks are quite extensive. There's no outrunning them."

"You've tried?"

"Yes, but I never get very far."

"How do they find you?"

"Seriously?" she smiled, relaxing her features. "I'm a young Black woman with freckled cheeks and red-tinted hair. I'm not very good about blending into a crowd."

"If it's a question of money—"

She touched his shoulder lightly, shaking her head.

"It isn't. It's just I have nowhere to go. No one on the outside—"

"The outside? You really do make it sound like a prison."

"No friends. No family."

"There's your other grandmother," he pointed out. "Have you considered staying with her?"

"That would spark a war. Between the two of them. I'd be caught in the crossfire, and I'm afraid my Grandma Waxman would come out on the losing end. "

"How so?"

"My Grandmother Warner owns half the county. It's perfectly within her power to bankrupt my other grandmother and drive her right out of town."

"I guess I don't understand. Why is your Grandmother Warner so intent on keeping you locked up?"

Essence sighed.

"It's her reputation. I'm an embarrassment to her—always have been. When I was younger, she wouldn't even bring me along when Jenkins took her shopping. She refused to be seen with me in daylight. Even my coming-out party—"

Will couldn't help but let out a low whistle.

"You had a coming-out party?"

Essence gave him a nudge.

"A really dismal affair. The only people invited were three ancient members of her garden club."

"Sounds like you need to broaden your social network. Ever consider online dating?"

He wanted to point out it was safer than the course she was taking, as well.

Without warning, she rolled over on top of him, straddling his midsection, and he found himself responding immediately.

"What about you?" she asked. "What brought you to such a Podunk place as this?"

"An online job posting," he admitted.

"No, really." She gave his shoulder a shove. "If it wasn't for love, it couldn't be for money. You could find a much more lucrative job, I'm sure, in a big city. So what was it?"

Will put his hands behind his head and attempted to smile.

"You don't seem the criminal type, but let me guess," she persisted. "You're on the run from something or someone. Oh, I know! You were falsely accused and now you're a fugitive, just like the guy in that movie. What was it called?"

"*The Fugitive*," Will said, less than humorously.

"Right," Essence laughed. "Like, duh. But that's what it is, isn't it? You're being hunted, chased."

Will remained tightlipped, silent, shifting his gaze to the branches of a tree past her head.

"Not so talkative, are you, when the tables are turned?" She pulled his hands from behind his head and placed them on her hips. "But you're right," she said, lightly. "Enough talking for one night." She leaned over him, swaying her breasts, soft and supple, against his mouth, where he caressed her with his lips, teasing her nipples with his tongue. If her goal was to stop further discourse, it was working.

"I almost forgot to thank you," she said softly, as she pulled herself upright and lowered herself onto him.

"Thank me?" He was lost in a wash of feeling, satiated, fulfilled, as though he had completed a quest that had been hidden from him in his own mind all this time, but also with strings of guilt running through it, so that his mind refused to settle in any one place for long before it was jerked back to thoughts of the life he had left behind.

"For the flowers."

Chapter 13

Waking came slowly. It started with birdsong that blended with a dream he was having about Abbey. She was whistling blithely, as he followed her through a grocery store, aisle after aisle. They didn't have a cart, and she kept loading his arms up with a growing tower of boxes and cans and cartons.

He kept trying to apologize, to ask her forgiveness. It was an accident, unplanned, just something that happened. It didn't mean anything. He had thought of her the whole time. He knew all of his excuses sounded like so many empty clichés, and Abbey just kept whistling along, ignoring him.

As he fell farther behind, he had a horrible sense of losing her. He knew if he lost control, if just one item fell, it would be like his life falling apart. He needed to catch up with her before she disappeared. But he felt something tugging at him, holding him back. Finally, he gave up and let the tugging pull him awake.

Essence?

That was his first thought. But he found himself staring up into the face of a boy. It was the same urchin he had encountered outside the gate to the Warner mansion who held a bag of popcorn for the tigers. Now he wasn't holding anything. He was simply bending over Will, shaking his shoulder.

"Okay," Will said. "I'm awake. You can stop now."

The boy stopped, and Will sat up with a jerk.

"You've been asleep a long time," the boy stated. "You kept twitching like a dog having a dream chasing rabbits. Were you chasing rabbits in your sleep?"

Will glanced at his watch. A quarter past eight. That gave him time to run like a last little piggy all the way home to his apartment, change, and rush back out again to—maybe—be in time for opening the museum.

"Thanks," Will said. "For waking me. Lance, isn't it?"

The boy nodded.

"It's all right," Lance said. "But why are you sleeping out here? A bear could have eaten you."

"Unlikely," Will said, standing up.

"Yes, sir, but I saw a squirrel. It was nibbling at your ear."

"It's a good thing you were there to save me. Are you sure you're not my guardian angel?"

"I don't know about that, but I do know something else."

"Oh? What's that?"

The boy held his hand over his mouth to restrain a giggle.

"Your zipper's down." So it was. And not just his zipper, but his pants. He loped off across the park, pulling them up and buttoning his shirt as he raced toward the bridge.

From the top of the arc, the bridge provided a parabolic descent that propelled him to the Victorian Arms. As he pulled open the heavy oaken door to the foyer, Mrs. Gossett stepped out of her apartment to intercept him.

"You can't go to work like this," she said, tsk-tsking. "You're all covered in mud!!"

"I'll change. Do you happen to know what color day it is?"

"A green day," she said. They had formed an alliance with Mrs. Waxman to have emails copied to his landlady's computer, as a backup to Will's laptop, its connection was so fickle.

"Thanks!" Will rasped, rushing past.

Green! Will thought. *Green!* What did he have that was green?

As he came up to his door he found it ajar. Cautiously, he pushed it open, giving up a quiet entry, as it let out a long squeal on squeaky hinges.

"Anyone here?" he called uneasily.

No one answered, not even the ghost.

What caught his attention as he rushed past was a glint of yellow. On the red velvet cushy chair sat a tenor saxophone, gleaming a wondrous, lustrous gold. Not just any sax. He knew at once whose it was: *Jamaal's!* The calligraphic inscription along the rim of the bell confirmed it: *May Your Tone Never Waver – Love, Mama.* This was the inscription Mrs. Waxman had engraved on it, he had learned, when she presented it to her son on his seventeenth birthday. Yet on the recording—the one that played on its endless loop in the museum—Jamaal's wavering tone was a hallmark of his sound, a studied vibrato.

Although he was tempted, Will knew better than to touch it. He gave it a wide berth, as he went to the Hex Room to change. By the time he was done lacing his shoes, he made a decision.

He picked up the sax carefully by its long stem with a dish-towel and set off down the long and winding stairs. At the bottom, he knocked at Mrs. Gossett's door.

"My, my," she said, in the kind of admiring tone people use to appraise the appearance of newborns. "Jamaal Waxman's sax. Who'd have thought his mother would ever relinquish it."

"That's just it," Will explained, "she didn't."

His landlady drew her eyebrows into a wedge of puzzlement. "No?" she prompted.

Will told her how he had just come across it in his room.

"Did you notice anyone strange coming into the apartment? An old tenant? Someone who would already have a key?"

"Not offhand. Although some of my tenants make spares. Entirely against the rules. But they do like to have their house-guests stay over."

"Would you mind taking it for a while? Until I can figure out what to do with it?"

"I don't know," She shook her head on a stiff, wizened neck. "Stolen property and all."

"It's not necessarily stolen."

"Misappropriated," she affirmed. "All the same."

"I don't know where else to keep it. I'm afraid if I leave it in my room—"

"Why not call the police? Let them know the circumstances."

"What circumstances?"

"That you're being framed—apparently."

Will contemplated this line of reasoning for a mere half-second, during which he attempted to quell a surge of panic.

"There would be too many questions. I don't want to be the subject of an investigation. The publicity. The press."

"And you wish to keep a low profile." She lowered her head, granting him a sympathetic gaze. "That's one thing I've known about you from the very start."

"So you'll help me?"

"Much as I would hate to lose you as a tenant, wouldn't it be easier just to quit your job? Pack your bags? Move on? I could turn in the sax. Explain what happened. Give you time to escape questioning."

"I couldn't," Will stammered. "Not now. I can't."

She took a moment to light a cigarette from a pack in her robe's pocket. She inhaled deeply and expelled a blue stream of smoke toward the ceiling.

"It's because of Essence, isn't it? That's where you've been till this morning, am I right?"

Will didn't give a response to this, but there must have been something in his demeanor that made his landlady cave.

"Oh, here!" She suddenly reached out and took hold of the dishtowel. "But only until you get back, understand."

"Thank you, thank you," he gushed. "And if anyone asks, I

was here all night."

"Of course you were," she said with a knowing smile, as Will moved toward the front door.

***

At the museum, a police cruiser sat out front, misaligned against the curb. As Will entered, he took in a trio of Mrs. Waxman and two officers: a uniformed young man inspecting the glass case for fingerprints, the other a plainclothes woman taking notes.

"There he is now!" his employer exclaimed. Both officers turned their heads at her outburst.

"Hello," Will said meekly, approaching the glass case with caution. "What's going on?"

"Is this the employee you were talking about?" the detective with the notepad asked.

"This is my curator," Mrs. Waxman said. "William Archer."

"Archer is it?" the detective confirmed, jotting down his name. "Do you mind telling us your whereabouts between eleven p.m. and eight o'clock this morning?"

"I was at home," Will answered levelly. "Asleep mostly. I had a migraine."

"It's true, detective," Mrs. Waxman confirmed. "He left here with an awful headache. Just look, Will. Just look at what someone had the nerve to do."

"A professional job," the officer inspecting the case observed with a meaningful glance in Will's direction. "Seems to have been done from the inside."

"Indeed," Mrs. Waxman remarked. The glass hadn't been shattered, merely cut, as though with a laser. Later, Will would learn that the alarm system had been disabled upon entry.

Will raised his index finger to outline the precision of the cut glass in the perfect shape of the stolen sax, but the officer at the other end of the case yelled at him, making him lurch.

"Don't touch it! I'm still collecting prints."

"But William's fingerprints are probably all over it by now."

"And how long has he been working for you?" the detective with the notepad asked.

I'm right here, Will thought. *You could ask me.*

"Six days."

"Six whole days, huh? Not even a week."

"A full week if you count his day off."

The detective jotted this information, then exchanged a glance that was easy to read with the officer continuing his inspection of the case with powder, tape, and brush: *Person of interest.*

The glance was noticed by Mrs. Waxman, too.

"But surely, officers, if William were guilty, would he have shown up at work at his usual time today?"

The officers redirected their gaze at Will, making him feel like a lab rat in a cage, something meant for observation.

"And wouldn't he have just used the key to the case rather than go to all the trouble to cut through the glass?"

"Maybe," the uniformed officer responded, evaluating Will's expression, which Will tried to keep neutral.

"Case in point. William, do you know what color it is today?"

"Green," Will intoned robotically, wondering where this line of questioning was heading.

"And are you, in fact, wearing green?"

Will lifted a trouser leg to show off a sock.

His employer narrowed her eyes.

"Khaki is not exactly green, but I suppose close enough. There!" she concluded, turning her gaze toward the officers. "He could only have gotten this information from my email. There-fore," she said, sounding more and more like a public defender, "he must have been home to open it."

"He could have used his cell," the investigating officer said.

"True, if he owned one."

"No cell phone?" the detective asked doubtfully. "We'll be wanting his address in case we need to …"

"Question him," the officer lifting fingerprints interjected with a smirk. "You have other employees?"

"Just one. Amanda Anders."

"She goes by Mandy," Will offered, drawing the gaze of both officers, as though to determine whether he was trying to deflect guilt from himself.

"Let me offer another possibility," Mrs. Waxman said, as though the notion had just come to her, and maybe it had. "What if I were the perpetrator?"

"You?" both officers asked in unison.

"Maybe I've staged this whole thing for publicity. Have you ever considered that?"

The officers exchanged glances.

"Very funny," the detective commented, folding up her notebook. The other officer began packing up his fingerprint kit. "We'll be wanting you to come down to the station to give a statement."

"Thank you, officers," Mrs. Waxman said with an official politeness intended as a dismissal. "I'll be there shortly."

"If you can think of anyone who might have motive," the forensics officer said. "That would be helpful."

"I'll bring a list."

The officers took one last, suspicious look at Will and walked out the front door.

"You covered for me," Will noted, once they had gone. "Why?"

"Why indeed," Mrs. Waxman agreed. "If not for fear of losing yet another curator. Plus, I received a phone call before you arrived from Phyllis Gossett, who filled me in on your …

activities last night."

"Oh. You know about that." He braced himself for a lecture about the inappropriateness of his actions. Would last night's rendezvous cost him his job?

"So," she said, allowing a little room for sweetness to pucker her voice. "Just how is my favorite granddaughter?"

Hadn't she meant "only"? he thought. Unless there were others? In any case, he decided to share what he had learned.

"She's preparing to jump."

"Jump?"

"From the bridge. In two weeks—or just under. On July 4th. The anniversary of—"

"I know very well what anniversary it is," she responded humorously, as though struggling to swallow a digestive wafer. "But jump?"

"She's intent on killing herself."

This made his employer pause as she studied Will, eye for eye, seemingly to inspect his vision for a cataract.

"Nonsense!" she concluded. "You don't know my granddaughter the way I know her. She is only seeking attention."

"What about the other two times?" he asked. "She tried to, I mean she attempted to—" He felt he was fumbling a verbal football.

Mrs. Waxman pooh-poohed the notion with a hand she flourished with remarkable grace, like the wing of a butterfly.

"Attention, mere attention."

"What if she's sincere this time?"

"What if she is?" she answered, folding her arms across her heavy chest.

"Shouldn't you call the authorities? Notify a hospital?"

"And what would I say? And what would *she* say if cornered?" She paused to let Will think about this, but not for long.

"She would deny it. She would pass any battery of tests they might give her. She would know how to fake psychological health to elude the clutches of the medical profession. This is why it is so very, very important that you keep an eye on her."

"But what can I do?"

"Find a way to prevent her, if she's as determined as you say she is. And now, if you'll excuse me, I have a lecture to give. A Ladies Aid group. One of my many obligations to the community. In fact, I arrived here early to gather my notes. And you, I believe, have work to do."

With that, she pulled her green, silk scarf around her neck and, like an aviator, made her exit along a runway through the front door.

Chapter 14

With no further instructions except to keep his hands off the crime scene, Will proceeded directly to item #4 in his list of assignments: answering emails. There was one he almost overlooked, as it had no subject line. This alone made him hesitant to open it, and when he did, he realized too late his intuition proved correct.

DEAR CURIOUS CURATOR, it began, using ALL CAPS— the first time an email had been directed at him.

I hope you're enjoying our little charade with the sax as much as I am. And you can tell the QUEEN BEE that as for her beloved son having a golden tone: HAH! Again, I say, HAH!!!

Have you listened to the tapes? Or are you tone deaf??? So much more like ordinary brass.

Signed,

Yours Truly

The email said "our." *Our*, he considered. *Our?* Was there more than one perpetrator? The email was obviously taunting him, but rather than respond—which he was prohibited from doing by Mrs. Waxman's policy, in any case—Will retreated to the privacy of the video room within its enclosure of velvet curtains. It seemed a perfect place to consume a late breakfast of popcorn he shoveled out of the machine that was meant for the culinary pleasure of younger guests. He hit PLAY on the VCR and took a seat.

Should he delete the email? Print it as evidence? Would it

exonerate him with the police? Or would they think he had sent himself the email to provide an alibi?

When he focused on the television screen, Jamaal was playing on a small, cramped stage with a pianist, upright bassist, and drummer. The sound was tinny, buzzing at times, probably due more to the quality of the tape than the playing. A banner that spelled HOMECOMING hung as a backdrop. Jamaal seemed so relaxed, so confident. What was it about a young man, so bright, so full of energy, which would cause anyone to hate the museum that celebrated his life and times?

During a lull in the action, Jamaal was leaning over, speaking in low tones to a young woman in profile, her face illuminated like a crescent moon by a spotlight aimed from the foot of the stage. Their conversation was masked by the background noise of the crowd. Why had the videographer continued to keep the tape playing? Will wondered. He hit PAUSE, and the tape stuttered in place. In freeze-frame, she was a grainy miniature of the portrait in the Warner mansion, her luxurious red hair piled in a beehive with loose strands gracing a slender, white neck.

"Pretty, wasn't she?"

Will started and turned, as though caught in some guilty act.

"Mandy! You're going to have to quit creeping up on me like this."

"Sorry," she said, spinning to show off her lacy skirt and satiny blouse and sheer stockings all in a brilliant green. She could have stepped directly out of the Emerald City of Oz. "You like it?"

Will shrugged, then nodded enthusiastically to cover up his faux pas.

"Where's *your* green?" she asked.

Will pulled up his trouser legs to show off his socks.

"Oh," Mandy said. "We really need to work on your wardrobe if you're going to continue working here. Any news about

Jamaal's sax?"

"No, not yet. So you've heard?"

"Mrs. Waxman called me early this morning, but I had to go to classes, so I couldn't come by till now. Quite an escapade, wasn't it?"

Escapade. Such an odd word to use to describe a crime. It rhymed with "charade," the word the emailer had used in his message. Or what made him think it was a "he"? Could it be a "she" instead?

"Yes," Will said slowly, eyeing her for any hint of a hidden meaning.

"When you're through ogling Fortune, would you be so kind as to give me a tour of the crime scene?"

Side by side, he and Mandy stood in front of the glass case as though paying respects to a sarcophagus that had held an Egyptian mummy.

"There's something different about you," she said, turning her head and sniffing. "You smell different."

"I do?" He wondered if he had put on deodorant this morning, he had been in such a rush.

"Yes, like jasmine."

"Yeah, well, I've never been into cologne," he said, trying to ward her off the scent, so to speak.

"I know what it is!" she exclaimed brightly, taking his arm and spinning him about so he had to look her full in the face. "You're getting laid!"

Why did she have to conclude so many of her sentences— even questions—with exclamation points?

"Uh," Will uttered, unsure of how to proceed.

"You are! Admit it! We're friends." She had hold of both of his hands so he couldn't exactly squirm out of her inquiry without physical violence. "Who's the lucky lady? Anyone I know?"

"You're mistaken," Will stated bluntly, hoping to forestall further inquiries. "I better get back to work."

***

After his shift, it was a weary walk home. The sky was overcast, textured with dark gray strata resembling the contours of an archeological dig. The museum had been phenomenally busy all that afternoon. Once the forensics expert had departed, Will had spent the rest of the day ringing up an endless queue of customers. It seemed word had got out and everyone wanted to take a gander at the crime scene, filing past the glass case as though at a funeral with an absent corpse.

On the porch, he found Mrs. Gossett smoking a cigarette, swinging idly in a glider in a bathrobe—her standard attire. Did she never change into regular day clothes?

"It's been quite a day around here, let me tell you," she said, blowing out a stream of smoke in uneven bursts between pursed lips. Will had never seen her agitated like this.

"Is something wrong?" he asked.

"The police raiding my house. Searching every nook and cranny. You'd think I was running a brothel. I'm sure I'm the talk of the neighborhood."

"And the sax?" Will felt a coil of apprehension. What if his landlady had been pressured? The term "squawked" went through his mind. What TV crime show had he got this verb from?

"I'll show you." She snubbed out her cigarette and ambled across the porch, through the foyer and up the stairs. "It was just a precautionary measure," she said, as Will trudged behind. Passing the door to apartment #5, as they made a turn on the landing, it opened a crack. A pair of nervous eyes peeked out, taking them in. The eyes sprung out of a face with a goatee on the bottom and a beret on top.

"Sorry," the little man said, "I thought the police were back."

"This is Will Archer," she paused to introduce him.

"Charmed," the man said and closed the door.

"You mustn't mind him. He's a director. Eccentric as they come."

'Stage or film?" Will asked.

"Film," she replied, leaning in confidentially with a whisper. "And blue ones at that."

"Blue?" Will had an idea of the kind of films she meant.

"Very. In fact, he's planning a new film he intends to call … oh, what was the title? *Wait Your Turn*—a comedy, no doubt. He's recruiting participants. All amateurs." She paused a moment on the stairwell to size him up and down. "I don't suppose you have an acting bug in your bloodstream?"

They arrived at the one door he had been warned about when he first moved in, the one that opened on nothingness, just empty air two stories above the spiked fence below. She turned the knob and pushed it open.

"See anything?" she asked, eyebrows raised high.

"Nope."

He watched his landlady produce a handkerchief and reach around the door, struggle for a moment, then bring the sax into view by its strap.

"I hung it on the other side." She seemed proud of her deception.

"So I see." Will wished she had done something else with it: thrown it in a dumpster, lobbed it into a neighboring lawn, melted it down and poured it down a drain. "And the police? They didn't search outside?"

"Oh, no, they did. They prowled around. They even had a dog from their canine unit sniffing the shrubbery. But I was counting on just one thing."

"What's that?"

"People rarely look up." Handing the sax to Will along with the hanky, she pulled the door closed. "I'm afraid your room has been—oh, how should I put it?"

"Any way you wish," Will encouraged her.

"Ransacked. Would you like me to show you?"

"It's been a long day. I'm sure I can take it from here."

Her choice of adjective turned out to be right, although there hadn't been much to ransack. His duffel bag opened and searched, its innards strewn about haphazardly. The few condiments he kept in the medicine cabinet had been rearranged. The futon had been flopped over like a beached whale. His yellow ledger had been riffled. The one thing they hadn't discovered was his handgun, which he had had the foresight to hide in a plastic bag taped behind the toilet tank when he first moved in—a trick he picked up from *The Godfather*—although he had meant it as a countermeasure to snooping landladies, not prowling cops.

But there was something, else. The desk drawer—the one immovable feature in the apartment—had been pried open, splintered apart with hammer or crowbar, revealing its contents. Will gently removed a stack of red envelopes bound by a pink ribbon. Had the police simply glanced at the top envelope, seen a woman's handwriting, taken in the addressee, and left the stack intact, as having no relevance to the case at hand? It appeared so.

Untying the ribbon, he shuffled through them in order. They were all in the same hand. No return address, except for a single heart inked with an arrow through it in the upper left corner and the initials F.W. beneath. The addressee was the same on each: Jamaal Waxman. Only the addresses changed: Memphis, Chattanooga, Knoxville, Louisville, Lexington, Charleston, Wheeling. There were a couple dozen in all. The one on top had no address and no stamp. It simply read: *Jamaal, My Love. Home at Last!*

It took him less than an hour to read through the stack.

Chapter 15

The first letter was dated July 1st, an ominous twelve months before her and her lover's deaths. In it, she remembered a night of affection—presumably their last before Jamaal struck out on the jazz circuit.

My dearest, it began.

Its salutation assumed a level of intimacy that made Will feel he was intruding on Fortune's privacy, although this didn't keep him from reading.

You are always in my thoughts. I can so vividly remember our last night together before you departed on your journey. I understand you must make your way in the world, but oh, how I long for your embrace …

It went on and on in this vein for three more pages, the references to their lovemaking thankfully vague and abstract, leaving large, empty rooms for the imagination should the reader wish to enter. The letter was signed:

Affectionate regards,
Fortune

How many degrees short of "passionate" was "affectionate" on a thermometer of romance? Perhaps it was the Warner reserve, the height of the Warner station in life, which kept Fortune at an "affectionate" distance?

July 14

I imagine you happy, as I am happy, remembering you. I don't want you to think I am a prudish type of woman. I know the kinds of temptations you are privy to "on the road." Even were I to be so perverse as to imagine you with a bevy of women at your beck and call—

"Bevy," Will noted. Such an odd choice of word. It made these imaginary women seem a herd of cows.

—I would wish you all the happiness in the world. Am I jealous? I would be lying to say I am not, but I also know how it is with a young man who has certain physical needs, and so I encourage you to "sow your wild oats," as it were.

Such a maternal tone, as though Fortune had placed herself in the role of "older woman." Will couldn't help but wonder about Fortune's own "wild oats." He knew from the obituaries on file at the museum that Fortune would have been only 18 to Jamaal's 22 when their romance began.

July 30

You haven't called, as I begged you to. It's been weeks now, and I've spent every minute of every day anticipating the sound of your voice …

Is it because of Mother and her insidious habit of screening calls?

I know she expressed her dissatisfaction—to put it lightly—with our relationship, but you mustn't take Mother too seriously. She has her moments, as all of us do, but in the end, I can bend her to my will. I always have …

In lieu of a phone call, when can I anticipate a letter from your hand? I must admit, I have always found something more intimate about pen on paper than the spoken word. Don't worry about Mother intercepting them. I'll instruct Jenkins to make sure your letters are delivered safe and sound.

The next one was addressed to the Brass Pineapple in Charleston, SC. The same hotel as appeared at the top of the stationery Will had used to take dictation from the Ouija board.

August 12

I hope this letter reaches you before you move on, having only your itinerary to go by. Your dear, dear mother has been so very gracious in divulging your rest stops. Of course, I've had to beg and beg. Why have you not written, as I asked? No calls, no letters … it would be so much better if I could relay what I am about to tell you in person, face to face, and eye to eye.

Are you sitting down? I don't know how else to announce what I am about to announce except to plunge right in and announce it: I'm pregnant!

August 21

The money you wired was … unexpected. I know you know I am in no need of money, but how to interpret this gesture? Is it meant to encourage me to do the unthinkable? You know I couldn't do anything so horrendous to an innocent life-in-waiting, so fragile, so vulnerable. My doctor tells me she can determine the sex of it. However, I'd like to keep it a surprise. Nevertheless, I do think of her as a "she"—our little girl.

P.S. My doctor is sworn to secrecy. My mother believes my visits are for just a little "woman trouble."

September 19

If Mother should discover I'm pregnant … Selfish of me to say, but thankfully her eyesight has quite deteriorated, and so I may disguise my "little bundle" from her prying eyes.

Aside from you, Jenkins has become my only confidante in this time of trouble. I know he harbors affection for me, but I could hardly be expected to reciprocate. I have known him as our "butler" since my mother hired him when I was barely fifteen. He is only eight years my senior, but I can only think of him as an uncle—an uncle from Down Under with a funny Aussie accent. Odd, his being a house servant with such a royal first name: Earl. Please don't be jealous, dearest, that I have a man-friend to hear my deepest thoughts. He is only a temporary prop, someone to lean on while you are away, but he could never, ever take your place in my affections.

October 5

Mother has found out I'm "with child" as she likes to phrase it. As though I could be pregnant with anything else. A moose? A cat? A chameleon? Needless to say, she is not very pleased … I don't believe it was Jenkins who told her. It must be one of those female things. Her antennae must be able to sense the changes in my daily habits. I am so, so addicted to chocolate, I am afraid I shall balloon into a hot-air zeppelin by the time you arrive home for Christmas! I am counting not only the days but the hours …

Taking this as a cue, Will jumped ahead to the end of the year. This particular letter was addressed to the Victorian Arms, c/o Mrs. Phyllis Gossett. The return address on the envelope had been inked out. It seemed an act of censorship designed to conceal the sender's whereabouts.

December 26

I am so thankful for your Christmas gift. A heart to place next to my own. I shall wear it always. And the engraving—so sweet. I so, so wanted to be there for you to give you a gift of my own, but I am writing this from a place my mother has sent me … the home of an elderly cousin once removed on my dear departed father's side of the family. I don't even know the address. Somewhere in Connecticut is as much as I can tell you, in case you were thinking of rescuing me.

She tells her garden club friends that I am "studying abroad." I can imagine them rolling their eyes as I am sure they know the code words all too well. I wish I really were attending college overseas. At least I would be learning something, developing, growing. I feel so useless, just sitting here, skimming the magazines my nursemaid brings around to keep me entertained. I've read more back issues of Glamour *and* Cosmopolitan *than I could wave a stick at. And the women in these magazines, their bodies make me so jealous. Do supermodels ever have babies?*

"Studying abroad." Just what Abbey had done the year before he met her, on scholarship—not a Rhodes, but what did it matter? She was in England, a lifelong dream. After that, she returned to the States for her senior year, when he had met her at college. Luckily, her pregnancy hadn't interfered with her studies. Nevertheless, Will had to wonder. Had Abbey let their hurry-up marriage keep her from other dreams, unspoken ones, even so?

February 1

Mother wishes me to put the baby up for adoption and return to our domicile post-delivery as though nothing out of the ordinary has occurred. How she could suggest such a thing—it is too horrid to contemplate. The baby is mine, she is ours!!! I shouldn't let Mother upset me so, she always makes everything so much more difficult than it has to be.

It shan't be long now. She is kicking so hard to get out into the world, I know she will have a fighting spirit, just like her father …

February 19

Congratulations, my dear, dear love!! You are the proud father of a baby girl!!! Oh, how I wish you were allowed to visit, to see our daughter. The little trickster arrived three weeks too soon. She is so small, so tiny, so beautiful a baby, with the richest coffee-and-cream complexion (I believe you know which of us is the coffee, which the cream—and together we have created a perfect blend!), the frizziest head of hair (already) with a hint of ginger, and the widest, deepest eyes. They are your eyes, I am sure of it, the way they seem so earnestly to take in the world. And now I must go nap. Nurse and nap, nurse and nap—it is all I am good for at present.

The remainder of the letter began on a new page with a new color of ink: blue exchanged for black.

I have convinced Mother to allow me to bring the baby home after all. Too bad I had to resort to a threat of suicide ... More than a threat. I actually slit my wrists in the bath. And now I am under 24-hour psychiatric observation. So I am allowed only limited time with the infant, our child. I have named her Essence, thinking of the time we've been apart, and how time is always of the essence, so they say. I do hope you can come see your daughter sometime very soon!

A long gap in correspondence ensued, or it could be that the intervening letters had not been preserved. It's possible that Fortune was too preoccupied with the responsibilities of being a mother, except for what the letter revealed.

March 15

A most unexpected visit from your mother on this of all days—the Ides of March! She has brought welcome news that you are returning home!!! I am so happy you will see our little Essence before she outgrows her babyhood. She is so small, so sweet, a ripe little plum. I am sure you are not sorry about missing the late-night feedings, although we have hired a wet nurse for this, as well as the diapering. You might think I am getting off easy being a mother, but it will be so good to have you home again. In my arms, and me in yours. Our lips together, our bodies ... oh, but my imagination runs wild at the very thought. I know it is only another few days, but I feel like a schoolgirl, impatient for the last day of school, when she will be set free.

Another long gap, during which Will assumed they had become reunited with no need for written correspondence. Yet the next, and final, letter was addressed to the Victorian Arms, room #9, Will's very own, what used to be Jamaal's. How strange to send a letter from a place within walking distance.

June 25

I know our argument was only you trying to protect me by shutting me out of your life. If only you knew how it hurt … I know you don't think it will work, you don't believe you would be a good father, so you say. A life on the road is no life for a wife and baby … Alas, that I could persuade you differently.

So you're determined to venture forth again? Do you think me incapable of coming along with Essence? Of following behind on our own, if need be? We would keep a low profile, stay out of your way. Your late nights with your orchestra—

Funny, Will thought, she used the word "orchestra" for what he knew was Jamaal's jazz combo, a scaled-down quartet.

—will be way past Essence's sleeping time. I know how to wait by myself in a room. I have been doing it all my life so it seems.

I know you believe that the gulf between us is insurmountable. That you cannot provide for me the supposed riches you think I enjoy. But I can tell you honestly, I would rather live with you in a tarpaper shack than spend another minute in this house of mirrors.

Please, oh, please, Jamaal, I must speak with you again. It is so important you don't throw away what we have!

Your dearest, truest soul,

F.

Will couldn't leave it hanging here. It was like a novel with the last page torn out. He knew of only one person who might round out the story. Maybe it was time to take up his landlady on her standing invitation of joining her for an evening meal.

Chapter 16

"So nice to have a guest for dinner," Mrs. Gossett enthused. "A willing guest, at that. And so clean shaven, I barely recognize you as one of my tenants compared to the day you first moved in."

Was this another one of her puns? *Will-ing?* Will smiled, just in case.

"Have there been unwilling guests?"

"Only my husband Walter, God rest his soul. He was never one for dinner."

"How did he die?"

"From side effects," she answered, spooning another heap of mashed potatoes on Will's plate. "Of medication. Ironic, don't you think, his being a pharmacist?"

At this, Will felt prompted to propose a toast: "To life!"

He raised his glass that contained just a wee percentage of alcohol by volume, perking up a homemade brew his landlady referred to as an herbal medicine: *A mead for those in need.* She promised the alcohol content had been kept to a minimum. Ever since the accident, Will had sworn off alcohol along with cell phones—the two factors he blamed on the collision.

"Heavens, a bottle of cough syrup holds far more!" she had assured him.

After dinner, Will asked for a refill—the concoction was proving addictive, so warm and mellow on the throat—which he sipped while he and his landlady smoked cigarettes on the porch. It had a honeyed flavor that could induce humming like a bee in a grown man, with an aftertaste of blackberry or currant, he couldn't quite tell.

"Ah, the lost art of letter-writing, what a shame." This was her assessment, as she sorted through the letters.

"How do you suppose they've managed to stay locked away all this time?" Will asked.

"Probably because no one ever asked me for the key."

She skimmed them quickly, horn-rimmed spectacles on the bridge of her nose, which made Will question their usefulness since she seemed not so much to look through them as over.

Her head on its thin neck bobbed in rhythm, it seemed, with the words, the language, the flow of ink across a page. He was reminded of the movement of a gobbling turkey.

No, she hadn't known about the letters. But she wasn't surprised that this was how they corresponded, or rather how Fortune preferred to correspond. She was old-fashioned, that way.

"You must understand that Fortune was a prisoner in her own house—her mother's house, that is. Except after she had attempted suicide—yes, I knew about that. The threat of a repeat attempt—this is the leverage Fortune was able to wield over her mother to escape night after night for the months that Jamaal spent here, resting, drying out."

She took a long drag on her cigarette as though to aid her recollection before continuing her narrative.

"It's true he had a drug habit that he was trying, truly trying, to overcome, for Fortune's sake. The baby's, too. No one would guess—a young man on the road, playing gig after gig, having women visitors to his hotel rooms—that he might consider turning his life around, might consider becoming a father. He could have run at any time. There was nothing keeping him here at the Victorian Arms. Certainly not his own mother. It was her overprotectiveness he was always trying to outdistance. No, it was only Fortune. In short, I believe he was smitten."

She paused, refilling their goblets, then lit another cigarette.

"So she got away from her—her mother?"

"Only to a point. You see, she was chauffeured everywhere by Jenkins. Florence Warner permitted her to visit these 'premises,' as she called them with that overriding arrogance, on the condition that Jenkins wait for her, which he did—dutifully."

She turned her head toward Will, blowing out a stream of smoke from the side of her mouth. "Who do you think took care of Essence during her mother's liaisons with Jamaal?"

Will hadn't considered the affair from the perspective of the infant, but as soon as the question was posed, he knew the answer, betraying it with a raised eyebrow.

"Yes, yours truly," she said. "You couldn't expect blind Florence Warner to take care of the baby. Nor Jenkins, who preferred to wait in the car—the long, black hearse of a limousine—on the street curb with the radio for company."

Will could picture it: the feeding, the burping, the diapering. He had gone through it all before with Joel.

"And you were okay with taking care of the baby?" He couldn't help grinning. How old would she have been at the time? Mid to late forties? Fifty maybe?

"Let me assure you," she confided, patting Will's knee, "playing nurse is not all it's cracked up to be."

"Your husband must have helped?"

"No, I'm afraid not." She took a moment to iron a crease in the sleeve of her robe with her thumbnail. "Poor Walter died the year before. We had always wanted children, but as much as we had tried, we had never been able to conceive."

She paused, as though letting the past flow like perfume through her mind, and Will found himself imagining her as a young woman. Smooth out the wrinkles, dye the hair—and she became an alluring woman with dark, secretive features.

Picking up the baby the next morning, Fortune would spend a few minutes talking with her over a cup of tea: oolong, no sugar, just a squeeze of lemon. She would confess her hopes for her relationship with Jamaal. She couldn't confide in her own mother. Florence Warner could never understand love as a fountain of feeling, she was such a cold, remote figure, very much like a statue in her own garden.

Once Jamaal awoke, he would saunter downstairs, often in his PJs, and join them for breakfast. Except for these occasions, only rarely did he visit with his child when Fortune stayed over. He didn't want to become too attached. Or vice versa. He wanted to remain a soloist, not participate in a duet, never mind a trio. As much as Fortune wanted the relationship to flourish, he spent the three months of their newfound togetherness trying to find a way to ease her down gently.

"So they had a falling out," Will nudged things along, thinking of that final letter.

"Oh my, yes, and then some."

It began in room #9 behind closed doors. You could hear the shouting through the floorboards. The stomping. The other tenants peeking out of their doors as if afraid the house were infested with a hive of killer bees. The bees emerged, stinging at each other as they descended the stairs, barbs flying, Fortune in tears, Jamaal running after her, trying to console her, even as he stayed firm about breaking up. It was truly quite a scene. It spilled through the foyer and out the front door and onto the street like a torrent. She joined her tenants on the porch. It was as though they had box seats at an opera or ballet.

The movements of protagonist and antagonist—and without taking sides, it would be impossible to say which was which— were choreographed in silhouette against streetlights. Fortune got into the back of the waiting limousine and slammed herself tightly inside. But instead of taking off, her chauffer—that's right, Jenkins—kept the car idling on the curb.

Her younger self wondered, at first, what could possibly be the holdup. It occurred to her at the same time it did Jamaal, who went inside and came back out with the baby. It might have been only the second time in the four-and-a-half months since her birth he had even held her. But instead of hurrying back with her to the limo, he paused, pulling away the corner of the blanket so as to see her better under the porch light.

He rocked her back and forth, descending the steps slowly to stand on the curb, cradling her. Handing her over through the rolled-down window, he let go of her reluctantly, fingertips still touching the blanket while the baby stared wide-eyed.

Phyllis. Gossett closed her eyes, remembering Jamaal's parting words, choosing not to share these with her guest, who seemed satisfied her reminiscence had reached a logical end.

"Fortune, wait," Jamaal had said softly as the limo sidled away and the window was rolled back up. He watched it glide down the street toward the bridge, evaporating in the mist that had risen from the river. Only after it crossed, did he turn and accept the umbrella she offered, ducking beneath as she hooked his arm.

"Phyllis, I think I made a mistake letting her go," he had said to her that night and repeated it the next morning at breakfast, which he barely touched, so she knew it was true.

***

After Will left, she took her time clearing the table and setting the dishes in the sink. The leftover stroganoff she scooped into a Tupperware bowl for tomorrow's lunch.

Retreating to her bedroom, she drew the blinds and turned on the light. Like a burglar in her own house, she went straight for the jewelry box on her dresser, except this burglar happened to own a small golden key on a chain around her neck. Inserting the key, she gave it a twist and popped open the lid. There was an odd-and-end assortment of rings and earrings, cufflinks and pendants, in various compartments constituting the top layer, which she lifted out and set aside. In the bottom of the jewelry box lay a single letter of the same variety that Will had been so eager to share with her.

It bore the same careful cursive on the envelope, with herself, Mrs. Phyllis Gossett, identified as the addressee. Fortune had delivered it to her care via Jenkins, knowing that if she sent it to Jamaal directly, she took a chance on his discarding it without reading it. This way, she reasoned, there was a greater chance he would accept the message if it came from someone he trusted, someone older, supposedly wiser. And this is what the short note said:

My dearest,

This will be my last correspondence. I will wait for you on the bridge at midnight tomorrow with Essence wrapped in swaddling clothes …

I have made my decision. I won't be returning to the Old Manse no matter the outcome. I will be leaving with Essence, our daughter, even if you are not with us. But I pray, I believe, you will do what you know is in your heart and join us.

Think of it as our independence day …

Such drivel, she thought to herself, her opinion unchanged from when she had first opened the envelope and read the contents. *Such a poor, forlorn, foolish girl.*

She folded the letter back into thirds and, with the cover note instructing her to hand it personally to Jamaal and to make sure he opened it and read it, placed it back in the envelope and deposited it at the bottom of the jewelry box, where it had remained untouched and unread all these long, long years.

Chapter 17

The civic authorities had decided the time had come. There was no use waiting to see if the bereaved husband who had leapt in after his wife would reemerge from the hole into which he had disappeared like a gopher. And since the hole posed a hazard to passersby and traffic, it had been decided to take action by filling it in the very next day.

As he approached in the darkness, Will saw the outline of the backhoe that had been recruited for the job. He decided to hook the sax in plain view on the lip of the large metal bucket. Will figured the operator of the digger was bound to see the glittering sax and rescue it from oblivion. Or not. And if not, it would be buried forevermore in an unlikely grave.

He didn't know where else to put the sax where it might attract public attention with minimal risk of someone stealing it all over again. As he was the first one to open the museum each morning, he didn't think he could be the one to discover it planted outside the door without incurring more suspicion.

Relieved of his burden, he could almost describe his step as "jaunty." Or would that be pushing it? Let's just say he had a new bounce to his gait.

It carried him all the way to the park. But then he hesitated. They hadn't made definite arrangements. He was half afraid—all right, more than half—that he would find her in the act with some other man, if the rumors he had heard about her proved true. He scanned the playground. Not on the swing. Not on the merry-go-round. Then he saw her on the seesaw, laid out upon it as though a sacrificial victim.

"There you are," she said, stretching her arms above her head as he crept into her field of view. "I was beginning to worry."

"So, you were expecting me?"

He pushed down the end of the see-saw so that she began to slide headfirst, upside down.

"Hey!" she called out.

But Will only laughed. It felt good to let out a laugh. He had been boxing in his emotions so long.

"I have something for you," he said.

"Yeah?" Essence batted her lashes, looking up at him. "Like an engagement ring already?" Her question startled Will. He wasn't used to her sense of humor. In fact, he was still getting used to the idea that she could even have a sense of humor when plotting her suicide only a couple weeks away.

Bringing it out from behind his back, Will showed her the sheaf of envelopes.

"Am I being subpoenaed? I've been subpoenaed before, you know. A huge custody battle between my two grandmothers. I had to choose one or the other, just like My Friend Flicka. Or was it Black Beauty?"

"Letters," Will announced. "From your mom. Your mother's letters. Fortune's."

Essence righted herself on the seesaw and pushed herself to standing.

"What letters?"

"To Jamaal. Your father."

A moment of complete silence. This wasn't the reaction Will had been expecting.

"Here, don't you want them? They span a whole year, the whole time you were in your mom's, you know, womb. And even after—"

Essence walked off toward the perimeter of the playground,

but Will was undaunted.

"—all the way to when you were four months old," Will blustered on, following her. "You need to read them. They prove—"

"Prove what?" Essence asked, turning sharply in the darkness. "That my mother was so much in love with my father, she forgot all about my existence?"

"No, just the opposite. She was hoping to elope, I think. She wanted to go with Jamaal on the road. But she was going to take you with her. With them. Don't you see?"

"See what?"

It was exasperating, Essence's refusal to comprehend such a clear point.

"You don't have to go through with it now. There's no reason you should do what your mother did."

"That's where you're wrong. My mother still chose to abandon me. She jumped off the bridge, didn't she? She still went through with her suicide."

Will hadn't anticipated this line of reasoning. He had felt so sure he was making an airtight case for the continuance of Essence's existence.

"Yeah, well," he fumbled. "What if she didn't kill herself? Your grandmother—your other grandmother—happens to think her son was murdered. Why not your mother, too?"

"That's crazy," Essence blurted. Her body went rigid, as though preparing to fight—or flee. Will braced himself for more argumentation. But then something in her softened, her frame slumping in silhouette. Her lower lip jutted out in a pout. When she turned to face Will, her expression was lax, like wet leaves after the passing of a storm. "Isn't it?" she asked, softly.

"I don't know. Did she have any enemies?"

"By all reports, she was the sweetest woman alive—at least

in New Bloomfield."

"What about the other side of the river in East Orange? That seems to be where she was spending most of her time before she died."

"Let's not talk about my mother all night."

She seemed put out of a sudden, the opposite of what Will had intended.

"What did you have in mind?" he asked, changing tack.

"Come on," Essence said, pulling his hand. "I'll show you."

"What? Where?"

"Just hurry up and come on."

Will followed after as she let go of his hand. He had trouble keeping up. It was like trying to follow a deer through the woods.

They reached the gated entrance in minutes with Will bent over, winded, while Essence punched in the code. The gate swung open and she went inside, where she turned.

"Are you coming?"

"What about your pets?"

"Crimson and Clover? They won't bother you. Although I must admit, they are fond of water."

"Water? What does water—"

"I want us to go swimming," Essence stated, reaching out for his hand.

"Swimming? But I don't have a suit."

"Who says you need one?"

With this invitation, Will cautiously crept inside the grounds as the gate automatically swung closed behind him with a final clank that shivered his spine. And just as he had anticipated in a worst-case scenario, here came Crimson and Clover, bounding across the open lawn, sticking to the shadows between flood-lights, darting and dodging the statuary.

Will backed up against the cold, rigid metal of the fence.

"Freeze!" Essence commanded.

"I am frozen," Will managed to utter.

"No, not you, the tigers."

They immediately sat down on their haunches, as Essence gave each a rub behind their ears.

"Come closer," she beckoned. "They won't hurt you. They're just overgrown pussycats, aren't you?" she cooed, lowering her face, so that the tigers took turns licking her cheeks with sloppy kisses.

Standing a good three feet away, Will was as close as he wanted to get. His automatic reflex was to close his eyes, shutting out the threat, so he had to struggle to force his eyelids open. So far, he hadn't wet his pants.

"Come on," Essence said. "They won't bite."

Obeying, Will took one step, two steps. The tigers eyed him, and before he could take a third and final step, they came over and began rubbing themselves against his legs, just like a cat would, except they came up to his waist, while he stood as tree-like as possible.

"Give them a pet," she encouraged him. "Once they have your smell on them, they'll accept you as one of their own."

Skeptical as he was, he did as instructed, gingerly patting each on the head as they sat back down.

"Okay," she said, standing, "introductions are over. Now run off."

Will began to move away, as directed.

"Not you, silly."

She gave each tiger a gentle shove, and off they went, wending back the way they had come through the clutter of statues.

"But you didn't give them my name," he tried to joke. His jaw was quivering, so that his words came out in spasms.

"No name necessary," she said, taking his hand. "Let's go.

I'll show you the pool."

For a mansion so large, the pool was rather small, shaped like a lima bean. A sliding door allowed entrance onto the patio below a balcony. No lights were on except the ones beneath the surface, casting a bluish glow through the water.

Essence stepped quickly out of her sandals, shirt, and shorts, and dove right in. Will was more sheepish about removing his clothes. He set the letters under an ashtray on a glass table, then joined her by slowly sinking into the water while hanging onto the side of the pool. Testing the temperature, he was pleased to find it on the warm side.

Essence came up to him, floating on her back, and Will joined her. It was possible to imagine they were in the bottom of an enormous canyon staring up at a patchwork quilt of clouds, obscuring the moon. Essence took his hand and pulled him over and under, where she gave him a luxuriant underwater kiss that threatened to drown him from surprise.

"Why can't we get together in the daytime sometime?" Will sputtered, as their heads bobbed up.

"Like for coffee?"

"Well, yeah. Coffee could be nice."

"I'm not a big fan of coffee."

"Something else then. It doesn't have to be coffee. A milkshake."

"With french fries? I just adore french fries."

"Sure, whatever you want."

"But no ketchup. I'm morally opposed to ketchup."

She gave him a push that sent him backward. Before he could recover, she had disappeared under water, then reappeared at the far end of the pool, supple as a porpoise.

"It's just that my grandmother," she explained. "She wouldn't like my going out in public unchaperoned. And when

Grandmother doesn't like something, well then, you know how it is."

Actually, Will didn't know how it was. His one encounter with Mrs. Warner had been off-putting, true. But perhaps her demeanor was a façade, a form of upper crust stiffness.

"What is it you do all day?" he asked. He imagined her lounging in bed until nighttime came back around.

Essence lay on the water, her breasts breaking the surface like twin islands. The clouds parted, sending a moonbeam down her midriff.

"Oh, this and that. Mostly, I assist my grandmother."

"Your Grandmother Warner? Like with meals and getting dressed and such?"

"Nuh-uh. She's quite capable of doing all that on her own. I'm a sort of parttime secretary." Essence rose into a vertical position, treading water with her arms, even though they were in a shallower part of the pool. "I help with her charity work: research foundations to make sure they're legit, take dictation, handle online correspondence, send out checks …"

"What kind of charities?" Will asked, cutting her short.

"Oh, the usual: feeding the hungry, ending cancer, rescuing animals."

"Like abandoned kittens?"

"More like endangered species. You know, elephants, rhinos, tigers …" She came up to him, smiling, and draped her forearms over his shoulder. "Men who respect a girl's privacy by not asking so many questions."

"Sorry, just one more. You said 'parttime.' What about the other part of the time?"

Essence pushed off from his chest, back into the water.

"Well, there's her memoirs."

"She's writing a book?"

"We both are. I add little details here and there to make it more exciting. We're up to husband number two. Husband number three died before I was born, so I never got a chance to know my step-grandfather. She comes from old money, so there's always someone wanting to marry her. I'm surprised Jenkins hasn't proposed by now."

Will took a couple slow-motion steps toward her.

"I can see where this would take up a lot of your day."

"Not all of it. Speaking of books, did I mention I like to read?"

"Let me guess. Romance novels?"

"Actually, I'm working my way through Western philosophy. Right now I'm on Nietzsche."

"Well," Will reflected, "that would explain your nihilism."

Essence splashed him with a backhanded tsunami.

"I'm not a nihilist," she countered. "I'm an idealist. A Platonist, if you must know. I believe in a hidden world of ideal forms."

Will glanced around into the night, half expecting such forms to materialize. What shapes would they take? Conversely, he half wished he could disappear into such a shadowy world at this very moment. Clearly, he had underestimated Essence's capacity for depth of thought. He felt chagrined by his own condescension.

"I didn't mean to offend you," he said.

"Admit it. You thought I'm some empty-headed bimbo."

"No, it's not that. It's just—"

Will fumbled for words to express reassurance: that hers, as she described it, was a life not worth giving up.

"Don't worry about it. I get that all the time."

If Abbey were here, she would reprimand him for his latent chauvinism. Of course, he'd have to explain what he was doing in a swimming pool with an attractive, naked, younger woman.

If Abbey were here ...

"Guess how long I can hold my breath under water," Essence said, playfully, pulling him out of his reverie.

The sudden change in mood and topic caught him off guard.

"I don't know. A minute?"

"Longer."

"Two?"

"Three and a half," she boasted. "I've been conditioning. Here, I'll prove it to you." She reached down and under, grabbing hold of him. "By the feel of it," she said with a sly smile, "it shouldn't take that long."

In preparation, she heaved three long breaths, bobbing up and down. Will maintained his footing in anticipation. Just as she was preparing to go under, the floodlights came on.

"Is someone out here?" they heard Mrs. Warner's voice.

"Sh-h-h," Essence quieted him, but he knew enough not to call out.

"Essence, is that you?" her grandmother asked.

"Yes, ma'am," she announced. "Just me."

She must have super hearing, Will thought, if she heard them through the glass door. But what good would the floodlights do her? That's what he wanted to know. Maybe they came on automatically. "Who is it you're with?"

"She's not with anyone, Mum." The voice came from above, but Will already knew whose it was before he turned his gaze toward the balcony. "Mum," Will thought, as though Mrs. Warner were the bleeding Queen Mother. Jenkins rested rolled-up sleeves on the balcony ledge. He stared down at the two of them with the stab of a smile tightening the already sharp outline of his features.

"Jenkins? Is that you?"

"Yes, Mum."

As though it would be anyone else with that unmistakable Aussie twang.

"Is she telling the truth? Is she with anyone?"

"No, Mum. No one. I think it's safe to go back to bed."

"Where you should be, too, my dear," she directed her voice toward the pool. "I do wish you would reduce the number of these midnight swims of yours."

Ah, Will thought, feeling deflated. So she has these midnight swims often, then. With whom? he wondered. Who else?

"I'll be in as soon as I dry off," Essence told her.

Will waited quietly while Mrs. Warner made her way back inside in her wheelchair. The patio door slid closed behind her.

Jenkins, for all the nerve, chose this moment to light up a cigarette and continue his observation from above. Will wondered how long he had been there, critiquing their lovemaking.

"You can go now, Jenkins," Essence called up to him.

"I dunno," Jenkins said. "I'm rather fancying a bit of night air. Refreshes the lungs."

This, before taking a long drag on his cigarette.

"Well then, if it's a show you want."

Essence climbed out of the pool, the water shimmering down her well-lit body. She walked toward a pile of towels stacked on a glass table. Aiming the full-frontal nudity of her pose at Jenkins, she leisurely dried off, pulling the towel back and forth behind her from shoulders to buttocks, shaking back and forth so her breasts shimmied in the light.

But Jenkins was already gone, having disappeared before her "show" began.

"Come on, Will," Essence said. "I'll escort you out. This way." She led Will by the hand, once he gathered his clothes. "There's a back entrance."

A path led through the trees. Will felt a moment of panic

when he brushed against something descending from the branches, which turned out to be a vine. He had a momentary fantasy of Tarzan and Jane.

Essence walked in front, surefooted, never once losing her balance, until they came to a fence. She was still naked, her buttocks round and firm, her legs long, her shoulders narrow. Her hair snaked down her back, clinging in wet, curling strands.

Every now and then she turned and flashed a smile.

"Still behind?"

Will didn't know how to interpret that. Would he forever be behind? Would he always be merely a follower?

At the rear gate, the width of a common door with another combination touchpad, Essence stopped abruptly, and Will bumped against her. He dropped his clothes and held his hands around her waist. She leaned back into him, her hair wet against his neck, her eyes closed.

"You know this is going to end badly, don't you?" Essence said quietly.

"But why does it have to?" Will countered, letting his hands slide down and around and beneath her breasts.

"Have you ever known a life to end happily?"

"No, but the chapters, the pages, these can have happy endings, can't they?"

"You don't want to get involved with me."

"It seems a little late for that."

"I'm nothing but trouble."

"I don't mind trouble."

"Let me guess. It's your middle name?"

Leaning forward to grasp the fence posts, she arched her back and pushed her buttocks into him, mashing against his hardness, making it easy to enter. Each thrust lowered her down the fence posts, and he was lasting so long this time, that by the end, she was on her knees, and he was crouched over her, cradling her breasts. His thrusts became slower, longer, and she let out a series of moans. With one last thrust, he came and let out a shout, a vocalism that took him by surprise.

Afterward, they lay spooning in the grass of a narrow lawn. He ran his finger between her breasts and down along her torso. She was as slippery as a fish.

"Still think you're going to save me?" she asked, turning her head to find his eyes.

"From drowning?"

Could he when the time came? And how would he if he tried? Would he leap off the bridge after her? Would he wrestle her away from her clutch on the cables, her foothold on the rail? And what would prevent her trying again? Would he call the police? Would he kidnap her and take her to the ER to have her admitted to a psych ward?

"Not from drowning," she whispered, snuggling close, inducing a pause. "From myself."

Chapter 18

After Will left, Essence walked back to the pool. There was something clean and natural about walking naked through woods of a starry evening. Her skin prickled all along her arms and legs, but not from any perceived coldness. She crossed her arms over her breasts, hugging herself. Could it be nervousness? If so, it was one of the first times ever she felt it so.

All the way, she thought about Will in a way she wouldn't have with any of her other male "friends" who met her for quick five- or ten-minute "sessions" in the dark of night. She had never been in a relationship—except for a brief affair with a sorority sister at the local college that dwindled and died after her grandmother pulled her from classes—and she didn't think of Will as a boyfriend. But was this the way her mind was leaning? Somehow, he made her feel differently than she had with other men. He made her feel innocent in some way. That was it—innocent.

He had a sexual history, she presumed. And for the first time, ever, she had allowed her male companion to proceed without protection. Impulse had overridden caution. She made a mental note not to let this happen again.

Poolside, she dressed back into her shorts and shirt, both loosely fitting her frame. Her first order of business was to read through the letters from her mother Will had given her.

But the letters weren't there. Could be the wind had blown them, but there wasn't so much as an agitation of a breeze. It's possible they were knocked off the table when she and Will had grabbed towels. But Will had used an ashtray as a paperweight. And the ashtray was still there—with a telltale cigarette, crumpled in it and smoldering.

She looked up at the balcony and saw Jenkins's light was still on. His was the suite immediately above the pool.

She huffed up the stairs inside and strode down the hall with a purpose, banging on his door. It opened within seconds, as though he had been waiting for her.

"The letters," she said, fuming. "I want them. Now!"

"Won't you come in?" he asked, all sweetness, sweeter, that is, than his cologne, which smelled like battery acid, astringent, as though a coat of armor—or aroma—to ward off enemies.

"The letters!" she demanded from her side of the threshold.

"So you've said," he reminded her, backing into his living quarters. All very spare, very Spartan. On the wall dangled a pair of golden boxing gloves, memento of his time as a prizefighter Down Under. "Come on in, I'll fix you a drink."

The way the night was proceeding, she had a hard time resisting the offer of a drink, so she stepped inside after a slight hesitation. This was one of the rare occasions she had ever been permitted access to his quarters.

"Close the door behind you," he said, turning around with two tumblers of bourbon from the sideboard. "And have a seat. No need to be shy."

There was always something compelling about his voice, a self-assuredness that set her at ease, dispelling her wariness. She reprimanded herself for being so prone to the suggestiveness of his voice. But she did as she was told—or invited. She took a seat in a chair to avoid having him sit next to her on the couch.

"I found them lying around by the pool. Didn't want them to get wet now, did you?"

"I'd like to have them," she said, more politely, now that she was seated opposite him, sipping her drink.

Jenkins produced them from inside his nightshirt, which was

unbuttoned to his navel, and set them on the coffee table.

She reached out for them, but he took hold of her wrist.

"Not so fast, my dear. Dunno know why you'd be wanting to see them after all this time. Nothing but heartbreak in them, I'm sure."

He eased her hand back to her lap, although she put up a Pyrrhic war of resistance.

"You've read them," she observed, noticing the pink ribbon that had tied them so neatly together had unraveled. Jenkins picked up the envelopes, arraying them like a fan of cards.

"I find them fair sentimental and foolish. Your mum's affections were—how best to say it?—misplaced."

"Shouldn't you leave that for me to judge?" Essence half rose from her seat. "What is it you want from me anyway?" she asked, although she suspected the answer. In all the time she had known him, meaning forever, he had never laid a hand on her physically or sexually. But she had been reading his looks of late.

Jenkins stood, dropping the clutch of letters to his side, and Essence took up a position in front of him on her knees. She undid the snaps that were sealing the fly of his pajama bottoms, but as she reached inside, she felt a sharp blow on the base of her chin that sent her sprawling backward with such force she hit her head against the far wall.

She sat up slowly, feeling dazed, her vision spinning. It took her a moment to realize what happened: Jenkins had brought up his knee in a sharp uppercut, perfectly aimed.

Now he was kneeling beside her, taking her arm, helping her sit up, even as she backpedaled like a crab away from him against the wall.

"Sorry, love," he said, sounding sincere. "I didn't mean to. It was just reflex. I would never mean to hurt you. You must know by now, this isn't what I want from you."

"So what is it you want then?" she asked, acerbically, massaging her jaw.

"Here." He extended a handkerchief. "Your lip's bleeding."

She accepted it grudgingly and touched it to her mouth, then brought it away with an imprint of blood. She wadded it up and threw it back at Jenkins.

"Bastard," she said, more as a calculated commentary.

Not for the first time, she wondered how their relationship had reached such a low ebb. When she was little, she had followed him like a pull-toy on a string, helping him with odd jobs around the property: waxing the car, polishing the silver, setting traps for ants, fixing a rail. But she had always sensed a disconnect, which had widened with the onset of puberty. The sensation she was feeling now, however, was new. She had never felt afraid of him before. Distant, yes. Fearful, no.

"I'm sorry, Missy. Truly. You may not believe this, but I'm only trying to protect you."

How she hated this pet name for her.

"Protect me? You've got a strange way of going about it."

"Not all your problems can be solved with a quick shag in the bush," he said solemnly, as though delivering sage advice.

"Please, spare me the lecture. You're not my father."

"How very true. But if I were, I'm afraid I cannot approve of this gentleman caller of yours."

"Gentleman caller? Really? How eloquent."

"What do you want me to call him: a bogan, a bloke, a grifter? I assume you're intent on seeing him still."

Licking the blood from the corner of her mouth, she gave her shoulders a shrug.

"What's it to you?"

"It's information I'm after. I want to know his game."

"Game? What makes you think he's playing one?"

"Because you're playing one, Missy. And the sooner I find out his, the closer I'll be to finding out yours."

To this, Essence made no answer. She was merely surprised at how open Jenkins was being with his intentions. She suspected a trick of reverse psychology.

"Here's the deal, Missy. I will ensure you receive one letter for every evening you spend in our Mr. Archer's company."

He handed her a letter from the top of the stack that he had folded back into a pack and placed on the table. As she took hold of it, he held it firmly pinched in his grasp.

"Aren't you forgetting something?" he asked blithely. "I need information. For every night you provide information, you get one letter."

"What kind of information?"

"I want to know anything and everything. From the length of his donger when limp to the diameter of his clacker when doing a poop on the dunny."

His smile relaxed into a frown when Essence didn't respond to what she supposed was his attempt at humor.

"Sorry, that came out rather ruder than I intended. Here." He let go the letter, and she took it calmly, without tearing into it as she had wanted to do earlier. "We'll consider this one a first installment, a gesture in good faith."

One a day meant only twelve letters until the time she had set for her leap of faith.

"The rest I will just tuck away for safekeeping."

Essence slowly got to her feet, starting with her hands and knees. A drop of blood dripped onto the immaculate white carpet, unnoticed by Jenkins, who had his back turned as he went over to open the door—her cue to leave. She placed a bare foot over top of the drop to hide it from view as he turned back around at the threshold.

"All right," she murmured, contemplating the "deal," as he called it. "However, I have a condition of my own."

"Oh?" he asked with raised eyebrows.

"No more following me. No more spying. I don't want you lurking about when I meet him."

He lowered his head, smile gone, giving her proposal his full consideration.

"If you think I take any pleasure in looking out for you—"

"Then I guess the deal's off."

"I wouldn't be too hasty," he cautioned her. "That is, if you want to continue seeing him."

"And how will you stop me?"

"Aren't you forgetting?" he reminded her good-naturedly. "I have the keys."

She knew he meant two keys: the key to the cage barring her patio doors and the key to her bedroom. It was perfectly within his power to keep her locked in at night.

"No hard feelings?" He extended his hand, but Essence only spit a glob of saliva into his palm.

"I suppose I deserved that," Jenkins commented.

Essence turned with a huff and walked out of the room. She mulled a single question in her mind as she proceeded down the hall: How badly did she really want to read her mother's letters?

She decided the answer could wait until morning.

Chapter 19

At the museum, Sybil Waxman made an early appearance—
bursting through the front door with breathless haste.

"Have you heard?" she exclaimed.

"About it being an orange day?" Will said laconically. He
wore an orange-and-black tie striped like a candy cane that Mrs.
Gossett had loaned him from her deceased husband's wardrobe.

"No, no, not that, my dear." She proceeded to inform him
about the recovery of the sax. "I imagine the perpetrator was
going to bury the evidence but lost his nerve about climbing
down into the pit." She seemed confident of her theory, and Will
didn't contradict her.

"Where is it now?" he asked.

"Being held as evidence. Dusting for fingerprints and all that.
Though I daresay the only fingerprints they'll find, if the thief
was good about his business, are my son's or my own, the only
two people in existence who I know to have handled it with bare
hands."

Her phone went off and Will tensed. He felt another migraine coming on, like a thundercloud on the horizon. He braced
himself for a bad one. Maybe he should just call off for the day
as a preemptive measure.

"Yes," she said into her phone. "Uh-huh. No I wouldn't
have a problem with that. Anytime today is fine."

She turned back to Will.

"That was the police. They'll be returning the sax this afternoon." She reached into her handbag and pulled out a bottle of
champagne.

"I thought we might celebrate."

"The finding of the sax?"

"Are you feeling all right? You don't look well."

"I'm fine," Will said, taking a step backward, as his employer peeled away the foil from the top of the bottle and untwisted the wires.

The cork exploded with a loud pop that drove a railroad spike into his brain. It wedged between his eyes with the heavy blow of a sledgehammer, and his vision went blank like a white-out in a snow squall.

When he woke up, Mandy was beside him, holding his hand. He noticed she was wearing black. Shouldn't she be wearing something orange? Had someone died? And was that someone him?

"Do you remember anything?" she was asking. It sounded like a question in the middle of a conversation, the beginning of which he couldn't recall.

"Have I been awake?" he asked, trying to sit up.

"You don't remember waking up?" Mandy said. "Wow, you really are a case."

He saw he was in a hospital gown in a hospital bed in a hospital room. Everything—the sights (lime green walls), smells (antiseptic mixed with calamine lotion), textures (stiff bleached linen sheets), sounds (various beeps coming from monitors) spelled hospital—and one past its prime at that. This just left taste, and he already knew what hospital food tasted like. He would skip the tapioca pudding, though. The clock on the wall said 11:00. It must be AM, he decided. Daylight seeped through the blinds. He had an IV in his arm.

"It wasn't me this time," she said. "I wasn't anywhere near you with a flash."

He was glad she hadn't been there to see them again—his

convulsions. His wife had described them to him. They had only started occurring after the accident. His doctors—there had been a team of them—thought it had something to do with head trauma. Duh! But that's as good a diagnosis as they were able to provide, despite the number of tests they had run.

"How are you feeling?" Mandy asked, frowning with concern.

"Like I've been shot out of a cannon against a concrete wall. How do I look?"

"Like you've been shot out of a cannon against a concrete wall."

"Not worse?"

"Bad enough."

"What are you doing here anyway?" He tried not to sound impolite.

"I thought you might like to see a friendly face. You know, when you woke up. And now, here you are, awake!"

Same old Mandy, after all, full of exclamation points.

He tried sitting up, but his body felt leaden, as though held down by weights. He wondered what they were dripping into his arm to make him so drowsy.

"Here, just use the push-button thingy," Mandy said, handing him a control unit on a cord. "See, there's this button for 'up' and this one for 'down.'" She sounded like an elementary school teacher explaining how to do simple arithmetic. He wanted to tell her it wasn't that his brain was befuddled. Just his body felt like slumber.

"I really shouldn't be here. My clothes," he asked, looking around.

"In the closet. There," she said, pointing.

"And my wallet?"

"Mrs. Waxman took it, I'm afraid. She had to give them your personal information."

No doubt she would come across his other identity, that of Alan Paxton, his former self. He relaxed against the bed, pushing the arrows up and down until he found a comfortable position. He would have to think up a story.

But he wouldn't have time. Because here she was. In the flesh. Right on cue. She entered the room like a train conductor, come to check his ticket. Will noticed she was dressed in black, too. Had they dressed preemptively, in case there should be need for a funeral?

Mandy rose to give up her chair but hovered near the bed as though preparing to watch a boxing match, a giddy expression on her face.

"I thought you might like some magazines," Mrs. Waxman said. She plopped several onto Will's lap: *Time, People, Ebony.* "Mandy, you have my permission to leave."

"I thought I might be of some help," Mandy sounded a muted note of rebellion.

"Mandy!" Mrs. Waxman's voice cut sternly as though she could scissor through steel.

"Yes, ma'am," Mandy bowed her head, leaving, but gave Will a sly and subtle wink before heading through the door.

"You had another attack," Mrs. Waxman observed. "Have you had them this badly before?"

"Not often. This was just a headache in comparison."

"William, please," she said, resting a hand on his shoulder, "I do know what a headache is. And what you had, I can assure you, was no headache."

"I'm really fit to leave. I shouldn't be here."

"The doctors want to perform an MRI."

"They won't find anything. I've had MRIs, X-rays, CAT-scans—there's nothing to see."

Will noticed the flowers at the foot of the bed.

"From your landlady," she said, reading the card. "Phyllis Gossett, bless her tiny heart."

"How long have I been here?" Will asked.

"Just overnight."

"Two days! But I thought …" He looked again at the clock on the wall. It read 11:15. But now he knew it was 11:15 on the second day of his stay. "Two days," he repeated, as though digesting an inedible biscuit. Might as well come out with it. "You've had to go through my wallet?"

"Oh, yes," she said, blithely, as though it had only just now occurred to her. "Let me return it to you." She rooted through her purse, rearranging the contents, which seemed mostly to comprise a cluster of tissues, crumpled with lipstick marks. "There was only this one little blip, registering you at the hospital."

"Is that right?" Will braced himself as best he could against his pillows.

"You seem to have two identities."

He gave up the attempt to focus on her face and peered off above her shoulder, where he noticed a crucifix for the first time, hung like a horseshoe above the door.

"Does the hospital know?"

"For all intents and purposes, the hospital believes you to be William Archer."

"Will you be turning me in?"

She stared at him for a long moment, her eyes coming into focus.

"No, I don't believe so. Whatever pact you've made with the devil, I'll leave it for you to resolve."

"Thank you," he said, relieved, then had another, even more alarming thought. "You've told others?"

Mrs. Waxman arced an eyebrow.

"If by 'others' you mean my granddaughter, then no, I'll

leave it to you to divulge such information. And if you should feel well enough to return to work on Monday," she added, rising to leave, "it's an aquamarine day."

That evening, after an exit discussion with his doctor, the man formerly known as William Archer began packing his belongings. He didn't have one scrap of aquamarine clothing in his wardrobe.

Chapter 20

The only thing he didn't pack was a slim 9 mm handgun advertised as "scaled for self-defense." But nothing about self-offense. It was flat and light in the hand. It contained fifteen rounds, and he'd fired it fourteen times at a practice range, reserving the last bullet for a night such as this.

In the Hex Room, he set out a stack of towels from the bathroom to help whoever it was who found him to mop up. Then he changed into pajama bottoms and tee as though preparing for sleep, which he was—the big one.

He was afraid it would come to this one day, and now that day was here. The day he was found out. The day his former identity was researched, as it was bound to be, Mrs. Waxman being such an inquisitive sort. He felt trapped in a trifecta of dead ends, unable to move in any direction, save the one he was contemplating now.

There was no going home again, not after a year apart. That option seemed closed for good. How could he face Abbey? What explanations could he give? Neither had he an inclination to leave East Orange, go to some other strange city or town and start all over again, borrowing some other dead man's identity. He dreaded the whole process. It would be soul-draining, tiring beyond endurance. That left staying put, but he wasn't sure he could continue working at the museum, despite his employer's assurances. At very least it would feel awkward, at most unbearable, being an object of perpetual suspicion, scrutiny.

He thought about leaving a note, but what would it say? And to whom would he address it? Abbey? He thought not. Hadn't that one parting note already been enough?

He took a large plastic tarp—one he had packed for just such a continency—from his duffle bag and unfolded it over the futon. He could picture the aftermath, how easy it would be for the examiners to simply wrap him up like a burrito.

As a farewell gesture, he turned the photograph of his wife and child around to face the great outdoors where it was propped on the windowsill of the Hex Room. The frame was intact, but the glass was cracked because of that time with the ghost.

And where was Jamaal on this eve of the ending of Alan Paxton's life as well as the second demise of William Archer's?

"Come on out and show yourself, old mole!" he dared it. "Not sure if you could use any company, but soon enough …"

Kneeling on the tarp, he brought a pillow up to the side of his head and pressed the muzzle against it, finger on the trigger. He waited for some intervention. Wasn't this the point in a movie version of his life when someone would knock at the door or ring the telephone or drop out of the sky on a wire to tell him, *"No, wait, you have so much to live for. Don't do it. The dance will go on without you, and you haven't even learned all the steps."*

He heard music—Jamaal's?—droning through the pipes like a funeral dirge. He wished he knew more about jazz than what he absorbed off the vinyls from the museum. It sounded mournful, so he supposed a minor key. There was a song in there somewhere, but that was the whole trouble, he felt, with jazz. It kept returning over and over to its same, old, safe melody. After all of that clever improvisation, it always came back home.

With twilight, the room was growing dark, dark enough that no one would see in with the lights off. A steady rain was streaking the windows, giving the bridge a bleary look, its strings of lights wavering. His eyes searched the length of it, pausing at the center to seek the figure of a woman with wild chestnut hair.

Save Essence! went through his mind.

He dropped the pillow but kept hold of the gun. He leaned forward, pressing his forehead against the pane, hand shaking.

Before he could stand, there actually was a knock on the door, which confused him. His mind had been occupied with Essence, and he wondered how she could have crossed the bridge without his noticing. On his way to the door, he deposited the gun in a desk drawer.

But it wasn't Essence. It was Mandy.

"I've already signed the guest register and everything and cleared it with Mrs. Gossett," she said, barging in, "so there's no need to worry."

"What are you doing here?" he challenged her.

"Never mind that, what are you doing, dressed in pajamas? Turning in early?"

"You could say that."

"Oh, and what is that?" she asked, peering around his shoulder at the tarp. "Planning a picnic?"

"I was thinking of painting," Will fumbled.

"In a room full of windows?"

For this, Will didn't have an answer.

"Is there a place I can sleep?" she asked, spinning around.

"What makes you think you'll be staying here?"

He didn't mean to sound rude, but …

"See? I even brought pajamas." She drew a skimpy, frilly thing out of her handbag like a magician producing a rabbit.

"But, but …"

"My employer insists I stay with you overnight."

"Your employer? You mean, Mrs. Waxman?"

"Nuh-uh. My other employer. Mrs. Gossett."

This bit of information astounded him. "I didn't know you were close."

"We're not. I help her out from time to time. Little odd jobs around town. Just for some extra money."

"And that's what I am? An odd job?"

Mandy smiled.

"She's worried about you. She didn't want you to be alone tonight."

"Okay, but …"

"No more 'buts,' all right?"

She brought two bottles out of her handbag and held them up to view. One was alcoholic, the other not—one of Mrs. Gossett's homemade brews, she explained. So Mandy knew about his prohibition against alcohol? As she twisted the cap off the wine bottle, he was half-tempted to intervene. Maybe eighteen months of abstinence had been long enough.

"Cheap, but effective," she said. "Got any glasses?"

Surrendering, Will produced two goblets from the kitchenette.

"So what do I call you, anyway?" she asked, filling each glass two-thirds full out of separate bottles. "Will? Or Alan?"

So she knew. Mrs. Waxman had obviously told her. He wasn't upset. He supposed she just had to divulge his secret identity to someone. In a sense, he felt almost relieved.

"Just call me Will. It's who I think of myself as. I never really went by Alan, except for my wife, it's what she preferred to call me. My friends called me Pax."

"Pax? Really? Like Pax Romana?"

"A leftover from college days."

"So," Mandy said, sitting cross-legged on the small settee, leaving enough room for him to squeeze in beside her if he chose, which he didn't.

"So?"

"Aren't you going to tell me what happened?"

"What do you mean?"

"How you went from being Alan Paxton to William Archer."

Will delayed his answer, taking a seat on the hard-backed chair at the desk.

"All right," he said, slowly, tentatively, "but just remember, you asked for it."

Besides, Will thought it might offer some release. He hadn't told anyone else, all these long months. Except for the ghost of a jazz musician, he had had no one else to tell.

***

Two officers were there to question him when he awoke in the hospital. They were sorry to report that the driver and passenger in the other vehicle weren't so lucky. It was a mother and daughter. The girl was only nine years old. They were on their way home from a gymnastics class the girl was taking.

His blood alcohol level was within the legal limit. He had only had two beers in the course of an hour—retirement party for a coworker. That he worked as an auto claims adjuster was an irony that would come to haunt him. The roads had been cleared of snow, and the temperature had been above freezing, so he couldn't blame the accident on a rogue patch of ice. His cell phone was found. He had been in the middle of a text to his wife—just to tell her he'd be home soon—the aborted message of which ended with "luv."

One or both of the vehicles had crossed the centerline. However, from their positioning after the crash, it was difficult to tell who had been at fault. There were no skid marks. It looked as if the vehicles, like charging rams, had simply locked horns, danced a brief waltz, then disengaged, ending up on opposite sides of the road. Now the officers wanted to hear his side of the story. There was no other side to be had.

He wished he had been the one who had died.

The only trouble was the two people who were glad he was

alive: Abbey and Joel. But he was no longer alive to them after the accident. Whenever he played with Joel, he could only think of the other man's daughter; whenever he made love to Abbey, he could only think of the other man's wife. For weeks, he moped. He couldn't concentrate. There was nothing wrong with the hardwiring of his brain. He had what a psychologist called "survivor's guilt."

Except for a lengthy letter affixed to the refrigerator with a magnet, he left without good-byes. In the middle of the night, like a thief in reverse: escaping a house rather than breaking into it. This was a week after he met with the widower, prompted by the man's insistent invitation, at a local restaurant.

Abbey had tried to talk Will out of meeting this man. No good could come out of this, she had told him. Will would only feel guiltier. Perritt would only feel more upset.

"You owe him no explanations," she had advised.

"I don't have any to offer," he had responded.

"He probably wants to settle the score."

"Or just talk things out. Find some closure."

In hindsight, he wished he had listened to her.

Don Perritt was in his late thirties, although with a balding pate, recessive chin, and thick round eyeglasses, he looked a decade older. If he didn't know he played for the symphony, Will would have guessed math professor or dentist. He had been married ten years he told him as he showed photos of his wife and daughter from his wallet.

Perritt's wife, he learned, had been on her cell phone with her husband, just as Will was texting his wife. The last thing Perritt heard from her was the exclamation: "Oh, shit!" And this was the aggravating part of it, that these should be his wife's parting words, engraved forever on his memory.

"Why?" was the question Perritt started with. "How?" was

the question he ended with. The "why" was for the gods or fate or chance, and of course no answer would be forthcoming. The "How?" was a question directed at Will. But all he could answer, truthfully, was what he had told the police: "I don't remember."

"You're lying," Perritt said accusingly. "You must remember something of how it happened. You are only saying you don't know so as to collect what's yours from the insurance."

Could he help it if Perritt didn't believe him?

"Why you?" he asked Will, taking a handkerchief from his pocket. "Why should you be the one to survive? Why should you get to enjoy your wife, your child, while I have nothing left, no one—"

He couldn't fault the man for being resentful, but he wasn't prepared for what Perritt said next.

"I wish it had been you, I wish you were the one who had died. I've often thought, if there is any justice in the world, if the gods care at all about mortal suffering—" He wiped his eyes with the hanky, although the sockets appeared to be dry. Will noticed how soft, how delicate his hands were. "I have thought so long about retribution."

Will knew he would have the same thoughts, the same feelings, had the situation been reversed. He wasn't sure, though, that he would have spoken them aloud. The effect was chilling.

"I can't," Perritt said, relenting, his shoulders sagging. Their meals had arrived, but they didn't touch them. Perritt studied his plate as though it held a hidden message. "I wouldn't. I am not that kind of person." He looked back up, hooking Will's attention with an ominous stare. "But I do know people who would."

"What do you mean?" Will asked, half rising. "Are you threatening me? My family? Because if you are—"

Would such a genteel, respectable, mannerly man know anything of an underworld of hired assassins?

"I am talking about balance, symmetry, harmony," Perritt said, looking at Will directly, his thoughts gathering momentum. "If you were an honorable man, you would do the right thing."

"Which is?"

Was he advocating suicide?

Perritt leaned forward, interlacing his fingers on the table.

"You should not be entitled to your wife and child. You should be dead to them. They should be dead to you."

It was a seed, a small kernel, but it had been planted, and over the course of a week, it grew. He waited for the settlement check to be deposited before making his departure.

And then, for all intents and purposes, he died.

***

"Here, you really do need this more than I do."

Mandy handed him her bottle, but Will shook his head.

"So what do you think?" he asked, refilling his goblet with the nonalcoholic variety.

"I think for a quiet kind of guy, you have a lot to say."

Will set the bottle aside.

"For a talky kind of girl, you do a good job listening."

"Very funny," she sounded a note of mock indignation.

Will took a sip of his drink.

"But what do you really think?"

"I think you have a very strong sense of conscience." She leaned over and kissed him lightly on the cheek. "However, I am wondering a couple of things."

"Such as?"

"You just up and left?" Her brow narrowed in concentration. "Your wife? Your child? It just seems so ... cold."

Will didn't have an answer for this. From her perspective—hell, from any perspective—he knew it must seem a cold-blooded act of desertion.

"Haven't you ever been tempted to go back?"

This time, he did have an answer.

"All the time."

"Why don't you?" Mandy asked, reaching for her bottle. "Is it because you're afraid of this Perritt character and what he might do?"

"No, it's not that."

"He sounds pretty unstable. You could always get a restraining order."

"It's just that, it's been so long. I've thought about it. The very first night I was away—my wife and I hadn't been apart for even a night since we were married—it was difficult, but one night became two and then three, and now … I don't see how I can. Besides, she's probably moved on by now."

"But you haven't," she noted. "Well, you know what they say? Time heals all wounds."

"If it doesn't kill you first."

Will stood up. He went through the door into the Hex Room. The rain had stopped, and he wondered if Essence might be hanging out at the park, waiting for him.

"It's a Saturday night," he said, turning about to find Mandy had followed him into the room. "You should be out and about. Meeting up. Hooking up. Don't you have any friends?"

"No, not really. I tend to study a lot."

"What is it you're studying?"

"Psychology."

That seemed to make sense.

"And what about you?" Mandy asked point blank. "What were you in your former life?"

"Insurance," he answered simply, not wanting to be reminded of his previous line of work. The only upside had been being spared processing his own claim, as well as that of the other vehicle. He started back toward the living room but paused. "There's something else that makes it hard to go back."

"Oh?"

"There's a woman."

"Essence Warner?"

"Have you ever met her?" Will asked, turning around.

"Not officially. She stops by the museum Sunday mornings. That's their time to spend the day together, she and her grandmother."

"Which grandmother?"

"Mrs. Waxman, of course."

Will brightened with a brainstorm.

"Maybe you could help me."

"I thought that's what I'm doing now."

"Tomorrow. Come with me to the museum. Help me talk with Essence. Talk her out of—"

"Out of …?"

"She has this crazy plan to kill herself. On the anniversary of her mother's death."

"And you know this how?"

"She told me."

"That's what I was afraid of."

"How so?"

"She has a reputation for exaggeration."

"Really?"

"You can't believe everything she tells you." Mandy downed the dregs of her wine. "Are you sure you're not using her?"

"Using her how?"

"As an excuse, a way of sabotaging your marriage, so you can't ever go back, even if you wanted to?"

"Psychology, huh?" Will tried to evade the accusation. Or was it more of a diagnosis? "You're pretty good at it."

Chapter 21

That evening, across town in a modest house of her own, Sybil Waxman crouched over her laptop perched—where else?—on her lap as she reclined in bed, propped by several pillows. She had been checking the museum website, posting an item in its newsfeed to the effect that she was very grateful for the return of her son's saxophone.

Not for the first time, she focused on the impromptu photo Mandy had taken and posted of her new curator, having in mind to replace it with a more polished portrait, if she could get William to pose. Or should she start thinking of him as Alan?

Two curators in two years. And was it because she had hinted to each that her son had been murdered? Had they seen something, caught onto something, sinister? Their deaths had been far from natural. Unreasonably she felt responsible somehow—but nowhere near the degree she felt she had let down Jamaal. She had been so very close, yet so goddamned out of reach when he died, in a boarding house just a hop-skip across the river.

She had never been a big fan of his moving into his own apartment in the first place, and for this, she blamed herself: that she hadn't put up a convincing enough argument for her son to stay put at home. Once he had moved in and settled down? Then her tune changed. She became an advocate of it as a permanent residence, not as a base for gigs played out of town. She'd rather he played closer to home.

Her biggest concern was what he would find to eat, but his landlady obviated this worry. Phyllis Gossett had followed up the two curators' deaths with home-cooked meals, real down South cooking, delivered to her doorstep. She had done the same following Jamaal's demise. Apparently, she had felt guilty, too. Maybe too guilty? The stereotypical cuisine had been almost insulting, but the food was delicious and, oh, the desserts! If Jamaal had been shacking up with his landlady on the side—a suspicion she entertained from time to time—it was easy to understand how he would have been lured by his palate alone. But that would have been all pre-Fortune, of course.

Now she was working on her third curator, a most interesting specimen. Not the William Archer she thought she had hired. Before handing back his wallet, she had photocopied his driver's license, the one that said he was Alan Paxton. The license was three years old, and he looked much brighter, less ghostly, in this photo—much more alive. A head full of brown hair that hedged his ears in a neat trim. Eyes squinting at the camera. An expression that seemed caught in the middle of some private joke.

But what was that joke? What was the truth? Should she violate his sense of privacy by digging into the Internet for it?

Hah! What a question! Of course she would …

It didn't take long to find what she was looking for: a social media account for an Alan Paxton out of Utica, NY. Deactivated, but there was another link to one that was live. Such an odd page. As with the driver's license, the profile photo showed a face that was smiling, friendly, a tad camera shy, the smile crooked, the head cocked, chin trying to flee into the open collar of a lemon polo shirt. And a single posting in all caps:

HAVE YOU SEEN ME? I AM LOST AND ALONE. I MAY BE GOING BY A DIFFERENT IDENTITY. I HAVE LEFT MY WIFE AND SON AND AM WANDERING THE PLANET, PERHAPS WITH AMNESIA. IF YOU SEE ME, PLEASE RESPOND TO THIS POSTING. THANK YOU.

Whoever this "you" was, she didn't believe it could be her curator, but she decided to play along with the imposter's ruse. As a typist, she was slow, methodical, having never graduated beyond a hunt-and-peck method.

I have found you. You are alive and well. You can find me through my employer, Sybil Waxman, at …

She decided against revealing her identity, always a risky venture on the Web. She backspaced through her name and changed "employer" to "place of employment."

… at the Jamaal Waxman Memorial Museum in West Bloomfield, OH. Web site at: www—

She typed out the URL in full.

But you are staying at the Victorian Arms apartments across the river in East Orange, WV.

She decided to add a footnote:

You are going by the name of William Archer.

***

In a motel room outside Pittsburgh, Daryl's phone buzzed, waking him out of a light sleep, even though he had put a pillow over his head to drown out the sounds of a lovemaking session through the thin wall of the adjoining room. It was so seldom he ever got a message.

His own lovemaking session with Asuka had ended an hour ago, after which she had promptly fallen asleep. Somehow, she was immune to the thumps and bumps, the moans and groans, coming through the wall.

Asuka had become his steady partner in the repo trade—*partner*, he wished to emphasize, not girlfriend. Their relationship—strike that, *partnership*—hadn't progressed to that level. This was their third assignment since the fiasco with the wrong Porsche, the repossession of a late-model, fully equipped, state-of-the-art Jaguar, which like the Porsche had required a late-night rendezvous with the owner's residence.

The Jag had been protectively tucked in a garage for the night, but earlier in the day, Daryl had recorded the numbers the owner had punched into the access panel through his telephoto lens. Technically, with the code in hand, absconding—his favorite word—with the Jag hadn't been the result of breaking and entering, which would have constituted a breach of the peace. Using a copy of the key fob from the dealer, he had simply started the car and backed out.

But it had been another long day. Asuka was the one who suggested a motel, where they had pulled both vehicles, the repossessed Jag and the getaway car, Daryl's faithful, old-model Chrysler, into an out-of-the-way parking lot illuminated by a temperamental neon vacancy sign.

Rising in bed, he saw that a social media message had come up for him—or rather for Alan Paxton. *The Pax-Man. Six-Pax. Pax!*

He was at a juncture. His plan had been to take the Jaguar—which he had retrieved without gunfire this time—back to the dealer in Utica.

But like a newly hatched fortune cookie, this message changed everything, including his route. He clicked on the link to the Waxman Museum, anticipating a house of wax, a la Madame Tussaud's, a mausoleum of mannequins in various poses.

Instead, he came across the waxen image of the new curator, frozen in shock, as though he had been surprised by the camera flash. His hair was longer—much longer. He had always been so preppie, so clean-cut, like a Ken doll, just one more reason to dislike him. Now he seemed a regular rock-and-roller. No facial hair. No tattoos. No piercings. Just the long hair and a much, much thinner face with more jagged lines. The term "haggard" came to mind.

There was an email link and he typed in a "Hello, my name is …" before deleting the message. What if Alan—or should he think of him as Will?—was in charge of answering the museum's online correspondence? Daryl didn't want to tip his hand and alarm him, spurring him into flight mode with another change of identity, as he had apparently done back in Erie.

Sure, he could leave right away, but he was in no hurry. He had the rest of the night to decide what to do. Tell Abbey? Or wait? His instincts told him to wait.

"What is it?" Asuka asked, lifting herself onto an elbow, turning toward him.

"Nothing, change of plan."

"Oh?"

"I'll need you to drive the Chrysler back to Utica."

"The Chrysler!" Asuka sat up straighter, covers falling around her waist, exposing her naked torso. Like Daryl, she preferred sleeping in the raw. "That old smelly thing. You promised me I could drive the Jag."

"Well, you know what they say about promises." Daryl flashed her one of his trademark smiles, as though applying a salve to her grievance.

"Is it that Paxton guy?"

"What do you have? Sixth sense?"

"You've only been adding to his fake Facebook page every chance you get."

This was true. Any time they had a layover in a bar or restaurant or Internet café, every time they had a long stretch staking out a residence, he had played with being Alan. It had become a hobby of his: sharing photos, posting updates, enhancing his profile.

"I need to take a little detour with the Jag."

"Why can't *you* take the Chrysler and *I* take the Jag?

What Daryl didn't divulge was that he didn't fully trust his partner to drive the repossessed car back to Utica and turn it over to the dealer—at least not right away. In fact, he couldn't be positive she wouldn't outright steal it or even sell it before he could return home.

It took her a while to overcome her disappointment. She sat there with her chin resting on her upraised knees, sulking.

Another bout of lovemaking flared up on the other side of the wall, and Asuka raised her pretty head, her long, black hair falling around her shoulder.

"What do you say we give them some competition?"

Daryl knew exactly what and whom she meant. He reached over and stroked her cheek, but she didn't return his gentleness. Instead, she grabbed his wrist, twisting it painfully, flung him onto his back and, straddling him, placed her forearm across his neck, forcing his head into the pillow.

It was all Daryl could do to breathe. His breath came through his clenched teeth as a thin, shrill whistle.

"You know I could kill you right now if I wanted," Asuka informed him, her voice calm, cold, without rancor or bitterness. Just a statement of fact, which he believed at face value. She lowered her head, whispering fiercely into his ear. "I need you to promise that next time, I'm in charge."

Daryl would have nodded his head or uttered more than a grunt if he could. Instead, he blinked twice, hoping that conveyed a positive response. Asuka appeared to understand.

"Good," she said, lifting her arm and rolling off of him. She lay on her back, knees raised, preparing to receive him. "Make it loud," she instructed.

And Daryl did as he was told.

Chapter 22

By the time Will awoke, it was going on eleven. Mandy was already gone, so he hoofed it alone, arriving at the museum just in time to see Sybil Waxman and Essence leaving together. In fact, his employer was just locking up.

"Mrs. Waxman!" he called out, running up to her out of breath, startling her so badly she dropped her ring of keys.

"William! For heaven's sake! You just about gave me a heart attack. What are you doing here? I believe I made it clear there's no overtime connected with this job. As for the days you missed, we'll just consider them sick days, since that's what they were."

He stooped to retrieve her keys to save her the trouble. As he did so, he tried catching Essence's eye, but she was evasive, keeping her head turned away, down the street, where daylight was breaking like an egg across the sidewalk.

"Nevertheless," she continued, sorting through her keys, "it's good to see you up and about." She gave him an odd sort of look, odder than usual, as though estimating how far his eyes were set apart. Lips half open, she seemed about to add something more, something revelatory, but a glance at her granddaughter appeared to change her mind. "Essence, I believe you've had the pleasure of meeting my new curator?" Will detected a smirking sense of insinuation in her delivery of the line.

"Yes, I've had that *pleasure*," Essence emphasized with a subtle smile of her own.

"I do hope to see you at work tomorrow," she said. "Now if you'll excuse us. Brunch awaits."

Essence caught Will's attention with a wink and a nod of her head toward the museum.

"Actually," Will said, taking the hint, "is it okay if I stay here for an hour or two? I'd like to catch up with my work."

His employer cast him a doubtful look. She turned her head back and forth between Will and Essence, but Essence maintained a picture-perfect straight face.

"What possible work would you have to accomplish on a Sunday?"

"You know," he fumbled, "checking emails, dusting, resetting the VHS. That sort of thing."

Mrs. Waxman gave him one last, scrutinizing look that penetrated his eye sockets. It seemed she was turning over something in her mind.

"Now that I think about it, there is some correspondence you could help out with by email." She leaned in closer and lowered her voice. "Don't be surprised if you come across a special message or two coming your way."

"My way?" Will asked.

She gave him a knowing wink in response.

"I'll trust you to lock up then," she said, then turning toward Essence, "Coming?"

Essence followed along in her grandmother's footsteps, and Will watched them recede as they treaded upon slabs of sunlight, their shadows puddled around their ankles like hoop skirts. He was perplexed by his employer's mannerisms, she seemed so full of hints and whispers.

Upon entering the museum, Will noted that the sax had been returned to its case, although the glass cover hadn't yet been replaced. Taking a seat in the back, Will checked through an assortment of emails. No death threats today. Otherwise, he didn't see anything out of the ordinary as his employer had implied he might find. He switched off the computer.

Watching it wind down, he was just about to give up on Essence reappearing, when the bell dinged, and Will turned to see her rushing through the museum. She fell into his arms as he stood, almost knocking him backward, coiling him in a hug, which warmed him to his bones.

"I circled back around as fast as I could," she said, releasing him. She was as out of breath as he had been. "It's so hard giving Nana Other the slip, I had to fake feeling sick to get out of our lunch date. Speaking of sick, I'm so glad you're better. I hope you're not mad I didn't come visit you at the hospital."

"Yeah, well, no. I was unconscious most of the time, so no hard feelings."

"I'm glad," she said, placing her hand on his arm. The hand traveled up to his neck and curved around his head, bringing his face close to hers. They maintained a long, luxurious kiss while shedding each other's clothes.

"Here?" Will asked as Essence pulled him down to the floor.

"Where else?" Essene responded, pushing him onto his back and straddling his midsection.

"It's just—"

But Essence leaned over him, soft breasts grazing his chest. She lay a finger against his lips as she reached back and around with her other hand, fitting him inside her.

"Shh," she whispered, moving her hips in rhythm with the beat of the bass underlying the music filtering through the museum's sound system.

Her father's music, Will reflected. But he let the thought dissolve along with the refrain of Jamaal Waxman's sax.

***

"This theory of yours that my mother was murdered," Essence brought up the subject while dressing. Not exactly a romantic turn of conversation, Will thought. "I was looking at the photos of her. Wait just a sec." Buttoning her blouse, she went into the archive room and brought out a sheaf of photographs, which she spread in her hand like peacock feathers. They were pictures that included her mother, ones that Mandy hadn't got to with her X-Acto knife. Did Essence know the extent to which her grandmother was literally cutting Fortune out of the picture?

"As you can see," she emphasized, pointing, "in the later ones, she always wore a locket. And my grandmother tells me— my Grandmother Warner—that all of my mother's personal effects were collected together in a Manila envelope that I have in my possession. But no locket." Her face made a serious frown. "Strange, isn't it?"

"Yeah, I guess." Will was wondering where she was going with this line of reasoning, as he resumed putting himself back together, one piece of clothing at a time.

"I'll bet you anything Jenkins has it."

"The locket? Why would he have it?"

"He was the one who found me, supposedly. On the bridge. How do I know he wasn't the one to push my mother off of it?"

Will smiled at her logic.

"And he asked for her locket first?"

"What if he did?" Essence jutted her chin defensively.

"It's just you're saying the butler did it. It's funny, that's all. Any crime novel you read—it's almost never the butler."

He was aware of making this same observation before, to her grandmother, Sybil Waxman.

"But what if it's true in this case. Besides, Jenkins isn't really a butler. He's more of a general caretaker and handyman. He does everything from fixing dripping faucets to chauffeuring my grandmother around town."

"Like Driving Miss Daisy?"

Essence laughed. "When she's out doing her charity missions."

"Doesn't sound like much of a murderer. What motive would he have?"

"Who knows?" Essence shrugged. "Jealousy? Anyway, the locket. I want to be wearing it when I—"

The way they were talking, so casually, it was hard to take seriously the idea that she would be jumping off a bridge in another a week or so.

"Why don't you just ask him for it?"

"He wouldn't give it to me if he had it, and he would never admit having it if he did."

"So?" Will felt there was something being left unsaid.

"Tonight, I'll create a diversion."

"What kind of diversion?"

"To give you enough time when you come by the house."

"The 'house'!" Will responded, both alarmed and amused. It was ten times the size of any house he'd ever encountered.

"While I'm keeping him busy, you can explore his rooms."

"Rooms?" How many does one person need? he wondered.

"There are only two of them."

"Only?"

"Except for the en suite," she added.

"Why can't *I* create the diversion and *you* explore his rooms?"

Essence came up to him and placed her hands lightly on his shoulders.

"Trust me. It's better my way. He would suspect something's up if it's you."

"Can't you just explore his rooms when he's not around?"

"He keeps his quarters locked up tight when he's away from the house or not in the monitor room down the hall."

He didn't quite believe she had never had a single opportunity over the years to infiltrate Jenkins's locked quarters but didn't call her out on the lie.

Essence squeezed his shoulders firmly and gave him an equally firm look in his eyes. "You can do this," she assured him.

"How would I get inside?"

She dropped her hands to her side.

"I'll give you the code."

"To the back gate?" Will hoped.

"No, the front. You'll need to arrive at precisely 9 p.m. It's important. That'll give you maybe fifteen minutes, tops. I can't promise I can hold his attention any longer than that."

"But Crimson and Clover?" Will shuddered.

"They know you now. Just take along their favorite treat: a ribeye steak apiece."

"Not popcorn?" The museum kept a heady supply of it for visitors, young and old. So much cheaper than a pair of steaks.

"Don't be silly," she chided, giving him a playful push. "I'll leave my balcony door ajar for you. Jenkins's quarters are just down the hall, second door on the right."

Will felt out of his depth, as though he were treading water on dry land. He looked into Essence's eyes. They seemed so intense, glistening.

"So you want me to break into your house," he sought confirmation, taking a step back. He wanted to make sure this wasn't all some sort of joke.

"You won't be breaking in. You'll have free access."

"And I'm supposed to search his rooms for this locket? It sounds like a terrible plan."

Essence gave his shoulder a friendly shove.

"Come on, Will. It'll be fun."

"Fun?"

"Where's your sense of adventure?"

"Is this some kind of test? To prove my love for you?"

"You said 'love,'" she observed, smiling up at him and

fluttering her eyelashes. "Does this mean you love me?"

Love? He had to wonder. *Was* he in love with this young, impetuous woman? Fond of her, yes. Worried about her, true. But love? He had to remind himself he was still in love with his wife. Wasn't he?

"Okay," he said, breaking down his resistance from within, one link at a time, as he played out the scenario in his mind. "I'll do it on one condition. If I do retrieve this locket of your mother's, you'll give up this idea of drowning yourself."

This induced a long pause in the conversation.

"I promise that I will consider it," she agreed, finally.

"Just consider it? That's all?"

She came up to him, wrapping her arms around his waist.

"You'll just have to trust me," she breathed into his ear. "Do you trust me?"

Before he could answer, she undid his belt and slid it out of its loops with a sharp, snapping sound, like that of a whip.

"Here," she said, handing it to him. "It works both ways."

Where was this coming from? Is this what she meant by trust?

She held out her arms, wrists together. Her eyes closed; her lips parted. Her breathing was deep and regular, her breasts, contoured by the thin fabric of her half-buttoned blouse, rising and falling. Will hadn't much experience with this type of thing, and he felt nervous. Aside from Abbey, he hadn't much experience at all.

"Too tight?" he asked.

"No," she breathed in a sultry whisper, leaning back and away, as he lowered her to the floor. "Tighter."

Chapter 23

After work, Will prepared himself as though to plunge into the future as a dead man. He bought a set of clothes—all black. Black turtleneck, black pants, black socks, pair of black gloves, and even a black ski mask that he found at a Salvation Army store.

He stopped by a butcher's and ordered two thick, juicy, red ribeye steaks all wrapped up, separately, in wax paper and tied with a string.

That evening, he treated himself to a last meal—which he hoped it wouldn't turn out to be—with his landlady. Strangely, she seemed preoccupied, not much given to conversation.

"Is something wrong?" he prompted.

"No, no, just wondering where I'll put the new boarder."

"Boarder?"

"There's a room below yours that's empty, but I'd hate to put someone in who makes too much noise. You know how some of these single male tenants can be."

Will took a stab of his broiled shrimp, deveined, just the right touch of garlic in butter, all leveraged on a pile of wide noodles.

"He's not here yet?"

"He'll be arriving tomorrow."

"By bus?" Will asked, forgetting there were other ways to reach East Orange.

"By car. From Pittsburgh. Walter and I passed through it on our honeymoon. After that, Walter claimed he wouldn't give you a plugged nickel for visiting a big city ever again."

After dinner, to pass the time, Will joined Mrs. Gossett on

the porch for a cigarette. He really needed to cut back on his smoking.

"I suppose Miss Anders will be coming to see you again?" she asked.

"Mandy? No. Not tonight. I have plans tonight."

"Oh?"

He felt the urge to tell, to reveal. And so he did, detailing the plan of attack, as he conceived it, just in case something went wrong and he needed someone to bail him out. Mrs. Gossett listened while smoking intently, focused on the glowing tip of her cigarette.

"That certainly is audacious. Do promise me you'll be extra careful? I would hate to lose another tenant before his lease is through."

Joking?

"And now, if you'll excuse me, my dear, I have some correspondence to catch up on."

***

As usual for this time of evening, Jenkins sat in the video monitoring room, his feet propped on a table, his chair tilted back, hands clasped behind his head, as he reviewed the several black-and-white monitors.

This was the part of the job he enjoyed most. It offered luxury to daydream, to chew over past experiences, mull old regrets, plot a different future. It was his main worry that he would end up a permanent manservant for life—but only the life of his employer, after which he hoped to receive a healthy percentage of her estate as an inheritance, part of which he knew she kept in a white vinyl satchel in cold, hard cash.

She couldn't last that much longer, could she? And then his ambition was to return home, back to the land of Oz, a rich man, so unlike the foolish young scamp who had come to America hoping to make a go as a professional boxer.

One last review of the monitors. All quiet on the Western front … It had just turned nine o'clock. The old bat would be inside her bedroom listening to her favorite British television show, her eyes locked on the screen as though she could see it.

He began flicking off the monitors one by one: front gate, statuary, tiger cage, balconies, pool …

Ah!

There was Essence, climbing the ladder to the diving board, thankfully in bathers this time, although her stringy two-piece required little imagination to fill in the gaps, which Jenkins was loth to do. As usual, he worked to suppress such intrusive feelings. Nevertheless, he compared her favorably with her mother. She had a similar shape: high waist, long legs, firm shoulders. Her mother had been a redhead with ivory skin, whereas Essence was a brown goddess with dark auburn curls.

He watched her dive with an appreciative eye, assigning her Olympic-size numbers in his head, as she progressed from simple to complex with each launch from the board: from Crouching Tiger, jackknife, and Nestea plunge for fun to backflip, cartwheel, and even a double somersault.

He was proud of her dexterity, almost as a father would be of a daughter's. He had taught her to swim, had been the one to coax her onto the high dive, helping her overcome her anxiety with heights by dangling her from the board and lowering her into the water to show her how little she had to fear. He had never quite taken his place as a father figure, however. Such paternal feelings were quenched by her mere existence, always reminding him of her mother, whom he had doubly lost: first to a jazz player, then to the river. Not to mention the guilt he harbored at not being able to prevent her death-drop from the bridge.

Not for the first time, he felt he had failed Fortune's daughter in trying to achieve a balance between permissiveness, on the one hand, by granting her the freedom her mother never enjoyed, and protectiveness on the other, by keeping her locked up from time to time per her grandmother's wishes. Then again, it's not like he had been the one to raise her. That's what nannies and tutors had been for.

It was refreshing, though, watching her do something wholesome, healthy. Better than what was on the telly. Maybe tonight would be a good time to fire up the barbie, put on some prawns. Try to smooth over their recent misunderstanding. It would be nice having a drama-free evening for once.

Balanced facing backward on the edge of the board, Essence stared steadily at the poolside surveillance camera, as though to make sure he was watching.

I am, love. I am.

Three bounces sprang her high off the board. He watched her perform a complicated dive, a triple freeform spin off a gainer like a bird in flight, but she must have tensed up, twisting and contorting, then splatting face down where she floated for a count of ten, twenty, thirty … Instead of recovering and stroking toward the side of the pool, she started sinking into its blue depths lit from below with wavering palm fronds of light.

No, no, no! This wasn't right. This couldn't be. He sped down the back stairs, charged through the patio doors, and plunged headfirst into the water fully clothed.

***

At precisely 9 p.m., by his watch, Will pulled his ski mask over his face. Feeling so much like a burglar, he left the park and crossed the street to the front gate of the Warner estate, as planned. What he hadn't planned for was the popcorn-crunching kid. Dusk had settled, turning the boy into a silhouette.

"Hello, Lance," Will said, cordially. "Don't worry, it's just me."

"Why the disguise?" the boy asked. "It's not Halloween."

He was afraid to lift up his ski mask to reveal his features to the security camera trained on the entrance. Already the mask was giving him an itch. Add to that the warmth and humidity of a summer evening, and his discomfort was doubled.

"Have you seen them tonight?" he asked, choosing to bypass the boy's interrogation. He was hoping against hope the kid would say some form of no, nugatory, not a sign of the marauding tigers, but Lance politely informed him of the opposite.

"Yeah, they're in there all right."

"You still think they like popcorn?"

"Think it? I know it! They come right up and eat out of my hand, don't you know?"

Will took a step toward the gate to type in the code on the keypad, and there they pranced, bleeding into visibility out of twilight, black and white stripes providing a perfect camouflage as they approached in crisscrossing paths. He hadn't expected to see them so soon and wasn't prepared for what to do when he opened the gate. How was he to keep them inside? He would hate to spring them loose on an unsuspecting public through fault of his own.

"Don't worry," Lance said confidently, "I'll distract them."

He ran along the fence shouting, "Here tigers, here girls!"

Responding to the boy's calls, or else catching a whiff of buttered popcorn, the tigers hurried along after him, seamlessly, their stripes alternating with the vertical iron bars as they moved, animating the fence, making it seem the bars were in motion.

Once inside, Will crossed the lawn cautiously, moving from statue to statue, behind each of which he took momentary cover, peeking around or above, before goosestepping on to the next.

Halfway across the wide lawn, no tigers in sight, he decided to set aside the two hunks of meat wrapped in wax paper. He placed them in two of the open palms of an eight-armed deity—his offering to the gods for a propitious outcome.

Vaulting a low hedge, he made it around the right side of the mansion, where he found the drain spout Essence had mentioned. Without ado, he shimmied up to her balcony, as though reliving his worst nightmares of seventh grade gym class when he failed rope climbing.

He loitered longer than he should in Essence's room, drawing in the smell of perfume and flowers. The room was all powder and fluff, with the aura of a harem or opium den, cushions scattered around the floor, pell-mell, no apparent order prevailing. All were garish colors—neon pink, lemon yellow, incandescent orange. Lamps were lit in tiffany shades.

But no sign of Essence.

Enough lingering.

He opened the door and trod lightly down the carpeted hall afraid of making the slightest sound. He counted the doors. Easy enough: one, two. Freeing himself from a moment's paralysis, he opened the door to Jenkins's room before fright could make him change his mind.

The room he entered was spare in its furnishings. Forget feng shui. There was virtually nothing to arrange: just a settee and reclining chair that, oddly, was set to recline, illuminated by a floor lamp. A couple of magazines on a coffee table: gentlemen's mags, to put it politely. On the wall hung a pair of golden gloves. Another wall held a poster: *Surf Australia!*

The farther room was the bedroom, beyond which was a balcony. It was dark, but enough light was streaming through the French doors from floodlights outside that he could make his way around without bumping into anything. As with the sitting room, there was almost nothing to bump into: a twin bed, a nightstand. Above the bed was a portrait: a miniature of the one over the mantel downstairs. In the half-light, Fortune's features seemed ghostly, yet he could trace the petite nose, the long throat, the pile of red hair in a hive on her head. The picture was crooked, and when he went to straighten it, it fell off the wall, revealing a small inset safe.

The safe was locked, as was a nightstand drawer. He hadn't any expertise at cracking combination locks, but he was so through with locked drawers. He yanked hard, and the frontispiece of the drawer ripped loose of its nails with a loud screech. Inside, he found a thin sheaf of letters in plain envelopes—not the scent-laced ones of Fortune's. The return addresses on these were hotels up and down the southeastern United States—and all were addressed to Fortune. There was nothing else in the drawer. Unless there was something hidden under the floorboards—a human heart, he had little doubt—he considered his investigation of the premises complete, except for the absence of a locket.

Will stuffed the letters into his waistband and hurried out of the bedroom. Backtracking across the living area toward the door to the hall, he thought himself safe, except for the muzzle of a handgun.

***

"Hello, Mr. Archer," the matriarch of the house said calmly from the comfort of her wheelchair, blocking his path. "I've been expecting you."

How? Will wondered. *Who?* There was only one person he had divulged his plan to.

Mrs. Warner held the gun as levelly as she maintained her voice, so Will had no doubt she knew how to use it. There was no getting around her except by leaping or climbing, as her wheelchair was planted on the threshold, filling the doorway. Without her sunglasses, her eyes exhibited a whitish gloss like poached eggs.

"Mrs. Warner, please," he said as calmly as he could make his voice sound. "I can explain."

"Save your explanations for Jenkins. It's his quarters you have violated, after all."

Violated, he thought. What an odd choice of word.

Before he could conjure a response, she pressed a button on an armrest.

"Jenkins," she said loudly, "if you would be so kind as to come up to the second story, there's a ... situation that needs your attention."

Jenkins's reply followed a burst of static.

"Sorry, Mum. There's a bit of a situation down here at the pool."

What Will had had interpreted as static became a series of spluttering coughs and hacks.

A situation?

"As your employer, Jenkins, I must insist. It's urgent."

A long pause. Will knew Jenkins's balcony overlooked the pool, and he listened attentively for telltale sounds coming through the French doors.

"Jenkins?"

No response. Whatever was occurring poolside sounded serious. Serious enough for Will to investigate. He took a soft, padded step backward.

"Hold still," Mrs. Warner commanded. "Not another step."

Maybe she really did possess super hearing. She waved her gun around, freezing him in place. Who knew where a stray shot would end up?

Jenkins's voice broke through the intercom.

"Be right there, Mum."

"You have no right to hold me here," Will protested, testing his captor's resolve.

"I think I have every right," she responded, aiming the gun at Will's midriff. "In fact, I believe I'm within my legal rights to shoot you on sight. So to speak," she added, as though catching the misnomer.

"There are people—"

"You'll have to speak louder," she said, wheeling forward, gun still in place.

"There are people who know I'm here."

"People? What people?"

"Mrs. Gossett," Will said, "for one."

"That nosy old biddy?" she said, smiling widely with her thin lips drawing the skin tautly over her cheekbones.

"And me."

Will was surprised to hear Essence's voice and even more surprised to see her draped over Jenkins's shoulder like the carcass of a deer, except this carcass was animated and wriggling.

"You can set me down now," she said. "Thanks again for rescuing me, but I already told you I'm fine."

Jenkins did as instructed, setting her upright on the carpet. Both were wet and dripping.

"What have we here?" Jenkins asked. He reached over and pulled off Will's face mask. "Archer?" He didn't seem overly astonished. In fact, he cast an accusing look at Essence, as though to say, "I might have known."

"Hello," Will said, meekly.

"I found this gentleman snooping," Mrs. Warner explained. "Jenkins, you may wish to make a survey of your premises to make sure nothing is missing."

"I think you can safely set aside the gun, Mum," Jenkins said, carefully wheeling her backward to get past her into his quarters. "The situation, as you called it, seems well under control."

"Did you find it?" Essence mouthed.

Will shook his head and watched her hopeful expression melt into a frown.

"Now, we can make this very easy and have this business concluded before my normal bedtime in … Jenkins, what time is it?"

"Nine twenty-three, Mum," Jenkins called through the door.

"… in precisely thirty-seven minutes. All you have to do is explain to us in as few words as possible what you are doing on my premises."

"I can answer that," Essence piped up. "Will is here as my guest."

"Guest?" Mrs. Warner asked, her gun lowered safely onto her lap.

"Yes, guest. He was here at my invitation. To go swimming."

"In a ski mask?" Jenkins put in, returning to the hallway, eyebrows arching with menace or amusement.

"Can I help it he didn't want to be recognized on the way over? Now, Grandmother, this charade of yours must stop. You've got to stop intimidating every person I bring to the house."

Every, Will thought glumly. More evidence he wasn't the first.

"Ah, Mr. Archer," Essence's grandmother said with a sigh. "I appreciate your need for secrecy. You may not believe it, but I used to be young once myself—and in love."

There it was again, that notion of love.

"Grandmother, please," Essence said. "This isn't the time."

Closing her eyes, Mrs. Warner waxed sentimental in a warbly voice. "In love with the wrong sort of person, however. Or let's say someone of whom my own parents didn't approve. A person they thought was far, too far, beneath my station in life."

"And how did that work out?" Will asked, curious, in spite of the circumstances.

He watched her open her eyes, fixing him with a steady gaze, belying the fact she couldn't see.

"It didn't. I was carted off to a boarding school. When I came back home for summer recess, my beloved had moved on with someone new. Which is why, Mr. Archer, it is best to nip these mismatched romances in the bud. And so Jenkins, if you'll be so good as to escort our guest from the premises?"

"Never mind, Jenkins, I'll do it," Essence said, wrapping her arm around Will's.

"But your grandmother's orders, Missy," Jenkins pointed out, taking hold of Will's other arm, firmly around his bicep. Now Will knew what it must feel like to be a wishbone.

"Jenkins, I already said—"

"I'm only thinking of your health, Missy. The night air. You'll catch your death, dressed as you are. You've already had one close call."

"Jenkins is absolutely right, my dear. Please let him perform his duty."

Essence let go of Will reluctantly, her fingers slipping from his arm, as Jenkins pulled him loose.

"And Mr. Archer," the Grandmother called after him, as Jenkins manhandled him down the hallway, a hand clutching his elbow in a vise. "I hope you'll harbor no hard feelings?"

Will decided the best course of action was just to keep walking without comment. Besides, what was there really to say? *"Thank you for your hospitality"*?

He was marched down a narrow staircase, from which they burst upon the foyer through a side door. Will was ushered onto the front portico, from which he stared at the lawn full of statues.

"Thank you, Jenkins," Will said, shaking himself loose, "you can go now."

Jenkins apparently didn't appreciate the humor.

"Normally, I'm opposed to violence," he said, advancing as Will backstepped. "But in your case, I'm willing to make an exception."

Without further warning, he landed a blow to Will's stomach that bent him in two. The pain was as real as a burst appendix. Will understood this was a warm-up exercise, as Jenkins raised his fists for another round.

"On your feet, Archer."

Will chose to stay where he was. When it came to fight or flight, he was grateful his amygdala consistently chose flight. He scooted backward on the cement walkway, as Jenkins advanced, relaxing his pugilistic stance and extending a hand, palm up. Will didn't mistake the gesture for a helpful tug to his feet.

"The letters," Jenkins demanded, hovering over him.

"Letters? What letters?"

"Quit with the games. You know which letters."

"All right, all right."

Will held his hands out defensively as he scrambled to his feet, then backpedaled across the lawn managing to keep just out of range of the man's jabs.

Faced with a standoff, Jenkins brought his fingers to his lip and emitted a high whistle. Within seconds, the tigers came bounding to his side, where he reached down and petted each behind the ears.

"I believe you're acquainted with Crimson and Clover," Jenkins said with a smile that promised an adventurous sendoff. "I'll let them finish escorting you to the gate, unless …"

"The letters," Will finished for him.

"Why, it's like you've read my mind, mate."

"You mean these, I suppose."

Will reached around and removed the letters from the waist-band of his sweatpants. His hands were still gloved.

"The very ones," Jenkins said.

"You kept them from her, didn't you?" he asked, backing away.

"From whom, may I ask. Essence?"

"No, Fortune. You wanted to keep Jamaal from her. Why?"

"There's no need to get all inquisitive now, is there?"

"Was it at the orders of Mrs. Warner? She wanted you to dispose of them. But you didn't. Why not?"

"Why, why, why … So many questions at once."

"It's why you couldn't ask for them in front of her, either of them. They don't know you have them. And they'd be angry if they found out."

To this, Jenkins had no answer, as Will kept retreating, glanc-ing left and right at the statuary. There, to his right, was the large-breasted goddess in whose cold embrace he had spent a long, frigid night. But it wasn't the statue he was looking for.

"You read them at night, don't you? You read them before you go to sleep. But you can't sleep, can you? You stay awake, thinking of her."

It was a long shot, but it seemed to hit the mark. Will deftly tucked the letters back into his waistband to hold them in place. It was a signal of defiance that Jenkins didn't so much misinter-pret as misunderstand. Will simply wanted his hands free.

"Enough of this idle chit-chat, Archer. I'll gladly collect the letters when my two beauties are through with you."

"But they're pussycats," Will reminded him. "Just as you said. Wouldn't harm a flea."

"Yes," Jenkins agreed with a tortuous smile, "unless they're ordered."

Jenkins gave each tiger a nudge, and they bounded forward, like twin statues guarding a library entrance come to life.

To the left, just ten paces away, was the Hindu deity with the outstretched arms. Will reached it just as the tigers were at his heels. Finding the packages he wanted, he grabbed them out of the deity's clutches and turned, holding one in each hand.

Instead of springing, as they had seemed poised to do, the tigers sat on their haunches, anticipating a treat.

"Nice tigers," Will cooed, walking backward. "Nice girls."

The tigers advanced as he retreated. His back came up against the iron cold bars of the fence before he was ready, and he almost dropped the steaks. Recovering, Will waved the packages back and forth, saying, "Here girls. A couple of nice steaks for you. Hope you're hungry." The tigers swung their heads in unison, entranced. He flung the packages outward in opposing directions, and the tigers bounded—fortunately, toward their intended snacks.

This left Will with a quick opportunity to tap in the code. Slowly, the gate swung inward—too slowly! *Come on, come on!* Finally, there was enough room for him to slip through the opening, after which, he had enough presence of mind to punch in the code a second time, halting its progress, and forcing it to creak back closed.

***

By the time Will reached the gate, Jenkins had ensconced himself back in the surveillance room, watching the episode play itself out on a black-and-white monitor.

Watching the look of terror on the young man's face gave Jenkins an enormous sense of satisfaction.

The letters? Archer could keep them, for whatever good they would do him. Jenkins had read them enough over the years to have memorized them. He only wished it was he who had been

Fortune's correspondent. He envied Jamaal's way with words, his turn of a phrase the hallmark of a true poet. If only Fortune had lived long enough so that he could have duplicated her lover's words in love notes modeled after those of the master. Just like that guy in the play. Who was it? *Cyrano de Bergerac.*

His only worry was what Essence would think about him when Will showed her the letters. Their relationship was on tenuous ground as it was.

After he watched Will leave through the gate, he retreated to his bedroom where he brought out a small heart-shaped locket on a silver chain from the wall safe. He tumbled the locket over and over between his thumb and forefinger. Like a rosary, it brought him solace. He didn't have to open it to see whose visage resided inside. Its occupant was identified in the engraving:

For my good Fortune.
Love, J. W.

Chapter 24

Daryl flew across a landscape of hills and vales—at least it felt as close to flying as possible while keeping all four tires on the road. The Jag, a silver F-type sports coupe, hummed along like a bird. He'd had more difficulty operating a washing machine than this top-of-the-line, latest-in-technology marvel of engineering.

Crossing into Ohio, he'd found flat, straight stretches of empty interstate between rolling hills where he'd risked speeding along as he would on an autobahn—pushing 120 mph. But only for short distances. He was deathly afraid of the cops. For one thing, this wasn't his car. He didn't have the proper registration. Of course, he had the documentation for legal right of repossession—notarized. Nevertheless …

The Jag almost drove itself. He only had to keep one finger poised on the steering wheel, and lightly, at that. Sensing all pits and holes, cracks and crevasses, bumps and grooves in the road, it autocorrected itself, much like a computer word processor.

How he hated this feature on his phone. It always second-guessed everything he meant to text. Like this one he was composing to Abbey. He knew he shouldn't be composing a text while flying along the roadway—a jet fighter skimming the surface of clouds—but he couldn't resist. He was on his way to track down her renegade husband on a very good lead this time.

Hey, Abs!

"Abs" had been his nickname for her back in college, when Abbey had been stomach-crunching her way to a fitness regimen combined with stairs and regular jogs.

Closing in on you know who. Can't say much more at present. Will let you know when I …

He swerved onto the shoulder to avoid colliding with the rear end of a slow-moving diesel climbing a hill, then jackknifed back and around. On impulse, he slammed on the horn as we went by. His cell phone flew into the space behind his seat, and he twisted his neck around to make sure it was still in the car. The trucker was giving him the finger when he looked back, bringing the car under control, maneuvering it smartly into the slow lane. And slow down he did. He reached back and found that the phone had deleted his text. Which was just as well. He didn't want to raise her hopes. And that's when it hit him: No, he really didn't.

Son of a bitch! On the downslope, the trucker had sped up and was still issuing the middle finger out his window. Daryl returned a goodwill gesture of his own. Unfortunately, he happened to be passing a cop at the same time. He kept driving, lowering his head, but it wasn't long before the swirling blue and red lights were right behind him, egging him to pull over.

He could have sped up, easily outgunning the police cruiser, which was only a hyped-up Ford Taurus—pshaw! But he thought prudence would work best in this case. He pulled to the side, the truck passing with a loud blast of its horn that dwindled like laughter with the Doppler effect.

It took a while for the cop to step out of the cruiser, so long that with the warmth of the sun and all, Daryl felt in danger of nothing more catastrophic than a nap. Eventually, he emerged, a tall, lanky, Barney Fife of a deputy. County officer, not a state trooper, so there was a chance he would get off with a warning.

Except he sidled up to the window with his hand on his holster. That was a bad sign. He approached the car along the fender, side-stepping, one cautious step at a time, then lowered his head toward the window.

"Hands on the wheel, where I can see them!" he ordered in

a high-pitched kid's voice.

First thing out of the cop's mouth was a command. Another bad sign. It meant any number of apologies or explanations Daryl might give would be ignored in favor of a narrative the cop had already formed in his head. It had happened once before when all the politeness he could muster hadn't prevented Daryl ending up face down with a cop's knee pinning him to the cement as he was handcuffed.

Daryl immediately and calmly complied. As long as he didn't do or say anything out of line from this point forward—

"License and registration," the cop demanded in the same squeaky voice. Was this his natural soprano or the product of anxiety, like that of a frightened mouse? "Well?" he asked when Daryl didn't do as instructed.

"You told me to keep my hands on the wheel."

Stupid, stupid, stupid!

If he had his hands free, he would have banged his forehead repeatedly. Daryl's worst weapon, he knew, was his mouth. And his mouth had betrayed him once again.

"Are you trying to be smart with me, boy?"

Oh, brother. Was he really pulling the "boy" routine? Daryl knew he should have anticipated this level of implicit racism north of the Mason-Dixon line, but that didn't remove the sting.

"No, sir," Daryl responded more solemnly. "But about the registration, let me explain."

The cop held up a hand.

"Save it for the judge," he said.

"The judge? Am I being arrested?"

"Just remain in the car," he advised, after demanding Daryl hand over the key fob.

Apprehensive, Daryl watched the cop move toward the rear of the Jag, apparently to stand guard, where he kept glancing back and forth, speaking into his walkie-talkie from time to time, until another squad car arrived. A third cruiser, unmarked, came out of nowhere and parked at a diagonal directly in front of the Jag, boxing it in. Daryl took note of a police helicopter hovering at a low altitude, in case there was some special button he could push on the dashboard that would enable the car to levitate or his seat to eject.

"Son of a bitch," Daryl muttered under his breath, as he saw what was taking place.

Once the other officers had all got out of their respective vehicles, Daryl was instructed to exit his—no funny business. He kept his hands in plain view as he was escorted to the original cop's car and placed in the back seat, grateful that the only physical contact was the obligatory hand on his head as he was guided beneath the roof of the car.

He watched with anxiety as a van labeled Canine Unit pulled up and a German Shepherd on a leash seemed over-eager to perform assault and battery on the Jag. All his other fears for the situation melted away, leaving him with one major worry: dog claws! He had pitched the last of a joint he'd been toking half an hour ago, but he knew what would happen if the dog smelled a suspicious odor: paint would start flaking!

His employer had stipulated only two rules: repossess the Jag without breach of the peace, and please, please, please, no dings or dents or scratches. In fact, he had been required to take digital photos of every square centimeter of the car as surety against physical damage.

***

So here he was at the Victorian Arms, without a car, sipping tea in the cozy dining room of the proprietor, Mrs. Gossett, althhough she asked him to call her Phyllis, which he had already tried out experimentally one or two times, just to see how it rolled off his tongue.

The tea was sweetened with honey that she said came from a local beekeeper. Her face looked like it was enmeshed in a fine netting, the way it was so finely creased and lined. Her hair, which hung in loose curls to the nape of her neck, as though it had just been released from hair rollers, lent her a sort of Medusa look, giving Daryl a shiver that he had to fight off with more sips of hot tea.

He reminded her of someone, she told him. Someone who had lived here in this house a long time ago.

"Jamaal," she said. "Jamaal Waxman."

She said it with a wistful smile emerging from thin, parched lips.

"Right," Daryl commented, "the fellow the museum is named after."

He was starting to feel drowsy, effect of the tea—and all he had gone through that afternoon.

He suspected the trip to a holding cell while his story was checked out was simply a ruse for the cops to take pleasure rides in the Jag. How often was it that they had the opportunity to flag down such a high-performance vehicle?

He guessed as much because the cop who had been assigned to escort him to the police station—the same tall, thin, lanky, pimply kid—grumbled all the way down the interstate about missing all the fun.

They had decided to impound his car and impound him, as well, by confining him to the police station while they investigated his claim that the car was in his care as a repo man. The paperwork proved it wasn't stolen. However, they were awaiting verification from Daryl's employer, who had so far been incommunicado.

"Oh, you poor, poor boy," Mrs. Gossett—Phyllis—cooed in

a very motherly fashion, taking a hand in both of hers and patting it with affectionate care. "Best to put all of that unpleasantness behind you and get a good night's rest. Everything will look better in the morning, I guarantee it."

He was so relaxed, he did indeed feel like bed, even though it was only going on eight o'clock. He suspected a sedative in the tea. He let her lead him out of her apartment into the foyer, where she showed him the guest register.

"In case you have guests," she said with a sly wink, which let Daryl know exactly what type of guests she was talking about.

The only recent entry was for a Will Archer in room #9: the guest's name, Amanda Anders.

"This Will Archer," Daryl began to ask.

"Oh, a very nice man." She paused, as though reconsidering. "Except for certain habits."

"Habits?"

"He's a bit of a night owl, you could say. In fact, he had a very rough time of it the evening before, from what I've been told. Nevertheless, I'm sure the two of you will get along, should you happen to meet on the stairs."

Speaking of which, she began leading him up the staircase as though guiding the movements of a somnambulist. Up and up they climbed, she in the lead, Daryl behind, until they arrived at #7. The door opposite his was an infamous "door to nowhere," which she demonstrated by opening. It overlooked a perilous drop to the sidewalk below, impalement on the spiked iron fence lining it a near certainty.

At his door, she stretched up and gave him a kiss—light and leathery—on the cheek. The kiss startled him. He lurched back, bumping his head against the doorframe.

"For being such a good sport in having a cup of tea with a poor old woman," she said.

"Thank you," he mumbled, turning his back on her, while he fumbled his key into the lock.

"I should tell you about the ghost," he heard, much too close behind him.

"The ghost?" he asked, turning about.

"He comes with the house, but he shouldn't disturb your slumber. He inhabits the room above yours: number nine."

"Will Archer's?"

"I'll tell you all about him sometime," she said, smiling, while slowly making her adieu.

Did she mean the ghost or her tenant?

"But not now," Daryl said. "I'm feeling rather tired now."

"Yes, of course."

He watched her descend the stairs, with frequent backward glances, as he opened the door to his new apartment. He was only hoping he wouldn't have to stay very long.

Chapter 25

The news came in the form of a short text.

"Damn!"

Joel looked up from his Crayola masterpiece on a large rectangle of unrolled newsprint spread on the living-room floor.

"That's a bad word, Mommy."

"Sorry."

She hadn't heard from Daryl in a couple of weeks and assumed his radio silence was due to his uncovering no new clues as to her husband's whereabouts. She reread the text, and read it yet again, afraid to even touch her phone more than it took to keep the screen alive, in case it should disappear.

Hey, Abs, I think I've found Alan. Just need to confirm. Won't text more till I can figure something out. Love ya, D.

She read it slowly, word by word, taking it all into her mind, where it registered with the pressure of a ballpoint pen. First the salutation: *Abs.* How funny, her nickname from college days when she had abs to actually brag about—pre-Joel. Then the "I think" part of the next sentence. Why didn't he know for sure? And where was he that he needed to "confirm"? Why hadn't he pinged his location? Finally, what did he mean he wasn't going to text anything further? Just what was it he needed to figure out?

Taking a seat in the breakfast nook, she texted back.

Daryl, where are you? Let me know now! Please?

If only he would reveal his location. She waited a minute,

another minute, a third minute, each one longer than the one before. She sent another text, all caps, a yell through cyberspace that she hoped would impact his brain:

DARYLLLLL!!! ANSWER ME! PLEASE!!

Still no reply.

"Bastard!" she muttered, but Joel picked it up immediately.

"That's another bad word, Mommy," he reminded her. "That makes two." He formed his small fingers into bunny ears.

"Come on, Joel," she said, crouching next to the boy, "Mommy needs to take a walk."

"Playground?" he asked.

"Not today."

She felt too restless to sit passively on a bench watching Joel slide and climb and swing. She needed to work out her nervous energy.

"Aw," he complained, but she gave his head a tussle as she steered him out the door. His hair was a tangle of tight curls that would need a haircut soon.

From the back patio, they cut through the parking lot and crossed a courtyard past the neighboring complex of townhomes. Abbey took in the clouds, gray, low stratus, threatening drizzle. She should have checked the weather forecast on her phone before stepping out without an umbrella.

Her phone!

She checked it one more time for a response from Daryl.

"Shit!" she said aloud.

"That's three bad words," Joel reminded her, keeping track. "Something wrong, Mommy?" he asked, taking her hand.

"No, nothing's wrong," she said, smiling down at him.

Everything's wrong! her mind screamed.

Joel led the way, hopscotching a series of flat rocks across a thin trickle of water that bordered the complex, as though someone had left the tap on upstream while brushing their teeth. They took a trail that edged off the far side into a patch of woods.

Joel skipped ahead, tackling the undergrowth with a stick. Civilization popped up briefly in the form of a cluster of houses against the farther shoreline of a community pond, wild and untamed on this side, manicured and subdued with boat launches on the opposite shore.

"Why don't we have a boat?" Joel wanted to know.

"Someday we'll get a boat. But for now, let's go back."

"The trail keeps going," he pointed out, tugging her along by her fingertips.

Not much of a trail, though. More a trial than a trail.

"Ouch!" Joel said.

"See, I told you we should turn back. These are nettles. They sting. They'll make you itch the rest of the day."

"Okay, Mama." He reached up his hands. "Okay."

Back to "Mama," she noticed. He was alternating "Mama" and "Mommy" of late, but she wasn't sure what to make of it. Did it indicate progress or regress?

She lifted him, even though he was getting harder to carry, heavier day by day. A good thing. A healthy thing.

As she spun them around, she came face to face with a man.

"Donald!" she shouted.

"Hello, Abigail," he said, in that soft-spoken manner that was his trademark.

She would have fallen if Don Perritt hadn't been right there to catch her, even though it was his presence that had caused her to lose her balance in the first place. His grip was firm, too firm, and once latched on, he didn't seem eager to let go. He helped steer her back into a perpendicular line, and she had to shake him off her upper arm like she would the clenched jaw of a pit bull.

"May I accompany you?" he asked politely. He was always so gentlemanly, peering at her with myopic eyes magnified owl-like by the round lenses of his wire frames. His stare gave her a chill, as though he were a wax figure come to life out of Madame Tussaud's. "I see you are out for a stroll. Or am I mistaken?"

"No, no, you're not mistaken," she informed him. "Joel and I were just out—strolling! In fact, we're heading back home."

"This way, then," Perritt advised, pointing out a side path. "I know a shortcut."

She set Joel down, and they let Perritt lead the way. Like Joel, he used a walking stick as a machete, slashing at branches that crossed the path.

"You seem agitated," he said, casting a backward glance. "Is something wrong?"

It's just what Joel had asked. Was her uneasiness, her jumpiness, so noticeable? She took a deep breath, clenched and unclenched her fingers, then let out a long stream of air from her lungs. Why not tell him?

The path recrossed the creek and opened out onto a green space, a wide lawn dotted with malnourished saplings. Perritt held back a branch, like holding open a door, to let her walk past.

"It's my husband," she remarked.

"What's a husband?" Joel asked, looking up.

The idea, the purpose, of a walk evaporated. She felt listless, directionless, aimless. When she turned around, she saw she wasn't the only one. Perritt had turned into an ice sculpture of immobility.

"Donald?" she asked, concerned. There was a park bench within a few steps. "Here, let's sit," she suggested.

They had arrived at the playground from a different angle than usual—nirvana for Joel.

"Can I, Mama?" Joel asked, pointing.

"Go ahead. Go play."

Coming back to life, Perritt wiped the seat down with a handkerchief, a gesture either gallant or obsessive-compulsive. He allowed her to take her seat first, then took up a position close—too close. But he was always too close, wasn't he? It was just his mannerism. Always having to touch her arm as they talked. And now, shifting closer, even as she tried to edge away.

"Your husband," he said, "you were saying?" He seemed eager to hear—too eager. His head inclined just enough to accentuate his interest. But of course he would be interested in the man who had taken the lives of his wife and daughter. She regretted bringing it up. This must be an unbearably painful subject for him.

"He's been found," she announced.

A look went through Perritt's eyes that Abbey found hard to describe. It was as though windows had become suddenly glazed with frost. His lips thinned into a horrid smile, corpselike in its artificiality. All the blood drained out of his face, giving him a masklike quality. At the same time, his hand clamped hard around her wrist, his fingernails digging into the soft flesh where the tendons were most vulnerable.

"Ow! Donald! You're hurting me!"

It was a spontaneous outburst, loud enough to be overhead. Joel popped out the opening of a plastic chute and trotted over.

"Are you okay, Mommy?"

Perritt let go, and Abbey rose quickly and went to her son.

"Yes, Mommy's fine."

When she turned, she found Perritt standing there, eyeing her curiously, as though he had never seen her before. Her initial fright dissipating, she thought he might be having a heart attack or stroke.

"Donald?" She approached him warily, as though he were an animal with lockjaw. His eyes blinked once, twice, thrice.

"I'm sorry.," he said, coming back around. "You were talking about your husband."

She decided to come right out with a sentence she had been formulating in her head for the better part of a week.

"I'm not so sure it's a good idea for us to be seeing each other ... at least for now," she added to soften the blow.

"I see," Perritt said icily. "At least, let me walk you home. We can talk about it."

"That won't be necessary. We can manage, the two of us."

"Mommy? I'm hungry. When's lunch?" Joel was starting to complain.

She rubbed her wrist where Perritt had grabbed it. She glanced down to take in the fingernail marks that had gouged her flesh, leaving a series of half circles all in a row.

"Let me come by this evening. I'll bring dinner. Chinese?"

"No, it's just—" She came to the hard part she didn't want to have to explain, but now she had a way to bluff herself out of an unpleasant situation, thanks to Daryl, despite the murkiness of his information. "It's just, with my husband coming home ..."

"So you believe he will be coming back to you?"

This was said sternly, barely concealing an ill temper.

"Yes, I'm hopeful, so you see—"

"I do," Perritt snapped. "I see all too well."

"I'm sorry," she said. "Come on, Joel."

As she walked hand in hand with her son, she had the uncanny feeling that Perritt's eyes had left their sockets, slithering after her like snakes. She looked back only once before reaching her apartment to make sure he was still there, safely behind her, but he wasn't. The spot where he had been standing was empty, as though he had been nothing more than an illusion.

Chapter 26

The letters Will had worked so hard to keep in his possession, braving man-eating tigers in the middle of the night, produced more evidence that Essence's parents hadn't been planning to abandon her. Maybe this handful of letters was all he needed to persuade Essence to remain among the living.

Most had been written during that first separation when Jamaal set out on his own—young, confident, full of life. Sent from various states: Kentucky, Tennessee, Missouri, Alabama, Georgia, and then back up through the Carolinas. The first series of letters were polite, lightweight, noncommittal, holding Fortune at a distance. Mostly, they detailed the odds and ends of his life on the road.

First and foremost, there was the food, an introduction to a Southern palette of greens and grits and gravy. Secondly, the gigs themselves, the raucous atmosphere, the dark, smoky stages.

By Christmas, with Fortune committed to giving birth, his tone had warmed, the letters sprinkled with reminiscences of his earlier rendezvous with her, poetic descriptions of her hair and eyes and mouth and chin and throat and shoulders and—this was where Will chose to skim ahead. He described her in terms most tender, reverential, as though he were holding his breath so as not to disturb the delicate soap bubble image he was fostering.

Fast-forward to the following spring, and his mood has changed. It's darker, more introspective, more somber, as he wrestles with the issue of parenthood, what kind of father he would make, how he could provide for a family at his young age, the infringement on his plans, his freedom. Massive apologies for not being able to live up to the ideal that Fortune held in mind for him to embody.

In the last letter, on the threshold of his return home, enter another woman, a mystery woman whom Jamaal refers to with personal pronouns only. He confesses he must settle an old score with this woman before he can make good with any promise to take care of Fortune and her baby. Will noted that he was careful to call Essence *her* baby, not theirs.

At breakfast the next morning, Will showed Mrs. Gossett the letters.

"Ah, so your little quest last night bore results?" she said, arching a brow. "You found your Holy Grail?"

"Not quite," he answered. He considered confronting her with his suspicion that she had been the one to tip off Mrs. Warner, although he detected no sign of uneasiness, just curiosity. "Did you happen to tell anyone about my ... quest?"

"Just my new personal assistant," she replied forthrightly. "Amanda."

"Amanda? You mean Mandy?"

"If you prefer silly nicknames."

"Oh, that's right. She told me she's been helping you out with ... errands. What all does she do for you anyway?"

"Returning overdue library books mostly. Surely, you don't think her prone to gossip?"

Thinking of her talkativeness, Will answered, "I wouldn't be so sure about that."

He made a mental note to question Mandy at the museum, although he couldn't imagine her being in contact with Mrs. Warner. Then again, he was still slightly unnerved by her affiliation with Mrs. Gossett.

Change of tactic.

"Was Jamaal involved with anyone else?"

"You've seen the ledger? There were dozens of others."

He recalled his landlady's rule about guests. Permissible, as long as they sign in, no matter the length of time, whether for five minutes or five days. The registry on the lectern in the foyer, the type of guest book you would find at a wedding or funeral, went back in time 20-plus years. He had examined the pages, scouring them for names coupled with Jamaal's. During the months preceding Jamaal's setting out on his tour of Southern states, there indeed had been dozens of women's names interspersed with Fortune's.

"But not during all the time he had come back home," Will observed. There were no other names beside Fortune's during the last few months of his residency at the Victorian Arms.

"It's anyone's guess," she said, eyeing Will over the rim of her cup of tea, a look that Will allowed to go unreturned, absorbed as he was in his thoughts. "I imagine you'll be wanting to stay inside tonight? Rest up after last night's misadventure? I thought you might like to meet our new lodger."

"So he's arrived, has he? I don't know," he said, referring to her previous question. "I haven't made any plans."

***

But, as it turned out, other plans had been made for him.

At a quarter to midnight, Will left the Victorian Arms.

Having crossed the bridge, he wandered the town of West Bloomfield, pausing beneath a streetlamp to study the email he had printed out at his workplace providing directions.

The subject line read: UR INVITED!!!

Cute, but who was it from? It wasn't signed. The "From" line read: wonder-woman_19. He could only assume Essence. She was 19 years old. But why so mysterious all of a sudden? Why make him wonder, as it were? And why the need to shout out the invite?

HEY WILL! COMING TO THE PARTY TONIGHT? SEE U @ MIDNIGHT OK? DONT BE LATE. BUT DONT BE TOO EARLY EITHER ☺

The details were vague, but he had replied to the email, trying to initiate a slowpoke version of texting. Wonder Woman hadn't responded. He'd thought about calling using the apartment's landline, but of course the Warner residence was unlisted, and Essence hadn't divulged her cell phone number … yet.

He wanted so much to show her Jamaal's letters to her mother. Here was confirmation that her father really had contemplated settling down, to take up a life with Fortune. He couldn't wait to see her reaction.

A police cruiser turned a corner, and he stepped into the shadows, waiting for it to move past, a silent, white shark on the prowl, always in motion or die.

The thumping of a bass, undercutting the natural noises of the night, led him like a piper down a street marked: NO OUTLET. At the end of the street, set apart from its neighbors by a vacant lot, sat a large, rambling, two-story clapboard house with a wide front porch, its roof held up by makeshift two-by-fours in place of pillars. Will confirmed the house number against the address provided in the email, just to be sure. He didn't know about Essence, but it didn't seem like his type of party.

Music boomed through a screen door, about which several figures mingled in the porch light like so many moths. Cars were stuffed into the end of the lane four or five deep. A row of motorcycles edged the front yard like a row of dominoes. As he approached, the cluster of people on the porch, drinking out of plastic cups, fell into an observant silence that seemed neither hostile nor encouraging.

"Looking for Essence," Will said to no one specific face or

person. He seemed ridiculously attired in polo shirt, jeans, hi-tops, at least compared to some of the others: all black leather, chains, piercings, tattoos, shaved heads.

"Inside," one of the men said, flexing the tattoo of a Confederate flag on his bicep as he hooked a thumb over his shoulder.

Will pushed through the storm door, shuffling around the man, who appeared to be stationed there as a bouncer.

He entered a hazy, smoky living room crowded around a plywood stage where a band's instruments were grouped post-break. Three partiers were gathered around a coffee table, snorting lines of cocaine, heads bowed as though in prayer. Will noted a queue climbing a flight of stairs along a banister.

"Long line for the restroom," Will observed.

"Hah!" a man near the foot of the stairs exploded with a laugh that launched a speck of saliva.

"By the way, have you seen Essence?" he asked, as though she had left his side only a moment ago.

Three or four heads turned.

"My, but you're a funny one, aren't you?" a woman snickered. "You'll have to wait your turn like any other participant."

Participant?

Curious, Will took his place in line, which shuffled along in single file. It was like being in a bread line or one of those convict lines you see in movies. Their ankles might have been shackled with chains for all the progress they were making.

He saw a man in business attire plodding down the steps, stuffing his shirttails into his waist and tightening his belt.

Participant!

A path along the banister had been cleared for the sharp-dressed man's descent. Will took advantage to begin climbing past the others before the pathway closed over.

"Hey, Mac, what do you think you're doing?" a man asked

sharply, jamming an elbow into Will's side.

"What's the hurry?" someone else said more amicably, gripping his shoulder, and a couple others laughed.

"Wait your turn, why don't you?" a Goth-attired woman complained, trying to trip him up with a boot full of spikes.

"Bathroom!" Will let out, stretching a thin smile that he hoped signaled discomfort. He was starting to feel alarmed by the pushes and shoves as he climbed.

"What's wrong with the one downstairs?"

"Handle's broken," he said, grasping for an excuse.

"So?" A distinct challenge to the authenticity of his lie—this from a man with huge arms and a beer belly to match, at the top of the stairs.

"Overflowing," Will said hurriedly, trying to squeeze past, through, or under.

Clearing the top step, Will began working his way down the hallway, barreling through an obstacle course of arms and feet.

"Bathroom's that way," a small, thin accountant of a man with thick, round eyeglasses pointed out. It was the kindest voice that had addressed him so far. It just wasn't the direction he wanted to go.

Flattening himself against the wall, he made his way by fits and starts down the rest of the hall to a bedroom doorway, navigating a gauntlet of jabs to his ribs, kicks to his shins, a slap of knuckles that made his gums bleed.

At the far end of the hall stood a young wisp of a woman in a devil's outfit, as though dressed for Halloween, with a clipboard. Despite her attire, she seemed nothing so much as a barista taking coffee orders.

"Watch or perform?" she asked, blandly.

"Huh?" Will responded.

"Watch … or … perform? Either way, you get five minutes.

Anonymity guaranteed. There are masks in the changing room. Here, you'll have to sign this either way." The demon girl handed him a form to fill out. "Did you bring your own protection or do you need the house blend?" She held up a condom, as Will stared wide-eyed and uncomprehending. "But you'll have to go back to the end of the line. You can take your time deciding back there. Or have you decided? Watch or perform?"

"Neither," Will said and wedged his way past.

"Hey!" the sentry called after him.

Stepping through the doorway was like moving through a portal into the '70s. The floor was carpeted with a thick red shag. The lighting was also red-tinctured, filtered to produce a smarmy effect. A disco ball slowly rotated from the ceiling, reflecting myriad diamonds of light revolving about the room from racks of flickering candles. There were large-leafed plants in Grecian urns. The music was a Muzak rendition of smooth jazz.

For a few moments, Will was completely mesmerized. He found he wasn't the only spectator. There were others, men and women, fully clothed, standing along the perimeter of the room, in the shadows, like wallflowers at a dance. Their faces were masked as though for a costume ball: feathered masks, gilded masks, gladiator masks.

The centerpiece was a Queen-size bed, a four-poster. On the bed lay a woman, utterly naked, donning a black Zorro mask. Will noted her light-brown skin, freckled shoulders, jazzed auburn hair.

Essence!

Her arms were stretched out above her head, wrists tied loosely to the headboard. Her ankles were similarly tethered with braided, velvet ropes, slack, not taut. Her body was likewise slack, listless, passive. As Will moved toward her, he was joined by a young scarecrow of a yokel stepping out of a side room, naked except for a ninja mask. The man grabbed hold of Will's shoulder, trying to move past, but Will shoved him aside, boxing him out as he climbed onto the bed next to Essence.

"Hey! I'm supposed to be next," the man complained, stepping back and covering his crotch with both hands.

Behind the mask, Essence's eyes were open, but lax, vapid. The pupils, dilated, were aimed at the ceiling, but they seemed to focus on something farther, more distant, invisible to the ordinary eye, until he brought his face into view.

"Will?" Her voice rose plaintively, her eyes struggling to focus. "Is that you?" Her eyes went wide, then narrow. "Oh, my God," she said haltingly. "Are you here for the same thing?"

"What? No—of course not! Hold on," he said, fiddling with the knot at one of her wrists, prying at it with his fingernails, but it was deftly tied. "Let's get you out of here."

"It's no use." Her words came at him as though from a distance, expressionless, emerging from a hollow cocoon of despair. "You're too late."

"No, don't say that. just give me a—"

"Hey, buddy!" a shrill voice cut in sharply from behind him. "Mind moving? You're ruining my shot!"

"Shot?" Will echoed.

He turned his head, taking in the owner of the voice: a small, delicate man, his head capped with a beret and his chin with a goatee. His eyes were myopic behind glasses with glitzy frames.

"On second thought, scratch that. Keep on doing what you're doing. Shining hero coming to the rescue of the helpless maiden. But would you mind taking your clothes off first?"

Will took in the high-end video camera on a tripod that the man was operating. It only took a moment for it all to finally fall into place, and when it did, he carefully covered Essence with a sheet and then lunged—not at the man but at the camera, knocking it down in a tackle, and throttling it by the neck of the tripod, bashing it repeatedly against the carpeted floor as though he were attempting to eradicate consciousness from the casement of a skull.

"You'll pay for that!" the man in the beret promised.

"Yeah?" Will sneered up at him. "Well, let's see what you have to say when I call the cops."

"The police?" the man said, stroking his goatee. "Why would you involve the police? We have waivers. I have signed permissions, releases. We're doing nothing illegal." He turned his head to the side. "Will someone please get this madman out of here?"

Within seconds, Will was hoisted off the floor. Two burly men, clothed not naked, grabbed him under the armpits, and started to carry him away.

"No," Essence called from the bed, struggling to rise against the tethers that bound her, "please don't take him. Will!"

He tried to resist, but it was no use. He was overpowered, dragged along the hall past the line of waiting men and women, at whom he could only shout: "You're animals! All of you!"

At the top of the stairs, Will was given a push that sent him flying. He landed at the bottom in a heap, where another set of hands hauled him up and hustled him out the front door.

He was dragged past the row of motorcycles to a car with an opened trunk, where Will renewed his struggle. He kicked hard, catching his foot on the lead motorcycle. It fell over, and the rest of them toppled in sequence, like a house of cards.

"You've got to be kidding me," one biker said.

As Will wriggled and squirmed, he saw a long metal tire iron rise into the night.

"No," Will said. "Not that."

It hit him hard on the back of his head, and it was the last thing he felt before it all went dark.

Chapter 27

Whip-poor-will … whip-poor-will …

He awoke to birdsong. But his name wasn't Will, it was something else. He was someone else. And he wasn't poor. He was … who was he? Where was he?

Squinting into sunlight, he sat up in an oozing stream of muck at the bottom of a gully. The movement of the water suggested it had rained recently—overnight? But he hadn't felt any of it. As he attempted to crawl out of the ditch, slipping and slithering, he realized he was completely naked.

Looking around, he saw he was on a country lane. Pine trees bristled overhead shading him from the full, harsh disk of the sun. Across the road lay a quarry, abandoned, gouges clawed out of treeless hills.

A few pieces of litter marred the bottom of the ditch: crumpled cigarette package, opened condom wrapper, a man's sock.

But what about his clothes? His wallet? His keys? The pocket-size photos of Abbey and Joel? The loss brought out a thick sob.

It made him feel sick thinking of the process ahead of him of cancelling his credit cards—both the new one under his assumed name and his old one for his and Abbey's joint account he had hung onto like a scrap of memory—then telling Mrs. Gossett and Mrs. Waxman he needed new keys, replacing his ID—but which one? Will? Alan? Both? The irony of someone stealing an identity he had himself stolen struck him as absurd.

It made him feel worse when he realized he was thinking of his personal effects ahead of Essence. The letters he had intended to give to her, the ones from Jamaal addressed to her mother, had been confiscated as well. But this loss seemed minor compared to the gravity of the night's events.

What had become of her? Where was she? Still in that horrid house? Still tied to a bed? Was she some sort of sex slave? Or had she been a willing participant? Had there truly been permissions, contracts? Had she signed her privileges away? Her freedom?

And that director—a small weasel of a sexual predator. He remembered seeing him before on the landing of the stairwell at the Victorian Arms. Mrs. Gossett had introduced them.

Gingerly, he felt the back of his head. It was throbbing, pulsating. Tender, but not excruciating. A distinct lump, though. Still, he was alive. He should be grateful for that. He recalled with sudden clarity the image of a wrench. He hoped it hadn't caused a concussion.

A car approached slowly, crunching the gravel. Out of a husk of misery, he found himself raising his hand in a vague sort of salute, as the car swiped past his vision: a long rectangle of green.

But then, far down the lane, it stopped.

Now he felt exposed, vulnerable. Finding his footing, he climbed out of the gully and hid behind the wide trunk of a tree. The car came back, and he heard its horn, blaring like the loud call of a shore bird. He peered around the trunk to spot Mrs. Waxman, standing turret-like outside the open driver's side of her green Lincoln, the car splattered with mud from the road. She was wearing a tight outfit of stretchy purple spandex, her lips compressed with a violet shade of lipstick to match.

"William, will you please come out? I would hate to have to come in and fetch you."

Will made a motion to show himself, then thought better of it, letting a branch sashay back in place as though touched by a breeze.

"I'm not decent!" he called out, testing his voice. It came out as a hoarse rasp. He coughed and repeated, "I'm not—"

"Yes, yes, I heard you, but seriously now, do you think this is the first time I've seen a man naked? I've brought you some clothes to change into. They're arranged on the back seat. You can change while I drive. I promise, I won't so much as look in the rearview mirror."

Just to be sure, Will clutched a large sycamore leaf in front of his groin. It was only when he got in the back seat that he let go of it. Mrs. Waxman kept her promise as she began driving without so much as the flicker of a rearward glance.

"Essence?" he asked, his mind replaying the surreal events of the previous night.

"Recovering, thanks to you. You're the reason the party— if that's what you can call such a gathering of degenerates—broke up when it did. Before things went too far."

Too far? How far was too far? Hadn't "things" already progressed far enough by the time he had arrived?

In any case, he was grateful for the clothes.

"My ex-husband's," she confided.

They were clean, pressed, but a size too long in the sleeves, an inch too short in the leg. Not exactly his style: a silk lavender shirt, black wool trousers that itched in all the wrong places. As for the shoes, they were black leather with pointed toes, a size too small, but he managed to squeeze his feet into them.

"Sorry about this morning," he apologized into the mirror.

"Tut, the museum isn't important at a time like this."

"What color day is it?" he just had to know.

"Why, the color of your shirt, of course. Please don't tell me your little bump on the head left you colorblind."

"Oh, so you know about that?"

"Are you sure you don't have a concussion?" She threw a concerned look into the rearview mirror. "We probably should get you checked out."

"I'm fine," he claimed, although he didn't quite feel it. "How did you know where to look for me?"

Mrs. Waxman emitted a sigh.

"An acquaintance of Essence's—some sorority girl from the Bible college, if you can believe that! She overheard the men who drove off with you boasting about it when they came back. Apparently, it's a road famous for drag racing and drug deals late at night. She was the one who called to tell me about Essence."

They came to an intersection where she turned onto the highway.

"Where are we going?"

"Why, the hospital, of course. To visit my granddaughter. You do want to see her, do you not?"

She glanced into the rearview mirror for confirmation, and Will nodded.

"How is she—really?"

"She's as well as can be expected," she said, putting her eyes back on the road. "For having been left at the door of the ER as though she were no more than a dog."

"What was wrong with her?"

"Hemorrhaging," she said simply.

Will winced, filled with a sense of helpless outrage.

"But nothing too serious, as it turns out. It's the drugs that are more worrisome." she continued. "The competing drugs in her system made it seem like Essence was trying to set a world record—her doctor's words, not mine." She lowered her voice into a confidential tone. "Do you know the saying, 'To find yourself, you must lose yourself'?"

This seemed an inappropriate time for a lesson in quotations.

"New Testament?" Will wondered.

"It's no matter the source. There is no one—let me repeat— no one as lost as Essence."

***

When he went in, the hospital room was darkened, the blinds drawn. Essence was hooked up to an IV and heartbeat monitor that sounded a steady beep. The flat screen on the wall was showing a home shopping network channel without sound.

She had a sheet pulled up to the neckline of her gown, but her arms, long and bare, rested outside the cover. Will had the strange feeling he was viewing an open casket, except as he approached her bedside, she opened her eyes.

"You came," she said, struggling to sit up. "I wasn't sure you would want to see me after—"

"Don't strain yourself," he said, coming to her aid.

"What a horrible, horrible night. I don't remember all of it, but what I do remember—"

Her sentence ended with a choked sob, and Will reached out to stroke her shoulder with light fingertips.

"It's all right," he managed to say. "It's all going to be all right."

"I should thank you for trying to rescue me."

"I wish I could have pulled it off—the rescue, I mean."

"But what I don't understand is what took you so long."

She looked up at him, searching his eyes for an answer.

"I'm sorry?" Had his rescue attempt been anticipated?

"I waited and waited, and the people there, they kept pouring me drink after drink."

Will took a tentative seat on the edge of her bed.

"I guess I don't understand. Why did you think I might be there?"

"Your text."

"Text?"

"You said you'd be there by nine. You gave me directions and everything. I thought—well, what I thought was, 'How nice.

It's like he's asking me out on a date.'"

"Are you sure it was from me?"

"I thought maybe you got my number from my Grandma Waxman. I texted back. I tried calling. But there was no answer either way."

This part made sense. She wouldn't know he didn't own a cell phone with which to send a reply.

"I received an invitation, too," he told her.

"You did?"

"By email. Someone going by Wonder Woman. I thought it was you."

"Not much of a superhero, was I?" she lamented. "I'm sorry you had to see me that way."

She retreated inside herself. He could tell by her eyes. Maybe she was trying to puzzle it out: who would have invited him to such an event? It was a puzzle challenging Will, as well.

"They kept telling me you signed something," he told her. "A waiver. A permission form."

"Maybe I did. When drugged, something in my drink. There was this director."

"Director?"

At the utterance of the word, Will squinted his eyes against the picture of the small man with the beret and goatee, struggling to suppress an upswelling of anger—pure rage—that threatened to unmoor his senses.

"I guess you could call him that. He offered me a part in this amateur movie he was directing. I didn't even know what it entailed. It was all very vague. All he told me was mine would be a starring role. I just went along with it. I thought it was all a big joke." She half-closed her eyes and sank back onto her pillows. "Seems I was the star all right."

Will took her hand, which offered no return response. It was warm but lifeless, folded into his palm without resistance.

"It wasn't your fault," he tried consoling her. "You were drugged, like you said. You didn't know. You couldn't have known—"

"Don't you see? They did all of that to me because of my reputation. They know—or think they know—that I'm that kind of woman, the kind that looks for that sort of—"

She broke down with a subdued cry and turned her head away, hiding her face. Will didn't know what to say, how to respond.

"Those men," she continued, "I recognized some of them by their eyes, their voices, their bodies. I thought they were my friends. I didn't expect them to—I never thought they would do what they did. It's like they thought they had the right to my body. That they owned it somehow. Could do what they wanted with it. That it was their property. So you see," she trailed off, looking up at Will plaintively through curling strands of hair, "I'm not who you think I am. I really am that kind of woman. I don't deserve to be rescued. Not by you. Not by anyone."

"That can't be true," Will countered, pulling her toward him.

"No, but it is!" She pushed away, placing hands on his chest, as though to hold him at a distance. "On some level, I knew what was happening, and I let it happen. I didn't fight back when they led me up the stairs. I didn't resist when they—when they tied me to the bedposts. But then—when they came and kept coming, like some kind of fucking ..."

She lowered her head onto his shoulder, suppressing tears.

"Maybe I deserved it—maybe I deserved what happened."

"No!" Will stated, a firm rebuttal. "You can't say that. You can't let yourself believe it. Did you report it? To the police?" He felt he needed to ask.

"The police!" Essence scoffed, lifting her head. "For all I know, the police were taking part—a couple of cops at least.

Besides, she wouldn't let me. My Grandmother Warner. She's much too afraid of the scandal it would cause her reputation."

She stared past him, through him, wiping her eyes. He held her close, running his hand through her hair.

"When will you feel good enough to leave? Did they tell you? After you're released, maybe we could do something … simple Together. The two of us."

At this, she gave a weak smile.

"Like what? Go on a date?"

Will took her hand and kissed her forehead, gently.

"Sure, a regular old-fashioned date."

"Will …"

"We'll go to a movie."

"Will …"

"Go out for ice cream. What's your favorite flavor? See, I don't even know that about you. There's so much to learn."

"Will," she said, withdrawing her hand, taking all of the warmth with it. "It's not going to work. I can't just pretend—"

"Why won't it?" he asked, cutting her off, although he knew what she was trying to tell him.

"You're wrong about me. You—you're the shining hero. And me—I just don't have that heart of gold you keep looking for."

"Yeah, well," Will said, teasing out the words, "maybe gold is overrated."

"You're funny." She turned to face him with soft but steady eyes. "I can't promise I'll reform. I'll still be the same woman. So there's really no chance for us—you and me. You know what I'm saying?"

"Look, if it's about what happened. Last night. I know you didn't mean to get yourself involved in—" He stopped short, unsure how to proceed.

"No, it's true, I didn't, but don't you get it?" she asked, the wail of her voice muffled by her stack of pillows as she curled up on the bed facing the wall. "We can never be together. Even if we wanted to. I can never be with anyone. They—the two of them—would always come between us. They would harass us to no end."

Them? The two of them?

Then Will understood.

"But surely you don't think it was your own grandmother? Jenkins, maybe." He could never be sure about Jenkins. But Mrs. Warner? Her kith and kin? It didn't make any sense that she would engineer an encounter so devastating to her granddaughter and make sure Will was on hand to witness it, just to—what? Break them apart?

"Maybe not," she said, turning back around. Will handed her tissues from a box on the nightstand. "But it doesn't matter, does it? She's already told me, she wants me to have nothing to do with you. And not just you. With anyone!"

She wiped her eyes with clenched fists and Will reached over and brushed her hair back away from her forehead, which was damp with sweat.

"You need your rest. I'll come back. Or—" He had another thought. "I can stay here, if you'd rather."

"No," she said, lying back down against the pillows. She sounded tired, weak. "I don't want to be a bother."

"It's no bother," he tried to assure her.

She was drifting, fighting against closing her eyes, but losing the struggle. Will pulled the sheet up over her shoulders, tucking her in.

"Listen," she said, almost a whisper, "I want you to promise me ..." Her eyes were closing, her voice becoming an echo, her eyelids getting heavier, as though responding to the spell of a hypnotist. "Promise you won't stop me when the time comes."

"Oh," he said, understanding. How many nights were left until the anniversary of her mother's death? Six? Seven? He was losing count.

"You have to promise me, promise me, promise …"

There were no more words, just a regular breathing through her nostrils, her eyes closed now. She looked peaceful this way.

"All right," Will said, making the promise as much to himself as to her. "I promise."

He thought he saw it now. He thought he understood what it was she wanted so badly to escape. With both of his identities taken away and facing the need to start over, he felt just as despondent, his situation just as hopeless.

Hell, he thought. *I won't stop you. I'll join you instead. We'll do it together. We can give each other courage that way.*

Chapter 28

As though wearing an albatross around his neck, Daryl had been lugging around his digital camera on a strap for three days now, following on the heels of Alan Paxton—or maybe he should start thinking of him as Will Archer? It was only a hunch, but an entry in the guest ledger for one Amanda Anders raised his hackles. He wanted so much to offer concrete, physical proof to Abbey of her husband's waywardness.

If he could show her that Alan or Will—Will-Alan?—had not only abandoned her but had entered into an extramarital affair, he felt he could set her mind at ease. She could stop all her misspent longing for the ghost of the man she had once known and open herself up to other men … other relationships.

For two nights in a row, the subject of Daryl's safari had him across the bridge and into a park, where he investigated a playground. Leaving the park, he crossed a street and stood in front of the entrance gate to a huge estate, peering through the iron bars. By midnight, Will-Alan had returned home—alone. All Daryl heard were footfalls of a lonely man pacing back and forth on the floorboards and the long wailing moan of the pipes.

This night, however, provided a welcome break in his routine. Instead of Will-Alan leaving his apartment, someone else entered, clicking up the stairs in high heels. After the heels passed by, Daryl crept downstairs to look at the guest ledger. Sure enough, a second entry for Amanda Anders. He snapped a photo of the ledger entries—two of them now, beginning of a pattern. Back in his room, he listened for telltale sounds of amorous activity from the apartment above. After an hour … nothing. Just murmurs of conversation punctured with laughter. And then, thankfully, silence. The silence lingered, widened, deepened.

Daryl couldn't just sit there, waiting for an incriminating sound to emerge. Camera dangling from its strap, he began an assault on the stairs, taking them two at a time.

"Just thought I'd introduce myself," he said, when Will-Alan answered the door. "I'm new here, just moved in."

Peering through the doorway, he saw a young, attractive woman, holding a goblet of red wine. Unfortunately, she was fully dressed. More than fully. She was outfitted in a vivid green taffeta gown.

"Frank," Daryl said, holding out his hand, "Frank Owens."

"Will," he responded with a firm handshake. "Will Archer."

"I heard tell of a ghost," Daryl said, giving a know-all grin.

"Yeah, well, he isn't much of a ghost anymore."

This was unexpected. He had anticipated Will-Alan sharing the joke at their landlady's expense, not a suspension of disbelief.

"Nice camera," Will-Alan said.

"Camera?" The young woman stood up at the mention of the word and joined the two of them on the threshold. "Mind taking our picture?"

"Mandy," Will-Alan scolded. "We just now met. I'm sure Frank here doesn't want to——"

"Happy to," Daryl interrupted, raising his camera. This was better than he could have hoped for. Mandy snuggled in close to Will-Alan, her arm around his waist. At the last second, she held up her hand.

"But no flash, OK?"

"Got it," Daryl agreed. "Smile!" He waited for Will-Alan to struggle his way out of a frown and fired off a sequence of shots.

"Here, let me give you my number," Mandy said, pulling out her phone. "So you can send the photos."

Even better, Daryl thought. Now he not only had a face and

a name but a contact number as well.

"Sorry about Mandy," Will-Alan said. "She tends to be a little sensational."

"Hey!" Mandy complained.

"Speaking of sensational," Daryl said, hoping to keep the conversation going, "seems you've made national news."

"Yeah?" This caught Will-Alan's attention, just as he was about to close the door.

"That man who disappeared down the sinkhole, looking for his wife? They found him. And his wife." It was something he'd found out on a trip to the police station to check on the progress they were making with the Jag.

"What do you mean?" Will-Alan asked. His gaze became more intense, like concentrated laser beams. "Found him? Where? How?"

"They both popped up in a cavern near Athens, about fifty miles north of here, in the middle of a guided tour. Crept out of a hole, both of them."

"But that's impossible!" Will-Alan shouted. His eyes seemed to dance with a wild light.

"Not so impossible apparently. What I heard, the wife had been living on moles and bats. Gruesome to think about, really. But they're alive now. And together."

"Thank you!" Will-Alan said, taking Daryl's hands in both of his. "Thank you. You don't know what this means! The hope for a future, a life."

And with that, he took off down the stairwell, racing at full gallop, leaving Daryl rubbernecking on the landing.

The girl came out: Mandy.

"Where'd he go?" she asked, her lower lip curling into an offended pout.

"Don't know," Daryl shrugged. But he intended to find out.

***

Fueled with optimism, Will didn't care if the tigers greeted him or if Jenkins spotted him with the security camera. He entered the code into the keypad next to the gate and waited for it to swing open just enough to admit his body. He didn't look back to make sure it closed properly once he was through.

He crossed the wide lawn, dodging statues, making his way to the terraced side yard that ascended toward Essence's balcony.

Down below, he found the rainspout was missing. He debated climbing the trellis, but one touch let him know it was embroidered with roses, and roses had thorns. Fortunately, the foundation of the house was lined with decorative pebbles.

He threw a single pebble into the air, but it only landed on the other side of the balustrade. Selecting another, he arced it just right, so that it banged against a windowpane.

Still, no appearance. Maybe he was wasting his energy on a phantom pursuit? Next, he grabbed a handful of pebbles and threw them like birdshot. They rattled a hard rain against the panes before rebounding onto the balcony floor.

And there she was, still dressed in white, except this was a sleeping gown, not a hospital garment.

"Hello!" he called up in a voice competing with a plethora of night noises.

"Will? What are you doing here?"

"This is the part where you say, 'Romeo, Romeo,'" he joked.

"Seriously."

"I need to come up. Can I? I need to talk with you."

"Oh," is all she said, as though she somehow understood the motive behind his urgency. "Well, I—"

Before she could object, he reached in for the trellis despite the thorns. Climbing hurriedly, he reached the balcony and grabbed onto the balustrade.

"You know you could have used the ladder," she said, smiling, leaning against the doorway in such a way that made him worry about her physical health.

"Ladder?"

She pointed, and he looked over at a metal ladder leaning against the house on the farther side of the balcony.

She began to laugh.

"Jenkins left it propped up. For repairs." Her look turned more serious. "Look at you, you're bleeding."

"So I am."

"Come on inside, I'll nurse your wounds."

He followed her through the French doors and entered her large, luxurious, rose-colored room. She motioned him to sit on the edge of her bed with its quilted comforters. Tiffany lamps, flickering candlelight, incense, dark recesses, shadows in corners—all gave the room a magical aura.

She went into the en suite and came out with a damp washcloth, which she dabbed at his face and arms and hands, holding the latter on her lap, as she sat beside him, thigh to thigh, so close it made his insides twist with electricity.

"I have a proposition," he said, taking her all in. She was pale, her hair tied back in a bow. Her gown was transparent. He could see right through to the delicate curves of her breasts. He felt a dull ache in his chest, knowing there could be no acting on desire.

"Your proposition?" she reminded him, still smiling in a vague, distant sort of way, as though she had other things on her mind. He hoped it didn't have anything to do with that last horrible night. He turned to face her more directly.

"Come live with me. Let's give it a try. We really should make the attempt to live, don't you think? And then, well, if you don't think it will work, if you still feel life is not worth it, then, all right, we can end things, however you like. But at least we'll know we tried."

She pulled back from him, staring in apparent disbelief.

"I don't get it. You haven't tried to get in touch with me for days."

"I haven't had a way to. I tried to find you. I looked. I waited."

"I thought you were blowing me off because of what—because of what happened." She closed her eyes in sync with a shudder of her shoulders. "Not saying I'd blame you, but now here you are, all hyped up with some crazy scheme?"

"Not so crazy," he said.

"What's changed?"

"Nothing's changed." Or maybe he had. He wasn't sure what had come over him either. "It's just that I'm tired of running."

"Not that you're deeply in love with me and want to stay with me forever?"

"Well, yeah. There's that."

She leaned toward him, cupping her chin over his shoulder. She felt so warm. She was all sweaty, as though damp after a bath. He could feel her heart beating strongly against his chest.

"Stay here tonight," she whispered in his ear. He had been expecting an argument, not an invitation. She pulled away from him, slowly, and he helped ease her onto the bed. She kept hold of his arm, though, and tugged on it, beckoning him to stretch out beside her.

"But your grandmother. Jenkins."

He looked around for any sign of a security camera.

"He already knows you're here," she said, her eyes half closed. "He knows everything."

"All right," he said, lying back on the bed but feeling ill at ease. "So you'll think it over? About coming to live with me?"

"Uh-huh," she responded, snuggling against him.

"We don't have to stay here. In this town. We can go somewhere else, anywhere you want. Change our names, our identities, so no one would find us. Just as long as we're together. Essence? Are you listening?"

He shook her gently by the shoulder, but she was already asleep. The silence of the room was disturbed by the sound of her breathing, light and airy. He lay awake thinking, listening to her breathe. This room, this mansion, her way of life—it all seemed so foreign. He might as well be lying next to her in the Taj Mahal.

Eventually, the candles flickered and died, and the shadows dissolved. Or else it was his mind dissolving into a strange, new darkness that seemed merely an alleyway to his dreams.

***

Standing outside the gate, Daryl trained the long telephoto lens on the balcony, adjusting the focus. The lens came in handy when documenting the location of a vehicle designated for repossession.

Now, said "vehicle" was on foot, having climbed a trellis—how romantic—into some strange young woman's window. He had snapped off a dozen shots, catching them as they both went inside. There was just enough light spilling from the interior of the mansion to illuminate their faces. So here he was, positioned outside the gate with a clear shot, waiting for one or both of them to reemerge. He heard footsteps, and Mandy joined him, a bottle of wine in hand. Without hesitation, Daryl took a long swallow right out of the bottle.

"So who is she?" he asked, tossing his head toward the mansion. He invited Mandy to join him cross-legged on the sidewalk outside the fence.

"Essence," Mandy informed him. "Essence Warner."

She told him as much of the story as she knew about Essence

and Essence's mother, Fortune; about her father, Jamaal, the Wax of Sax; about her grandmothers, Mrs. Warner and Mrs. Waxman; and about Will Archer, new curator of the Waxman Museum.

Curator! Daryl still couldn't get over it. It seemed a bit of a career stretch from auto claims. "And your relationship, if you don't mind my asking?"

"Just friends," she said with a shrug.

Done with her wine, Mandy put her head in Daryl's lap and fell asleep. Daryl must have nodded off himself while seated. It was just breaking daylight, when there he was, Will-Alan emerging like a cat onto a hot balcony roof. And there she was, in all her lithe, beautiful essence. An appropriate name, that. A slim tarantula of a woman, no doubt, who had spun Will-Alan into her web.

Setting Mandy's head gently aside, Daryl stood up and raised his camera.

Snap, snap.

He zoomed in closer. The image was clear as gold, and he snapped away, afraid to lose his catch of the day. First shots, darkness. Last shots, daylight. Add in the date and time stamps, and what further proof would Abbey need?

"Come on," he said, crouching, nudging Mandy's shoulder.

"Huh?" she said, waking.

She looked up at him and smiled, then extended her hand, which he took to lift her to her feet. She stumbled forward and he clutched her around the waist to keep her from falling.

The only question was how much, if anything, should he tell Abbey about her husband. And the photographs, the digital images of Will-Alan's infidelity. Should he keep a lid on them? Or expose them to the light of day?

Chapter 29

At the museum, it was a blue day, and this is how Will felt as he went through his ordinary morning routines, preparing the museum for its lack of visitors: blue. It was a Saturday, so there were no field trips, no school visits, planned for the day. But he set up the viewing room, anyway, with its VHS cassette and put the background music on, the one disk that played over and over throughout the day, then took a seat in the darkened area, ruminating.

Will had left Essence at dawn, crawling down the ladder this time and racing across the lawn ahead of feeding time for Crimson and Clover. If he timed it right, Essence said, he could take the shorter route and beat it to the back gate before Jenkins opened their cages. This way, he could make his exit unobserved and, more importantly, undevoured.

The idea of her staying with Will in his apartment was left suspended. Will was afraid to broach the subject, fearful if he brought it back up in the light of day, Essence would challenge it, and it would dissolve like a lozenge.

He was about to leave the viewing room when he heard the tinkling of the bell. Emerging through the curtains, he came across Essence in the doorway, wearing a long skirt and short-sleeved blouse. In one hand she clutched a small white vinyl traveling case with a braided handle and brass snaps offset in her other hand by a larger cloth valise of a carpetbag variety.

"Essence!" Will shouted, taking three giant steps to come right up to her, reaching out his hand to make sure she was real.

"I've never had a reason to pack before," she said, looking down at her luggage.

"Never?"

"To tell you the truth, I've never even crossed the river. I've always stopped halfway, where my mother—"

Will wasn't sure what to say. He just stood there staring at her, smiling, feeling he was taking part in a fairytale, a reverse Cinderella, where the maiden has found her prince, although he didn't exactly feel like one.

"Maybe I should go," she said. "You've work to do."

"Not at all. Come on in."

He took her luggage from her. The vinyl case felt strangely light.

"So this means …"

"I've thought about what you said and decided to give it a try. Surprise!" she said meekly.

"I am surprised. Have you had breakfast?"

Essence shook her head.

"Me either. I'll make popcorn."

At this, Essence laughed outright.

"Popcorn for breakfast?"

"I'm afraid it's all we have."

While Will prepared the oil and placed dry kernels in the popping machine, a brightly lit carnival-type contraption on wheels with red stenciling, she stared at the display case that held the gold-plated sax, the glass restored to offer full protection. Then she moved over to another case, this one with Jamaal's extensive collection of used reeds.

"He used to pocket them, on the road," she said. "He thought it good luck if he had something to take home with him, to add to his collection. He thought it guaranteed a safe journey."

"How do you know that?"

"My grandmother told me."

Will didn't have to wonder which grandmother, but he asked

anyway.

"Sybil Waxman?"

"She's told me all about him. We've had long sessions, she and I, where he was our only topic of conversation. All pre-Fortune, of course."

"Are you sad? That you never knew him?"

"You can't miss something you never had." She brushed her hair from her forehead and leaned toward him. "Kiss me," she beckoned.

He did as asked, chastely, until the popcorn started popping. Drawing back, Will opened the door to the machine and filled up a bag with the trowel.

"Butter?" he asked.

"No, I'm on a diet."

"Seriously?"

"Of course butter." She gave his upper arm a light punch with her fist.

"Take in a movie?" he asked.

He turned off the overhead soundtrack and held the curtain open for her while they went into the darkened theater. Essence took a seat in the back as Will started the videotape. Then he joined her, pressing his leg against hers. She leaned her head against his shoulder, putting one popped kernel at a time into her mouth. It was as though they were on a first date, watching a home movie. The tape was somewhere in the middle, where it had left off from the previous day's showing as bored patrons made their exit. Jamaal stood center stage with his quartet, playing a local gig for an anniversary or family reunion. The sound was low-quality, but the tremulous tones of the sax carried through.

"Wait a second!" Will exclaimed. He jumped up, bumping Essence off his shoulder.

"What gives?" she protested, but he was already at the recorder, rewinding a few frames, then pressing pause so that the tape stuttered in place.

"Look," he said. He pointed to a woman who had just turned toward the camera. "I've seen this film a dozen times. I guess I never paid much attention." Will studied the features of the face, the sharp nose, the high cheekbones, her hair in loose curls. Give her a set of wrinkles and her hair a blue tint and you'd have …

"Well? Are you going to keep me in suspense?"

"Mrs. Gossett," Will said, staring at the screen.

"Your landlady?"

"I didn't know she was this big of a fan."

"My father had a lot of … followers," Essence said casually.

"It's funny thinking of her as one of Jamaal's—your father's—groupies."

"More like a cougar," Essence surmised.

Will rewound the tape, then played it forward, this time keeping his eyes on the woman he had singled out, watching as she bobbed with the music. Abruptly, a man entered the frame from the left and took hold of her arm, pulling her away from the stage. They pantomimed an argument, the man tugging, the woman resisting, their mouths moving but the words an indistinct grumble overdubbed by the blasting volume of the sax. Within seconds, the woman was gone, yanked directly across the camera lens in closeup, but not before registering a grimace of disapproval—or anger?

"Wonder if that was Walter," he thought aloud.

"Walter?"

"Her husband. I'm getting the impression he didn't care for his wife's infatuation with Jamaal."

Will was still trying to fathom his landlady as a groupie when he heard a cough from behind.

"Mandy," he said. "I didn't hear you come in."

"I came in the back way," she said.

"But it's a Saturday," Will reminded her.

"Thought I'd catch up on some work."

"Have you been standing there long?"

"Oh, I don't know, sort of." She sounded caught off guard, as if she had been doing something she shouldn't. She stared at the television screen in a contemplative sort of way.

"Mandy?"

"Sorry. It's just I heard what you were saying about Mrs. Gossett and—"

"Hello, Mandy," Essence said, rising. "I've heard a lot about you." This struck Will as funny since he didn't think he had ever mentioned her. Perhaps Mrs. Waxman had filled her in.

"Oh," Mandy said, looking even more embarrassed, her face flushing. "I didn't know it was you."

Will stopped the tape and turned on the lights.

"Mandy, this is—"

"Oh, you don't need to introduce me to Essence Warner. She's like royalty around these parts."

"And Essence, this is—"

"Mandy, so I gather," Essence said.

Mandy crossed the floor briskly and, stopping deftly in front of Essence, held out her hand.

Essence, chewing kernels of popcorn slowly, like a wad of gum, studied it, then held up her hand to indicate it was coated in butter. As though prompted, Mandy handed her a handkerchief out of her purse. The handkerchief was blue.

"What brings you here?" Mandy asked.

Essence flashed her eyes at Will.

"Oh," Mandy said, seeming to understand. "Well, I have work to do."

"I guess I do, too," Will said. He took a seat at the computer to process emails. Mandy went to her archivist's desk, and Essence wandered over to observe.

"Still chopping my mother out of their pictures, are you?" she asked, after a time.

Mandy looked up, locking eyes with her antagonist.

"I've got a sudden headache," she said, gathering her things. She gave Will an air-blown kiss, then blew through the museum like a whirlwind, removing her phone on her way out the door.

"She doesn't like me," Essence observed.

"She doesn't know you," Will replied.

He escorted Essence to the archive room, where she began sorting through the photos Mandy left on display.

"I've looked through them," he admitted. "Why is it there aren't any pictures with you in them?"

"Most of these are pre-baby. Pre-me. The ones with my mother and me are at home. These are ones my Grandmother Warner donated. She didn't want any reminder of the two of them together." She heaved a heavy sigh. "There aren't any with me and my father in them either. Apparently, when I came along, he didn't want anything to do with me."

"I think you might be wrong about that," Will told her. "I'm pretty sure he had been intending to settle down. You know, make a go of it with your mother—and you. All three of you together as a family."

Essence studied him with narrow, questioning eyes.

"What makes you say that?"

"His letters. To your mother. From his time on the road. I found them in Jenkins's bedroom when I was searching for your mother's locket."

"You read them?"

Will decided it best to bypass the subject, delicate as it was involving a potential breach of trust.

"I was planning on giving them to you. But they sort of got misplaced on the night of the—"

Essence cut him off sharply.

"Let's not talk about that night. Ever." She turned back to the task at hand. "It might take a while, but I'm going to match up and tape them all together, the way they should be. I don't care what my Nana says. She can't go around cutting my mother out of my father's story just to please her version of the past."

Taking a seat at the computer, Will left her to it. He didn't want to be intrusive, but, as it turned out, he hardly let her get started.

"No way!" he exclaimed as a new message popped up.

"What is it?" Essence asked, coming over.

"Another email addressed to N.L."

"N.L.?" she inquired, peering over his shoulder.

"The L. stands for 'lover.'"

"And the N?"

"The first couple of emails were much more explicit with their terminology. Lately, they've settled for acronyms."

"Oh," she said, comprehending, then read out loud:

So the s-h-i-t's finally hit the fan, has it? And you think you're being so smart in harboring a fugitive. Well, I've got news for you, buck-o, you're in for a big surprise if you believe in happy endings. P.S. Always watch your back. There are people who don't want you to be together and who will prevent it at any cost. Who do you think you are, anyway? Tony Orlando & Dawn???!!! Yours, in all matters of color.

"Colorful character, huh?" Will observed.

"Somehow, whoever it is, knows our plan." Essence turned around, as though to catch someone standing behind her. Will looked, too, stretching his gaze past the lobby and through the glass door to the street, where he caught sight of a couple passersby. Nothing to raise an alarm.

"Who would write such … tripe?" Essence wondered.

"They've been sending these things every other day. You get desensitized fairly quickly."

"But who would know? My grandmother? Jenkins?"

"Mandy, for one. And anyone, really, who saw you arrive at the museum with luggage and who knows anything at all about us."

"Like the whole town?"

"Probably, but who's this Tony Orlando?"

"That, I do know. My mother left behind a huge collection of CDs. I've listened to most of them. Surely you've heard 'Tie a Yellow Ribbon 'Round the Old Oak Tree'?"

"That was him?"

"Them. You're forgetting Dawn, two beautiful Black women. They were the real talent. Tony was just this Italian-looking guy with a mullet and cheesy moustache." She took a knowing look at Will's hair inching over his collar. "At least you don't have the moustache anymore."

"What are you saying?" Will smiled in mock defense.

Essence took a seat beside him and put her head in a nest formed by crossed arms.

"Wake me up when you're ready to leave," she said, her voice subdued by her own embrace.

"Then you'll be coming to my place?" he asked, just to make sure.

"Mm-mm," she murmured, and that was good enough for Will. He took it for a "yes."

Chapter 30

A disturbance in the foyer woke Daryl from a late afternoon nap. The breeze stirring the curtains made him drowsy, warm as it was, and he had fallen into a light doze on the divan. Ordinarily, the Victorian Arms was quiet, tranquil, this time of day. But now he heard a ruckus coming from way down below, echoing all the way up the stairwell.

Shouts! Oaths! Curses!

Was this part of his dream?

He descended the stairs quietly, catlike, sneaking around the final corner overlooking the foyer, where he paused, catching the finale of a scene that seemed scripted out of a soap opera.

At the foot of the stairs sat an elderly woman in a wheelchair, her gray hair partially covered with a silk babushka, large opaque sunglasses giving the impression of an owl. Behind her stood the visage of a bodyguard, well built for a forty-something, clad in a dress shirt that showed off taut, muscular arms and out the top of which sprouted a neck the size of a small tree trunk. Before them, as though seeking admittance to a stronghold, were Will-Alan and the young woman he had seen through his camera lens: Essence.

"Well, then," the woman was finishing up a tirade, "if you're so determined to play the harlot, I have no more business here. But keep in mind, young lady, I have full power of attorney over you, and I can decide to have you put away again at any time. Jenkins!"

Observing from the safety of her apartment doorway was Phyllis Gossett in her standard blue bathrobe. Another observer was peering out of her separate apartment on the ground floor as well, a thin spindle of a middle-aged woman with a ghostly pallor, who also preferred to remain half-hidden.

"I do wish, Florence, you would change your mind and come inside with me?" Phyllis proposed. "I could fix you some tea?"

The woman named Florence tightened her mouth into a thin, compressed seam, giving the impression of a lip-sewn corpse that made Daryl shudder. Even Phyllis retreated a few steps into the haven of her apartment.

"No thank you, my dear," she said. "I'm so sorry to have disturbed the peace of your … establishment. Please be so good to look after my granddaughter. She seems incapable of looking after herself."

And with that, the bodyguard wheeled her around Will-Alan and Essence, who stood mute, impassive, side by side, the girl holding a carrying case that made her look somehow all prim and proper, as though she were boarding a bus.

"Careful, Jenkins," the woman commanded as he navigated her through the front door. "How I do hate a scene."

Daryl chose this lull in the action to continue his descent on the stairs, making his entrance seem as unpremeditated as possible.

"Everything all right?" he asked.

"Huh?" Will-Alan seemed coming out of a daze. "Yeah, sure. Everything's fine."

He took a step forward, past Daryl, who gave way. But then, when the girl remained stationary, he turned.

"Essence? Are you coming?"

His voice seemed plaintive, not pleading, but at the same time unsure.

Without speaking, without looking up, the girl lifted her leg to the first step. Will-Alan held out his hand, and after studying it a moment, Essence took it and let herself be led up the rest of the way. Daryl watched them disappear, rising into the cathedral gloom of the stairwell.

"All clear?" Phyllis said, poking her nose back through her apartment door.

Daryl shrugged. He assumed so, but he couldn't be sure.

***

In the apartment, there seemed a coldness in the very air, as Essence walked around slowly, examining this and that. She paused a long while in front of the sofa, staring at it as though at a wake.

"So this is where it happened," she observed quietly.

"Yeah," Will said. "It's where Mrs. Gossett found him."

A moment more and she turned to Will with a calm, steady look. Her eyes held no tears.

"One thing's for sure. I won't be sleeping on the couch."

Will took hold of her hand in both of his, playing the part of a sympathetic undertaker at a funeral, until she excused herself to the bathroom. As soon as she closed the door, Will ducked into the Hex Room, removed the photo of his wife and child from the windowsill, and put it in a desk drawer just before Essence came back out. There hadn't been a toilet flush, just running of the tap, and her face was all wet.

"Couldn't find a clean towel," she said, giving a slight smile, as though the previous exchange had never happened. "Typical bachelor pad."

"I'll get one for you." He made a move toward the closet, but she stopped him with an outstretched arm.

"It's all right, I like the feel of the water."

"You must be famished," he said.

"Very."

Will scrambled some eggs and made some toast, and they sat side by side on the futon, as though at a picnic.

"Do you think we're at a point where I can get your phone number?" he asked.

"Sure," she laughed. "I thought you'd never ask."

It seemed everything might relax between them after all.

***

That evening, they sat side by side on the futon, staring at the river and the doomed suspension bridge, talking about her father, as Will divulged what he had gleaned from Jamaal's letters: descriptions of hijinks from his life on the road, pranks he played on his bandmates, episodes designed to amuse.

"That sounds about right," Essence said. "One thing I know from my Nana, he was a rebel at school. Sort of a class clown. Always getting into trouble. Joking with authority. There was only one thing he took seriously."

"His saxophone?"

"Yes, that's right. His music. It's how he and my mother met. His combo was hired to play at a debutantes' ball thrown by my Grandmother Warner. Funny, isn't it, that my grandmother inadvertently was the one who brought them together?"

"Ironic," Will agreed. "Very."

"Come here," she said, so calmly Will had the impression he was the visitor and she the host. "Sit beside me." After he sat, she whispered, "Closer." And he moved closer, so they were touching, attached at the hip.

The futon had cushion-style pillows to act as a headboard, and they leaned against these, without saying anything for a while. Will tried to calm his breathing to match Essence's. Hers was so even, so regular. Will's was nervous in comparison. He felt self-conscious.

She yielded as he pressed himself more closely against her. He was wearing his usual polo shirt, she the same short-sleeved blouse, the two top buttons unbuttoned. He began by kissing her earlobe.

"That tickles," she said, pulling her head away, and he ran his fingers through her hair. Taking hold of her jaw, he drew her back to him and kissed her on the mouth, her lips responding, open now, her breath coming in bursts, her eyes half-closed. He ran his fingers inside her shirt and felt the roundness of her breasts. Dipping a finger within the fabric of her bra, he plucked at a nipple, massaging it between thumb and forefinger until she moaned, but then she leaned forward, pushing his hand away.

"We can't," she whispered. "I want to, but we can't. I'm just not—right—down there. I don't feel—ready. I'm not sure when—if ever." She leaned her face onto his shoulder. He stroked her hair over and over, feeling her body convulse, then lowered his hand and rubbed her back in gentle circles, letting her break over and over against him.

"I know," he said, softly, as she grew quiet and her breathing became more regular. "I'm sorry, I shouldn't have."

She pulled away and wiped her eyes on her sleeve.

"Don't look at me," she said, her voice muffled in the crook of her arm. "I hate myself this way."

He ran the back of his hand down her cheek, brushing away the wetness. He wanted so much to show her that he valued her as she was, that in his eyes she was a whole person, but now he worried they would never be the same after the scarring of that one unspeakable night.

"I'm sorry," she said, drawing back. "I know you were just trying to—"

"It's all right."

He kissed her lightly on her brow. They lay down on the futon, facing each other, holding each other, foreheads pressed together at an angle, enclosed within the deepening twilight.

Will didn't fall asleep right away. He lay in a daze. In a way, he felt content simply lying beside the one he loved. The drone of the pipes played a steady, calming note that made him believe the ghost was content as well.

"It's like a lullaby," Essence murmured in her drowsiness.

"Yes," Will agreed. "Very soothing."

Maybe Jamaal was finally at peace now that his daughter had been rescued, as he had beckoned Will to do when he first moved into the apartment.

And Will was beginning to feel at peace, too.

***

Sunday was theirs to spend together—the entire day. They kept a low profile, choosing to hang out in Will's apartment without venturing out except to grab bagels from a delicatessen around the corner.

That evening, Essence sketched portraits of Will as he read excerpts from his yellow ledger—snippets of poetry, the odd haiku, notes to self—journal entries he had never shown anyone, not even Abbey. He complimented her art as she did his writing, maintaining straight faces for as long as they could. Then they broke down laughing at what poor liars they were.

"It's good to hear you laughing," Essence said. "You're always so serious. How come?"

"I don't know," Will answered. "I've never thought about it." But now he was considering it as he might a fault in his complexion, a leftover pimple from his acne days as a teenager.

"Tell me about you," she said, turning her head slightly, so that her hair brushed his cheek.

"What do you want to know?"

"Tell me about your wife."

Will felt taken aback.

"You know?"

"I've always known."

"How?"

"I can always tell when I'm with a man who's married. I can

tell when he's holding something back. There's always a feeling of guilt in the air."

"It's not quite like that."

And that's when Will decided to take the photograph out of the drawer.

He told her everything except for his name change, his exchange of identity—it was just another complication in a complicated tale. After he was through, she just sat there, staring at the photograph, which she held with both hands.

"I didn't know you had a child. Will you go back to her? To them?"

"No, I can't. It's hard to explain, and I know it sounds cruel. It's just that, I made a promise to myself."

"You're punishing yourself. That I get. But have you ever considered how you're punishing them?"

"Yes, but it's never been my intention. It's just, I'm dead to all that. And I wanted to make it easy on them, my wife especially, to let go, if she can just think of me as dead. I'm dead to everything that happened before. To who I was. Who I used to be."

"Dead, but not reborn." She gave the photograph back to him. Now he wished he hadn't told her about his past, about his family—the family he used to have. All that knowledge seemed a blunt wedge.

"I feel like I'm coming between you," she said. "You and them. You and your past. And I don't like feeling that way."

He moved over beside her. He put a hand on her thigh. The other hand he placed behind her back, feeling her ribs, her breathing, her lungs pressing against his palm.

"You aren't," he said. "You're what I have now. You're what I have in this moment. And that's all that matters."

She placed a hand on his, pressing it firmly.

"I don't want to lose you," she said.

Gradually, as the evening deepened, Will felt able to let down his guard. There was no need for him to look out the windows of the Hex Room. No need to study the bridge for the supple form of the woman who lay beside him.

There was just this one night to get through until July 4th. Independence Day. It would be a different sort of independence now that he and Essence were together, for better or worse. He would be free of his past life, his past self, and she would be free of her captors.

Except, when he awoke in the morning, Essence was gone.

Chapter 31

True, he had woken late. It was going on nine o'clock. He wondered if a hunger pang had taken her to the bakery around the corner, and when she didn't return after another half-hour, he went to see for himself if she had ever popped in. The owner shrugged off his inquiry in broken English. No one of her description had been in this morning, "No, sir!" By her tone, it was quite possible to infer she felt herself wrongfully accused.

Back at the Victorian Arms, it took him another half hour to decide to use the landline to dial her number. Four rings took him to Essence's voicemail, but how should he answer? What should he say? He hadn't thought it through, and after a few seconds' hesitation, he burbled, "Hi, Essence. Just calling to see—" Mercifully, a long beep signaled the cutoff, and he decided those words would be enough of a request for a return call.

Had she left him for good? Had he divulged too much about his past, about Abbey and Joel? Maybe he had scared her off.

"I don't like feeling that I'm coming between you." Isn't this what she had said—or something to that effect? Maybe she had decided to remove herself from the equation. Or maybe he was overreacting? It's possible she just needed some space.

That she had left behind her valise reassured him—it held a couple changes of clothes—but the other item of luggage, the white vinyl carrying case with the brass snaps, made him wonder what it contained. She had neither opened it nor referred to it. He thought it over before clicking the latches, recalling Pandora's box, but figured a glance couldn't hurt. What he discovered dumbfounded him. The case was packed solid with banded bundles of twenty-dollar bills.

Why would she leave so much money behind? Where would she have gotten so much cash in the first place? He could only assume it was stolen, so wouldn't this make him an accomplice? It seemed more important than ever to find her and try to get some answers.

Downstairs, he knocked on Mrs. Gossett's door.

"Don't you know it's a holiday?" she complained. By the length of time it took her to answer, he must have pulled her out of bed. Her hair was disheveled, her bathrobe askew.

"Has Essence been by?" he asked, trying to keep the urgency in his voice to a minimum.

"Don't tell me she's flown the coop already?"

Disregarding the barb, he asked, "If she should happen to stop by—"

"Yes, yes, I'll tell her you're desperately in love with her and can't live without her," she interjected with a smile, which Will didn't return.

"Well, yeah," he said, drily, "something like that."

Before turning to leave, he eyed her curiously, trying to imagine her as a younger woman, picturing her in Jamaal's arms.

"Something wrong, dear?"

"No, nothing." He shook the image out of his head. "I was just thinking I've never seen you out of your bathrobe."

"Trust me, Will." She gave a coquettish toss of her hair. "If only I were younger, I would certainly give you the opportunity."

"I'm sorry. I didn't mean to imply—"

She cackled at his obvious discomfiture.

"Oh, Will," she said, placing a hand on his shoulder. "I am so going to miss you when you're gone."

Gone? he wondered. Gone where? What an odd thing to say. Did she know something he didn't?

Bowing sheepishly out of her presence, he made his way to

the bridge, pausing at each booth and food stand and sideshow game that had been set up, as though magically, overnight. Crowds were already starting to form. The last Bridge Day Celebration, advertised on flyers stapled to telephone poles either side of the river, was underway, coinciding with the Fourth of July, which is why the museum was closed.

Already, large jackhammers had been erected on either end of the bridge with backhoes and dump trucks positioned nearby, making the bridge impassable to vehicular traffic. And today was the last day for foot traffic as well before demolition commenced the day after by breaking up the roadway.

Unsure where to look for her next, he passed a combo on the Ohio end of the bridge playing jazz.

Jazz!

Of course! Her Grandmother Waxman's. It seemed a logical choice of destination.

***

The cab let him off in front of a two-story Cape Cod in an upscale neighborhood he wouldn't have guessed belonged to the town, it seemed so new and well-kept.

"Need me to wait up?" the cabbie asked, making change, which Will handed back as a tip.

"No, that's all right," he answered, calculating the distance back to the main part of town and the bridge.

It took all of a minute to walk up the drive. A stone goose dressed in a Bengals uniform greeted him at the front door where he rang the bell. After a moment, Mrs. Waxman opened it with wide-eyed surprise, which seemed genuine, not a stage act. It was so unusual for her to be caught unawares.

"William? What brings you here?"

"I thought I might find Essence."

"Essence? Why would Essence be here? She never visits

here. And why are you looking for her in the first place?"

She seemed to be regaining her old, confident, bullying self, but Will didn't let himself get flustered.

"I'm afraid for her. I'm afraid she's going to do something terrible tonight and she doesn't want me to stop her."

"Terrible? Such as?"

Yes, this would be a typical Waxman approach to a problem, adopting a schoolmarm tone and arching an eyebrow.

"I'm afraid she's going to kill herself." There, it was best just to state it directly, his worst fear. "I'm afraid she's going to jump from the bridge."

His employer stared at him for a moment with a serious frown, then broke into a grin that widened into a laugh, short and abrupt.

"Tut, there you go with this wild theory again. If you think my granddaughter capable of such an act, you don't know her very well at all. To do herself in on the anniversary of her mother's death? How maudlin. Essence is not what you would call the sentimental type. If she were planning such a thing, don't you think she would have confided in me?"

Will wavered on the threshold, not daring to contradict her.

"Have you tried her other grandmother's house?" she suggested. "I can drive you over there if you'd like." She remained standing in the doorway, a wax figure, her visage unreadable, as she waited for him to make up his mind.

This was something he was having a hard time doing. If Essence had abandoned him, it made sense she would retreat to her Grandmother Warner's. It was her home, after all. But why hadn't she left him a note? Why hadn't she left a message with Mrs. Gossett? And why had she left behind all that money? That was the big question.

"I won't need a ride," Will said, taking his leave. "I just need to—" Actually, he wasn't sure what he needed, aside from trying to clear his mind. "I just need to walk."

And that's what he did, along the little cobbled path, down the concrete drive, and out to the curb.

When he turned around for one last look, he thought he saw a curtain flutter, but it was that time of morning when the sunlight could play tricks on a windowpane.

✳✳✳

For a second, Essence was afraid he had seen her behind the curtain. She stepped back, away from it, and let her vision of Will walking so forlornly down the street linger in her mind's eye, like an evaporating cloud.

It hadn't been her intention to desert him. She had woken up early. Birds were chirping outside the Hex Room, as Will referred to it, their shadows fluttering against the blinds. Instead of falling back asleep, she gently prodded herself away from Will and placed her pillow in the space she had left, smiling when she saw Will put his arms around it, cuddling it as though it were something alive.

She dressed quietly and slipped out the door, trying to keep from creaking the stairs as she descended to the foyer. She thought she might, in fact, visit the bakery around the corner. She was drawn by the aroma of fresh-baked bagels but found out she was a half hour early. She watched the baker mixing dough behind the counter, but the woman, middle-aged and matronly, hadn't looked up, absorbed in her work. Wouldn't it be nice to have something that absorbed all her worries and fears and doubts like a vat of rising dough?

Instead of returning to the Victorian Arms, she kept walking, arriving at the bridge. Usually such a sleepy town of a holiday morning, there were already quite a few people moving about. Large walled tents were being pitched along the doomed thoroughfare, the vendors setting up their wares for the bridge closing carnival. How odd to be so visible in the predawn hours of a lightening sky, but no one cast her a second glance. They were too busy getting ready. The fair would start later this morning.

A moment of panic jolted her. She had left behind the white carrying case and all the money it contained—the $100,000 of her grandmother's emergency fund. Originally, she had intended to convince Will to cover for her as the sole "eyewitness" of her plunge into oblivion. Together, they would carry out a plan that would enable her to elude the grasp of her Grandmother Warner. Once the authorities had concluded their futile search for her body, Will would join up with her in some other city—far from New Bloomfield and East Orange—hopefully long before her grandmother ever became aware of the worthless paper she had substituted.

The only question was whether Will would agree to her plan on such short notice. What if he felt she was only using him to play his part in the ruse? She kept walking, her thoughts turning over and over. Only after she crossed the bridge did she realize where she was going, and she let her footsteps take her there.

And now, tucked away in her Grandma Waxman's house, a plan began to form in her mind that appealed to her sense of fair play. She would notify Will to meet her at the bridge at the stroke of midnight, and make sure to bring her luggage. But she would instruct him to open the carrying case to check and make sure its contents were still intact. Discovering what was inside, would he show up for her as prearranged? Or would he take the money and run? She didn't think so, but this way, she would know for sure. On top of that, leaving the money for Will to discover would seem a sign of good faith on her part. Then he would know she wasn't just taking advantage of him as a foil.

The trouble was relaying the message. As she picked up her

phone, her Nana appeared in the doorway with a tray of tea.

"I thought you might like something warm," she said, her eyes made of glass, so it was impossible, as always, to read her emotions. "I'm surprised you didn't leap out the window after him," she added with a wry smile as she poured two cups.

"It occurred to me," Essence replied, taking a cup with both hands, observing her grandmother over the rim.

"So why did you let me shoo him away like some pesky moth?"

She took a chair across from her granddaughter, leaving a comfortable space between. That was one thing Essence liked about her Nana Other: she didn't press, she worked by innuendo.

"I wasn't ready to face him."

"And will you be?"

"I'm not sure. I have an idea I might."

"One can never be sure in matters of the heart, no matter what the poets have to say."

"Is that why you hate my mother so, because she was sure, and your son wasn't?"

Sybil sipped her tea quietly, eyeing Essence through thick lashes.

"I don't hate your mother," she said quietly.

"So that's why you've been cropping her out of all their pictures together? Because you like her?"

Her Nana looked startled, but only for a moment, before her eyes went back to their typical slits.

"The biography of Jamaal Waxman is about my son—not his many consorts."

"She was more than just another consort. Is that why you hate her?"

"I repeat, I do not—did not ever—hate Fortune Warner."

"She was sure about Jamaal, wasn't she? But she threw

herself off the bridge when my father didn't show up. And it was his despondency that drove him to heroin. If only *he* had been sure about *her*, the two of them, in return."

"Your father did not die of a heroin overdose!"

"I know, so you keep telling everyone. The whole town knows you think he was murdered. But who would have murdered him? The case has been cold for twenty years."

"Nineteen to be precise." Having finished her tea with a delicate slurp, her Nana rose onto her stout legs done up in sheer stockings. "Stay as long as you want, I won't give you away, not even if your other grandmother"—and here she allowed a sneer to cross her face—"comes around snooping with that Aussie bodyguard of hers."

"I won't stay long."

Her grandmother halted at the bedroom door.

"What is it?" Essence asked.

Her Nana turned in the doorway and cast a low, level gaze at her granddaughter that raised the hairs on the back of her neck. "Promise me something. Promise me you'll stay here tonight, the whole night through?"

There was a worry in her eyes she had never seen before, her grandmother always seeming so self-possessed.

"And miss the fireworks?"

"You've seen fireworks."

Her grandmother waited for an answer until Essence nodded her head.

"Thank you," she said and left, closing the door behind her.

But before it swung shut, Essence made up her mind. At midnight, the actions of one Will Archer would decide her fate. She would let him decide everything.

Chapter 32

It took less than an hour to make it to the front gate of the Warner grounds where Will confronted the security camera positioned atop one of the gateposts. He wasn't sure if there was audio, but he called out anyway.

"Jenkins, hello! It's me!" he shouted, waving his arms. "It's urgent, so if you'll please let me in."

He waited, feeling very exposed and quite vulnerable. Who knew? Aside from changing the keycode, it's possible Jenkins had installed a machine gun nest in one of the sycamores towering over the fence since his last escapade. He had confidence, though, that he was being watched, observed.

Soon enough, he spotted Jenkins in his Crocodile Dundee hat with its bent-back brim and dressed in baggy khakis traipsing across the lawn with Crimson and Clover harnessed on two long leashes, giving the impression he was being pulled across by powerful steeds on an invisible chariot. Why leashes? What did Jenkins have in mind to do, open the gate and sic the tigers on him?

"Hello, old boy, what brings you to this neck of the woods?" he asked jauntily, coming up to the bars of the gate.

"Essence," Will stated matter of fact. "Is she here?"

"That depends on who's asking."

What sort of absurdity was this?

"I'm asking. That's who's asking."

Will felt impatient. He wanted nothing so much as to punch Jenkins in the nose through the bars, then open the gate and step over his prostrate body, but he knew how that would turn out.

"Well, she's not here, Mac—and that's a fact."

"Could you give her a message? If she does turn up?"

"Your little romance not working out then, heh? Lost the filly before she was broken in?"

Now he really wanted to lunge at his adversary but held his stance.

"Just tell her I'm not giving up on her. I'm not going anywhere. And I'll keep her … property safe until she comes back for it."

"Property, you say? What property would that be?"

What was he thinking? He shouldn't have used such a big word to describe such a small package. He watched Jenkins sink the corners of his mouth into a full-blown frown. He had only meant to let Essence know he knew about the money.

"Nothing. Just something she's left at my apartment."

"Describe it." A firm command.

"Nothing really. Luggage. That's all I meant to say."

Jenkins lowered his head, contemplating nothingness, it seemed. The tigers, bored, strolled back and forth, crisscrossing their leashes, so Jenkins had to keep changing hands to prevent their tangling.

"You mean that white satchel she was carrying up to your flat?"

"Satchel?"

"The one with the brass snaps."

So Jenkins had his suspicions as to its contents, Will surmised. Otherwise, why be so concerned about some dumb piece of luggage?.

"Never mind," Jenkins said. "No worries. I'll be sure to pass on the message—if she shows. But you know our Essence, always out and about with someone or other on her arm."

Now that Will was used to the goading, he chose to ignore Jenkins's jibe altogether. He chalked this up as another fruitless path. Was Essence at home as Mrs. Waxman had suggested? Had

Mrs. Warner instructed Jenkins to turn Will away? Either way, the effect was for Will to retreat.

"Hey, Archer!" Jenkins called through the gate. Will looked over his shoulder without pausing. "You be careful with that satchel, eh? You be very careful, all right?"

Without breaking stride, Will gave an uncertain shrug and moved on.

***

Dusting off her husband Walter's urn on the mantel was always at the top of Phyllis Gossett's to-do list, but today she found she had neglected her wifely duty till late in the day.

"So sorry, my dear," she cooed, feathering the thin film of dust that had accrued since the day before. She was still in her robe, but what of it? She only had three tenants who might take notice and she didn't believe any of them would take offense.

There had been a fourth tenant, a self-proclaimed director of "nature" films, but he had left town in a hurry, skipping out on his lease, shortly after Will Archer pounded insistently on his door in a rage, demanding he show his weaselly little face. It was just as well. He had never been a particularly sociable guest, despite the conversations they had had about his need of a "model" for a film he was directing. This left just the three of them: a Miss Lonely-Hearts on the first floor, the delightful Daryl Harris on the second, and the problematic Will Archer on the third.

As she steeped a pot of tea, she thought about their previous encounter, marking the beginning of his search for the missing Essence Warner. She had begun to think of Will as a son, one of her own, as she had adopted other tenants his age in the past—the two previous curators came to mind—but now, of a sudden, she could detect a strange disconnect between them. There was something in his gaze that hadn't been there before, a suspicious scrutiny, as though he were trying to husk the nut of her to get at her kernel, her core.

The phone rang as she added a dribble from her flask to the teapot.

"Hello, Mrs. Gossett? This is Essence. You know, Essence Warner."

How odd to get a call from the very person she was only just thinking about. What did Jung call it? Serendipity? No, it was some other term beginning with an "s."

"Yes, dear? How may I help you? You know your … beau is looking for you?"

"My beau? That's funny. What a funny thing to call him. Anyway, yes. About Will. It's very important I get a message to him. Can you take this down for me? Do you have something to write with?"

The poor girl was obviously in some distress.

"Of course, dear, of course. Let me find a pen."

There was a pause that lingered for a count of one, two, three . . .

"Tell him to meet me at our usual place at midnight tonight. Midnight sharp. It's vitally important that he knows to meet me."

"I'll make sure to post it to his door," she said without writing it down. "At midnight tonight. Your usual place. Oh, and where would that be?"

"He'll know, just make sure he gets the message." Then, as an afterthought: "And there's one more thing. Tell him to bring my luggage. And ask him to check the contents of the white carrying case. Okay? It's very important that he check the contents first, to make sure it's all there. Did you get all of this?"

Such manners!

"I will, dear, I will. But this 'usual place' to which you refer? Is it the bridge or the playground?" This had the effect she intended of catching Essence's breath in her throat. "Oh, come now, my dear. It's a small town on both sides of the river, you can't expect to keep your rendezvous so secret."

She heard a distinct swallow on the other end of the phone.

"The bridge," she was informed in a low voice. "Tell him to meet me at the bridge."

The phone went dead in her hands.

After two sips of tea, she made up her mind to make a call of her own. For this, she would need to go back to her address book. It was a number she wasn't used to dialing. And this is exactly the phone she had used all those years ago to dial it. The message back then had been to report that she knew where to find her daughter, Fortune. And now she could happily report something eerily similar, so similar it made her recall the word she had been searching her brain for: *synchronicity*.

"Yes, Florence, hello. This is Phyllis Gossett. The purpose of my call? I happen to know where you may find your granddaughter at precisely midnight tonight."

This should have been her only social call of the afternoon, except she had one more to make. She had a final favor to ask of a sweet, young, flighty moth of a girl whose favorite color was pink.

Chapter 33

There was no mistaking the voice of the person he had come to label Will-Alan. Daryl didn't even have to turn around. The urgency in it was compelling.

"I'd like to report a missing person," it declared.

Daryl was sitting at the sergeant's desk—the entire station took up no more floor space than a convenience store—minutes away from being in formal possession of the key fob to the Jaguar. The police had finally been able to contact Daryl's employer. Son of a bitch had been vacationing, sans phone, in Costa Rica. Given Daryl's prior mishaps with repossessions, he hadn't appeared too surprised to learn of the situation with the Jag. Arrangements were being made for the release of the car from the impound lot. It was just a matter of paperwork.

"Missing, huh?" This was the officer on duty at the front desk, a platinum blonde who had made eyes at Daryl when he first walked in. She was chewing a wad of gum with the deliberation of a heifer. "And who would that be?"

"Essence," Will-Alan said, "Essence Warner."

The woman took up a ballpoint pen, scribbling furiously with it on a yellow ledger to get it to work, then tossing it in a trash can below her feet.

"Funny, but that's the second report of her missing this morning," she said.

"Who else was it reported her missing?" he asked.

"Let me see, a Mr.—wait a sec, I've got it here." She flipped a page of the ledger. "—Jenkins. Earl Jenkins."

"Jenkins! But I just talked with him."

"So she isn't missing?" Transferring her wad of gum from

one cheek to the other, the woman was still looking for a pen that worked.

"No, she is—at least I think she is."

"All I can tell you is what I told him, if it hasn't been twenty-four hours and the person alleged to be missing is over eighteen and there's no suspicion of foul play, there's not much we can do." She waited a moment, pausing with her chomping routine. "Has it been twenty-four hours?"

"No," Will-Alan said, looking down at the floor. "It hasn't."

"Relax, dear," the woman said with a sudden shift to a motherly tone. "She always shows up some time or other. It's not like she hasn't pulled these disappearing stunts before. Am I right, Harry?" she queried with a toss of her head.

The officer handling Daryl's release forms at the desk behind her nodded, but looked flushed, or at least Daryl noticed a burgeoning redness fill his jowly cheeks.

"Just sign here," he said, pointing with a thick forefinger. Daryl signed, and Harry gave him the key fob.

"How do I get in?" Daryl asked.

"Fence is unlocked," Harry informed him. "We've always had trouble with the combination."

"Thanks." Daryl leapt out of the chair and raced after Will-Alan, who had just exited. "Hey, buddy, wait up!" He caught up with him on the sidewalk. Will-Alan was standing there, looking from one end of the street to the other.

"Hey," Will-Alan said. "Frank, right?"

"Right," Daryl said, recalling the pseudonym he had given him. "Owens. Wherever it is you're going, I thought I might give you a lift."

"That's all right. I'm just going—I'm—well, actually, I'm not sure where I'm going."

"All the more reason," Daryl said brightly, "till you figure it out. Plus, I guarantee"—and here he held up the key fob as evidence—"it'll be the ride of a lifetime."

***

This Frank Owens fellow was right. It really was that sort of ride.

They whizzed through the countryside, going around curves through the woods, uphill, downhill, without slowing, taking the hills fast at the summits to create a feeling of floating in air, sailing weightless, along with Will's stomach, for the stretch of roadway it took to get to the next rising patch of asphalt.

He was impressed at how well the driver handled the car, maneuvering with such a light grip on the steering wheel, downshifting and upshifting with no more effort than it would take to navigate a computer mouse, the gearshifts as subtle as sighs. Most importantly, Will took note of the fact that Frank, no matter his speed, always stayed on his side of the dividing line.

At one point, Frank had offered to change places, but tempted as he was, Will declined.

Frank pressed the brakes, and the car slowed to a crawl. This snapped Will out of his reverie and forced him to look at the road. There was the explanation: a speed limit sign for 25 mph. They were reentering New Bloomfield with its danger of speed traps.

"Grab a beer?" Frank suggested.

"Sure," Will agreed on impulse. He figured he would never find Essence unless she wanted him to, and evidently she didn't want him to. He would stick by his plan to search her out that night, on the bridge. This seemed the likeliest of destinations. Until then, there was nothing but time.

He still had his prohibition against alcohol, which Frank found amusing when Will ordered a water with lemon.

"On the wagon?" Frank was drinking a rum and Coke, easy on the Coke. "Where you from, anyway?"

"Nowhere special," Will said. The bar was nearly empty this time of day. A couple of rednecks playing darts, an old-timer at the far end on a stool. "Erie," he decided to confess. "Erie, PA."

"Erie, huh? Fact is, I'd have taken you for a New Yorker myself. Upstate, am I wrong?"

"No," Will said, "you're not wrong."

It felt good to say something about himself that was actually true for a change.

"Thought so," Frank said. "I've got a knack for accents. I'm starting to pick up Appalachia, but I won't be here long enough to master the dialect. Be leaving tomorrow."

"Tomorrow!" Will said loudly enough for the dart players to give him a dirty look. "But you only just got here, what, a couple of days ago?"

"Yeah, but it was always meant to be temporary. Just till I got the Jag out of hawk."

Frank went ahead and told him the story about his most recent experience as a repo man.

"Funny, you mentioned New York. Dealer I'm taking it to is in Utica."

Will gave an involuntary start.

"Utica! But that's where I'm from," he announced before he knew whether it was information he wanted to divulge. It was just—someone from Utica, sitting right next to him in a bar, elbow to elbow. It took a moment for him to regain his reserve. "I mean, that's where I lived until recently, before Erie."

"My, my, so you've been all over, sounds like. A regular drifter, huh?"

Will chose not to answer this.

"So what brought you out this way if you were heading to Utica?" he asked instead. This was the one point of the story he couldn't cipher. It seemed to catch Frank off guard too.

"Love interest," Frank answered, a little too quickly. "You know how it is."

"Yeah." Will knew all too well. If nothing else, this he knew. "Is that where you're from?" he wondered, hoping not to sound too anxious.

"No, I'm from all over really. But I went to school at SUNY."

"Which campus?"

"Albany. Seven-year plan. Still paying off the loans for it."

Will watched him down the dregs of his drink and make as though to go.

"Wait a second," Will said. "What years were you there?"

He listened to Frank rattle off a series of years that overlapped Will's own enrollment.

"That's when I was there. I can't believe we were there at the same time. Did you happen to know a woman named Abbey?"

He asked it with an explosiveness that revealed it had been a name held in check for a very long time.

"Abbey? Not sure if I do. It's been a while."

"Abigail Winston. Medium height. Dark hair about shoulder length, keeps it tied back in a bow, but it's always breaking free. Birthmark on her cheek like a small map of Ohio."

"Ohio, huh?" Frank seemed amused.

"She started out majoring in business administration, same as me. Except she ended up going into art history. Scholarship took her overseas. Oxford, England. But that was before I knew her. We only met—I mean to say, I only met her—our senior year. When we were both seniors. And now she has her own art studio." Will took a breath to slow down. He took a sip of his ice water. "Last I heard, anyway." He gave his shoulders a shrug, a last-ditch effort to appear impartial, realizing the attempt was futile.

"I seem to have a recollection of someone matches that description. It was a pretty big campus, though. I could try Googling her name, see what comes up."

Frank brought out his phone and began pressing the screen.

"No, no, that's all right." Will reached out, tapping his forearm. He knew what he might find: Abbey's social media site. Was she still begging for his return? He couldn't bear to think so. "It's just it's been a while, like you said. There's no going back."

Frank put his phone away and ordered a beer.

"Sounds like she's the one that got away," he said, eyeing Will in profile.

"Yeah," Will agreed, sinking back into his normal state of being, giving his appearance a onceover in the mirror behind the bar. "I guess you could say that."

Unless it was the other way around, he thought. Unless he was the one who got away. But not really. Now he knew he could never get away from his past. Not fully. Not completely. There would always be Abbey's face any time he looked at his reflection.

The man who called himself Frank blew the head off the flagon of beer that had been set before him. *Beer on whiskey*, Will thought. *Very risky.*

"Sure I can't tempt you with a drink?" Frank asked.

Will gave it a moment's thought, then settled on an answer.

"What the hell," he caved in. "I mean, why not? Right?"

Chapter 34

Ever since the backfired encounter at the playground, Don Perritt had been unsuccessful in maintaining his bond with Abigail Paxton. Now that he realized how spidery a thread connected them, he spent his waking hours trying to find ways to strengthen it, to make it binding.

The next day, he had stopped by her apartment with a present, a ruby necklace. Abigail kept him on the threshold, from where he could see a cup of coffee—a single cup—on the dining table and could hear Joel singing a pop song at the top of the stairs. Contemporary music—a pet peeve of Perritt's that made him cringe, even as he handed her the gift.

She expressed surprise when she opened the box but didn't remove the necklace from its cotton padding. Instead of completing the picture he had in his mind of her accepting his offer to connect the delicate chain at the back of her neck, so brown and smooth and supple, with her holding her luxurious head of hair in place up and away, she had pushed the box back into his hands and begun to shut the door. He could still see the marks on her wrist, where his fingernails had dug into her flesh.

"I know you mean well," she said, so formally, so firmly, although her tone, as always, couldn't help but be so soft, so pleasant, "but I don't think it's in either of our best interests to continue seeing each other."

"No?" The question had come out as a whimper, and for a second, he thought he saw her eyes softening.

"No," she said without further explanation, and began closing the door, as though he were nothing more than a solicitor.

"But," he said, wedging his foot against the edge of the door, applying pressure, keeping her from closing it all the way. He saw her eyebrows flare up, and her eyes concentrate into a determined stare. "Couldn't we talk about it? Now. Over coffee?"

"I'm sorry," she said, giving her voice a cold edge, "but if you persist in trying to see me or Joel," and here she turned her gaze up the stairway, "I'll be forced to take stronger measures."

"I see," he had said, removing his foot as a gesture of goodwill, but before he could think of anything to say in his defense, the door closed with a thud, and he was left alone on her doorstep. That was the last he had seen of her face to face. However, it wasn't the last he had seen of her from a distance.

The orchestra was taking a summer recess, and he took advantage of the time at his disposal to begin following her. He felt compelled to know what she was doing, where she was, whom she was with, at any given moment. His number one fear was that she would rendezvous with her husband. That was something he couldn't allow.

He began consuming caffeine in bulk quantities, and when this failed to keep him awake, he began using amphetamines he got secondhand off a spare prescription from the third violinist.

He bought a pair of high-power night-vision binoculars, a necessary expense. He traded in his old car—a blue Volvo that Abigail knew by sight—for a used gray Toyota, something inconspicuous.

All was going well, until one night, parked behind Abigail's townhome, as he trained his binoculars on her upstairs window, his peripheral vision was interrogated by the harsh beam of a flashlight. He had forgotten about the night patrol, a young Hispanic man in uniform.

"Hola," Perritt said, trying to recall his high-school Spanish. "¿Cómo estás?"

"Mind telling me what you're doing?" the security guard asked in standard English, making Perritt feel rather foolish.

"I know what you must be thinking."

"So what am I thinking?" the guard asked in a level voice, no sarcasm detected.

"That I must be some sort of prowler." Perritt gave out a short laugh. "Nothing could be further from the truth."

"And what is the truth?"

"I'm a private investigator. I've been hired to observe a person of interest and keep a record of her comings and goings."

"Is that so?" The guard maintained a monotone delivery, and Perritt worried he would ask to see his professional license next, which of course he didn't have.

"Look, isn't there some way we can work this out?"

He knew what he must look like: the epitome of a madman. His hair, a bird's nest of a scraggly tangle, fell past his collar. His beard had blossomed into a modest shrub. His eye sockets were drained reservoirs, his face all pale and sweaty.

"We can work it out by having you leave the premises."

"But I live here," Perritt pleaded.

"Then the best you can do is go home, get some sleep. I'd hate to have to report you."

And that was it. The guard walked away, leaving an unsettled feeling in Perritt's gut. No, he didn't want to be reported to the police. And yes, he needed a good night's sleep.

Except it wasn't a good night's sleep at all. He lay awake, staring at the variegated plaster ceiling with its imprints of either flowers or snowflakes—it frustrated him that he couldn't decide which—illuminated by the streetlight through the curtains.

He knew his life was falling apart, and that he was letting it cave in, like a landslide. But he wasn't able to dig his way out of the memories that kept piling in on him. He conjured images of his wife and daughter. His Jenny would have turned eleven. Would she still be into gymnastics? Or would her interests have shifted? Maybe to soccer or dance. She was good at chess, even at age nine. So good that sometimes he really had to concentrate to avoid her feints and forks. This made it seem real, instead of pretend, when he let her win. How happy she had been whenever she could yell out, "Checkmate!"

And his wife. True, their marriage had been undergoing a strain. But they were working on it. They had been seeing a therapist, and they were making progress. It came down to his controlling nature, which she was finding harder and harder to abide. And he had been trying, up until the end. He had been working hard on letting go the little things.

But now, every time he tried to think of his wife, he saw Abigail's face instead. And when he tried to concentrate on his daughter, his imagination came up with Joel.

He gave up his nighttime vigil and began monitoring his quarry's activities during daylight hours only. He woke up when she did. Followed her to the daycare center where she dropped off Joel. Followed her to her place of work, a combination photography studio and art gallery. Followed her back to the daycare facility, then back home, observing always at a discreet distance.

And what if the worst were to happen? What if he saw her in the company of Alan Paxton?

He made a pilgrimage to a gun show to make a purchase from a private dealer. It was a small silver handgun that fit neatly in his palm. The dealer assured him it would do the trick for self-defense, especially if the intention was to wound, not necessarily kill.

"It'll still deliver a nice-size hole," the man said, ringing up the sale. "It may not stop him cold, but it'll give him something to think about."

And that's exactly what Perritt wanted to do in case Alan Paxton should show up at his wife's doorstep: give him something to think about.

Chapter 35

Keeping vigil, Will sat in the Hex Room in the swivel chair he had pulled over from the desk. How quiet the desk was tonight. Its drawer, glued back together, no longer rattled. The pipes were silent, too. All he heard was a vague humming, possibly of frazzled wiring behind the walls, the electrical connections being so ancient.

But he kept the lights off this night and placed his gaze firmly on the center of the bridge, visible through the parting of trees, as if nature were lending a hand to his night's watch. He was afraid to lower his gaze to check the time on his watch—last time he glanced it was a quarter past eleven—in case he should miss Essence's arrival.

Earlier, he had begun to cross the bridge, ignoring the barricade that had been put in place warning CLOSED TO FOOT TRAFFIC, but a security guard with a gun and a badge had told him no one was permitted across.

There's the new bridge, the guard pointed out unhelpfully. He could always take that if he had a dire need to get across. It lay a mile upstream, glimmering in the distance, its silver cables and steel buttresses lit up with spotlights. Instead, he had returned to the crow's nest of the Hex Room, whose panoramic windows offered greater visibility than waiting at the foot of the bridge would. Plus, he wouldn't arouse suspicion by being so noticeably in one place.

The fireworks had gone off early, at dusk, and he had loitered until the crowds had dispersed. He had hoped for a glimpse of Essence, but if she had turned out for the display, she must have been part of the onlookers on the far side of the river. Earlier, he had observed the dismantling of the booths and tents and games and stalls and the arrival of heavy equipment and machinery for breaking up the bridge beginning tomorrow morning.

When he came back from his failed attempt to cross the bridge, he had found Mrs. Gosset sitting in the swing on the porch, smoking a cigarette.

"Still no news?" he asked regarding Essence.

"No news, I'm afraid."

"And you're sure she never called?"

"Cross my heart," she replied. "How were the fireworks? Wonderful, I'm sure."

"You didn't see them?"

"I heard them, and that was enough. I needed to soothe the nerves of my cat, she gets so frightened, the dear thing."

Will looked around for it, but it must have left the porch.

"And the bridge?" she asked. "Lovely at this time of evening, isn't it?"

It was going on ten-thirty, long past dusk.

"Not really," he admitted. "They aren't lighting it up as usual." Instead of its traditional string of light bulbs, a number of floodlights had been placed at random along the roadway, guarding the demolition equipment, casting sharp shadows.

"No, I imagine they aren't, not with it being torn down tomorrow." She made it sound as though the bridge would disappear all in the course of a day instead of over the next several months.

"You'll let me know if you see her?"

"Essence? Of course. And where will she find you? You'll be staying in your room tonight?"

Will nodded.

And this is where he was an hour later, in the Hex Room, when a knock came at the door, three soft taps. He lurched out of his seat, thinking it was Essence come back to him.

Instead, it was Mandy dangling a bottle of spirits—two bottles, actually, one from each hand. She was dressed in typical Mandy attire: a fuchsia skirt with magenta leggings and a purple top to match.

"Hi, Will, doing anything tonight?"

He didn't open the door fully, unable to conceal his disappointment, never mind his irritation. Mandy was not on his roster of events.

"No, not at the moment, but—"

It was a hesitation he should have learned from experience constituted a fatal lapse with this young woman.

"Fine, then you won't mind my barging in for a little while?"

And barge in she did, ducking right under his outstretched arm, and swinging the bottles in wild arcs as she whirled over to the kitchenette and found a corkscrew in a drawer.

"Have a seat," he said, defeated. "Anywhere you like."

But he didn't join her. He retreated to the Hex Room and took up his post in front of the windows.

Mandy followed him in.

"Why so dark?" she asked, clicking on the lamp and plopping down on the futon. She sat like a pet cat, staring expectantly up at him as she proceeded to uncork her bottle. The one she handed Will had a twist-off cap.

"Why two?" he asked.

"Yours is nonalcoholic. Courtesy of your landlady. She caught me on my way up when I was filling in the guest register."

As much as he'd rather have a drink, now that his ban on alcohol had been lifted, he felt it more important to keep a clear head. Maybe a little diversion would help pass the time. He liked Mandy. In some ways, he thought of her as a kid sister. Her personal life always seemed on the brink of disaster with news of one aborted date or other. She took a small sip directly from her bottle, wrinkling her nose.

"Girlfriend trouble again?" he asked, eyes back to the window. Still no one on the bridge. Neither could he make out the lone security officer. Maybe this would be a good time to try the bridge again, repositioning himself where it counted in dead center. But he didn't want to be turned back again. In the lapse of time between going and returning, what if he missed Essence?

"Yeah, same old, same old," Mandy confessed. "Anyhow, cheers!"

She held up her bottle and Will clinked his against it. He sniffed the opening of the neck dubiously. It smelled of apples, pungent yet sweet.

"Homemade cider," Mandy said, flopping onto the futon.

He took a swig, testing it.

"Not bad," he remarked. Like a wizard, Mrs. Gossett had a talent for potions.

The second swallow was even tastier than the first. There was a distinct aftertaste, a tang that excited the back of his throat and warmed his gullet.

Mandy took a sip of her own store-bought variety, then lowered the bottle, staring into it as if searching a crystal ball for an answer to the riddle of life.

"I have something to confess," she said quietly.

"Yeah?" Will wanted, craved, another sip of the bottle. Whatever it contained was addictive.

"I've been spying on you."

"Huh?" Will's immediate reaction was to glance at the windows of the Hex Room. They were too high up for peeping Toms—or the female equivalent. "What do you mean, 'spying'?"

"It's not something I'm especially proud of," she said, "but since this is my last assignment, I thought you should know."

She took a drink from her bottle, and Will followed suit. It seemed an elixir to medicate all his worries away, to massage them right out of his brain. He wiped his mouth with the back of his hand. Why was his arm feeling so numb of a sudden?

"Assignment?" he asked, but the word came out a tad slurred. His lips were feeling numb, too. Something wasn't feeling right, or else it was feeling too right—he couldn't decide which.

"You have to understand, Will, I come from a family of very modest means."

Family? He had forgotten all about Mandy having a family. It always seemed she had sprouted directly out of a peony.

"When I was offered a chance to have my education—the next two years—paid for, all the way through to graduation, well, it didn't take me long to jump when she said, 'Jump!' I'm sorry, Will, but I had to."

"Jump?" he asked, but the word came out thickly, and he started to laugh, it seemed so ludicrous, everything she was telling him. He took another swig from the bottle, but he couldn't really tell if the bottle was connecting with his mouth, his lips were so unfeeling.

"At first, it seemed so innocent, just to keep an eye on you, to report your comings and goings. Oh, and, yes, I observed you, in the park." She gave a funny sort of abashed smile. "I certainly observed all of your comings."

"Comings," Will slurred. And this word seemed strange to him, too. Strange, and somehow humorous.

"I never meant for you to get in trouble. But I guess that's when I thought maybe we were going too far. You see, it was me. I was the one who stole the saxophone. It was supposed to look like a burglary. That's why I cut the glass the way I did, which was fun to do, I should add. I planted it in your apartment.

I wasn't sure what the idea was except she told me she didn't want you to keep your job as curator, and she thought this would be a clear sign that you were mixed in too deep and that you would bail out. Personally, I didn't want you to get fired, of course. Or worse—arrested. But I really didn't know you that well. And she had just paid my summer semester's tuition, and—"

"She?" Will asked, having trouble forming the word. His entire mouth felt swollen, as though it had been injected with Novocain in a dentist's chair.

"Mrs. Gossett. She told me it was all for your own good. She didn't want to see you come to a bad end like the previous two curators had. She said she would make sure you didn't get in trouble with the police. That it would just be Mrs. Waxman who would be angry if she were to find out. But it wasn't just that, Will. She wanted me to keep you from her—Essence. Essence Warner. And that was the whole idea behind the party."

"Party?" Will tried to say, but it came out as a barely intelligible slur.

"I'm afraid that was my doing too. The invitations, that is, telling you to meet each other there. Mrs. Gossett arranged the rest. She wanted you to see for yourself what kind of person Essence is. Except I'm sorry about how it all turned out. Especially for Essence. But what else could you expect from a girl like that?"

Will had an urge to take hold of her neck, to strangle her, but his body felt immobilized. He had trouble sitting up straight in the chair.

"And that's what I'm doing here tonight," Mandy went on, blandly, "keeping you from seeing her. Mrs. Gossett believes she is a very bad influence on you, and I'm afraid I couldn't agree with her more!"

Will leaned forward. He tried to right himself, but the bottle slipped through his fingers. As though watching it in slow motion, he saw the remainder of its contents gush onto Mandy's skirt.

She rose up quickly, brushing the dark brown liquid from her beloved taffeta, even as his body, twisting round with gravity, fell heavily onto its back. He stared straight up at the ceiling. He found he couldn't move his limbs. He tried, but his arm wouldn't move above his head the way he wanted it to. He tried to lift a leg as well, but it, too, was immobile. His whole body, from his scalp to his toes, felt desensitized. He could still see and hear everything around him, although it seemed as though he were under water.

Mandy was crouching above him. Her face was close and round and terrified.

"Will?" She was shaking his shoulder, but he couldn't feel it. He could only see the motion of her arm. "Will? What's wrong? Is it another seizure? Will, speak to me!"

But he couldn't speak. He couldn't make a sound, except a low, gurgling, guttural growl from deep within his throat. In fact, he had a moment of panic believing he might drown on his own saliva.

"Hold on, I'll get Mrs. Gossett!"

No! He wanted to yell this, to take hold of her arm, but his jaw froze in place. *No!*

Her head had disappeared, and he knew there was nothing he could do now but wait.

The waiting didn't take long.

He heard Mandy call out at the top of the stairs.

"Mrs. Gossett!"

But it wasn't a call for help. It was a cry of surprise.

Will saw what Mandy had been surprised by as she backed into the room, Mrs. Gossett prodding her with the barrel of a revolver. Pearl-handled, too. Like a six-shooter right out of the Wild West.

Chapter 36

"Mrs. Gossett, please. I don't understand."

"Oh, you will, dear. You will. You'll see."

Mandy knelt next to Will. All he could do was stare in return. His whole body was humming with a dull ache of immobility.

"It's Will, he's—there's something wrong with him. He fell, and now, well, look at him! Will?" she asked, turning her eyes toward him. "Will? Can you speak?" She nudged his shoulder, picked up his arm, placing her fingers on his wrist to feel for a pulse. "What's wrong with him?" She sounded hysterical. "It can't be a seizure. He's had seizures before, and they were nothing like this!"

"Oh, he'll be all right in an hour or so," the landlady said, "depending on how much he drank." She took a seat in the swivel chair where Will had been sitting and crossed one leg over the other, exposing a bony knee and mottled shin. She began tapping her foot to an inaudible beat. As casual as she seemed, she kept her gun trained on Mandy. "I believe I've mentioned that my dear, departed husband Walter was a pharmacist, and a very good one. He taught me everything I know about anesthetics … and poisons."

"You've poisoned him?"

"The paralysis is only temporary. It'll wear off in time. You played your part well, although it would have been easier had you partaken as well." She picked up the half-emptied bottle, holding it up for inspection, before setting it upright on the floor. "Now if you'll move away from him, dear, and just stand over there." She waved her gun in the direction she wanted Mandy to move, and Mandy obliged, taking a stance against a thin section of wall near the windows. "That's fine, dear. Now let me explain what's going to happen so there isn't any confusion."

She studied the watch on her wrist for what seemed like minutes but was probably seconds. Time, for Will, was operating on a different level. Everything was moving so slowly.

"It is now precisely eleven thirty-seven. In twenty-three minutes, Essence Warner will be waiting on the bridge for her lover, one Will Archer, to show up. But he won't be there, I'm afraid. Her grandmother will be there in his place. And with the help of her manservant, she will be taking Essence and putting her away, lock and key, where she won't be heard from or seen for many, many years. Just as should have happened to her wretched mother."

Will caught the tail end of her tone: angry, vindictive, hostile. But it took a few sluggish moments for Will to process everything he had just heard, and when it registered, he summoned all of his willpower to make even the slightest movement, but nothing happened. He was as good as a corpse.

"And so, what?" Mandy cried. "We're just going to sit here and let her be taken away?"

The question seemed to withdraw Mrs. Gossett from a momentary reverie. Standing, she raised her gun level with the girl's chest.

"No, my dear. You still have one more part to play."

"But you said this would be my last—" Mrs. Gossett's intention must have dawned on her. "Oh, God. Please—"

"I'm so very sorry."

She pulled the trigger. The gun fired loudly. Mandy bent her head toward the entry wound from which a rivulet of blood ran down her blouse, her expression one of wonderment. Her knees crumpled, and she slid down the wall to the floor, silent and still, leaving a long streak of blood in her wake.

No, no, no! Will's brain shouted, but the words bounced around inside his skull like the wings of a caged bird.

"Tch-tch," his landlady clucked, retaking her seat, as though nothing out of the ordinary had just occurred. "Such a shame when they die so young, but I truly needed her cooperation to make it seem she was on the wrong end of a lovers' quarrel. And how on Earth can you make something look like a murder-suicide if there isn't a murder?"

The question was posed as though for philosophical debate. Will had no doubt as to what was coming next. He kept trying to move, to untie his arms, his legs, his tongue, as if to loosen a series of knots.

"Now," she said with her same, steady, kindly voice, "let me explain a few things, Will. You're probably thinking I owe you an explanation, and I suppose I do." She let out a sigh, turning her gaze full on him, making him feel as exposed as if she had stripped him naked. "How to begin?"

She sat there a moment, turning over her thoughts, as though seeking to loop a thread through a needle.

"The first thing you should know is that once upon a time I was a much more attractive—dare I say, beautiful?—specimen of womanhood than the relic you see here before you now. Yes, yes, all of twenty years ago, I was still in my prime, just shy of fifty, but I could have passed for a woman much younger, so I was told. Do you want to know who it is who assured me of my attractiveness?"

Will kept struggling internally, wrestling with the ropes that ensnared his nervous system. The way he was positioned, he couldn't help but stare at this wiry, older woman in a blue bathrobe and house slippers, her blue-tinted hair done up in curlers, and the gun she rested on her lap.

"Why, it was the tenant of this very room," she exclaimed,

as if discovering a long-forgotten fact. "Let me confess, I had an affair with Jamaal Waxman. Of course, to pursue such a reckless act of unfaithfulness, I had to get my husband out of the way. Poor Walter, finished off with one of his own poisons. You know what he used to call me? I'm too much a lady to speak it out loud. Suffice it to say, he used to refer to me with a set of initials." And here she looked at Will with a sly scrutiny. "Do the letters N.L. mean anything to you?"

N.L. Of course! So it was Mrs. Gossett who was the anonymous author of all those horrible emails. Will remembered Mrs. Waxman saying the police were stymied because it was library computers that were being used with temporary accounts. And Mrs. Gossett was herself a retired librarian.

"I loved Jamaal dearly, and I believe he, in turn, loved me. Until *she* entered the picture." She uttered the pronoun with the venom of a snake. "Miss Fortune Warner. What an unfortunate name, don't you think?" She eked out a titter at her own joke. "It would have all been so perfect with Fortune out of the way, but of course, the poor thing decided to jump to her death rather than let her mother and her manservant Jenkins interfere with her endless love.

"All he could think of was Fortune, Fortune, Fortune! For three days, he stayed locked in his room, the shades drawn, the lights extinguished, not eating, not sleeping, just grieving, grieving for a woman who was no measure for him. Just a frail wisp of a thing who had never known life outside her gated mansion. 'If only,' he kept moaning. If only he had been there to prevent her death instead of being detained in my apartment. I couldn't let this go on. I put a stop to it."

Will recalled his session with the Ouija board. Jamaal, if that's who had really been on the transmitting end, had been trying to reveal the identity of his murderer with her initials: P.G. Phyllis

Gossett. He had been too obtuse to make the connection.

"I tempted Jamaal with heroin. It was his old-time vice come back to haunt him. Given his state, he couldn't resist. He filled his veins with it. He didn't hold back. Except it was heroin I laced with an opioid. And then, and then," she concluded, "I was the one who grieved." She gave Will a calm, gray-eyed look, perhaps the saddest he had ever seen. "I've been grieving ever since."

She stood up from the chair with difficulty, as though lifted by a crane.

"Thank you for indulging an old woman her reveries." She studied him head to toe and back again, aiming, as she did so, the gun at various parts of his body, as though deciding where to put the bullet hole. "Oh, I do love you, Will, as I would a son," she lamented. "I do believe I loved you even more than your predecessors, the two curators who came and went before you. Yes, I can answer the question you're thinking. I was the one who helped them move on as well."

She came a step closer, then slowly bent at the waist, folding her legs beneath her at the same time, coming to rest in a kneeling position beside Will's head.

"The trouble is they got too close to the truth. It took them much longer, of course, to arrive at it, but I couldn't let them live thinking, as they did, that I had something to do with Jamaal's demise. And you were getting close, too. You and Essence, the two of you, together, I'm afraid, were getting much too close, according to my informant." She waved the gun toward the figure of Mandy. "So you see, I'm really left with little choice. It is with a fond farewell that I must bid you adieu."

She pressed the barrel of the revolver against his right temple. Will could feel its coldness and wished he could close his eyes against the propulsion that was about to follow.

"Oh, my," she said, "I seem to have forgotten you are left-handed. It's the little things that begin to slip from your mind at my age."

Without rising, she shuffled around to his other side and pressed the gun against his left temple.

"Good-bye, Will," she said, cocking the gun with a click.

With all his effort, Will tried to force his muscles to move. He went deep inside himself, shutting himself inside the box of his own mind. And then a strange thing began happening. The pipes, silent till now, began to wail with a loud vibration. The desk drawer started to rattle furiously. Books fell from shelves as though flung. Picture frames crashed to the floor. Pots and pans leaped out of cupboards. Figurines that had come with the apartment flew from nooks. A cuckoo clock fell off the wall, candlesticks leaped from the mantel. Curtains whirled like dervishes.

"Hold still!" she shouted, except it seemed she was speaking to someone other than Will, who could do nothing but hold still. The noise carried on with the persistence of a drumbeat, or many drums pounding all together in various rhythms. "Damn you, Jamaal. Let me finish this!"

Like magic, as though on command, the noise ceased at once.

She brought her eyes to bear on Will's face. She looked at him tenderly.

"I do wish—" she began to say.

And then Will discovered he could move his head.

Chapter 37

Daryl must have been dozing. It was easy to do. Even with the windows open to the night breeze, and an electric fan on the sill, the apartment felt like a toaster. Voices awoke him, overriding the low volume of a baseball game on the TV, a decades-old Zenith that came with the place.

Lying on the sofa, Daryl tried to decode them. He knew Will-Alan's, and there was a woman's voice, young. Maybe Essence had returned to him. He was tempted to make another excursion with his camera when another woman joined the conversation, and he felt reassured by the croaking voice of the landlady.

He was prepared to go back to sleep and let the voices subside through his subconscious, but a loud, sharp explosion pierced his grogginess and lurched him upright.

He was almost certain it was a gunshot. Whoever it was that had fired it didn't seem overly concerned about its being overheard. Maybe he had misinterpreted. It's possible in his muddled state he had only heard a truck backfiring. Or were the fireworks restarting?

He strained to listen through the ceiling high above. There was just the one voice now, the old landlady's, droning on and on, but no response from anyone else. Something in Daryl's gut just didn't feel right. And he was always one to trust his gut.

Wary of a trap, he crept to the top of the stairs, where he found the door to #9 not just ajar but wide open. Peering carefully around the door jamb, he took quick note of the layout of the apartment before withdrawing his face from view.

The living room was empty, but he had registered three figures through the farther door leading to a room filled with windows: Mandy, seated on the floor, and Phyllis Gossett kneeling by Will-Alan. The image he retained was of her holding a gun to her tenant's head, but Will-Alan himself was unmoving. She was on the opposite side of him, facing the door, so this would make approaching her rather risky.

Daryl took another quick look to double-check the situation and found that she had changed positions. Now she was crouched on Will-Alan's nearer side, her back to the entrance of the turret. This might be his only chance.

But as he started across the floor, the apartment came unhinged. It was like entering a cyclone. So still just a moment ago, the living room seemed intent on tearing itself apart. Books flew from shelves, pots clanked onto the kitchen floor, cupboards spewed boxes and canned goods, the chandelier swung in wild loops, the desk drawers shook like death rattles. Evading flying objects, Daryl moved swiftly, grabbing the first hard object that came to hand, a brass candlestick that had flown off the mantel.

The landlady raised her voice in a shout—a command. Just as abruptly, everything stopped at once.

He took one step into the small, turreted room and, seeing that the gun was primed to fire, brought the candlestick down on the back of her head. But gently. She was a senior citizen, after all. He didn't want to hurt her.

The gun fired in any case, and the landlady turned around, still holding the revolver, her head wobbling, her eyes crossing, a strange smile curling the ends of her mouth like the papers of a hand-rolled cigarette.

"Oh, Jamaal," she said, "Is it you? But you were only supposed to call 911, like a good boy, not come upstairs."

She brought the gun up unsteadily, aiming it at Daryl's chest. This time, he wasn't so gentle. He walloped her soundly on the side of the head as though serving a tennis ball. Her head snapped sideways with a crack, and she crumpled into a heap.

"Thought you might need a little help getting out of this fix," he said, coming over to the outstretched body of her intended victim. Will-Alan's head had turned to its side. The bullet had grazed his temple, and blood was seeping from the wound. His eyes were open, his mouth moving, but nothing was coming out. "Are you all right?" It was evident he was struggling to say something, and Daryl leaned his ear closer.

"Save her," he whispered hoarsely, keeping his head to the side. "Save her."

Daryl looked at the figure of Mandy, slumped against the wall, her eyes wide open, glassy, unblinking, the blood pooling around her midsection. He went over and pressed his fingers to her neck. Just as he anticipated, he couldn't find a pulse.

"There's no saving her, man, she's dead!"

"No," Will-Alan whispered, no more loudly than before. "Essence. The bridge."

Daryl stood up. He looked out a window through the wavering branches of a tree, obscuring his view. The wind had picked up. There was a scent of rain in the air. It was threatening to storm. He could make out two figures, there in the middle of the bridge, maybe three, but he couldn't tell for sure.

"Save her from what?" Daryl asked. "Seems I better save you first. You're wounded."

"No time," Will-Alan said. He reached up a clawed hand, with apparent effort, trying to grab Daryl's wrist, but falling short. "Go. Please. Now."

Daryl was ready to comply. But first he pressed a wadded-up pillowcase against Will-Alan's wound, soaking up the blood, assessing the damage. It didn't look deep. He took off his belt and wrapped it around Will-Alan's head to hold the compress in place. Then he picked up the gun that had sprung free of the landlady's hand, pinching its muzzle so as not to leave finger-prints. He carried it into the living room and deposited it in a waste basket.

"I'll be right back," he said, turning.

He ran out the door, pummeled down the stairs, crossed the foyer, and rushed toward the front door. He stopped short, doing an about-face at the threshold. The thin apparition of the single woman who lived on the ground floor was poking her nose out of her doorway.

"Is everything okay?" she asked in a timid voice.

"Call 911," Daryl commanded. "Now!"

Outside, the street was empty as he raced down the sidewalk, the streetlights casting shadows, and this is why he tripped over a man lying face down at the foot of the bridge.

Christ! Another one? How many men was he going to come across lying prostrate this night?

The man wore the uniform of a security officer. Daryl tried shaking his shoulder, but he couldn't get a rise out of him. Assured of a pulse, he began making his way carefully toward the epicenter of the bridge, where the figures he had spotted from the Hex Room resolved themselves into three people.

Essence was standing on the rail holding onto a cable with one hand. Below her was a man reaching out toward her with a woman in a wheelchair looking on. It must be the gruesome two-some he had encountered at the Victorian Arms a couple days before.

He hadn't anticipated playing the hero tonight. He always thought of himself as a secondary character, expendable, good for a chapter or two.

But this seemed as good a time as any to don a cape.

Chapter 38

The evening wasn't turning out as she had imagined it. Not at all.

Essence had little trouble slipping out of her Grandma Waxman's house, just as she had all these nights through the years of her Grandmother Warner's mansion. Her Nana Other had a habit of snoring lightly after falling asleep with the evening news. She didn't even need to go out a window. She merely left quietly through the back door.

Now here she was, balancing on top of the railing, right hand clutching a cold steel cable, high above the dark, slow-moving water of the Ohio River below, which she didn't dare look at for long, so uncertain was she of her balance. It would be so easy to fall. All she had to do was let go. And she hadn't made up her mind that she wouldn't.

It was still three minutes short of midnight. She had promised herself she would wait for Will until the stroke of twelve, which she would indeed hear, tolling from the churches on either side of the river.

It was a matter of mentally preparing herself, as though plunging into the deep end of a pool. She remembered her first foray into the swimming pool by the mansion. Her grandmother used to sun herself, and Jenkins would supervise her wading. He even had to rescue her once when she took a step too far and went under, pulling her out by her hair, which is when he took a personal interest in providing her with swimming lessons.

And here he was standing in front of her, holding out his arms, as though to pull her back to safety. But it wasn't safety he was offering, not with the Grandmother below her in her wheelchair, coaxing her to step down from her perch with gentle words, a soothing approach. Yet there was an underlying edge to her voice, which Essence perceived as a sign of the Grandmother's desperation. It wasn't her granddaughter she wanted to save but her own reputation. She couldn't abide another scandal, not at her age, so many breaths short of a grave.

"Let Jenkins help you down, my dear," she suggested with saccharine concern.

"So you can—what? Put me back in a psych ward?" Essence countered. "How long this time? For life? No thank-you!"

"Of course not," the Grandmother replied. "We'll bring you back home. We'll talk things out. Isn't that what rational people are supposed to do about their disagreements?"

What game was the Grandmother playing? Essence wondered. Whatever it was, it had her wavering.

"There'd have to be some conditions."

"Of course, dear. Of course."

"I'd want my freedom. To go where I choose. To be with who I want."

"The correct case is 'whom,' my dear. But freedom? Is that all? That can be arranged. Believe me, all I've ever wanted is what's best for you. To protect you."

"Protect me?"

"From your own worst instincts. Certainly you must know that I've done so out of love."

"Love?" This made Essence pause to reflect. "You've never used that word with me before."

"Well, it's true. I—love you, dear heart. Now will you please let Jenkins help you down?"

It was Jenkins she had mistaken for Will in the first place. What confused her is that he approached from the West Virginia side of the bridge. And she, like a fool, had run out to him, stopping just short when she saw his face emerge from intermittent shadows. She turned on her heel but knew she couldn't outrace him. Seeing the Grandmother coming from the other direction propelled by the motor of her wheelchair, she had climbed up onto the railing, as she was wont to do of a summer night such as this, usually without an audience—except that one time Will had come across her.

"Jenkins, is she complying?"

There was that word: "complying." A fatal slip of the tongue. It meant compliance, obedience, a bending to the old woman's will. She could never be free of the Grandmother's hold.

"No, Mum. She's not."

"You're just being obstinate!" her grandmother shouted. "Unreasonable. What would your mother say if she were here?"

This jab with her mother almost made her take the old lady's bait, letting go her hand. What point was there now in bringing her mother into this? It seemed reasonable to suppose her mother would only egg her on, encourage her to take a step onto a stairway to nothingness.

One more minute. Fifty-nine seconds. Fifty-eight, fifty-seven … She kept her eyes on the thin ticking of the second hand across the radial dial of her wristwatch.

Twenty seconds, nineteen …

She turned her head for one last sign of Will, but this time it wasn't in vain. There was someone coming, loping along like a gazelle, dodging behind the excavation equipment parked on the bridge for cover. He seemed too tall and dark to be Will, now that she saw him approach. It was the man she had met only briefly on the stairs of the Victorian Arms. One of Mrs. Gossett's new tenants. What was he doing here?

He brought himself up short of the floodlights, remaining half hidden in the shadows.

"Essence?" the man asked.

So he knew her name. Had Will introduced her? She couldn't remember. The church bells began tolling the midnight hour, reminding her she hadn't jumped. She was still balanced on the rail, holding onto the cable. Alive.

"What is it *you* want, mate?" Jenkins asked, his voice sounding tentative but, at the same time, authoritative.

"Jenkins, who is it?" the Grandmother asked, leaning forward in her wheelchair, peering through her useless sunglasses.

But before he could answer, the man said, "I've come for Essence. I've come to save her."

"Save me?" Essence whispered. It seemed such an absurd proposition, she wasn't sure she heard him right.

Her grandmother echoed her own dismay, except it came out as a derisive cackle.

"Save her? You have no legal right to her. Enough of this nonsense. Jenkins, please take care of this—problem."

Jenkins left his post in front of Essence. He took three long strides toward the newcomer, pulling back his fist, and let loose. The punch landed hard against the man's jaw, felling him, knocking him off his feet.

"What the hell you do that for?" the man asked, massaging his jaw and spitting a spool of blood through the grille of the walkway. He slowly stood up, regaining his posture, and Jenkins let him, which was unusual. He wasn't always known for a fair fight.

"Sorry, old man, but you heard the lady," he said, readying for another punch. "Brisbane, middleweight title, golden gloves."

But the man kicked out with his foot, sideways, landing a blow in Jenkins's midsection, which doubled him over, winded, clutching his side, and he fell to his knees.

"Sorry, old man," the newcomer said, standing over him. "Utica, tai kwon do, green belt."

He eased into the light, revealing his features: sharp, distinctive, yet tender. The man took Jenkins's place in front of her and held up his hand. "And now, miss," he said with a smile meant to charm, "if you'll allow me?"

"Enough is enough," the Grandmother sounded. Moving her wheelchair forward with the push of a button, she produced a gun from a fold of her cloak, which she aimed unsteadily in front of her. "Mr. Archer, you simply cannot have her. I won't permit it!"

"Archer?" the man said. "I'm not Will Archer. I'm Daryl—"

The wheelchair bumped over a chink in the grating of the walkway and the gun fired.

Essence felt it like a pinprick, the sting of a bee. She touched the wound with her free hand. The bullet had punctured the shoulder of the arm that was holding the cable, and reflexively, she let go. It was just as she had imagined: a slow-motion falling backward and away, the railing slipping past her vision, as she reached upward, grabbing, but coming up with only empty air.

Until something firm took hold: a strong hand, just as it began raining. Dangling in space, the river far below, she looked up into the face of the man who said he had come to rescue her. And here he was, rescuing her. Except he held her only by one hand, his other hand keeping him anchored to the bridge, and she could see in the tautness of the muscles in his neck that the strain was too much for him to hold on much longer. Her hand, slick with rainwater, was beginning to slither free. A sense of vertigo was spinning her vision, making the bridge move this way and that. Or was it her hero swinging her like Tarzan? She closed her eyes, even as she felt her hand slipping out of his clutch.

So this is how it ends, she thought, feeling resigned, leaning into her own emptiness, her mind feeling strangely free and unburdened. Except just as she began to slide away, something else took hold of her. It grabbed her wrist, wrapping cold, hard fingers around it like a clamp.

She opened her eyes and looked upward. Jenkins was straining, determined, pulling with all his strength. Sooner than she thought possible, she was hauled over the railing and onto the walkway, the corrugated metal of the grille gnawing into her backbone.

"Jenkins, what is it? What's happened? My God!"

The Grandmother was pleading for answers.

Leaving Essence with her first rescuer kneeling beside her, Jenkins walked over to the Grandmother's wheelchair. Without saying a word, he reached down and lifted her up, a frail bag of skin and cartilage wearing a housecoat against the night air, and carried her to the railing.

"Jenkins, what on Earth? What is it? Why are you—please!"

These were Essence's questions, too, as she watched him set her on the railing, as though she were nothing more than a bag of groceries.

"Jenkins?" the Grandmother begged, her voice quavering.

Gently, with hardly any effort, he gave her upper torso a slight push, and over the railing she went with a long, agonizing wail.

Essence winced. She couldn't believe what she had just seen. By the look of him, the man pressing his shirt, which he had removed and bunched into a compress onto her shoulder, the wound blossoming like a flower, couldn't believe it either. But when next she looked over, Jenkins had picked up the wheelchair, manhandling it up to the top of the railing, and over it went, too, following the old woman in her wake. Just as before, there was barely a splash. The river was too far below. All she could hear was the sound of traffic emanating from the new highway bridge a mile upstream followed by sirens in the distance. Essence was sure she heard sirens.

Chapter 39

Phyllis Gossett struggled to pick herself up off the carpet. It took all her effort to twist and turn until she was on all fours, like a horse.

At present, she felt so goddamned old. The blow to her head contributed to her sluggishness. Her vision was blurred. Fortunately, it didn't require perfect eyesight to bring her up on her knees.

Will was gone. Where was he?

She looked around, spied Mandy sitting all bloody and glassy eyed against the wall. For a moment, she was confused. What was Mandy doing there? It took her a moment to come back to herself, to recollect the instance that had transpired to turn her from a rather pleasant but airheaded girl into a stiffening corpse.

She heard him retching. She got up on her feet, steadying herself against the doorway and, peering out, her vision still swimming, saw that the bathroom door was ajar. Just inside she saw her favorite tenant crouched over the toilet.

The poor boy was vomiting something fierce. Such a consideration to put him out of his misery, wouldn't it be? But first she needed to find the gun.

She walked around the apartment. What had happened? It seemed a cyclone had blown through the place, knocking books and pots and statuettes and picture frames and bottles all to the floor in haphazard heaps, so she had to tread carefully, finding veins of carpet through the debris.

Where would he have hidden it? She opened a desk drawer, and there it was. Except it wasn't hers. It was someone else's. Will's? Oh, what did it matter? A gun is a gun is a gun …

She picked it up and checked the number of bullets: none in the magazine but one in the chamber. Well, one was all she required.

The poor wretch was still retching. *Oh, Phyllis, how droll*, she thought. She took one hesitant step forward, needing support of the desk edge. She was about to take another when she heard the sirens. They grew loud, louder, loudest. They swarmed outside the house, surrounding it. She heard car doors open, footsteps on the porch, then clattering through the foyer.

Oh, but she must go down and beg them not to muddy up her floors. There had been so much rain of late, they were sure to track in mud if they weren't careful. That was one thing about Jamaal, he was always so conscientious, the way he would take off his shoes at the foyer entrance. Then he would pad up the stairs in just his socks, and she would follow.

She must go and greet the officers. Perhaps they will want some tea, one of her special brews? It would be no trouble, really, none at all, officers.

Holding the gun loosely at her side, she hobbled down the steps to the first turn in the stairwell, from which she saw three uniformed officers on the very next landing below, staring upward, their faces illuminated like baby birds in a nest by the naked bulb that swung from a wire far above.

"Ma'am, put down the gun, slowly," one of the officers said. Her voice sounded so cold, so commanding, so inhospitable. That was one thing she always detested most in people, their impatience, their rudeness.

"Oh, this?" she responded, waving the gun carelessly.

"Ma'am, I'm not going to ask you again, put the gun down on the floor at your feet and stand up slowly."

So many directions. Couldn't they see she was just a frail, old woman, of no more harm than a flea? She opened the door behind her. It was always left unlocked for just such an emergency.

"Ma'am, don't move any farther, I'm warning you!"

The door swung open onto the night, and a stiff breeze hit her back, slicing into her robe with a cold rain. She took one look behind her and downward, observing through the drizzle the iron fence with its sharp spires, pretty maids all in a row.

She had contemplated this view once before, after she had lost Jamaal, that very night, on her way down the stairwell from room #9. She had opened the door and had thought of taking that one fateful step now that she had no one to live for. But the idea of surrendering her memory of him, her lover, kept her from an act so rash, so heedless.

She turned in the doorway to say farewell to her pursuers. All three had their weapons raised, ready to fire. Their leader had her foot on the stairs.

"Oh, officers, must you?" she said, before taking one small step backward, settling her slipper on sheer emptiness. The wind took hold of her, billowing out her robe, like the wings of a lark. It would be a two-story drop to the spiked fence below, and she let go of the gun as she fell.

***

The rain slashed like hashmarks as Jenkins watched the stranger kneeling by Essence on the walkway of the bridge. The man—what had he said his name was? Daryl?—was still pressing his wadded-up shirt on her wound, cradling her head in his lap. She was mute, unresponsive, but alive. And her eyes widened as he approached her.

She must think I've come for her next, Jenkins thought. *She has every right to be scared of me.*

This was no time to bother about a certain white satchel. To be honest, it was the prime reason he accompanied his employer to the bridge in the first place: his suspicion about its contents.

He had long known about Florence Warner's secret cache and had no intention of letting Essence deprive him of what he planned to make his own inheritance. Nevertheless, he was impressed by her ingenuity in substituting one case for the other. He only wished he had had the audacity to commit such a heist rather than follow his own plan, which was to wait for the old bat to croak. Now that he was the agent of her demise, what kind of future did this leave him?

"Let me see," he said to Daryl, torso stripped to a muscleman tee, and the man tightened in defensiveness. Jenkins persisted, peeling the shirt away from the wound. Inspecting it, he found the bullet had punctured cleanly below the collarbone. It was bleeding steadily but not gushing, which was a relief. It meant no major artery had been severed. Taking her shoulder, he raised Essence just enough to peer beneath. She made a sharp intake of breath, and he steadied his hand under her. In the floodlights, he saw the exit wound was also manageable. The bullet hadn't lodged inside her.

"Here." He took off his own jacket and stuffed it underneath her so as to absorb the seepage of blood. "She'll need an ambulance. You'll be staying with her until it arrives?"

Daryl nodded his head, and Jenkins took out his phone, shielding it from the rain with a curved hand. He made the call to 911, then handed the phone to Daryl after he made the situation and their location known to the operator.

As Daryl stayed on the phone, Jenkins leaned in toward Essence. She was lovely in pain, so like her mother in her stubborn resolve, her preference for suicide to capture. It would take only a moment to offer her an explanation; then he would leave her, as he had her mother, forever. He noted that Daryl was listening in, as did, he hoped, the 911 operator. He made his voice loud enough to ensure ear-witnesses to what he was about to confess.

Essence was faltering between wakefulness and sleep, but he stroked her hair, as much to keep her attention as a mark of tenderness.

"Listen," he said, looking into her eyes, "you have to understand. I loved your mum. More than that. I worshipped her. I wished her no harm. I wanted to make a life with her, to give her my hand. But your gran—your Grandmother Warner—" Jenkins wiped the rain from her forehead, brushing her hair to the side. "She found out your mum's plan to elope, and she had me bring her here. Your gran was determined to intervene, to take back Fortune, but your mum climbed on top of the rail, just as you did. And she threatened to jump, same as you. Your gran, she called her bluff and commanded me to bring her down bodily, but as I advanced—" He felt a lob in his throat, rising, and he had to swallow hard to keep it down. "As I advanced, she lost her balance. I reached out for her as she fell—if you had seen the look of terror in her eyes, it was clear she wanted to live—but all I came away with was this."

He reached into his pocket and pulled out the silver necklace with its small, heart-shaped locket. After a moment of watching it dangle, Essence took hold of it, and Jenkins let it slip slowly from his grasp.

"Thank you," she whispered, closing her eyes. "Thank you."

He heard a siren, whining through the storm. This prompted him to take off at a jog through the rain, descending to the Ohio side of the river quickly, just as an ambulance pulled up. One of the emergency technicians got out to remove the barricade. Then, seeing a uniformed security guard stumbling out of a bush, rubbing the back of his head, she made a motion to go to him.

"No, she's up there," Jenkins said, pointing, startling the technician as he went over to help move the sawhorses. "She's in the very middle of the bridge. There's a man with her—her friend."

The ET worker, looking alarmed, got back in the ambulance and Jenkins watched it maneuver around the equipment sitting on the causeway until it came to a stop midway up the bridge, as he had directed.

How strange to be reliving this so long after the fact.

Nineteen years ago, he had wheeled his employer, somewhat younger then, but still very much a matriarch, across the park carrying her grandchild, Essence. They had given their report to the police—their stories converged on the notion of suicide—and she had decided against any other form of transportation offered by the authorities back to the mansion. She had wanted to be alone with her grief, or as alone as she could be, pushed along by Jenkins.

And Jenkins had been absorbed in his grief, too, unable to quite comprehend that Fortune had fallen. This is why he still regretted, all these years later, having obeyed the older woman's command to grab hold of her daughter. If only he hadn't reached for her, she wouldn't have recoiled, she wouldn't have lost her balance. And there wouldn't have been a body to recover from the river below.

Crossing the park, he reached the front gate of the estate, plugged in the code, and waited for the gate to swing open. He walked slowly across the wide, rain-soaked lawn, listening to the squish-squish of water sponging beneath his soles. He rounded the mansion, coming back behind it where the tigers were kept.

It was hours past their feeding time. They were pacing their cage relentlessly. Seeing him, they came up to the bars, emitting low growls.

"Hello, girls," he said jauntily, unlocking the cage door. "Hungry, are we?"

They came out and began their common practice of rubbing against his legs in complementary figure eights, in reverse of each other, so that just as he was being jostled by one, the other corrected his balance by nudging him back the other way. All the while, he ran his fingers through their fur, while they generated their low, rumbling purrs. All in all, they were nothing but giant kittycats, waist high as they circled, vibrating like engines.

Ah, well, no time like the present, was there?

He decided the best course of action to anger a tiger would be to strike it on its most vulnerable part: its nose.

He did this first to Crimson, and she stopped cold, turning her head to look at him with eyes that were disbelieving or else curious. Her sister Clover stopped moving too.

"Sorry, old girl," he said, turning his fists on Clover, landing a one-two blow against her snout. She emitted a roar and lashed back with a large paw, nails extended, so that it ripped down his side, but none too hard, a mock-playful return of the favor.

"Come on, then," he said, striking her sister in turn, even harder. She didn't take kindly to this but sprung up against his chest, and he found himself backpedaling with all the enormity of her weight pressing against him, as he struggled for balance by taking hold of her forelegs, embracing her, as they danced backward from the cage toward the pool.

Pushing back from the water's edge, he kicked furiously at Crimson's underbelly, and this succeeded in driving her off him. She studied him quizzically with a cocked head. This time he lashed out with his right, an uppercut to her chin that stung his knuckles, and before he could withdraw his hand, she took hold of his forearm above the wrist and crunched down hard.

"That's it, that's it!" he shouted through his pain, and he began shaking his arm, pulling at his wrist, playing tug of war with the creature. Except it wasn't a game to her. She was moving beyond seeing him as her caretaker to viewing him as prey. He could tell these things. And when he changed tactics and pushed against her, pummeling her head with his free hand, it was too much for her sister. Clover leaped with open mouth, teeth sharp and exposed. She grabbed hold of his shoulder and almost tore his arm from its socket.

Searing pain shot through him and he lost his nerve.

"Help!" he screamed. "Help!"

But Crimson tightened her bite on his arm, gnawing at the bone, and Clover opened her jaws only to clamp down farther up, around his throat. The force of it toppled him backward, and the last sensation he felt before darkness closed over the pain was the cold, harsh smack of water against his back like a slab of concrete with the weight of the tigers on top of him, pushing him under, until his vision dissolved in rising streams of blood.

Chapter 40

Will spent the rest of the night in a holding area of the ER with only a curtain separating him from another patient who kept hacking. This made sleep difficult, but Will hadn't felt like sleep anyway. Too much had been going through his mind, churning over and over, like a waterwheel.

Yet it was difficult sorting out his thoughts. First off, there were too many interruptions—nurses checking vitals, interns going over his chart, all those beeps and gurneys and low murmurs of voices. Not to mention his neighbor's lung.

Plus, two detectives questioned him shortly after he had been admitted. Basically, they were there to obtain his statement about the occurrences in the Victorian Arms. They wanted to know how long he had been a resident there, how well he had gotten along with Phyllis Gossett, what kind of relationship he had with Mandy.

"None," he had said, possibly too sharply, too quickly. "No relationship. She was just a friend."

The male detective flipped backward through a pocket-sized spiral notebook.

"You were under suspicion not long ago for theft," he stated bluntly, looking up through heavy lids.

"Yes, but that was all cleared up," Will tried to assure him.

"Right," the detective said. "Just wanted to be sure you were the same person."

"Yes sir. Yes, I am."

Before they left, each handed him a business card—one immaculate, the other crumpled with a coffee stain—and encouraged him to contact either of them if he thought of anything new.

"It's been a long night," the female detective said, leaving the curtained room on a warm note.

"It couldn't get any longer," her partner agreed.

"But you'll be getting other officers in here. You'll have to give your statements all over again to them."

It appeared there was a question as to jurisdiction regarding the death of Florence Warner, since it had transpired right on the dividing line between Ohio and West Virginia. Also, the FBI was anxious to get involved since the cases crossed state lines.

"Just be cooperative," the female detective said.

"And available," the other one added.

Aside from the detectives, the man whom he knew as Frank Owens had been his only visitor, shortly after Will was hand-delivered by ambulance and checked in and administered oxygen and injected with three separate needles and hooked to an IV tube. This was around two in the morning. Frank filled him in on the events of the bridge. Then he renewed his offer to take him up to Utica.

"You might as well know," he confessed with a grin, "I'm actually a good friend of your wife Abbey. Ex-boyfriend, in fact. Name's Daryl."

This jolted Will wide awake, prompting him to sit up and ask all about her and his son. Daryl had been free with his replies, filling him in as best he knew that she was in a new place and she was trying to move on, but she couldn't, not really, because she didn't know what had happened to her husband. Then Daryl delivered his take on the subject: how unfair this was to her. Daryl advised him to see her, at least once, just to let her know—or let her go, if nothing else.

"Have you told her about me?" Will asked.

"No, not yet." He set on his bedside a Manila envelope. "A memento," he said, before leaving.

From it, Will withdrew several 8 x 10 glossy photographs of his coming and going with Essence on her balcony and an additional one of Mandy and him, the two of them caught in the crosshairs.

Hours later, an attending with two residents in tow checked his chart, asked if he had any recurring symptoms, then signed a form to release him before he even had a chance to gain admittance to a real room.

Will quickly found the exit to a stairwell, which he took to the second floor. At the entrance to a wing, he asked a receptionist behind a glass panel where he might find Essence Warner.

"Is she pre- or post-delivery?"

"Huh?"

"This is the maternity ward."

A couple of keystrokes tracked her down.

Upstairs, down the hall to the left, Room 305. She wasn't in critical or even serious condition. Just in a regular old room.

Inside the door, he found Mrs. Waxman sitting with her. Essence was awake, watching the bracketed television set, her head propped on a stack of pillows.

"We're on the news again," she said brightly. Her gown covered whatever bandage there might be beneath, but her arm was in a sling. She had the customary IV tube dripping fluids into her other arm. Her demeanor seemed drained but cheerful—more so than he had ever known her to be.

Will saw Daryl hamming it up for the cameras on the TV—labeled the "Hero of the Ohio" in a string of bold letters at the bottom of the screen—fielding questions with a wink and a smile for the female news reporter, an attractive brunette, who cued in a series of separate scenes: the third floor of the Victorian Arms, the lethal spiked iron fence below the door to nowhere, the Warner mansion and pool. No bodies were shown, just still images of various locations where the incidents of the previous night had occurred. It was bound to be one of the more sensational stories of the early morning broadcast.

"Rumor is we're going national," Essence said.

"That'll make Daryl happy," Will said. "He seems to enjoy the spotlight."

"I'll leave you two to get caught up," Mrs. Waxman said, rising stiffly, "but first, I'd like a word with you, young man."

She walked into the hall and waited for Will to join her.

"Hurry back!" Essence beckoned from her bed. "Don't keep him longer than you have to, Nana."

Once Will joined her, she closed the door the rest of the way gently.

"I think," she said, solemnly, "that given last night's events, you can be excused from work today."

"Yeah, well," he mumbled, "about that."

"I'm joking," she said. Extending her arms, she took a step toward him. "You've more than earned a day off. Now give me a hug."

Her wish was Will's command, and he obliged, getting a huge whiff of her eau de cologne. It took her a moment to let go, and when the hug was concluded, she held him at arm's length by the shoulders, beaming a bright smile with eyes to match.

"Thank you, thank you, thank you!" she exclaimed, thumping his chest three times for emphasis. "You did it, just as I knew you would."

"Did it?" he asked, bemused.

"Solved the case of my son's murder."

"I guess so, but—"

He wanted to explain that all he had done was eavesdrop on Phyllis Gossett's confession while immobilized and repeat the details to investigating officers.

"But nothing," she said, clinching her lips. "You solved it plain and simple and have freed this old woman from all her worries. Jamaal's name has been exonerated, and the museum can continue to function, funding permitting, with a clean slate, as it were. Speaking of which, tomorrow is a color of your choice."

"I'm sorry, but I won't be coming in tomorrow."

"Yes, I can understand that. Take a couple of days off to recuperate. You've earned it."

"The fact is—"

"I don't want to hear a word about you resigning your position," she said, backing away, turning her head and holding up her hands as though to protect her ears from anything Will was about to say. "You're the best curator the museum has seen in years. Not only that, you managed to stay alive. And I simply cannot continue running the museum without you."

"But—"

"No buts," she insisted and beat it down the hall toward the bank of elevators, clicking her heels sharply in retreat.

Of course, he wanted to point out, he was only the third curator she'd had since the museum opened. Plus, she was forgetting all about Mandy. It seemed, as the morning unfolded, that Mandy had been tucked away, an asterisk to the main course of events, a state of affairs Will found perplexing and sad. The girl hadn't meant for any of the tragedies to happen. She had been only a clueless pawn.

Will came back in. Essence had turned off the TV and was resting.

"So," he said, coming up to her bedside.

"So," she said, looking up at him with wide, warm eyes.

He leaned over and gave her a kiss on the cheek.

"We'll have to stop meeting like this."

"Yeah, really." She touched her wounded shoulder with her

fingertips through her gown.

"Does it hurt?" he asked.

"Not very. Why don't you sit with me?"

He took a seat on the edge of the bed, turning so he could face her.

"I won't stay long," he said.

"Won't? Or can't?"

"I don't want to tire you."

"Ah," she said, letting a silence stretch between them that seemed somehow natural and awkward at the same time.

"I'll be leaving town. Just for a little while."

"I see," she said, drawing up her knees. "To your wife?"

He explained everything—about Daryl, about the offer of a trip back to Utica. She listened quietly, calmly. It was hard reading her emotions.

"I need to see her," he finished. "For closure, if nothing else. We left so many things undone."

"Of course," she said, shifting her position. "And your son, too. You'll want to see your son again." She played with the bed's remote control, adjusting her angle of repose. "Damn hospital beds. They're always so uncooperative."

"What about you?" he asked when she settled.

"What about me?"

"What will you do?"

She pushed up with her hands and winced. The movement startled him, and he reached behind her back to support her.

"There's that whole big ol' mansion to live in for now. But I doubt I'll stay long. I'll need to find a place for the tigers, if they aren't destroyed. I don't suppose you'd like to take care of them? They seem to like you."

Will would have assumed this was a joke, except her tone was somber, and her face had lost its smile.

He placed a hand on her shoulder, the unwounded one. It was bare, brown, and soft, curving out of the gown, which was drooping, a size too large.

"Well," he said, doodling a pattern along her neck, below her ear, with his forefinger. He felt the need to linger. "I probably should—"

"You'll come back?" she asked, turning her face toward him, her eyes peering into his as though to peel back the truth.

"Of course," he said, brushing a stray lock from her forehead, which felt warm, feverish. "Of course I will. I promise."

"Will," she said, softly, and he took his hand away. "Please don't make promises you can't keep. No one knows what's ahead for you—for me. Not really."

"I'm sorry—" he began. "It's just that—"

"Maybe it's better if you just go," she said, adopting a quiet finality to her voice. "Maybe it's better if we—" She couldn't finish her sentence.

He hadn't wanted to leave her this way. But he had thought it over through the morning hours, and this was the decision he had arrived at. He had to see, had to find out, what was going on with Abbey, his wife—and their son. It had been too long. Like a penitent on pilgrimage, he needed to seek her forgiveness. He doubted she would grant it so easily. In fact, he didn't think she would give it at all.

Rising, he took one last look at her, but Essence had turned her head away, toward the wall.

"I can see you again," he said, standing there, listless. "I don't have to go right away. The police still have questions." No answer. No response. "Well, then, I guess—"

He took a breath and held it, waiting for her to look his way, then walked toward the door.

"Will?" he heard and stopped without turning his head. And

then, softly, "Thank you."

"For what?" he asked, after a pause, keeping his back to her. He was afraid if he turned around, he would lose what little willpower he had to leave.

"For believing in me."

There's still time to turn back, he thought. But the thought carried him down the hall to the elevators, then through the lobby and out the front doors. He heard a horn blast from the other side of the street. Daryl was waving out the window of the silver Jaguar.

"Ready to go?" he called.

Will took a hesitant step forward. When he stepped off the curb, he was still Will Archer. It wasn't until they were just inside the Utica city limits that he started to feel like Alan Paxton again.

Chapter 41

Ever since Daryl had called and told her he was bringing home Alan, Abbey had gone into a feeding frenzy of feeling. A kaleidoscopic array of emotions turned this way and that, flecks of thoughts, images, memories, all in knots, bunches, sparkling.

She had to leave the studio early; she couldn't concentrate. There was an exhibit tonight, a local photographer, but her partner could take care of it. Everything was arranged, the hors d'oeuvres, the punch bowl, the promotional flyers. It was the photographer's first public display, and she was nervous.

Not so nervous as me, Abbey thought. Taking the rest of the day off, she picked up Joel from daycare before lunch.

"Why, Mama?" he had asked. "Is something wrong?"

"No, I just thought we'd have lunch together. I haven't seen you all week."

"But it's only Tuesday," he observed.

Reaching over the back seat of the car, she handed him a brush. "Here, comb your hair."

"But I combed it this morning."

"It won't hurt to comb it again," she said, critiquing its frilliness in the rearview mirror. Did they have time for a haircut? What about her own hair? It hung limp as a rag. Had she forgotten to condition it this morning?

She couldn't help but keep checking her phone. Daryl had synced his GPS to hers, and she followed them across state lines: Ohio to Pennsylvania and, my God! Here they were crossing into New York already. How fast was he going, anyway?

At this rate, she gave them less than three hours.

"Come on, Joel! We have to go." She grabbed his shoes out

of the bin of the fast-food restaurant's play area and waited for him to climb down a spider web of ropes.

"Aw, do we have to already?" His typical complaint.

On the way home, she kept rehearsing how she would break it to him: *Your Daddy is coming home?*

But first, she would have to tell him all about his Daddy. She hadn't been very good about keeping his memory alive. At first, she'd pored through her photo gallery with him, but there had been so few photos with Alan in them.

What could she tell him about his father? She hardly knew who he was anymore. He had started to seep into crevices of memory, like bits of ribbon, swatches of color, hoarded, tucked away. Now, here he was resurrecting like a ghost.

Change of plan.

"Joel, I'm going to drop you at Nancy's, okay?"

Nancy was the full-time girlfriend, part-time sitter, who Abbey held in reserve for her nighttime work at the studio. She was on tap for tonight's showing, and Abbey texted at a red light to see if she could take Joel earlier than expected.

The return text was immediate:

Sure, why not? Bring the little tyke over.

This was a relief. First, she needed to become reacquainted with her husband. Yes, he was still her husband. She hadn't let go of the tie that binds, even though it had become severely worn and frazzled over the past year. Then she would see about reintroducing him to her son. *Her* son, not *their* son. This is how she thought of Joel now.

After dropping him off at Nancy's, she spent the afternoon busying herself with something she rarely did except when the state of the townhome finally demanded some form of action: housecleaning. She was more into tidying up on an as-needed basis, not major overhauls.

The cleaning was a product of sheer anxiety. Surely there wasn't a need to impress, was there? He was still the same old Alan, a man she had known for years. Or was he? How might a year apart have changed him? How had it changed her?

That he had declined talking to her over the phone in advance bothered her. Was he afraid of his voice betraying him in some way?

Every so often, she glanced out the kitchen window past the fenced-in back patio that abutted the parking lot where Daryl would pull up in … only fifteen minutes!

She got up, checked the window, sat down, got up, checked the window, sat down, more than a dozen times, until she looked out, saw an unfamiliar silver sports coupe, and a strange man emerge with long hair, sunken eyes, and a haggard look that was no doubt her husband.

***

"Well, this is it," Daryl said, waiting for Alan to exit his side of the car. "Want me to wait around?"

"No, that's okay."

Actually, Alan wanted for Daryl to coax him back into the car and drive off, back the way they came, to what had become familiar territory these past three weeks. Is that all it had been? Three weeks along the river, one year away from home, except Abbey was no longer living in the house he had left behind. She was in a new place now and presumably had a new life. What was he thinking in wanting to disturb that for her?

He didn't think she'd be welcoming after all this time given the way he had left. In fact, he was surprised she was agreeable to seeing him at all. He fully expected to be reprimanded, yelled at. Maybe she would throw things at him? Had he ever known her to throw things? Just that one time when she was late for a gallery showing and her hair dryer shorted out with the flash of an electric arc. She'd thrown it out the bathroom window.

He went ahead and knocked on the patio door, which was curtained inside with vinyl blinds. The rain was lessening but still steady, running coldly down his neck under the collar of his jacket. He could have pulled up the hood, but he wanted his face to be visible when she opened the door. *If* she opened the door.

He knocked again, and the door slid open partway, guided by an invisible hand. Now all that separated him from the person inside were the columns of blinds.

"Abbey?" he called softly.

A pause, nothing, silence.

"Come on in, Alan," her voice said, evenly, softly, but clearly.

He took a breath and, parting the blinds, stepped into a dining area. Abbey stood on the other side of the glass-topped table. She looked just as he remembered her. She was dressed in slacks and satin shirt, her hair drawn back. He took note of a layer of lip balm—her lips were perpetually chapped. Hoop earrings—these were a new touch. He was afraid to look into her eyes, the way she was staring at him so intently.

"I spent all day cleaning," she said. "I wasn't sure when you'd arrive. I didn't know what else to do."

"The place looks nice," he said looking around, glancing at her across the table. He was afraid to move, to breathe, to say anything more uninvited.

"How was the drive up?" she asked tentatively. "Okay?"

He nodded. His mouth, his throat, felt dry. He wasn't prepared for ordinary conversation. Where was this leading?

"Daryl dropped you off? I guess he couldn't stay?"

Alan shook his head.

He felt like a stranger in this place, with this woman—an actor without a script. He recognized her as his wife. She was wearing her wedding ring. Had she been wearing it all the time he was away? He was glad he had thought to slip on his beforehand, but it didn't make the moment less tense. He was waiting for something, some feeling, some cue, to make the situation feel right.

"Well," she said flatly, still staring at him, not smiling, not frowning, her expression inscrutable.

"Well," he said, echoing her sentiment.

She held his gaze a moment longer, then rounded the table, into the kitchen. She opened the refrigerator, its interior light illuminating her profile, accenting the smoothness of her cheeks, the sheen of her forehead, the mold of her chin.

"You're probably hungry. Are you hungry? I forgot all about making dinner. There's not much here. Leftover pizza. A couple cans of soda." She turned her head, looking in his direction without meeting his eyes. "You want a Coke? It's Diet."

"Sure," he said, although he privately desired something more potent now that his restriction on alcohol had been eased.

She grabbed two from the fridge and set one on the counter, snapping open the other for herself. Alan winced at the sound, but it passed innocuously along the wiring of his brain. Keeping the counter between them, she raised the can to her lips and took a shallow sip.

"You can set down your bag, you know. You don't have to just stand there."

"What should I do?" he asked.

"I don't know. Nothing. Anything. Why don't we go in the other room."

She moved quickly past, her body all one fluid motion, keeping her distance, as though to prevent a static shock.

"Joel's not here?" he asked, following her into the living room, where he set down his duffle bag, as she had asked.

"No, he's at a—" She broke off and took a seat on the edge of an armchair. She leaned forward, elbows on knees, staring into the opening of the pop can as though it held a secret. He moved to the couch and took a seat on the far end of it. He glanced at the coffee table: a couple of magazines. But that was it. The place looked as devoid of personality as a hotel room.

"Abbey, I—"

"What are you doing here anyway?" she asked, looking up. "Was it because of Daryl? Would you have come back if he hadn't found you? Were you ever planning to come home?"

"I don't know," he said, his voice barely registering to his own ears. He looked at her out of the corners of his eyes, afraid to offer a direct gaze.

"Well, at least you're honest. Was it because of your penance? Is this penance of yours over now? Or was there some other reason you left?"

"No," he answered. "It was guilt. I couldn't get through the guilt for taking away another man's wife and child."

"What about us? Joel and me? You didn't feel guilt for taking yourself away from us? Depriving me of a husband? Joel of a father?"

"No, of course I felt bad about—"

"It was just so selfish of you. The way you left with just a note. Are you sure that's all there was to it? Penance? Guilt? Are you sure it wasn't to escape your obligations to us? To your family?"

Up until this point, she had kept her voice under firm control. But now it was starting to break.

"I'm sorry." He stood and picked up his bag, holding it at his side. "Maybe I should go."

"So go," she said, her words sounding brittle.

He stood there, feeling as though he had evaporated into an abyss of time, unable to move.

"Are you going?" she asked. She stood, facing him, tears in her eyes.

"Do you want me to go?"

"No. Yes. I don't know." The words came out in rapid succession. "Hold me," she said, her shoulders drooping, her head lowered, locks of hair falling over her eyes.

He took a hesitant step toward her, then another, and then, carefully, delicately, he put his arms around her, clasping them loosely behind her waist. She leaned her head against his shoulder. He could feel the wetness of her face, her cheeks, her eyes.

"I hate you," she said, murmuring the words, her body tense, rigid.

"I know," he said, whispering.

"I hate you, I hate you," she repeated, the words faint, barely audible. "I will always hate you."

She pulled away from him, breaking free of his arms, and as she turned, he reached out, taking hold of her wrist.

"Abbey," he said, his voice beseeching.

"Don't," she said, but she didn't strain, she didn't struggle out of his handhold, exerting only the slightest pressure. Gradually, he let her hand slide out of his grasp.

As she withdrew, he collapsed onto the floor, ending up cross-legged, head down. His breath, which he had been holding in check all this time, came out as a series of heaves.

He recalled a time he had cried, long after his parents' deaths. The unexpectedness of it had left him in dry-eyed shock. It wasn't until years later, in the middle of diapering, when Joel looked up from the changing table into his eyes and said "Dada!" for the first time that he gushed real tears, as though a switch had been flipped in his nervous system. And now he was experiencing the same sort of release, the crying coming from deep within.

Then he felt it, a hand on his shoulder, gently, just lying there; it might have been a phantom, a shadow, for all the weight it gave. But the hand soothed him, gave him something to

concentrate on. He felt a hardness on top of his head and realized it was her chin, bearing down, not hard, not meanly, just
resting, but with firmer conviction than her hand, as she knelt
before him.

"I'm sorry," he keened, "I'm so, so sorry."

The hand began a gentle circular motion below his shoulder
blades, a calming tattoo. His breaths came out in jagged waves,
catching, holding, releasing. After a while, he began breathing
more easily, and it was when he felt sure of his breaths that he
raised his head and her chin moved aside. He stared into her eyes,
so wide, so dark, so knowing, and she returned his gaze.

He brushed a strand of jangled hair from her brow, where it
was varnished in place with a thin veneer of sweat. Lowering his
hand, he wiped her cheek dry with his thumb, then leaned toward
her so their foreheads touched. Eyes closed, he felt her fingers
rubbing up and down his back along his spine. Sitting together,
they maintained their embrace, their fingers touching, feeling, ex-
ploring, wordlessly, until their cheeks touched, then their noses,
lips, mouths, while, still silently, they began working their clothes
from each other …

But then she stopped him before he could explore any further. She rolled away as though prodded by an electric current.

"Who was she?" Abbey asked.

How did she know? Daryl? A woman's intuition? There was
no denying the secret knowledge building in her eyes, not accu-
satory but questioning.

"No one," Alan answered. "Someone."

"Will you go back to her?"

Alan sat up, looking at his wife in profile, tracing with his
eyes the shape of her nose, the contour of her face, the accent of
her collarbone.

"I'm here now," he said, reaching out a hand.

Abbey lurched upright, startling him.

"I should go get Joel," she said. "It's getting late."

"I'd like to see him," Alan said.

Abbey stood up in the semidarkness, bending to gather her clothes. She headed for the stairway, pausing at the base of it, hand on the railing.

"I don't want him to get his hopes up," she said. "What just happened—what was about to. It doesn't mean we're back together. It doesn't mean I've forgiven you."

Alan nodded, understanding.

"I don't want you staying here tonight," she told him bluntly. "I don't want you seeing Joel."

Alan worked to suppress a sudden surge of feeling. Remorse? Disbelief? Anger?

"Ever?"

"Not until you decide you want to be part of our lives again for real."

As she started up the stairs, he fought a moment of panic.

"Your hairdryer," he said, almost shouting out the words. This made her stop, two steps from the top, and she eyed him curiously over the banister. "Did you ever replace it?"

She aimed a questioning look at him as though he had uttered an absurdity.

"A year away from home," she said, "and that's the first thing you remember?"

She moved the rest of the way up the stairs, shaking her head, and Alan, gathering up his clothes, traced her footsteps overhead by the sound they made.

Chapter 42

Feeling so much like a spy, Alan waited in the twilight shadows of the hedges bordering a neighboring townhome Abbey had entered. The rain had stopped, and thin, translucent clouds were flirting with the razor thin profile of a new moon.

He couldn't bring himself to leave for the night, find a motel somewhere nearby, without seeing Joel, his son, even indirectly, from a distance, as he peered through the branches of the viburnum. He had watched Abbey go in an hour ago. His watch glowed 9:30, long past Joel's bedtime, unless that had changed since he'd been away.

He was about to leave his post when the front door opened and one large figure exited. No, it was a double image: his wife carrying his son—their son. The boy had his head slumped on his mother's shoulder in a state of repose. But so big! His legs dangled out of his mother's clasped arms, and it was obvious she had her hands full carrying him.

As they passed under lamplight, he made out Joel's face, asleep. A year older, but still the same sweet face he remembered, a small brown oval with a delicate chin and a coiled mop of hair.

On instinct, he took a step forward but caught himself in midstride. It crept up on him: certain knowledge that he wanted so very, very much to be with Abbey and Joel, to be part of their lives again, to make them part of his. He was about to take another step when he heard a cough, and he turned, feeling alarmed. A man was standing in the shadows wearing a trench coat and fedora, as though he had stepped out of a celluloid still of a film noir movie.

"Hello, Mr. Paxton," the man said. "A beautiful sight, is it not? A mother caring for her child, willing to carry him a long distance so as not to wake him?"

Although he couldn't make out the face, shadowed by the brim of the hat, he recognized something about the voice. It sounded thin, high-pitched, wiry—like a violin string drawn too tightly.

The man took one step closer, entering the beam of light from a walkway lantern, and Alan discovered a familiar face: sallow cheeks, mouth pinched at the corners, eyes squinting through round-rimmed glasses. He saw, too, that the man extended a gun, small and compact, with the barrel of it unequivocally pointed in Alan's direction.

"Mr. Perritt?" Alan asked, tentatively.

"Please, no need for formalities. Call me Don, won't you?"

"What is it you want?" He tried to seek a hidden meaning within Don Perritt's gaze.

"It's not what I want, it's what you want, Mr. Paxton. Alan, if I may. You want to be reunited with your family, and I have no intention of preventing this. In fact, if you will lead the way, I believe you know where they live."

"Let's leave them out of it," he said sternly, forcefully.

If he lunged, could he hope to avoid a bullet while grabbing hold of Perritt's firing arm and pulling the gun out of his grasp? Maybe, if he swung his duffle bag, like a weapon …

As if sensing this change in temperament, Perritt took a step backward.

"Please, no theatrics. Let us proceed calmly in a straight line, if you would. But first, set aside your luggage."

He waved the gun in a circle for compliance, and Alan set down his duffle bag.

Directed by the movement of the gun, as though it were a conductor's baton, he began walking slowly, trying to stall, hoping to formulate a plan. He had no doubt Perritt would know if he was being led off the path. He thought about making a run for it, but who knew what a vengeful man with a gun might be capable of? He didn't want to put his wife and child at risk, yet this seemed to be his only recourse as he moved closer and closer to Abbey's townhome.

"You don't have to do this," Alan said, half turning to catch a glimpse of how far back Perritt was behind him—not far.

"No? Just as you didn't have to cross the center line and strike my wife and daughter? You should not have come back, Alan. You should have stayed away. Everything would have been fine if you had just stayed away. I thought we had an agreement to that effect."

They continued navigating a series of sidewalks, interconnecting like a maze, until they reached their destination.

"This way, Alan. We will go through the front door."

Alan paused, contemplating shouting out, warning Abbey of their approach, but Perritt nudged him between his shoulder blades with the gun.

"Go ahead, Alan, ring the bell."

The command was so politely made, the use of his first name so casual, Alan wondered if Perritt really had any serious intention to harm anyone, or if the melodrama of holding a man at gunpoint was all just a ruse, an empty threat.

Alan did as told. He rang the bell, and within seconds, Abbey opened it a crack, her face crimping into a frown when she saw him. She didn't look displeased, just perplexed.

"Alan," she said, "what are you doing back? I thought we agreed—"

When he didn't say anything, she glanced behind her.

"Joel's asleep on the couch," she whispered, not waiting for an explanation. "I haven't carried him upstairs yet. I suppose it would be okay if you came in and took a peek at him."

She opened the door wider, but Alan remained on the threshold, declining to enter.

"Alan? What is it?"

"Hello, Abigail," Perritt's voice rang out from the shadows. Prodded, Alan stepped through the door before Abbey had a chance to close it.

"Donald!" she exclaimed.

"One and the same," he said calmly, moving into the room and closing the door behind him, as Abbey stepped backward and Alan turned, placing himself between her and the gun. "I understand the importance of putting your son to bed, but I suppose it isn't too late to receive company?"

"Yes, well, no!" she said, obviously flustered. "I mean—"
She took in the gun.

"Alan?" she asked, her eyes beseeching an answer.

"I'm sorry, Abbey," Alan said. "There wasn't anything I could—"

"Let's all take our seats," Perritt interrupted, as though a manager inviting his subordinates to arrange themselves in a boardroom. "Shall we?"

With separate motions of his gun, he beckoned Alan to sit in the armchair and Abbey to sit on the couch next to the prostrate form of her son. Perritt remained standing, and Alan gazed at Joel. His eyes were closed, his breathing deep and regular. He noticed Perritt was gazing, too, so long and intently that Alan thought he had been swallowed by a daydream.

"Please, Donald," Abbey said firmly, then softened her tone as he turned his head toward her, "Don, please. You don't need to do this. Think of what you're doing."

"I know what I am doing, Abigail," Perritt said sharply. Then he too relented: "Abbey, I should say, given that we've known each other so long. Yes, Alan," he continued, "don't look so sur-prised. Your wife and I have had a—relationship, shall we say?"

"Alan," Abbey said quickly, "it was nothing like that. We were just friends."

"Yes, until your husband showed back up. Just friends with so much of our relationship left unexplored. But it was I, not you," he said, directing his vendetta at Alan, "who stayed by her all this past year. I was the one who cared for her, watched over her, protected her—"

"Mr. Perritt," Alan said, cutting him off. "Don," he contin-ued, feeling it strange to be on a first-name basis, "I know you're upset. I'm upset, too. I never stop thinking about it, that night. How I could have reacted. What I could have done differently."

"This makes two of us," Perritt said. "I never cease to think of it either."

"If you could just put the gun down. We could talk about it. We could try to—" He didn't know how else to phrase it, not knowing what Perritt had in mind. "Settle this some other way."

"There's nothing to discuss. You took my wife and child; now I am preparing to take yours."

Abbey took a sharp breath. Her eyes went wide, wild.

"If you think for one second I'll let you hurt my son."

She was on her feet, but Perritt commanded her sternly: "Sit down, please!"

He didn't aim the gun at her but at Joel, and Abbey threw herself in front of him, shielding her boy.

"Mama?" Joel said, waking up.

Alan lunged from his seat, but Perritt waved him back with his gun.

"Please, there's no need to make a scene," he said, turning his attention back to Abbey. "All year long, I've tried to be your friend—or something more. I could have helped you move on.

We could have gone anywhere you chose. Far, far away, so he"—casting a glance toward Alan—"would never find you. But you spurned all my advances. And so I will give you one more chance—to redeem yourself and come with me. I have a car all ready and waiting. All you need to is pack your belongings and those of your son."

Warily, Alan took a single step forward.

"If you would kindly retake your seat," Perritt said, training the gun on him. "There is no need for anyone to get hurt."

Instead of doing as bid, Alan ventured another step forward. Perritt raised the gun to chest level, but Alan sensed a tremor in his hand—a wavering of intention?

"You're right," Alan said, trying to make his voice as steady as he could. "There's no need to harm anyone. There's no need to take them anywhere either."

"Please, Alan. As much as I'd like to, I don't want to hurt you."

"I know you don't," Alan said, taking one more step.

He reached out quickly and took hold of Perritt's hand holding the gun. He applied steady pressure, trying to force the gun down and away, but Perritt had more strength than he anticipated.

"Let's just put the gun down, okay?" he pleaded, cupping Perritt's gun hand in both of his.

"Alan," Abbey said from the couch, observing as though from a distant wharf on an unsettled sea. "Don't."

Perritt looked him evenly in the eyes. There was a lost, empty, forlorn look to his gaze, his eyes disappearing inside himself momentarily.

"I'm sorry, Alan," he said. "I truly am."

He blinked once, slowly, and fired.

Chapter 43

Darkness and sound.

Or nothingness, really—nothingness engulfed in sound. He heard the loud wail of his wife, Abbey, rising like a pillar of salt, and then it dissolved into the scream of a siren, and he felt himself transported.

He saw faces swimming as though in a goldfish bowl, a thick lip protruding, a squinting eye: "Stay with us, buddy. Are you with us?"

Yes, I am with you, I am always with you …

Except he wasn't. His eyes closed, he felt himself suspended somewhere high above, and when he ventured to open them, he saw he was facing downward, lying on a cushion of air, looking at his own mirror image far below. This other self was stretched out on a hospital table in an operating room. His body was still, his eyes closed, a tube down his throat. He counted two doctors, two nurses, plus the anesthesiologist, looking impartial. The doctors, one male, one female, were busy spreading open his abdomen and sewing up his insides, exposed to view. He felt distant, removed, a feeling of tranquility taking away all that former sensation of piercing pain.

It all seemed surreal, and he found himself thinking that this must be a hallucination or dream. The body below must have some sensation. Sound waves are impacting its eardrums. Bright light is filtering through paper-thin eyelids. Its brain must be piecing it all together, imagining a scene reminiscent of the time he peeked over the curtain when Abbey was undergoing a C-section for a difficult birth, her abdomen opened up like a slab of beef, and he had almost passed out. But now he didn't feel nauseous at all. He observed the scene below with objectivity, curious only to see if the surgical team would succeed in its task of sewing him back together.

"Quite a sight, ain't it now?"

The voice came from his left, and when he turned his head, he found himself in a brightly lit room, all its walls and ceiling and floor a brilliant white, almost blinding. It was hard fathoming its dimensions. It seemed just as likely he was encased in a sugar cube or suspended inside a bank of clouds.

"He did quite a number on you with that gun of his."

The same voice, masculine, but bright, lighthearted, almost playful, as though trying to engage him in banter. Now it came from his right, and when he turned that way, he saw a young Black man dressed in a pure white suit with a golden saxophone slung around his neck and a beautiful pearly smile accented by a gold tooth that transmitted genuine friendliness. The contrast between the man's smooth, brown face, free of blemish, and the immaculate whiteness of his clothes and surroundings was stark.

"So what do you say, Alan? Not pleased to see me? Or is it Will?"

The names—Will, Alan. It seemed he should know who they were. He should be able to sort them out, differentiate one from the other. But the harder he tried, the more they seemed intertwined.

"What's the matter? Cat got your tongue?"

Will extended a hand, forefinger pointing.

"You're Jamaal, aren't you?"

"One and the same, brother. One and the same."

One and the same—the thought that had just gone through his own head.

"So which is it? Will or Alan?"

"Alan," he answered forthrightly. "But you can call me Will."

"Ah, you're a funny one, aren't you? But why the long face?"

"Is this—"

"The afterlife?" Jamaal took a step back, his smile momentarily leaving, then returning, as though it hadn't been troubled. "There's just the one life, my friend. Wherever you happen to be. Here … or there."

Jamaal nodded, and he looked down, seeing his body still being operated on, the monitor keeping track of his vitals struggling against flatlining.

"I suppose this is where you'll tell me I have to go back? I have more work to do?"

"Hell, no! You're free now, brother. Free to do whatever you want. You and me, I think we've both been through enough to last us a couple of lifetimes. Wouldn't you agree?"

He turned away from the operating scene spread out below. This white room—it felt so comfortable. And Jamaal—it was like he had always known him, always known he would be the one to greet him when the time came.

"Stick with me, and I'll show you a good time." Jamaal came closer, his face rich in color, his smile intense. "I guarantee it."

Jamaal started walking away, and he had a moment of panic.

"Wait," he said, "wait up."

He felt so lightheaded, so … airy. Insubstantial. The sound of the saxophone lured him down a long corridor that narrowed in the distance, receding like a railroad track. Jamaal was far ahead, shrinking into a dot, but his music was clear and crystalline. He had heard this tune, so pleasantly mournful, else mournfully pleasant, before. It was the same tune he had heard through the pipes of the Victorian Arms. How funny that all of the time he spent there seemed as though it belonged to someone else's experience.

At the end of the corridor, he came to a portal, a rectangle of misty grayness—or not gray exactly. A nameless color. Formless, too. Intangible. He could hear the music emanating from it, through it, but starting to fade, coming through in snatches like scarves, wisps of shredded fog.

He knew if he stepped through, there would be no going back. But there was something holding him, keeping him from taking a step through the doorway. What was it?

A person? A place? Somewhere, someone, was waiting for him.

He turned away from the door and took a step, but the step took him across a different threshold.

He lost the sound of the saxophone. In its place was a rushing sound of air in his ears. He felt wind on his face. It seemed he was descending through a hurricane of clouds, floating, but falling. As he stared, squinting through the squall all around him, the mist began to clear, and he could make out the outlines of a river far below, concentrated within the eye of the storm. Crossing the river was a bridge. It lay stretched across the water like a gray thread, thin and spidery.

It looked insubstantial, too frail for human traffic, too delicate for a single footstep. As he descended, he saw it was only the skeleton of a bridge. Crowds of people clustered on either end. They were counting backwards. He knew it was vitally important he join them before they reached zero.

But at the rate he was falling, he doubted he would ever make it in time.

Chapter 44

… five … four … three … two … one!

The shouts went up from the crowds on either shore, kept at a safe distance from the bridge by police barricades in the form of sawhorses and yellow tape.

There was a second's delay, making Essence, along with everyone else, wonder if there was some misfiring, some problem with the fuse. She heard the collective inhalation of breath, a pause, so very pregnant, and then … BOOM! The first explosive went off in a huge puff of yellow and gray smoke on this, the Ohio side. It was followed in quick succession by a series of explosions, moving along the skeletal remains of the framework, traversing to the West Virginia side, one after another, like a baton being handed off in a relay race.

When the final explosion resounded along the banks of the river, there was another pause, no less pregnant, as the bridge appeared to waver between life and death as first, the underlying stone supports crumbled, then the bridge chassis succumbed to gravity, and the structure—what was left of it—fell like a children's rhyme into the river.

Over the past nine months, jackhammers and backhoes and bulldozers and dump trucks had gnawed and ripped at it, tearing into it like a decaying carcass, and carted all of it away except the steel girders, all linked together like the vertebrae of a long-necked sauropod. Essence had come down to the river religiously, day after day, for all of its dismantling, through October leaves and December chills and March winds, and now today, as though in testament to human folly, on this first day of April, where it all went up in a cloud of smoke and dust that settled on top of the heap of metal and stone in the river like a funeral shroud. As the cheering subsided, the crowd began to disassemble, but Essence lingered.

Her Grandma Waxman—she could no longer be called Nana Other, there being no other grandmother with which to compare her—hadn't bothered to come down. Too much hype and hoopla for her taste. She had closed the museum, giving its new curator—a music major at the college who played trombone—the day off.

"You go ahead," Sybil Waxman had told her. She had given up worrying so much about her granddaughter, not that she didn't cluck over her like a mother hen from time to time. "I'll take care of the little one." She hefted the baby out of her crib and cradled her against her shoulder, where Essence could observe the small, delicate eyelids, remarkably still closed in sleep.

Essence had surrendered the mansion for the small upstairs guestroom in her Nana's house, which suited her and the baby just fine. There wasn't a mansion to live in, anyhow. Not anymore. Following the estate sale, the place was all boarded up and awaiting its own demolition to make way for the construction of a Wal-Mart, as advertised in big block letters on the sign posted out front. All the statues had been carted off by collectors. The tigers Crimson and Clover, despite their joint murder of their trainer, had found new homes in an exotic zoo in Arkansas.

"Just promise me this will be it," her grandmother implored. "After this, there will be no more reason for you to go down there. Day after day in the elements—a woman in your condition. So soon after—"

"Giving birth? I'll be fine. It's already been two weeks.

But her grandmother only harumphed in response.

She had promised, and she meant to keep it. The demolition of the bridge satisfied her need for closure, and now she felt ready for a new beginning. She wasn't sure exactly which direction she should go, but she knew it would mean leaving New Bloomfield.

Even though her Nana had offered to take care of them both indefinitely, she didn't think she could stay any longer than necessary. She'd had quite enough of the place. And she had enough money in her account following dispersal of her Grandmother Warner's inheritance—not to mention all that cash in the white carrying case, which, following their investigation, the police had returned to her—to go anywhere on Earth she desired. The idea of somewhere exotic—Tongo, Bhutan, Singapore—crossed her mind from time to time like the teasing of a feather.

Essence spent most of her free time—and there was lots of it—at the museum, putting her mother and father back together again, taping the separate, jagged halves of each photograph on the obverse, and doing a little touchup work on the flip side with a thin brush and various bottles of ink, from blackest black to whitest white—reuniting them for inclusion in the scrapbook that was to become a pictorial of her father's life. Their reunion—it was sanctified, blessed, by her Grandma Waxman herself, now that she knew the whole story of their romance.

Plus, there was the curator to chat up. Even though he was two years older, a junior in college, he seemed just a baby. He was pleasant enough and jokey—at least, his jokes, bad as they were, made her smile. But he wasn't Will.

Did she long for him? She wouldn't go that far. But she had missed him. She wasn't even sure what it was she missed. His sincerity? He was the most honest person she had ever met, and yet, all the time they had known each other, he had been living a lie. She had waited on him to make good on his half-promise to return, even if it was for nothing more than a visit.

Did she want him to come back to her? Part of her was

absolutely terrified by the thought. What did they have in common besides a string of trials and tribulations and deaths? Was that enough of a history to rejoin them? And how would he react to her news? She didn't know. But after the first month with no sign of him, her hopes began to fade, and after the second and then third month, she let him drift through her consciousness the same as any other thought. Well … almost. She could still breathe in the smell of him, feel his touch on her skin, trace his spine through the small of his back, stare into the steadiness of his eyes, tease out a smile.

And then Daryl had shown up in the coldest part of February, driving a shockingly red Mustang, pulling right up to the curb and knocking loudly, asking just as loudly for Essence Warner when her Nana opened the door.

They'd gone out for coffee. He apologized, saying he'd meant to come through before this, but one thing and another. He was so different than Will, so self-assured, self-possessed. This was a man who knew just who he was: a joker, a clown, maybe even a fool. But a wise one.

And he had been the man who had rescued her from the bridge. Surely, she owed him more than a cup of coffee? But that was all he had time for. And in the 30 minutes they spent together, he had told her all about Will.

It had taken him a long time to recover from the bullet wound …

"Bullet wound?"

He described how Will had been shot trying to defend his wife and child, embellishing, since he hadn't been there himself to witness it.

"And the man who shot him?"

"In prison. Behind bars. Turned himself in."

Then he explained how the doctors had had to excise the

bullet from his spine and rearrange his insides to put him all back together, just like Humpty Dumpty, you know? Except he wasn't fragile as an egg, of course. He was Will Archer, or had been. And now, he was trying to become Alan Paxton …

"Alan," she echoed. "Yes, I know. My Nana told me."

"Pax to his friends."

"Pax?"

Uh-huh, and it's been strange, watching his transformation, sort of like watching someone trying to fit his hand into a glove that's shrunk so it won't quite fit. Okay, maybe a bad analogy. But now, with him going back to being Alan, he and Abbey …

"Abbey?"

Abigail—his wife. They were trying to make a go of it, start afresh, as it were. But it didn't work out, and now they're separated with joint custody of their kid.

Daryl handed over a sheet of yellow ledger paper folded in thirds.

"What's this?"

"Open it and see."

Essence was half-afraid to read it, afraid of what the note would spell out.

Dear Essence,

Hmph! Not exactly a romantic salutation, was it? But she let her eyes scroll down the page.

I'm sorry it's taken me so long to contact you.

Contact? Just "contact"? Another impersonal choice of words.

It's taken me a very long time to put my life back together, and I fervently hope …

Fervently? Really?

… that you are putting yours back together as well. Please believe me, I've thought of you every single day since we've been apart. Dreamed of you even.

This was more like it. She was relieved to see the letter warming up … finally.

And it's true, I've thought of coming back to you. Not just to visit. But to pick up where we left off as it were. It seems to me we left so much unsaid, unfinished. But …

She had anticipated this. There's always a "but" where these sorts of feelings are concerned.

One day led to another and the days became weeks, and the more time passed, the more it seemed I was doing the right thing in letting you go. You're young. Your life is brand-new now. You have every option imaginable. Only you can decide how to live it. I didn't want to be the one to trip you up, to get in your way.

But he wouldn't have stood in the way, she didn't think. Just the opposite …

So many things have changed now for me, but who knows? The only certainty is uncertainty as some old philosopher or other has said (but what do old philosophers know?) …

She was thankful he still had a sense of humor, just at the point she was afraid the schoolgirl silliness of a tear might slip out of her eye.

Maybe somewhere, someday, we'll see each other … although I have to warn you, you might not recognize me … life brings so many changes.
Until then, I will always be grateful for the time, brief as it was, we had together.
Love,

She was glad to see him conclude with a tender sentiment.

Alan (aka "Will")

Daryl took a sip of his coffee, lowering his eyes over the brim to where her waist would be if he could use X-ray vision to see through the table.

"Looks like you might have some news of your own."

"You can tell?" she asked, feeling her face flush.

"How long?"

"Twenty-eight weeks. Not that I'm counting."

She could tell he was doing a mental calculation, crunching numbers in his head.

"Is it—?"

He didn't have to finish the rest of his question.

"I don't know," she said, honestly. "I hope so. Will you tell him?"

"Nah, I'll leave that to you."

He surprised her by leaning across the table on folded arms. The steadiness of his gaze unnerved her.

"So how are you?" he asked. "Really."

"Did he ask you to ask me?"

"No. I'm asking. You've been through a lot."

"Well … my shrink tells me I'm making progress." There has been a proposal to step down their weekly sessions from two to one, she might have added, although the therapist keeps encouraging Essence to join a survivors' group to compensate.

Daryl smiled and sat back in his seat, seemingly assured.

"That's good. Progress is good. As long as you know what you're progressing toward."

Their conversation was interrupted by the loud exclamation of a muffler directly outside the plate-glass window of the café. The muffler belonged to an old-model, travel-stained, white Chrysler. The driver, a tall, slim woman with straight black hair, circled around and pushed through the door, marching straight to their table on a pair of stiletto heels.

"Ready?" she asked impatiently, glaring at Daryl. "You said thirty minutes and it's been …" She glanced at her smart watch, barely diverting her eyes. "Thirty-two. And remember, I'm driving the Mustang."

With that announcement, she stalked back out, throwing Essence an icy cold parting glance as she ducked through the door.

"Friend of yours?" Essence asked.

"Business partner," Daryl replied apologetically with the curve of a half-smile. "I've been trying to teach her better table manners. Here, before I forget." He handed over a thin curl of paper that looked as though it might have been drawn from a fortune cookie. "He wanted me to give you this. His cell phone number."

"So he's got a cell phone now, has he? I guess that means he really has changed."

She had kept the number in a coin purse in her handbag all this time. During long winter nights, she had unraveled it and stared at it, as though trying to decipher a code. Every day, she had thought about calling him. But then she would reread the letter. She didn't want to make Will's life any more complicated—or her own.

She still possessed it now that Spring had arrived in full bloom as she stared out at the length of space where the bridge had been. Work crews with massive cranes were already going to work with the process of cleaning up the riverbed below, depositing the debris on barges to ship downstream.

As she watched them pick like vultures at the wreckage, she felt prickles on the nape of her neck. This usually meant someone was staring at her, and when she turned around, she saw she was not mistaken.

He was only half a football field away. A few seconds' dash would have brought them together. Sooner, if they both launched themselves toward each other at the same time. Cue in slow-motion effects and instrumental music out of a Hollywood romance. But her fantasy dissolved when she saw he was balanced on crutches, the aluminum half-type of support that put cuffs around his lower arms.

He stood there, hunched forward, his trademark polo shirt—salmon, making her wonder what color day it would be if the museum were open—showing through the open collar of his jacket, looking very much like the person she had always known. Except his hair was shorter, his face fuller, rounder, as though he had been spoon-fed back to health these past several months, his eyes not so sunken, his jaw not so sallow. Still, in the tilt of his head, there it was, that same old sheepishness that set him apart from other men she had known.

She approached him slowly, and he walked forward too, more quickly than she would have predicted, an indication he had been used to the braces for some time. All along the way, Essence wrestled with her doubts, her fears. Should she show him the string of photos on her phone: from pre-delivery to homecoming in the baby's bassinet?

They met each other halfway, stopping within touching distance. Their eyes locked and stayed that way, and it seemed in the mutuality of their gaze that they were reunited, approaching each other gently, tenderly, their noses nuzzling, their mouths searching, their fingers groping, bodies pressing together, the heat between them rising, as their arms and legs entwined, as though swimming in and out of the consciousness of each other's embrace. She could tell by his expression that he was experiencing similar sensations, because he gave her a smile, warm and reassuring.

This made her smile in return, but the sun chose this moment to stab through an embankment of clouds, bleaching out external reality and giving the illusion her beloved had turned into a ghost, as though he had never been, even as she called out his name.

ACKNOWLEDGMENTS

Katherine "Kathy" Burkman has been my mentor throughout my academic and creative career. She served as my thesis and dissertation advisor at The Ohio State University and has since provided feedback on my attempts at novel writing, including this one. Her own work is eclectic and includes scholarly treatises, a mystery novel, poetry, children's picture books, and plays written, directed, and performed in collaboration with her group Wild Women Writing. When she gave an early draft of *Soft as Water* a nod of approval, I felt encouraged to keep working on it.

My spouse, Miona Jansen, picked it up from there and conducted an extensive chapter-by-chapter analysis, pointing out parts that needed more work. Point-blank honesty can often dissolve a marriage, but in this case I valued her insights as spot on. Miona has been writing a novel of her own, so when the time comes to provide feedback, I'll have an opportunity to return the favor.

Fiona Forsyth is a Classics scholar and book reviewer whose attention was caught by the placename of the town that was the central location of my previous novel. This was due to her fascination with Ovid, which has prompted her to write a series of mysteries with the Roman author of *Metamorphoses* as the detective. Her enthusiasm for the revised draft I showed her gave me the confidence, for better or worse, to proceed with publication.

ABOUT THE AUTHOR

B. Robert Conklin (he/him/his) lives, writes, and works, not necessarily in this order, in Columbus, Ohio, where he and his spouse are continuously surprised by their three Gen-Z kids, who seem determined to take less-traveled paths of their own. His career has included teaching composition and literature at several colleges. To pay the bills, he is currently employed as a technical writer and editor. In a different medium, he practices the art of cartooning.

Visit him at www.brobertconklin.wordpress.com